By
Christopher Nicole

A SIGNET BOOK
NEW AMERICAN LIBRARY
TIMES MIRROR

NAL BOOKS ARE ALSO AVAILABLE AT DISCOUNTS IN BULK QUANTITY FOR INDUSTRIAL OR SALES-PROMOTIONAL USE. FOR DETAILS, WRITE TO PREMIUM MARKETING DIVISION, NEW AMERICAN LIBRARY, INC., 1301 AVENUE OF THE AMERICAS, NEW YORK, NEW YORK 10019.

COPYRIGHT © 1975 BY CHRISTOPHER NICOLE

All rights reserved. For information, write: St. Martin's Press, Inc., 175 Fifth Avenue, New York, New York 10010

Library of Congress Catalog Card Number: 74-32503

This is an authorized reprint of a hardcover edition published by St. Martin's Press, Inc.

SIGNET TRADEMARK REG. U.S. PAT. OFF. AND FOREIGN COUNTRIES
REGISTERED TRADEMARK—MARCA REGISTRADA
HECHO EN CHICAGO, U.S.A.

SIGNET, SIGNET CLASSICS, MENTOR, PLUME AND MERIDIAN BOOKS are published by The New American Library, Inc., 1301 Avenue of the Americas, New York, New York 10019

FIRST SIGNET PRINTING, DECEMBER, 1976

1 2 3 4 5 6 7 8 9

PRINTED IN THE UNITED STATES OF AMERICA

Contents

1. The *Matelots* — 1
2. The Jungle — 29
3. The Scum of the Earth — 55
4. The Lady of Green Grove — 87
5. The Devil's Honeymoon — 116
6. Across the Water — 142
7. The Choice — 170
8. The Avengers — 208
9. The Traitor — 243
10. The Trial — 271
11. The Outcast — 307
12. The Challenge — 328
13. The Revolution — 352
14. The Master of Green Grove — 382

1

The 'Matelots'

The man panted. Partly because of the heat; the sun hung above the barren rock that was the island of Tortuga, and sucked the last drop of moisture from the volcanic fissures much as it brought the sweat trickling from human pores. But he had been running for some time, and climbing, away from the open beach which fringed the bay, and the worm-eaten ships which lay at anchor in the harbour, away from the shacks and lean-to tents of the town, over the uneven track which was called a road, toward the house which crowned the red-rock hill. The house was weathered now, with cracks in the wooden hurricane shutters and the roof of one wing fallen in, but none the less strongly built of stone, loopholed for defence on the lower floor, perched above the rest of the settlement, gazing south across the narrow strait at the immense bulk of Hispaniola, largest of all Caribbean islands, which blotted the horizon, a cloud which overhung life for those who would attempt to live so close to the mainspring of Spain's colonial empire.

At the top of the hill the man checked, to catch his breath. He fitted his surroundings. He wore cracked leather shoes with tarnished gilt buckles, and torn breeches; his chest was bare and burned mahogany by the sun, his black hair was lank and hung past his ears, from one of which dripped a gold earring. He was unarmed, but his big hands looked capable of twining themselves around a rope or a cutlass. His face was devoid of intelligence; only animal passion had ever illuminated the brown eyes, and his beard was more a few sprouts of untidy scrub than a uniform growth. He lived by haunting the taverns and boasting of his deeds when he had sailed with L'Olonnais, and waiting for some more fortunate seafarer to throw him a coin.

But if he had ever taken part in the raids which had first made the men of Tortuga famous, he had gained no courage from the experience. His feet dragged and his shoulders slumped as he made his way towards the verandah on which the woman sat.

And she was, after all, only a woman. Still tall, and still slender. The thick hair was more white than red, now, but her face was still sharp in its outline, her expression as lively as ever in the past. She had watched the man climbing towards her, as she sat here most days and watched the comings and goings in the harbour beneath her house. Whenever there were any comings and goings. Today was important, because last night's gale had brought a ship limping towards Tortuga, and even Susan Hilton's fading eyes could tell at a glance that this was no rotting pirate hulk, staggering home from a disastrous visit to the Main, in which wind and reef would all but have ended her career at least once in every day, and the Spanish gold of which her crew would boast had remained always nothing better than a dream. This morning's visitor was a well-found ship, and it was flying the Cross of St George.

As Bale was about to tell her. ' 'Tis the Governor of Antigua, Mistress Hilton,' he babbled. 'Himself, ma'am, with a sprung foremast. He's here for a refit, ma'am, and he sends his compliments.'

Susan stood up, only a brief downward twist of her lips revealing the spasm of rheumatism which accompanied the upward jerk. 'Warner?'

'Himself, ma'am,' Bale spluttered. 'Colonel Philip Warner, and asking to be remembered to your honour. 'Tis said his father first set the English flag flying in these islands.'

'His father and his brother. So that Philip could inherit, the name and the glory.' Forty-five years in the West Indies had not diminished Susan's Irish brogue. 'Ye'll return to the harbour, Bale.'

'Oh, yes, ma'am. In time.' He circled his dusty lips with a dry tongue. In the ten years since Tony Hilton had died there had scarce been anyone to investigate his well-stocked cellar. 'It's mighty hot on that hill.'

'I will write a letter. Ye'll wait, Bale.' She went inside, and Bale sidled up the steps, to check at the rumble of threatening noise which came from behind the door; the mastiff formed a shaggy shadow against the wall. Bale remained at the top of the steps. From here he could peer into the interior of the house and see the woman as she sat at the scarred writing desk, dipping her quill into the old silver well. Apart from the desk, and a few straight chairs, the room was empty. And of people, when a servant might have been instructed to bring him a drink. But Susan Hilton had to live for the rest of her life on what gold her husband had accumulated during his career as a pirate, and Governor of Tortuga. Estimates varied. Certain it was that she lived tight, seldom went out, and when she spent money, it was on that grandson of hers.

She stood up and held out two letters. 'There ye are, Bale. One for Monsieur D'Ogeron, and one for Colonel Warner. I wish these delivered within the hour.'

Bale took the papers, reluctantly. 'Sure, and the sun is fit to strike a man dead, ma'am, on that hill.'

Susan regarded him with a stare which had frozen better men to the floor, then nodded, and went back to the desk. From one of the drawers she took a gold coin, and threw it.

Bale grabbed the flying sliver of light with a certainty born of practice, turned it over, opened his palm. 'A crown piece, by Christ.'

'So drink yourself into the gutter,' Susan suggested. 'After ye've delivered those letters.'

'Oh, aye, ma'am. I'll be at it now. God bless you, Mistress Hilton. God bless you.' He eyed the dog as he backed down the steps.

Susan watched him shamble down the hill. The noise of his progress receded, and the house once again became still. It was a quiet she enjoyed. When Tony lived here, and ruled this accumulation of outlaws and debtors, pimps and whores, he had filled these rooms with laughter and with song, with the clink of bottles and the stamp of feet. Since his death the loudest sound had been the whisper of the wind through the rotting shutters. Susan never wore shoes about the house. It was a habit she had formed as a child in Ireland, how many centuries ago. Nor had she reason to change here in the unending summer. Her feet were as smooth and hard and flawlessly shaped. And as no man had known her bed for ten years, her figure was no less youthful. She lived with her memories, and only when these were not quite enough did she hate the silence.

But tonight there would be noise. Philip Warner . . . she plucked at her lower lip. Only a boy, when last they met, in 1629, in that tumultuous summer when the Spaniards had made their supreme effort to destroy the heretical colonies which had sprouted like weeds in their private paradise, and had failed, because of the courage and determination of the Warners—and their friends. Then Philip had been a short, thick-set youth filled with jealousy of his brother. But now he was a Deputy Governor, and of Edward's old colony, too; Edward's widow, Aline, had chosen to take her surviving children back to France rather than remain on the island where her capture by the Caribs continued to be a source of gossip. But surely forty years would have given him dignity, and more. And a reputation for trimming; it was said he found it as easy now to be an admirer of His Majesty King Charles the Second as he had found it to do business with Cromwell's commissioners.

But that was not a question on which Susan Hilton would pass judgement. Philip was here. He must meet Kit. She turned, in a flurry of skirts, moved silently through the entry hall. Rufus immediately rose, shook himself, and padded behind her. They went through the great empty kitchens to stand together at the back door and look at the few stunted trees which made up the orchard. There the two boys faced each other, wearing only breeches, feet and heads bare, sweat glistening on muscular shoulders and rolling down their cheeks as they presented their swords, crossed the blades, thrust and retreated, swept and ducked, grunted and smiled. They did nothing else with their time, except when they practised with their pistols or went fishing in the shallows. They dreamed of leading their own buccaneering expeditions, of following in the footsteps of Tony Hilton and Jean L'Olonnais, of seeking a fame to equal that of Mansveldt; perhaps of rushing off to join the new adventurer whose name was upon everyone's lips: Henry Morgan.

Time enough for that when they were older. She had no eyes for Jean DuCasse, although the French boy, at eighteen, was already as tall as a man and remarkably handsome, black hair smoothly wavy on his shoulders, cheekbones high and dignified, smile elongating the small mouth beneath the trim moustache and then as quickly fading to return the long face to its more natural solemnity. A good friend, Jean, as was his father; without DuCasse's warehouse Tortuga would be more of a sandbank than it needed.

But Jean was not her problem. Christopher Hilton, a year younger, already possessed an equal height. And with it her features, small and delicate, hardened only by the jutting chin. She looked in vain for the great gash of a mouth which had been Tony's principal characteristic. But then, Kit's father had not possessed the Hilton mouth either, and he had been her eldest son, conceived during those tumultuous weeks in the St Kitts forest, when Tony and Edward Warner had equally shared her embraces. That was not a riddle to which she had ever dared discover an answer. And all others who might be interested were long dead. Sufficient that of all her memories this boy was the sweetest, and were he Warner or Hilton, he was equally fortunate in his forebears.

'*Touché*,' Jean gasped, falling to his right knee as he thrust. But Kit had already moved to one side, and his blade cut the air immediately above his friend's head.

'You'd be a dead man, now.'

'Perhaps.' Jean thrust his blade into the sandy soil, used it as a crutch, looked up and saw Susan. 'Madame.' He bowed. 'I have just been killed, it seems.'

Susan pretended to frown. 'And so will one of ye be, soon enough; swords are for passes, not for thrusts and cuts after the fashion ye practise. Now away with ye, Jean, and tell your father and mother I have guests this evening, and should be obliged if they'd join me.'

'Of course, madame.' The French boy thrust his sword through his belt, bowed once again, and hurried round the house.

'Guests, Grandmama?' Kit Hilton came towards her.

'Colonel Warner, no less. He's a foremast needs shoring. We're poor relations, boy. I'd have ye at your best.'

Poor relations, Kit thought. There could be no argument about that. He stood beside his grandmother and wore a cambric shirt, the white turned yellow with age, for it had belonged to his father. His breeches were his best, in pale plum, with only a single darned rent; they had decided against stockings, as he possessed none which were not in holes, but he had polished his leather shoes, and attempted to bring some gleam back to the buckles. And Susan was wearing her blue satin gown, edged with white lace, with a silk sash and a tiered lace-edged collar; her shoulders were bare and the tops of her breasts swelled as she breathed; her magnificent grey-red hair was gathered on the nape of her neck, to fall in a cluster of ringlets down her back. Globules of sweat clung to her neck and cheeks, but he hoped these were caused more by the afternoon sun than by apprehension.

And behind them, Monsieur D'Ogeron, small and dark and busy, even when standing still, and his wife, and Monsieur

DuCasse and his wife, both tall, quiet people, with Jean behind them, were scarcely more elegant.

What then were they to make of the approaching party? The ship's officers wore plain blue coats, although there were no mended tears in their breeches; but the pair they escorted were dazzling. Colonel Warner was not a tall man; Kit could give him several inches. But he was well set up, broad without appearing stout, and he carried himself like a giant. His features were round and pugnacious, his brown eyes watchful; they darted from side to side like a startled humming bird. He wore a scarlet coat and matching breeches, with gold braid and gold buttons, and a lace edging to his cravat, and his sleeves, and no doubt his shirt waist as well. His stockings were also red, and his shoes were black, and he carried a pair of white gloves in his left hand. He looked into middle age, but it was impossible to be sure, for his own hair was concealed beneath a brown periwig which tumbled in curls on to his shoulders, while on top of the wig was a black tricorne. He wore a sword, suspended from a blue silk baldric, and prodded the ground with a gold-topped cane as he climbed. He looked hot, as well he might be, but he also looked utterly contemptuous of his surroundings. Again, Kit thought ruefully, as well he might be. But his attention was already wandering from the resplendent figure of the Deputy Governor of Antigua to the lady who walked beside him.

There were no ladies on Tortuga. Grandmama, even when she had been the Governor's wife, had made no such claim and neither had Madame D'Ogeron. But it never occurred to Kit to doubt that here he was regarding a superior being. Not merely from her looks, for she was obviously very young, certainly no older than himself, and was equally obviously related to Philip Warner; she had the same rounded features, regular enough, certainly, but hardly the sort of face one would look at twice if it had been carved in marble. The splendour came from her eyes, green, glinting with life, from the faint twist to her small mouth, from the widening of her nostrils as she breathed, the tilt of her chin as she observed, the flash of her white teeth as she smiled at a remark of her companion's. She exuded vitality, and that was a quality seldom found amongst West Indian women, nor could Kit doubt that she *was* West Indian; the sun had tanned her face, despite whatever precautions she might habitually take. And the vitality spread to her hair, long and deep brown and straight, separated into four strands, each tied with a blue velvet bow, the whole topped by a white lace head-dress at least as high again as her own head, which gave her a height to compare with any man's. And to her movements, which were tirelessly confident, even at the end of a stiff climb, suggesting that beneath her gown there would be the figure of an athlete. The gown itself was of white satin, pulled back from the waist to display her lace underskirt and secured by another dark-blue velvet bow. Her décolletage was far more extreme than Grandmama's, and plunged past the curve of the young breasts almost as to suggest a glimpse of pink nipple as she moved, but the promise of the flesh was obscured by the soft glow of the pearl necklace which lay against it; her earrings were also pearl, huge drops of seemingly translucent white which looked almost alive.

And now she was close, Kit could smell the musk of her perfume, drifting towards him on the faint breeze.

Grandmama had moved forward. 'Philip,' she said, her arms outstretched. 'I had not thought ever to have this pleasure again.'

Colonel Warner stopped beyond her reach, and stared at her, and then made a leg and removed his hat with a flourish. 'The pleasure is mine, Mistress Hilton. Allow me to present my daughter, Miss Marguerite Warner.'

'But she is absolutely beautiful,' Susan said.

Marguerite Warner made a shallow curtsey.

'And a Warner to her toes, I'll warrant. I could be looking at your sister. You've news of Indian Tom?'

The crimson cheeks of the Deputy Governor darkened. 'Ah, no, madam. That misfortune has taken himself and his squaw mother back to Dominica, where indeed our father should have sent him many years ago.' His gaze was drifting beyond her shoulder, flickering down to the sitting mastiff and then up to the waiting people.

'I am forgetting my manners,' Susan agreed, without embarrassment. 'I so seldom have occasion to practise them, ye understand. Ye have met His Excellency, Monsieur D'Ogeron?'

'Indeed I have,' Philip Warner said. 'He was first on board this morning, seeking to charge me for the privilege of dropping my anchor in this miserable apology for a port.'

D'Ogeron merely smiled. 'It is necessary for us to live, Colonel Warner. Even on Tortuga.'

'Faith, I have heard sufficient tales of how you go about that, monsieur. I do promise you that my cannon are all loaded, and the fires are lit. Madam?'

'Madame D'Ogeron, and Madame DuCasse, and Monsieur DuCasse,' Susan said. 'Monsieur DuCasse owns our warehouse.'

'A storekeeper?' Philip Warner looked scandalized. 'My ship's officers will have business with you, sir. Tomorrow. And these two pirates?'

'That is their ambition, to be sure,' Susan said. 'Jean DuCasse, and my grandson, Christopher Hilton.'

Philip Warner glanced at her. 'He also has a strong family likeness, madam.'

Susan continued to smile. 'Should he not, sir? Now, will ye come to the house and take a glass of wine? And your officers, and of course, your daughter. Or would she rather Kit and Jean showed her something of our island? From this hilltop most of it is well displayed.'

'By my faith, madam, I would appreciate such a tour myself. Is that not Hispaniola?'

'Indeed, sir,' D'Ogeron agreed.

'And how many cannon do you mount to command that passage?'

The Governor of Tortuga shrugged. 'We have four cannon to command the entrance to the harbour. For the rest, that island is so large, and fertile, and prosperous, and this island is so small, and barren, and poor, I doubt they know of our existence.'

Philip Warner led the way towards the house, Susan at his side. 'You may be sure they do, monsieur. And however insignificant your little band of cut-throats may be, you are none the less nuisances to His Most Catholic Majesty. And now that we are once again at war...'

The entire party stopped.

'At war?' Albert DuCasse demanded.

'England is at war with Spain, sir,' Philip Warner said. 'Why else do you think I cut short my visit to London and came hurrying back before the storm season has run its course? My daughter is to be married, you understand, and so we sought her trousseau. But 'tis scarce complete.'

'Allow me to congratulate you, Marguerite,' Susan said.

'As for this war of which ye speak, Philip, be sure that the Spaniards will not waste their shot on Tortuga.'

'Indeed, madam, I would say you are right. Was it not for the fact that this island has always been their first target in the past.'

'War,' D'Ogeron mused. 'Pardon me for asking, Colonel Warner, but on which side is His Majesty?'

'His Majesty? Oh, you mean Louis. Why, sir, at the moment he supports King Charles, God bless him.'

'Now there is good news,' D'Ogeron said. 'Had it been otherwise, we should have been enemies, monsieur, and I should have had to place you under arrest.' He burst out laughing, and as Philip Warner dropped his hand to his sword, clapped him on the shoulder. 'A jest, monsieur. A jest. In Tortuga English and French are as one. We need each other too much. We count Monsieur Hilton, madame's late husband, as our first govenor, and if the administration now has a French flavour, why, that is merely because we are presently the more numerous. But Madame Hilton will assure you of our respect for her, and for all the English.'

Susan's turn to smile. 'He does speak the truth, Philip, although of course he mistakes the situation, as I have the honour to be Irish. Now, ye'll take a glass of wine before dinner.' She paused at the foot of the crumbling steps, and looked at Kit. 'I'm sure Miss Warner would appreciate a walk, Kit. Betrothed she may be, but politics and talk of war cannot help but be tiresome to one so young. And we are going to talk of war, are we not, gentlemen? As the subject has been broached.'

She led the way up the stairs, while Marguerite Warner stared after her. 'Faith,' she remarked, when they were out of earshot. 'But she gives herself airs, for a servant.'

'A servant?' Kit asked.

'Did you not know? She was shipped to these islands as an indentured labourer, and like so many of her sort, was auctioned off to the highest bidder as a wife.' She continued to gaze at the house as the women disappeared inside. 'But is that not how Monsieur D'Ogeron provided wives for his colonists here in Tortuga also? Save that they are reputed to have been gleaned from the street instead of the prison.'

The two boys exchanged glances.

'Indeed, that is so, mademoiselle,' Jean said. 'But my mother, and Kit's grandmother, were alike fortunate in those who bid for them.'

'A storekeeper and a pirate. Oh, yes, indeed, monsieur, it could have been far worse.'

'We could have had a half-breed for an uncle,' Kit remarked. 'Is not this Indian Tom Warner of whom my mother spoke a Carib? Pray tell me, what does he eat at table? Human steaks?'

Marguerite Warner turned her stare on him. 'Faith, sir, you'd not speak so were my father present. As for the breed, be sure my grandfather himself lived to regret ever taking a redskin to his bed. That unhappy calamity brought much misfortune on my family, and may do so again, as your French . . .' her bitter gaze encompassed Jean, 'have seen fit to make the scoundrel Governor of Dominica. No doubt they sit naked around a council table and rattle bones to decide their policies. Believe me, sirs, I am not afraid to admit the black stains on my family.' She walked away from them, round the house. 'You are to show me your island. Or have I already seen it all?'

'Now she is angry,' Jean said. 'You were tactless, Kit.'

'And was she not tactless? Or downright rude, both to you and to me. As for Warner, I'd like to pull his ears as well. He'll have no friendship of a Hilton.'

'Then let the girl insult you to her heart's content, and forget about her tomorrow,' Jean advised. 'They are planters, we will be seamen. Come, let us entertain the young lady.'

For Marguerite had moved away to look at the rear slope of the hill, which tumbled in uneven rocks and gullies down to the beach and the still seething sea, two hundred feet below her. 'Although I wonder,' she mused aloud, 'if Madam Hilton indeed did so well. Faith, she'd have done better to remain in St Kitts than come to this barren islet. Poor woman, it was not for want of trying.'

'You'll explain that remark, if you please, Miss Warner,' Kit said. For by now his anger was difficult to control.

She turned to face him. 'You did not know that she attempted to secure one of my uncles as a husband? Why, is well known she was Edward Warner's mistress, amongst others. Before and after she bound herself to the pirate, Hilton.'

'By God,' Kit said. 'I'll have no more of this. I had thought you a lady, Miss Warner. But it seems you have come to my home only to insult me.'

'Your home?'' she inquired. 'Faith, is that what it is?'

'Kit,' Jean begged.

But Kit was already lunging forward. Marguerite saw him coming with an expression of incredulity which rapidly changed to alarm as he seized her arm.

'You'll let me go, sir,' she said. 'I'll stand for no horseplay. You . . .'

Her words disappeared in an explosion of breath as he ducked and drove his shoulder into her stomach, straightening as soon as he felt her weight, and lifting her from the ground. Marguerite's legs flailed and her head-dress fell forward as she kicked and fought, but he was twice her size and possessed twice her strength.

'You . . . you pirate,' she screamed.

Jean could not stop himself laughing. 'Well, now,' he said. 'Having got her, what are you going to do with her?'

Marguerite pounded on Kit's back with her fists. 'If you do not put me down, why . . . I'll have you flogged.'

'She's a proper scold,' Jean remarked.

Kit was slowly turning round, his right arm holding the girl in place on his shoulder, his left hand grasping her thighs through the endless folds of her gown. He was enveloped in a world of silk and satin and scents he had not suspected to exist, and his brain was bubbling with a desire he had not known he possessed, either; with an anxiety to take advantage of her flying skirts and discover what lay beneath, with a temptation to lower her to the ground without releasing her, but instead to hold her ever closer, to squeeze her so tight that she would become a part of him. But also with a knowledge that he dared not attempt any of these things, that in fact he was already sliding down a slope the bottom of which he could not see.

But she had been inexpressibly rude, and Jean had put his finger on it, with his usual accuracy.

'Aye,' Kit said. 'A proper scold. There is only one treatment for such.'

He staggered across the yard towards the huge water butt which stood by the back door; as water was always scarce in Tortuga and rain provided most of it, this was large enough to swim in.

'You wouldn't dare,' Marguerite screamed. 'You wouldn't dare. Put me down. You . . . you . . .' her body twisted and bumped on his shoulder, and against his arm. One of her shoes had come off, and this Jean picked up with a grave smile as he followed them.

'Kit,' Susan Hilton called from the doorway. 'Kit? Whatever are ye doing?'

'You'll put that lady down, sir,' Philip Warner shouted.

'Aye,' Kit said. He was standing above the vat and now he threw the struggling girl away from him. She rolled as she spun through the air, kicking as her skirts rode up, and then landed in the water with a gigantic splash.

'By God,' Philip Warner shouted, and ran down the steps.

'Kit,' Susan screamed, following him.

'Mon Dieu,' remarked Monsieur D'Ogeron, smiling.

Marguerite surfaced, gasping and choking, her hair a damp mat on her neck, her gown dissolving into a sodden outer skin, her head-dress a dribble of lace over one ear.

'Don't just stand there,' Philip Warner bellowed. 'Get her out.'

'Of course, sir.' Kit moved forward, checked at the expression in Marguerite's eyes.

'If you touch me, I'll kill you,' she said softly.

'May I be of service, mademoiselle?' Jean inquired.

She glanced at him. 'You can give me your hand.'

He obeyed, and she scrambled up, sat on the lip of the vat to swing her legs over, and slid to the ground, hastily dragging her skirts into place.

'By God,' Philip Warner repeated. 'And now, you young whippersnapper...' the cane twitched.

Kit rested his hand on his sword hilt. 'She insulted Grandmama.'

'She...' Philip glared from the boy to Susan to his bedraggled daughter. 'And you, sir? Have you not insulted my daughter?'

'I punished her, Colonel Warner. If you wish satisfaction, be sure I'll be pleased to give it to you. Jean?'

'Of course, Kit.' Jean stepped forward. 'You have but to name the hour and the place, and the weapons, of course, Colonel Warner. Kit has no preferences. All come equally to him, I do assure you.'

Warner gazed at the two young men, frowning. But he could scarce be expected to put up with two humiliations in one afternoon. Susan decided to rescue him.

'Fie on ye, Philip. Ye cannot really mean to fight a boy.'

'He must be whipped.' Marguerite was still shaking herself in a most unladylike fashion, while water ran out from beneath her dress and dripped from her hair.

'Be sure that he will be punished,' Susan promised. 'Now

THE DEVIL'S OWN

come, if ye will enter my house, Miss Warner, I am sure I can find ye something to wear.'

'*Your* clothes?' Marguerite demanded. 'You'll take me back to the ship, Father, please.'

'Oh, come, Philip,' Susan protested. 'There is a splendid meal awaiting ye. Ye'll not let a children's quarrel spoil our first meeting in forty years?'

Philip Warner hesitated, looking from his daughter to the obviously amused guests. 'It was my mistake in calling here at all, madam," he said gruffly. 'The wind has gone down, and my foremast is not so badly damaged. We'll put to sea.'

'And my dinner, sir?' Susan demanded, becoming angry in her turn.

'Why, madam, I suggest you and your friends eat it up,' Philip said. 'With the Spaniards breathing down your necks, it may be the last thing you will ever enjoy.' He still looked at Kit. 'As for you, sir, Tony Hilton was ever a spawn of hell, and you've the same cast of character. Be sure the devil will have his own, soon enough. Come, Marguerite.' He stamped down the hill, the soaking girl squelching at his shoulder. The ship's captain bowed towards Susan. 'You'll excuse us, ma'am.'

Susan nodded, and watched them go, before turning to Kit. 'Now, really, I wonder if the child was not right, and after all ye do need chastisement. Ye are a wicked fellow.'

D'Ogeron burst out laughing. 'Really, Susan, I must take issue with you. Was he not defending you? I say good riddance to Colonel Warner. As for your splendid dinner, it will mean the more for us. And who knows, your friend the colonel may have been right.

'Prophetic words, Bertrand,' Susan remarked. They stood together on the front porch and watched the sails, at least a dozen of them, and still several miles off. They had come round the north-east corner of Hispaniola, to catch the fair wind which invariably blew over the islands.

D'Ogeron chewed his lip. 'It will be no laughing matter, Susan. You must get ready to leave.'

'I have never left before.'

'I have no soldiers, and few ships. I have . . .'

'Ye have several hundred seamen who habitually make their living by robbery and murder,' she interrupted. 'Will they not fight for their home?'

'This rock? Already they are manning their ships.'

'And ye propose to go with them?'

'There would seem to be no alternative. Maria, and the children . . . we cannot remain here and be murdered.'

'Ye are far more likely to be murdered at sea, Bertrand,' Susan said sternly. 'Shall I tell ye what the Spaniards will do? Exactly as they have done the last four occasions. They will sail past the harbour, they will fire two or three broadsides, and they will cut out any vessels at anchor and set fire to them. So I agree it's a good idea to send the ships to sea, but with no more than skeleton crews.'

'They landed once,' D'Ogeron pointed out.

'Indeed they did. I watched them from this very verandah. They put two hundred men ashore. And Tony withdrew up this hill, and lined twenty men with muskets along that ridge. The Spaniards looted the town and came up the hill, and Tony gave the order to fire. One volley, that was all it took. I think three of the Dons were actually hit. But the order to evacuate was given. Why *should* they risk their lives to seize a rock like this? What value can it be to them?'

D'Ogeron sighed. 'Those were raids, Susan. This is war.'

'Then treat them as enemies in superior force and negotiate a surrender.'

'And you think they would honour a negotiation with pirates?'

'Now ye are contradicting yourself,' she laughed. 'If it *is* an act of war they must deal with us as French subjects.'

'You are a stubborn woman," D'Ogeron said. 'I have given the order to evacuate. If you are coming, you have half an hour to get your things.'

'This house, this body, are my things. I am staying here. But ye have my permission to leave, Kit.'

The boy stood in the far corner of the verandah, Jean at his side. They were sharing the use of a telescope. 'We will fight them, Grandmama. Have you not told me often enough how Edward Warner held St Kitts against thirty Spanish ships, with but twenty Irishmen at his back?'

Susan smiled, her eyes misty. "And half a dozen women," she said, half to herself.

'My God,' D'Ogeron said. 'St Kitts is ten times the size of Tortuga. There are forests in which to hide, mountains up which to escape. Oh, Monsieur Warner was a great man, as great, perhaps, as his brother is small, but circumstances were in his favour. The Spaniards could scour this entire rock from beach to beach in an afternoon.'

'All the more reason for them to leave without wasting time,' Albert DuCasse said. 'I will stay. Jean, you will help me move the main part of our goods up the hill to this house. If you will permit me, Susan.'

'Of course. Kit, you will help Monsieur DuCasse. Hélène, shall we not make up most of the spare beds? Faith, it will be like turning back the clock to have the house full again.'

D'Ogeron stood at the top of the stairs, his hands opening and shutting helplessly. 'I have the power to command you, madame. Your own husband insisted that the Governor has that power.'

'But ye'll not use it on Susan Hilton, Bertrand. Now be off with ye. We shall look forward to your return.'

Brave words. She wondered that she was not afraid. For the moment was close at hand. The rumble of the continuous firing still seemed to filter up the hill, and the dense clouds of black smoke still shrouded the ships; the wind had dropped, and they had had to be towed into position by their boats, the same boats which were now rowing for the shore, each carrying a crew of glittering pinpoints, seen from above. But she had seen such pinpoints before.

She had seen such destruction before, as well. The town looked like a scattered antheap. At best it had always been a haphazardly derelict accumulation of shelters, with D'Ogeron's house and the DuCasse warehouse looming large just because the others were so ramshackle. Now only a few walls stood, and the single street had disappeared beneath crumbled stone. There was little fire, one shack burned quietly to itself. In Tortuga there was little to burn.

But the Spaniards were, after all, landing.

Was that a cause to fear? What could they do to her? As a girl she had been taken by the English, when Papa, that mysterious, lecherous, wild, romantic and apparently villainous old chieftain, had fallen in the doorway of the single tower he had called his castle. *That* collection of pinpoints had torn the virginity from between her legs and those of her sisters, before placing her in a rotting hulk and sending her to sea. In St Kitts she had been held up to auction, and bought by the Governor as a servant. And when she had caused the Governor's son to fall in love with her, she had been whipped, standing naked between two stakes thrust into the ground, while the entire colony had looked on. For permitting that to happen she had despised Edward Warner; for rescuing her she had worshipped Tony Hilton. Yet Edward had been only a boy, then, and Tony already a man. As Edward had grown, there had been nothing to choose between the pair. Was any woman so blessed as to have known the love of two such human beings?

It had not allowed an end to struggle. With Tony and Edward she had fought the other colonists; with Edward she had fought the Dons in that memorable campaign which had become a legend; and with Tony she had gone to sea, and fought the Spaniards again, before coming to rest on this rock.

And as she had truthfully told Bertrand D'Ogeron, even since then she had fought the Spaniards on four occasions. She had watched her husband die, remarkably in his bed, and she had watched the battle-torn bodies of her two sons brought ashore, to be buried in the little cemetery behind the house, alongside their wives. Life on Tortuga was a short, violent business. Except for Susan Hilton, who had survived them all, and was now acknowledged by them all; first lady of the lowest society in the world.

Out of it she had rescued but two things; this house, which she would never abandon, and Kit, who she would never let away from her side. Never? There was a big word for an old woman when confronted by a young man brought up on legend and with the sea in his blood.

'It is finished, Grandmama.' He wore only breeches, and still carried a hammer; his chest gleamed with sweat.

'Ye've not forgotten the cellar window?' she asked. 'It could be our last refuge.'

'Two boards, Grandmama. And there are three muskets by each loophole, with powder and shot. They'll need a cannon to smash in here.'

'And they'll scarce drag a cannon up this hill.'

'Then why are they landing at all?' Albert DuCasse frowned down the slope.

'A gesture,' Susan said contemptuously. 'Hélène, I think we should prepare an early supper for our garrison, as they may not have time to eat later on.'

She led the way inside, but the three men remained on the verandah, watching the Spaniards disembark.

Jean glanced at Kit. 'Are you afraid?'

Kit thrust out his chin, sucked air into his lungs, and suddenly smiled. 'Are you?'

'Yes. But it is what we have always wanted to do. Are you afraid, Papa?'

'A little,' DuCasse confessed. 'I had thought to be finished with fighting when I came here. I am too old to find pleasure in killing people, when I know that too soon I shall myself be dead. One never knows who one will meet in Heaven. Or the other place.' He laughed, and slapped his son on the shoulder. 'Even Spaniards go to Heaven, you know, Jean. Some of them.'

Kit stood at the corner of the verandah, where the railing joined the wall of the house itself. The only time he ever felt jealous was when he heard Jean and Monsieur DuCasse talking together. There was so much friendship between them, so much unspoken understanding. He could not remember his own father. The face became confused with too many other faces. He recalled that it was a young face, scarce bearded. Like his own, perhaps. But surely older, as he had had a son. And he recalled the day the ship had returned, flying the black flag. Because young as he had been, Edward Hilton had commanded his own ship.

Father had been named after Edward Warner, the famous Warner, the man who had defended St Kitts, colonized Antigua, and led the no less famous expedition to Dominica to regain his wife from the Caribs, obtaining for himself a reputation which would live as long as there were white people in the West Indies. A reputation to which Philip Warner perhaps aspired.

And a name his grandmother had loved so well she had used it on her eldest son. There was a strange business. But human relationships were a mystery, to him. He possessed only two: his friendship with Jean, and his love for Susan. She was more a mother than a grandmother to him. She ruled him and she dominated his life. And occasionally she laughed with him and played games with him. Less often nowadays, as they both grew older. But she had taught him to read and write, and told him something of the world. Although always her talk came back to the Leeward Islands and the Warners. Perhaps she should have married Edward Warner. Had she done so, how different would life have been. Philip Warner would have been his uncle, and that girl would have been his cousin, and perhaps he would have worn fine clothes and possessed a similar contempt for those less fortunate than himself.

That girl. He could still feel her, on his shoulder, still feel her thighs, pressing against his chest, her fists drumming on his back. His hands could still feel her too, where they had wrapped themselves around her legs, where they had brushed across the front of her gown. Christ, he had wanted. Had he not thrown her into the water butt he would have thrown her on the ground and raped her in front of everyone. And still the thought of her could bring him up hard and anxious. He was no stranger to women. There were no morals on Tortuga. And often when he and Jean had grown tired of hanging about the tavern listening to the endless lies of the seamen, they had crept round to Madame Hortense, and watched the men lying on the girls, and when business was slack, had been allowed to try their own fortune. 'Make Bettine laugh,' Hortense would say. 'And I will give you a silver coin.' For Bettine had thought herself a cut above the rest; she had not been shipped from Nantes, but had been picked off a sinking ship, south-west of Hispaniola. He remembered the sensation she had caused when she had demanded a passage home. Passages must be earned, and for a woman, in Tortuga, there was only one source of income.

Unless she be Susan Hilton.

But Bettine had inspired no such feelings as had Marguerite Warner. Bettine had made him feel good, as when he had drunk too much wine. She had not made him want to possess *her;* certainly not her mind, which was mean and vicious. Perhaps Marguerite Warner's mind was also mean and vicious. But Christ, to look at a woman like that, and know she was all his, bound to his bed as and when he chose, bound to deliver his children, bound to sit opposite to him at dinner —because people like the Warners would sit down to dine every night, he was sure of that. No doubt Grandpapa had thought just that when first he had looked on Grandmama. And what had Grandmama thought?

'*Mon Dieu.*' Albert DuCasse was peering through the telescope. 'Susan,' he called. 'Jean, call Madame Hilton, if you please. Quickly.'

Kit hurried along the verandah. 'What is the matter, monsieur?'

'What did your grandmother say? That this house will withstand any assault, save that of a cannon?' He handed over the glass.

Kit focussed, watched the Spaniards forming into two lines outside the town. Two columns, of men wearing morions and breastplates, one half armed with pikes and the other with muskets. Their jackets were red and their breeches black. They looked splendid, so many men, all dressed uniformly, all obeying a single command. What must it be like, he wondered, to have command over so many men? And a single woman? It occurred to him that that was all he really sought from life, command, authority. Power.

But behind the two columns a dozen sailors were putting harnesses over their shoulders and round their waists, for being swung ashore from a large pinnace there was a cannon.

'Let me see, Kit.' Susan stood at his shoulder, and he gave her the glass. She watched without changing expression for several seconds, while the wind plucked at her hair. Then she closed the glass, and there was a tightness at her mouth he had not seen before. 'It seems that Bertrand was right.'

'What shall we do, Grandmama?'

Susan looked at the sun, dropping over the mountains of Hispaniola as it sank towards the western horizon. 'We will have to negotiate, I think. But so long as we conceal our strength, that should not be so very difficult. Now inside, everyone, and eat your meal. They will not reach here for at least an hour.' She smiled at them. 'Perhaps they will postpone their attack until tomorrow.'

'In which case we can slip away after dark,' Albert DuCasse suggested.

'And go where, do you think?'

'It is no more than two miles to Hispaniola,' Jean said. 'I am sure we could swim it, under cover of darkness.'

'You could swim it, Jean. And Kit, I have no doubt. And perhaps even your mother and father. My bones are too waterlogged for such a venture. Nor did I elect to remain here merely to sneak away at the first risk of danger. Besides, it will not be necessary. They will be pleased to accept our surrender, set a Spanish flag over us, and depart again. It has all happened before. Now let us eat.'

Not that she wished to. While the others forced themselves to digest she remained by the door, Rufus rubbing himself against her skirt, looking out at the column slowly toiling up the hill, dragging their gun. How slowly they moved, and how wearily. But how slowly the sun sank. And how tired she suddenly was. She had supposed she was too tired to run away again, and return, to pick up the pieces after the Dons had gone. But that had been pride. And earlier this afternoon she had doubted they could do anything to her that had not been done before. But then she had not been tired. So, perhaps tomorrow she would be less tired.

But they meant to assault tonight. The head of the column, disappeared for a while in the dip below the hilltop, now re-emerged. The distance was scarce two hundred yards. And soon the cannon would also be in place. Hastily she closed the door, seized the musket which stood by it, levelled the heavy piece, and squeezed the trigger. The flint ignited, for a miracle, and the force of the explosion made her stagger. She did not know where the bullet went. But the helmets stopped moving.

Plates clattered and chairs scraped behind her as the men got up.

'A general fire, Grandmama?' Kit asked.

'No,' she said. 'We have shown them that we are here and prepared to defend ourselves. Now is the moment to parley. Hélène, the tablecloth. Tie it to the end of this gun, and I will go out and speak with them.'

'You, Susan?' Albert DuCasse shook his head. 'I have no doubt you will prove a capable leader if we have to fight, but I think this is man's work. I will speak with them.'

She gazed at him for some seconds. 'Be sure ye give an impression of strength, Albert.'

'Be sure that I shall.'

'God go with you, Albert.' Hélène kissed him on both cheeks.

'He has, ever in the past, my sweet. Stand to your weapons, boys. I may well come back in haste. Now unbolt the door.'

Kit pulled the bolts, and DuCasse stepped outside. By now the Spaniards were deploying along the top of the ridge, just out of musket range, but well within earshot; the people in the house could hear every word of command, and the principal one was a repeated exhortation to make haste with the cannon. But at the sight of the man with the white flag the chatter ceased. Kit wrapped his fingers around the gun barrel, and found them wet with sweat. He glanced at his grandmother. She stood by the door, frowning with concentration as she looked through the loophole.

Albert DuCasse walked down the path, the musket held in front of him, the breeze extending the tablecloth. An officer, glittering in red and silver, left the ranks of the musketeers and moved forward. He carried a drawn sword. 'You will surrender?' he demanded in French.

THE DEVIL'S OWN

'On terms, monsieur,' DuCasse replied. 'There is a fort, more than a house, strongly defended. This is French soil on which you stand. We will surrender to superior force, in accordance with the accepted usages of war.'

'French soil,' the officer said contemptuously. 'Usages of war? You are nothing more than a pirate, and will be treated as such.'

'Oh, God,' Susan whispered.

'I warn you, monsieur.' DuCasse said, his voice steady—if he was afraid he did not show it—'In that house there are many determined men who will not easily be overcome. What value can there be in spilling the blood of your people to gain a victory when an honourable settlement can so easily be achieved?'

'I speak of no honour with cut-throats,' the officer said. 'Nor do I deal with them, or accept their flags of truce. I spit upon your flag, monsieur. And upon you.'

DuCasse stepped backwards, the musket still held in both his hands. But the Spaniard was already swinging his sword, and the Frenchman wore no armour. The blade flashed in the setting sun and blood spurted.

'Albert,' Hélène DuCasse screamed.

Jean said nothing, but they could hear him breathe.

Kit levelled his musket and squeezed the trigger. But the Spaniards were still beyond range. And now the pikemen moved forward, to drive their halberds into the writhing body on the ground, while the white flag fluttered for a last time before falling limp in the dust.

'Albert,' Hélène DuCasse whispered.

Susan turned back from the door. 'The fault is mine. As Bertrand warned, the Dons regard us as less than human. Jean, Kit, ye'll take madame and escape out the back. It will be dark in half an hour, and ye will be able to make the beach and that swim. But ye must hurry.'

'Leave you, Grandmama?' Kit demanded.

'For God's sake, boy, will ye help me by dying? What can those men do to me that has not been done before? I have lived in these islands nearly all my life. I know the worst they can offer me. And I will be here when ye come back. Now go. Hélène, ye must hurry.

Hélène DuCasse's face was hard. 'No. I will stay with you, Susan.'

'Mama...' Jean begged.

'I have said what I will do, Jean. Now take Kit and get

down to the beach. It is the men they wish to kill. What profit can there be in destroying women?'

'But they will . . .' Jean bit his lip.

'Oh, come now,' Susan protested. 'Ye'd think we were two blushing maids. Be off with ye. I'll have no argument in the matter. But be sure ye come back, when the Dons have gone.'

The boys exchanged glances, but she knew they would go. They were not yet men, and to die was still too large an adventure. A moment later the women heard the back door close.

'Will they get away?' Hélène asked. 'It is an empty hillside.'

'So we must provide a suitable distraction.' Susan unbolted the door. 'Are ye ready, Hélène?'

The Frenchwoman stared at her. 'Ye mean to go to them?'

'I think it would be better than having them come to us. And besides, if they are looking at us, they cannot possibly be looking at anyone else.'

She threw the door wide and went on to the verandah, Rufus panting at her side. The Spaniards had not advanced, as they were still waiting for the cannon, which at this moment made its appearance over the hilltop. But when they saw the women the line surged forward without orders, and the officer who had killed Albert DuCasse had to run to keep at their front.

They paused, panting, at the foot of the steps, staring from the teeth of the dog to the breasts of the women. 'How many men are inside?' demanded the officer.

'None,' Susan said. 'We had hoped to bluff ye, señor, but as it did not work . . .' she shrugged. 'My name is Susan Hilton, and this is . . .'

'Hil-ton,' the officer said, pronouncing each syllable with great emphasis. 'You are related to the pirate, Anthony Hilton?'

'I have the honour to be his widow.'

'And this woman is also married to a pirate, no doubt.'

'She is the widow of the man you have just murdered, señor. I should be more polite, were I you.'

'Polite,' the officer said. 'Polite.' He turned to his men. 'You may take them.'

There was a whoop of excited anticipation, and the red and steel wave flowed up the steps, weapons being dropped in their haste to be at their victims. A deep-throated growl from Rufus checked the leaders, but before Susan could silence the dog a pistol barked, and the mastiff gave a yelp and rolled down the steps. Hélène shrank against the wall of the house, but Susan stood her ground, was seized by anxious fingers which fastened on her arms and tore away the bodice of her gown, while others dug into her thighs as she was swept from the floor, to be returned there a moment later, all the breath gushing from her body, in a mixture of shock and physical force and fear. But this had happened before. When she had been young. Now her breasts hurt from the unaccustomed violence, and there seemed a great void at her groin.

A voice was shouting, and the fingers were sliding away, reluctantly and with final sly pinches and digs. She gasped for breath and rose on her elbow, gazed at Hélène, still pinned against the wall, her dress also torn and her hair dishevelled, but otherwise unharmed. Then she looked at the soldiery, gathered into groups, muttering amongst themselves, faces flushed and hands hastily straightening doublets and breeches, and past them, at the grey-haired senior officer, aquiline face lined and distinguished, and at the black-clad figure who strode at his side as they made their way through the throng.

'Have you no shame?' the priest shouted. 'Are you men, or beasts? Is there no crime of which you are not capable?'

'These women are surely not whores like those in the village,' the Commandant said.

'They are worse, sir,' the lieutenant declared. 'Admitted wives to pirates themselves. Why, the red-haired one is proud to acknowledge the scoundrel Hilton as her husband.'

'None the less, my son,' the priest said. 'That she is the wife of a pirate, however guilty that may make her before man's law, does not establish her as beyond God's mercy.' He stooped beside Susan. 'Do you understand Spanish, woman?'

'Indeed I do, Father. And I thank God for that, and for you.'

The priest pushed his crucifix towards her face. 'Will you take the cross?'

Susan sat up. 'Gladly, Father. I will not swear I have been a good Catholic. There has not always been time. But I have never lost faith.'

'Then kiss it, and beg God's forgiveness, and not a lustful hand shall be laid on your body.'

'May God bless ye, Father,' Susan said, and did as she was commanded.

'And now you, woman,' the priest said, turning to Hélène.

Susan got to her feet. 'And they would spread tales of the blind fanaticism of the Spanish priesthood in these islands. Be sure that I shall ever sing your praises, Father. And be sure too that from this moment forth I shall be the most devout of churchgoers.'

The priest smiled at her, but his eyes were cold. 'I am sure you will be afforded every opportunity, to be devout, señora.' He turned to the Commandant. 'I have done my duty. But mark me well, Don Rodrigo, the man who practises lewdness upon either of these women will suffer eternal damnation.'

The Commandant inclined his head in a brief nod. 'Be sure of that. But as they would appear to have confessed their guilt there need be no further delay in the matter.' He pointed at the roof. 'These rafters will do. Hang them here, and then set fire to the house.'

As Susan stared at him in horror, and felt her limbs turning to water, the sun dipped behind the mountains of the larger island to plunge the evening into darkness.

'Oh, Christ,' Kit moaned. 'Oh, God have mercy on me.'

Jean said nothing. He watched the house, clearly visible from where they lay hidden, as showers of sparks shot upwards from the collapsing roof and seared across the evening air. The interior also burned, and to aid the flames the doors and windows had been unshuttered and thrown wide, so that the breeze could get to the fire. Thus the holocaust gave off a vast glow, which illuminated the verandah and the steps and the soldiers grouped a short distance away. And from the rafters on the verandah, only now beginning to scorch, the two bodies swayed. Did one still kick, or was that the wind? Both had kicked when they had been hoisted from the floor, the ropes tightening around their necks, their ears singing, even as they had been filled with the obscene jeers of the cheated men below them. But now, surely, they were dead.

'Oh, Christ,' Kit moaned.

'He may help you,' Jean said. 'But not here.'

Kit raised his head; tears rolled down his cheeks. 'Had we stayed . . .'

'And died beside them? What do you think the two of us could have accomplished, against so many?'

'But that they should be hanged, like . . . Jean, you have a heart of stone.'

Jean continued to stare at the dangling bodies; now their skirts were starting to burn. 'Aye,' he said at last. 'As of this moment, Kit, I have a heart of stone. And you had best develop one as well. We shall make them pay. Swear that, Kit.'

'I swear it,' Kit said fiercely. 'We shall make them pay, Jean. A thousand times.'

'A thousand times. Or may God heap such a fire on our heads. Now come, we'll not do it by staying here.'

He rose to his hands and knees, and then stood up, began to find his way down the uneven slope.

Kit stumbled behind him. 'Where shall we go?'

'Hispaniola.'

'But what shall we do there?'

'Survive, in the first place, Kit. We shall be *matelots*, you and I. As we have no others left in the world, so shall we need no others. Back to back we shall face the world. And then we shall find, or if necessary we shall make ourselves a boat, and get away. Perhaps to your friends in the Leewards.'

'God forbid that,' Kit said. 'To the Warners? They'd probably hang us quicker than the Dons. Anyway, when I see that little upstart again it shall be with gold pieces overflowing from my pockets.'

'Which upstart did you mean?'

'The man, of course. But it goes for her as well. There'll be naught she understands so well as money.'

Jean felt the sand of the beach beneath his toes. 'And no doubt, by the time your pockets do overflow, she'll have learned some sense. Now come, we must shed our weapons.'

'Then how will we survive?'

'We'll not survive even the swim, encumbered by swords and pistols. Leave them here. We'll take a knife each, and make sure it lies in the middle of your back. Now mark me well, Kit, we'll go slow and steady, and we'll make as little splash as possible.'

'We'll not go down,' Kit said confidently. ''Tis scarce a mile from shallow to shallow.'

'A shade further, I think,' Jean said. 'And I was thinking more of sharks.'

He waded into the water, and the next wave lapped at Kit's toes. Sharks. He had forgotten them. So they swam deep and seldom attacked men who were not already injured. But a mile was a long stretch of water. For a moment he felt that he would not be able to do it. Then he looked over his shoulder, at the house, burning like a beacon on the hilltop. He was too far away for detail, now, and yet he felt he could see the two women, hanging from the rafters. How much did he hate? He did not know. At the moment perhaps not at all. He just wanted to lie on the sand and die. And weep while he died. And think of Grandmama. But if he lay on the sand he would not die, at least not until the Dons found him, and then he would die slowly, and painfully. So why not die in the sea?

Jean was already well out, swimming steadily, not looking back, and now that it was dark, the huge bulk of Hispaniola seemed close enough to touch.

So perhaps he would not die, but would live, to fulfil his oath. He ran into the water with great splashing bounds, allowed it to grip him at the waist, fell forward and began to swim, too quickly at first, exactly as Jean had warned him not to, so that he lost his breath. Then he almost turned back, but after a few moments he regained control of himself, and struck out after his friend. Then the night became endless. Only a little over a mile. How long does it take to swim a mile? Fifteen minutes? Half an hour? No longer, surely. He could pretend he was walking it. But that was too exhausting. It was necessary to blot out the sea, and the growing agony of his arms, and the lurking fear in his belly. Because the sea was so dark, and contained so many things of which a man might be afraid.

He thought of Marguerite Warner. Would she be married by now? He did not know. He knew so little about her, except that she was proud, and angry, and contemptuous of him. But he knew something of her feel. In that perhaps he was ahead even of her husband. Her feel and her smell. He dreamed of the softness of her flesh, the hardness of her thighs and the firmness of her belly, the tickle of her hair and the texture of her skin. Marguerite Warner. When he again saw her, with his pockets overflowing with gold, she would look on him differently. And together they would recreate a race of giants, like Edward Warner and Tony Hilton, because that was what their children would be, part Warner and part Hilton, destined to rule these islands.

But when next he saw her she would be an old married woman, and probably a mother several times over. He felt so disconsolate his legs drooped and his breath went, and he trod water, and looked up at the immense bulk of the island in front of him, It had not moved, had grown no larger and no smaller. So then, he lacked the strength to go on. He would drown here, disappear forever in the narrow strait between Tortuga and Hispaniola, and be totally forgotten. In all the world, there was no one who would wish to remember Kit Hilton. Jean? For a while, perhaps. Because Jean would survive. He had the gift of survival within him.

And Marguerite Warner? Would she ever remember the boy who had dumped her in the water butt? They had been happy that evening after the Warners had left. Grandmama had laughed and Madame DuCasse has sung to to them and Monsieur D'Ogeron and Monsieur DuCasse had told stories as they had drunk Grandmama's wine. Now all were gone, and all were forgotten.

'Kit? Kit?' Jean, splashing about close to him.

He opened his mouth, swallowed water, and went down, and touched sand. He bobbed back up to the surface, and Jean seized his arms and pulled him into the shallows.

He knelt, up to his waist in water, and panted, and listened to his heart throb. 'You should not have come back.'

'We are *matelots*. We do not exist, without each other. Listen. To the silence.'

Kit could hear nothing save the beating of his own heart. 'My throat is parched.'

'And mine also. But we had best not leave the beach in the darkness,' Jean said. 'We shall sleep here, and explore tomorrow. But we are alive, Kit, there is the important thing. We are alive, and we will stay alive.'

Alive. He crawled out of the water, and crawled and crawled and crawled, dragging each leaden limb after its mate until he was on dry sand, and flopped on his face. God, how exhausted he was. Only a mile, and he seemed to have swum for ever.

Jean fell beside him, was instantly asleep. Jean had saved his life just now, by reminding him that he could do nothing but live or die. His head dropped, and he dozed, and was immediately awake again. His tongue seemed cloven to the roof of his mouth. To sleep, without slaking that thirst, would be impossible. So once again he crawled, hand over hand, knee in front of knee, across the sand, until the sand changed to grass, and he heard the trickle of running water.

Now he got to his feet, staggered through the grass, ignored the branches which brushed his face and pulled at his hair, and fell, half into a flow of the most beautiful fresh water he had ever tasted. He drank, and buried his face in the sweetness, and drank again, and scooped it over his head and shoulders, and drank again. And at last pulled himself away. He must tell Jean about it. But Jean seemed soundly asleep. Time for him in the morning.

Kit Hilton slept.

And woke to a peculiar sound, such as he had never heard before. Snarling dogs. But these were not dogs. He had heard dogs often enough before. His own dog.

He sat up. It was daylight. His arms and legs still felt tired, but his brain was clear and his thirst was gone. And two human dogs were snarling and growling close to him.

On the beach. And now there was another sound, a shout of alarm, from Jean.

Kit jumped to his feet, pushed his way through the branches, arrived at the edge of the beach, gazed at Jean in horror. His friend lay on his back, arms pinned by a creature which sat on them and held his head. But the creature was a human being. Almost entirely shrouded in long hair, a beard with drooped to his navel, his skin burned to a mahogany colour, for he wore only a kind of kilt, from his waist to his knees.

And he was only one of a pair. His companion knelt above Jean, tearing at the boy's breeches, mouth slobbering with delight at having found something new, and unspoiled. *Boucaniers*. Members of the derelict outlaw population of Hispaniola who lived by smoking the meat, the *boucan*, of the wild cattle which roamed the plains.

But Jean was shouting for help.

Kit reached into the small of his back, pulled out his knife. It was a seaman's knife, nearly a foot long, of which seven inches were blade, two-edged and sharp-pointed. It was not intended to kill humans. But it could. And right this minute he wanted to kill more than anything else in the world.

Jean screamed as the claws of the *boucanier* reached for his genitals; his body twisted to and fro. Kit uttered a bellow of rage and vicious hatred, of all things living, and bounded from the trees. He covered the beach in a succession of tremendous leaps. The first man sat up, rocking back on his heels; the second released Jean's arms and turned, blinking at the apparition hurtling towards him. He stood up as Kit reached him, knife thrust forward; perhaps before Kit even intended it the blade was buried up to its hilt in the *boucanier*'s chest. He died without a sound, still falling backwards, and as Kit's fingers were wrapped around the haft the knife came out with a jerk, leaving a gush of blood in its place.

The second *boucanier* stared at his companion in horror, fingers still scrabbling at the cutlass which hung from his belt.

But Kit could not have stopped himself now. He had killed, and he wanted to kill again. The knife whipped back, and then forward; this time the man shrieked as he collapsed on to the sand. And Kit collapsed beside him, panting.

Jean sat up. '*Mon Dieu*,' he said, 'I had supposed myself handicapped by a boy, but now I think it is you who will be handicapped by me. And you have saved me from rape, no less. There is a fate I had never expected to experience.' He put his arm around Kit's shoulder, felt it tremble. 'What did Colonel Warner call you? The devil's own spawn? Aye, they sent our families to hell; from hell will we re-emerge to torment them, you and I.'

2

The Jungle

The sun sailed above the mountains of Hispaniola. It had risen some hours earlier, but then its true majesty, and its true heat, had been obscured by the mist which shrouded the hills. Now it would no longer be restrained, and suddenly the morning was hot, where before it had been no more than close. In seconds the moisture which had earlier clung to leaf and branch and made clothes and hands clammy to the touch, was whisked away in an upward gush of sweat and steam. And now, too, images became clear, and sound seemed to travel farther. From the trees which fringed the plain the herd of cattle appeared to have come closer, although it had not moved. But it could be heard, a hundred hooves pawing at the sparse grass, more than a score of double-jointed jaws rhythmically chewing, while the birds hopped behind in search of displaced worms, and a small cloud of dust eddied around the brown bodies. Imported by the Spaniards over a century before to ensure their food supply, the cattle had multiplied so vigorously on the rich grasslands of the huge island that they had been allowed to run wild, to the benefit of the *boucaniers*.

The dust was useful, for the drift indicated the direction of the slight breeze. Kit Hilton wormed along on his belly, his musket pushed in front of him, his powder-horn banging against his back beside his cutlass, moving parallel to the herd to get downwind of them. Behind him, Jean DuCasse paused for breath, and to count again.

'Seventeen, nineteen, twenty-one, twenty-three head, Kit. I have never seen so many in one place before. Do you think we will get two shots?'

'We'll try,' Kit said.

The responsibility was his. Jean was no hand with a musket, and powder was too scarce to be wasted. The little they possessed they had taken from two other *boucaniers* a week ago, in the same manner as they had got their cutlasses and their pistols. This was a violent world, in which only a man's *matelot*, the companion with whom he shared his food, his sleep, his every breath, and in time, no doubt, his death, was to be trusted, even for an instant. It seemed a long cry back over two years to the day he had knifed his first man, and vomited in the sand, and then wept. Since then he had killed again, twice.

He had killed to survive. He often wondered why. Those first two men had been repulsive to him. He had destroyed them as he would have destroyed two wild dogs. But was he any better, now? His beard reached the centre of his chest, and his hair the centre of his back. He wore an uncured skin, roughly cut into the shape of a pair of breeches, with an odour stronger than that of any dead animal. His feet were bare, and hardened to a quality of leather. He existed to hunt, like a wild animal, and to smoke the meat he managed to kill against the days, or sometimes weeks when the cattle were absent. He slept in the open, and cared nothing for wind and rain.

Jean was no different. Only when together in the cool of

THE DEVIL'S OWN

the dusk did they revert to human beings, did they ever remember the good times in Tortuga, the laughter of Albert DuCasse or Susan Hilton; did they ever still vow revenge on every Spaniard they could catch, as if they had ever caught any; and did they ever still dream of escaping this living hell, and becoming once again men, with a change of clothes and an upright walk.

And only then did they dream of other things, too. Of the girls on Tortuga? Of Marguerite Warner? He did not know of whom he dreamed. She was woman, with face and hair and legs. And she did not wear silk. When he dreamed it was of two naked bodies twined in a sweating, angry embrace, and when the woman spoke it was to scream. Jean also had dreams like that, and on those occasions they even reached for one another.

No, indeed, he reflected as he crawled through the grass; they were no different from the creatures he had slaughtered for being just such animals.

Jean wriggled level with him. 'Company.'

Kit watched the grass and the trees. There was something moving to his left, also downwind of the herd of cattle, also stealthily. 'Twenty cows will attract everyone within ten miles. We'll not give them time.' He was within range, just, he calculated. He aimed his musket, drew back the hammer, and released the lever.

Almost before the explosion had sounded, the herd was away, lolloping towards the distant fringe of trees. But now there were only twenty-two; one of them lay in the grass, half hidden.

'Bastards,' Jean growled, starting to his feet. For at least ten men had now appeared, in pairs, from different hideaways in the scrub.

Kit knelt, hastily reprimed the musket, ramming home another ball.

'Halloa there,' Jean bellowed, running forward. ' 'Tis our kill.'

The men checked, a dangerous semicircle, close to the bleeding, writhing animal.

'I fired also,' said one of the bearded *matelots*.

Jean turned to look. There was but a single puff of black smoke, rising above the grass which concealed Kit.

'Bah,' said another. 'It matters not. There is enough for all.'

'No.' Jean drew his cutlass.

'One against ten?' demanded the first spokesman.

'The boy is right,' said another man, small, dark and heavy-set. 'If he killed the beast, then it is his.'

'He is your *matelot?*'

'He made the kill,' said the small man.

'Bah,' said the challenger again. But his companion was already sidling away.

'I thank you, friend,' Jean said.

'You are alone?' asked the small man.

Jean smiled. 'Not so, monsieur.'

Kit stood up, the primed musket set against his shoulder.

The small man also smiled; he had very bright teeth. 'You are the two young ones. We have heard of you. We have travelled north to speak with you. I am Bartholomew Le Grand.'

'Portuguese Bart,' Jean said. 'We have heard of you also, monsieur. Jean DuCasse, at your service.'

'Armand Duchesne,' said the man beside Burt.

'And Kit Hilton,' Kit said, approaching. 'I understand your intention, monsieur.'

Bart continued to smile. 'So why fight about it, Monsieur Hilton? This cow will divide into four, where it will never divide into ten. And we have much to speak of.'

Kit glanced at Jean, who shrugged. 'That is true, monsieur.' He knelt, passed his knife across the throat of the dying animal; blood gushed, and the kicking ceased. 'Let us make haste.'

They laid down their weapons and got to work. The other *boucaniers* had retreated some distance, and watched them, muttering. But they would risk nothing.

'Because we are feared.' Bart's hands were red with blood as he sliced through sinew and muscle to remove the cow's legs. 'There is not a *boucanier* does not know of Portuguese Bart. And there is not a *boucanier* does not know of the two young men. We four, monsieurs, could rule this plain.'

'With you as leader,' Jean murmured.

'I am the oldest. I am most experienced. Now let us build a fire. Armand?'

His *matelot* nodded, went to the trees to begin collecting wood.

'Here?' Kit asked.

'I have a glass.' Bart took the eyepiece of a telescope from his pocket. 'This is good, eh? And the sun, pouff. We will soon have a huge blaze.'

THE DEVIL'S OWN

'What else do you have, monsieur?' Jean asked.

Bart grinned at them. 'I have a cache, monsieur. Pistols, and powder. We took them from a Spanish hunting party. Oh, they are there, too. We buried them alive, after we had played with them a little. I do not like the Spaniards, monsieur.'

'Neither do we,' Jean said.

Kit stood up, watched the other *boucaniers* running towards the wood. He turned, looked at the cloud of dust on the far side of the plain. 'And they do not like us.'

Bart scrambled to his feet, frowned into the haze. 'A squadron of lancers. Bastards. We must hurry. Bring what you can.'

He seized an armful of still quivering red flesh, and ran for the trees. Jean and Kit did likewise. Armand watched them come, his arms full of firewood.

'Make haste,' Bart shouted.

Armand dropped the wood, hesitated, staring at the dust; now the horsemen's cries could be heard, and now, too, the separate figures could be seen; they wore gay costumes and flowing red and yellow capes, and broad-brimmed black hats to protect themselves from the sun. They rode splendid horses, and they carried long steel-tipped lances.

Kit raced towards the shelter, while his blood pounded in his ears. Blood oozed against his chest and down into his breeches. Blood and sweat. He was afraid, and hated himself for that. They had vowed vengeance against the Dons. But the appearance of a single Spaniard, in all the arrogance of fine clothes and new weapons and good horses, had them running. As for a squadron ... but Bart had killed Spaniards. There was a man, if he was telling the truth. They had seen hunting parties, and carefully hidden until the danger was past; Bart had attacked, with his *matelot*, and scored a victory.

He had reached the woods, and stopped, panting. Because Jean and Bart had also stopped. They were looking back, at Armand, who was bending over the carcass, slicing away huge chunks of meat.

'Hurry,' Bart shouted. For the horsemen were close now, spreading out like a slowly opening fan, hallooing and cheering.

'Oh, Christ,' Jean said. And he meant it as a prayer.

Armand started to run, and the horses came up on either side. The Spaniards called out to the running man, laughing and jeering. Armand's head turned from side to side, and he staggered as he ran. But still he ran, without any longer knowing, or caring, where he was going, with the bleeeding meat still clutched in his arms, staggering into eternity.

A lance was thrust down, between his feet, and he fell, rolling over and over, for a moment lost to sight in the dust. Another lance went down, and they heard a scream, high and thin and wailing in the faint breeze. But it was not the scream of a dying man; the lancers were too clever for that. It was a scream of agony, and it was a scream of knowledge, too, that even more agony was on the way.

Kit leaned against a tree, and levelled his musket, bracing his arm. Bart reached across and slapped the barrel down. Kit gazed at him in surprise. 'He is your *matelot*.'

'And he is dead. If you kill one of those soldiers you must kill them all, or they will hang us all.'

Armand screamed again and again. Bart turned into the trees. 'Come,' he said. 'We must get away. Away and away and away. Listen. I have a plan, which needs only *men*. And you are men, young ones.'

Kit lay on his belly, on the sand, close by the water's edge. Close to where they had first come ashore. From here he could look at Tortuga, across the sea. From here he could even see the flag fluttering above the fort the Dons had built on the hilltop where Grandpapa had first built his house. Yellow and red, dominating the sky. Tortuga was now a Spanish watchpost, guarding the north shore of the larger island.

And he lay here, waiting to die. Because there was nothing else to do. Life was a kaleidoscope of agony and hatred, with only death at the end of it. He no longer believed that the happy days of his childhood had ever existed. It had been one of the good dreams. As for Marguerite . . . he suddenly realized that he could no longer truly remember her face. It was a patchwork of expressions, hating, fearing, dying perhaps. It was not a face he would ever see again.

Footsteps, on the sand behind him. He did not get up. Jean had said he would return on the fourth day, and this was the fourth day. So, if it was Jean, then it did not matter. If it was not Jean, then presumably he was about to die. He did not think he would care very much.

'It is foolish to lie here on the sand,' Jean said.

'It is foolish to do anything,' Kit said. 'It was foolish to swim across from Tortuga. It is not foolish to prolong misery?'

THE DEVIL'S OWN

Jean squatted beside him. 'So let us leave this place.'

'Let us flap our wings, and fly away. Where shall we fly, Jean? Antigua? It is not far. Scarce two hundred miles, as we should fly. Perhaps we could swim that distance. It would not take us longer than a week.'

'You are a melancholy fellow,' Jean said. 'I went for news of Bart. And I have come back with news of Bart. I would have thought such news would make you smile again.'

'He is hanged?'

'Not Bart,' Jean said. 'We wait for him, now.'

'We?' Kit rolled over, and sat up in the same instant, gazed at the three men who stood by the trees. *Boucaniers*, certainly; they might have been Jean himself.

But Bart was not amongst them.

'Where is he, then?'

'Out there,' Jean said.

Kit looked at the dark blue of the sea, and watched the pirogue come creeping along the shore, propelled by twelve paddles. Fashioned from untrimmed timber, it was hardly more than a large canoe, with a pointed stem and a pointed stern and a rounded bilge lacking a keel but very strong, careless of outcrops of rock or sand.

'We stole it,' Jean said. 'And have been coasting every night. Looking for men who would rather die with swords in their hands than lances up their asses. Are you such a man, Kit?'

Kit gazed at the boat. Their dream, come true. Had they the courage to seize it. How attached was he suddenly to become to this bloodstained sand. Because he knew too little of the sea. Always he had looked at it from the security of a beach. And that was an open boat.

'Where will we go?' he asked. And asked again, as they waded out to the pirogue, where Bart grinned at them with his magnificent teeth peering through the blackness of his beard. They were five, and there were a dozen men already in the boat, together with a few smoke-cured sides of beef. Enough for two days, perhaps. But no water. 'Where will we go?'

'Away,' Bart said. 'We leave this place, eh? Down there, to the east, beyond Puerto Rico, there are islands, sandbanks, creeks, those the Spaniards call the Virgins. We will go there.'

Kit sat in the stern and watched the water draining out of

his skin breeches. 'Windward,' he said. 'You'd go to Windward?'

Into the unchanging wind, the ceaseless current? Were they even more ignorant of the sea than he?

'Only fifty miles,' Bart said. 'We will row all night, and tomorrow morning we will be at Puerto Rico. We will rest there the day, and leave again at night. The day after tomorrow we will be amongst the Virgins. So we will only have beaches to comb. It will be better than this pesthole.'

They took turns at the paddles. They fought their way into an increasing sea, which pushed the prow of the pirogue into the air and set it shuddering down into the trough on the far side, each such dip being accompanied by a rattle of spray which soaked them and had them shivering. Soon the seasickness began, and spread. Undigested lumps of raw meat spewed on to the bilges with evil-smelling bile; men lay on their paddles and panted. Salt caked their lips and had them gasping for water. But there was only salt water. So instead they prayed for dawn, and a sight of the Rich Island.

It grew light, and Bart braced himself on the steering oar as he stood up. The wind had dropped to a flat calm, but the swell continued, making the pirogue rise and fall, tower above the waves and then disappear completely into the next trough. Bart shaded his eyes and stared to windward. 'Now that is strange,' he muttered.

Kit wanted to laugh, because he wanted to weep so very much. He pointed the other way. 'Look there.'

They had paddled all night, and Hispaniola lay perhaps ten miles astern of them, massive green-clad cliffs rising from the unending sea.

'By Christ,' Bart licked his lips, and gazed at his men. Not his men, yet. Not ever, now. They had followed him to escape hell. And he had led them into a waterless horror.

'We can be back ashore in an hour,' Kit said. 'The same wind, the same current, which has held us here all night, will sweep us back.'

'Back to Hispaniola?' someone muttered.

'What will you do?' Kit shouted. 'Sit here and die of thirst?'

'Oh, Christ,' Jean said. 'Oh, Christ.' Because he was in the stern, and still peering at the coast. They crowded aft, in such haste that the narrow craft rolled dangerously. They stared at the ship, not two miles away, drifting. Drifting because the wind had dropped. All her sails were set, but the

THE DEVIL'S OWN

canvas drooped against the yards. As did her flags and pennants. Those at the masthead were unrecognizable. But the great ensign on the jackstaff was familiar to them all. Yellow and gold, hanging limp.

'A *garda costa*,' someone whispered. 'We will hang this day.'

'She is no ship of war,' Bart growled. 'A coaster, from Isabel for San Domingo.'

'Is there a difference?' Kit was angry. With Bart, for leading them into this predicament; with himself, for agreeing to come at all. On Hispaniola he had at least existed. And then he had wanted to die. Now he was going to die, how badly did he want to live. 'She carries guns, and men with better weapons than ours. She will blow us out of the water.'

'She will not waste the powder,' Jean said. 'Why should she, when she knows that we are helpless?'

They sagged, with the pirogue, into the following trough. Bart alone remained standing, staring at the ship, his eyes narrow slits beneath the wrinkled frown of his brow. 'As you say, Monsieur DuCasse,' he said. 'They will not waste the time. She is not equipped for fighting. She will merely report what she has seen when she reaches San Domingo.'

'And *then* the *garda costa* will come,' Kit said. 'We must put back now. We have no choice.'

Bart did not move, but his tongue came out and circled his lips.

'Kit is right,' Jean said. 'This was a hopeless venture from the start. Even big sailing ships must work their way to windward, slowly. They say it takes a week from Barbados to Port Royal, and three weeks to get back. We shall not do it in this piece of bark.'

'A week,' Bart muttered. 'From Barbados. Two days, from here. To Port Royal. There is a place. Morgan is there. I have heard that he recruits, for another venture against the Main.'

Kit sighed. Morgan was nothing but a name. A dream, perhaps. A man who had already made L'Olonnais and Mansveldt and Hilton no more than memories. 'And we are here,' he said. 'So it is downwind. It is still far too long for us.'

'In *this*,' Bart said.

Their heads rose, and they stared at the drifting coaster. 'You are mad,' someone whispered.

'She will carry fifteen, twenty men,' Jean said. 'And passengers, no doubt.'

'And are we not seventeen?' Bart at last descended into the bilges where they crouched. 'Listen to me. We are forty. Sixty. Because what have we got to lose? You wish to go back to Hispaniola? To that stinking plain and those stinking cattle? To be treated as vermin? Hunted down whenever some *capitano* in San Domingo wishes to exercise his men? What do we there, but exist, and then die? So if we are going to die, why not let us die now? But die with the prospect of something better ahead of us. That ship may carry soldiers. But she may not. And if we take her, why, we'll be in Port Royal the day after tomorrow, and the whole world will be at our feet.'

They stared at him, their faces mixing incredulity with fear, with greed, with ambition. And with hope.

'By God,' Kit said. 'You are right.'

'Your name is Hilton. You've pirating in your blood. And you, Monsieur DeCasse?'

Jean chewed his lower lip, glanced from face to face. 'It would be better than putting back.'

Heads began to nod. 'But will they not see us approaching?' someone asked.

Bart grinned at them. 'Not even the Dons can see in the dark. Now lie down. Scatter yourself about the boat, that we may appear even more helpless than we are. And wait.'

Slowly, how slowly, the sun sank towards the horizon. There were no mountains out here to interrupt its imperious gaze. But yet the evening reminded Kit of the night Grandmama had died. Then too they had waited for the sun, and the sun had moved too slowly for them.

This time? The ship was about a mile away, still becalmed, still drifting. All afternoon they had watched the heavens, anxiously, fearing the slight puff of wind that might carry their prize beyond their grasp. But the day had stayed motionless.

Their prize. Kit lay against the pirogue's gunwale and stared at the ship. It was like a man, barehanded, setting out to seize a lion. Unless the lion slept. Then, perhaps, the man might have a chance. And certainly the ship had shown no interest in them. She drifted along, content in the knowledge that Hispaniola was close, that the next little wind would blow her around the headland and into port. Her crew had no reason to fear an open boat containing a few mad *boucaniers*.

Suddenly it was dark, with only the gigantic glow low on

THE DEVIL'S OWN

the horizon to mark where the sun had been. "Look to your weapons,' Bart said. 'And be sure you make no noise.'

He stood up, to peer across the swell at the coaster; she was easy to find because of the huge lantern dangling from her stern. 'Give way.'

The paddles dipped, and the pirogue started to crawl up and down the swell once again. Gone was the sea-sickness now, and even the fear. These men lived by violence, and here was the prospect of violence, with the prospect of rewards beyond their wildest dreams at the end of it. The ship grew ever larger.

'Stop.'

The swish of water stopped, and the paddles lay still. The men breathed, slowly and heavily, and Bart stared at the ship. It was only a hundred yards away now, turned downwind, for now too there were catspaws on the surface of the sea. Soon she would take off and leave them far behind. But now they were close enough; they could see the glow of the lanterns in the great cabin.

'Women,' someone muttered beside Kit. 'Do you think there'll be any women?'

Kit glanced at him, saw the saliva dribbling over the matted beard. By God, he thought, women. It hadn't occurred to him to want, or fear, that. But he wanted it, desperately. And feared it, too.

'Now,' Bart whispered. 'There can be no more stealth. Make as hard as you can for the stern. Give way, lads. Give way.'

The pirogue surged forward, the paddle-blades splashing. The ship remained a dark hulk on the water, its lanterns bobbing to the swell. Kit crouched up in the bow, his cutlass in his hand. He meant to be first on board. To seek women? To kill, and perhaps to be killed? He panted, and felt the sweat starting out on his body, making his hands slippery on the haft of his weapon.

He was afraid. But less of the thought that in a moment he might be killed than of the understanding that in a moment he would be killing. Always before it had happened suddenly, an act of desperate self-defence. This was premeditated. But those people were Spaniards. They had hanged Grandmama, those men or others like them. After doing what to her, first? They had heard a scream on that dreadful night, but it had been from Hélène DuCasse. She had been younger, and possibly more attractive.

And when they had finished, they had tied ropes around their necks and hoisted them from the verandah floor, legs kicking obscenely, bodies functioning obscenely. There. Now he hated. Now he would kill, and kill, and kill. And this time he would not vomit.

A voice cried out above him. The stern of the brig was immediately over his head, and a man looked down, for the first time seeing the dark shape of the pirogue as it sped through the water; he was shouting his alarm. But they were close enough. Kit placed his cutlass between his teeth, reached up, touched the ornate decorations which surrounded the stern cabin. And the great window opened, allowing a belch of light to flow over the sea and the pirogue, and the bearded animals who crouched there.

There was another shout, ended by an explosion as Bart fired his pistol. Kit wrapped his fingers around the lip of the open window, dragged himself up, swinging his legs through and seizing his cutlass as he opened his mouth to utter a gigantic shout. There were four men in the cabin, standing up, reaching for weapons, one just collapsing on to a seat; he was the one who had been looking through the window when the pistol had gone off.

Kit swung the cutlass round his head and then to and fro. He struck one of the men on the shoulder and blood flew. Another put up a sword, but it was a thin Spanish rapier, and the sweeping cutlass brushed it aside as if it had been a toothpick. The sword clattered against the wall and the Spaniard jumped behind it, his eyes bulging as Jean climbed through the opened window, followed immediately by Bart himself, brandishing a cutlass and roaring like a bull.

Kit was on top of the table, on his hands and knees as his back touched the low deck-beams. There was no one between him and the door, but the door was opening as one of the deck watch came in. Kit swung round, propelled himself forward, struck the man on the chest. He sat down at the foot of the companion-way to the poopdeck, and Kit stamped on him as he went up the ladder. There was another man at the top, just starting down. He held a pistol, and fired as he saw the *boucanier* beneath him. The flash filled the narrow space, and Kit fell against the bulkhead. But he felt no pain, and a moment later was lunging up the ladder, the cutlass held at the end of his rigid arm like a lance. The Spanish sailor took it in his belly, and made a frightful sound like an exploding bag of air. Blood cascaded over Kit's

THE DEVIL'S OWN 41

arm, and his stomach rolled, while the man came tumbling down the ladder to cannon against his legs.

'Deck,' Jean yelled behind him. 'Get on deck.'

Kit inhaled, scrambled up the ladder, checked as he emerged into the comparative light to see a dozen soldiers clad in breastplates and morions, and armed with muskets, still forming their line, having been dragged from below by the alarmed shout of the watch.

The muskets were levelled. Kit dropped to his knees, and a wave of heat seemed to shroud him, while a cloud of black smoke rose above the line of glinting morions. Someone stepped on Kit's back. No doubt it was Jean. Then there were others, scrambling by, howling with joy as they poured at the soldiers, who desperately dragged their swords from their scabbards as the *matelots* shrieked at them.

Kit got up, slowly. He was suddenly exhausted, and the blood-lust had gone. So had the exhilaration. Because the battle was over. He wondered how long it had lasted. A matter of seconds. The soldiers lay scattered; helmets rolled in the scuppers, swords and muskets littered the deck like the remains of a hideous feast.

And now the slaughter began. The crew, cowering in the hatchways and forward of the masts, wished only to surrender. To Portuguese Bart and his *boucaniers*?

The captain was borne to the gunwale, held in a dozen searching hands, fighting and begging for mercy. He was swung to and fro and launched into the air, to fall into the water with a tremendous splash. And as yet the sea was calm, and silent. He went deep and came up, shouting curses. But one of the *matelots* knew what was missing, and dragged a soldier's corpse to the gangway; the bloody flesh was rolled out, to fall beside the captain. Soon the *boucaniers* were pushing all the corpses overboard, while others seized the remaining members of the crew, and threw them, screaming and howling, after the dead.

Whom they were about to join. For the blood had spread across the sea, and the ever-present dark fins were creeping towards the ship. Now the living shrieked, in pain and in terror, and the water thrashed and seethed with horrible violence, and the night became hideous with sound.

Yet worse was in store. For lurking in the recesses of the after sleeping cabin the *boucaniers* had found a priest. With yells of joy they dragged the black-gowned figure on deck, into the glare of the lanterns others had lit, and threw him headlong into the blood and the slime that covered the deck, to roll on his back, arm and legs feebly kicking. Kit, still standing by the companion-way where first he had fallen, stared at him in horror, his mind a jungle of conflicting emotions. From the safety of the ridge behind which he and Jean had hid, he had watched the black-robed man thrusting his cross into the face of Grandmama, had understood what had transpired there, had watched her kiss the piece of wood. And afterwards had watched her pulled high to dangle from that beam. For how many tortured years would that scene haunt his memory?

And here was one of those same Dominicans. But here, too, was a man of age and dignity, grey-haired and restrained, even as he put his hand down to push himself into a sitting position, and then raised the hand to gaze at the red muck which clung to his fingers.

'A priest,' Jean breathed, his eyes alight with hate. For he too had watched the priest in Tortuga. And the woman who had been hoisted first had been his own mother.

'Aye,' Bart said, standing before the Spaniard. 'One of the blood-suckers.'

'Let's have him to the sharks,' someone shouted.

'Aye, let's hear him scream.'

'You don't want to be hasty,' Bart said, his mouth spreading in a terrible grin. 'He's a man of God. He'll give you a curse as he goes. He'll send you to eternal damnation.'

There was a yell of derision.

The Dominican was sitting up, staring at his captors with wide eyes, his right hand fumbling for the crucifix at his neck.

'He's a man of chastity, too,' Bart said. 'I'll wager he hasn't used his tool to do more than pee in twenty years, unless it's been to bugger some poor boy.'

There was another shriek, lust now entering the hatred as they understood their leader's meaning. They descended on the helpless man like a swarm of locusts, and he sobbed in pure terror; no doubt he even understood the bastard French spoken by the *boucaniers*.

Kit forced himself to move. The breeze was still gentle, and yet the ship seemed to be swaying and tossing, revolving around his head as he staggered forward. Bart looked up.

'Here's our hero,' he bellowed. 'Here's the devil's spawn himself, lads. We must give him the pleasure.'

The priest was below him, his habit pulled around his

shoulders, his legs twitching, his thighs pitifully white, his penis shrinking as if it would defend itself.

'Use my knife, Kit, boy,' someone offered, and a sharp blade was pressed into his left hand.

The priest stared at him; he no longer wept, but his lips moved, as if in prayer, or perhaps in entreaty.

'Come on, Kit,' someone howled in his ear.

He pushed the man aside, reached into his belt, pulled out his still unfired pistol.

'Hey,' Bart yelled.

But the pistol was already levelled; at this range he could not miss. There was a flash and a bang, and he was momentarily blinded by the puff of smoke. The limbs at his feet had ceased their twitching.

The *boucaniers* stared at him.

'Now why did you do that?' Jean demanded. 'You saw your grandmother hang. 'Twas after a priest had finished with her.'

'And now I have avenged her,' Kit said. 'Like a man. Not an animal.' He thrust the pistol back into his belt, dropped the knife to the deck, and faced them.

But there was more bewilderment than hostility in their gazes, and Bart shrugged. 'So you're not a lad for sport, Kit Hilton. You've the gut of a fighting man, spite all. Now let's get this ship turned. We're for Port Royal. And Henry Morgan.' He slapped Kit on the shoulder. 'He'll teach you what you're at, lad.'

Jean stood beside him on the foredeck as the anchor plunged into the translucent green water. 'By Christ,' he said. 'But there is a sight.'

They had thought the harbour at Tortuga the most sheltered in the world. But here was something beyond their wildest imaginings. North of them lay Jamaica, a smaller version of Hispaniola, mountains reaching up towards the sky like rows of gigantic teeth, blotting out the wind, while to the west, protruding from the shore, there curved a long, low spit of land, a natural breakwater which all but encircled the bay in which they lay. The spit itself was chiefly denoted by the row of palm trees which lined it, and which had given it a name, the Palisades, but at the end it widened into a peninsula, and here was the town. A strange town, hardly more substantial to look at than the settlement in Tortuga, with tumbledown shacks and a cluster of tents and only one or two real buildings—but dominated by a church, whose square tower rose above the surrounding debris like a watchdog.

And unlike Tortuga, even seen from the deck of a ship, this place teemed. It gave off an enormous hubbub, and it gave off an enormous effluvium as well; the faint westerly wind carried the stench of rum and sweat, sewage and perfume, across the huge expanse of water which was the harbour. Although perhaps much of the smell, and the noise, too, came from the ships. Not one of the *boucaniers* had ever seen so many ships in one place at the same time. Below the clear green water the bottom was obscured by anchors and trailing lengths of warp and chain. There were little rowing boats and half-decked sloops, trim, fast brigs and two-masted schooners, and more than a few big three-masters, dominated by two galleons, with twenty guns in a broadside and culverins peering forward and aft, capable of throwing a twelve-pound ball upwards of a mile with some accuracy. They presented a general air of neglect and even decay, with paint peeling from their topsides, with shattered bowsprits and tarnished giltwork, with sails carelessly furled and revealing many a rent, with long strands of worm-filled weed trailing away from their bottoms. But all possessed at least an anchor watch, and boats plied ceaselessly to and fro.

' 'Tis like a fleet of war,' Bart whispered. 'Preparing for an armada.'

'They'd not survive their first gale of wind,' Kit said contemptuously.

'But the storm season is over,' Jean pointed out. 'Why, it is all but Christmas.'

'I wonder what we must do,' Bart whispered, half to himself, 'to announce our arrival. Port Royal is but the seaport. There is another place somewhere on the mainland itself, where the Governor resides.'

'Spanish Town,' Kit said. 'I have heard of it.'

'It must be over there.' Jean pointed at the north-eastern end of the bay, where the roofs of houses could just be seen. 'But it seems we have to worry less about visiting them than having them visit us.'

They looked after his finger. A barge came towards them from the mainland shore. It was propelled by twelve oars a side, each manned by a half-naked, sweating Negro. Amidships and forward were a guard of a dozen soldiers, wearing long, red coats and wide, flat hats, and armed with pikes

THE DEVIL'S OWN 45

and swords. And in the stern were two gentlemen, from their dress; above their heads a gigantic Cross of St George floated in the breeze.

'You'll gather, lads,' Bart bellowed. ' 'Tis being visited by the authorities, we are.'

The *boucaniers* formed two lines on deck. They were still sufficiently elated by their victory of two days before to obey their leader without question. And they looked more like men, now. Most had shaved; Kit and Jean indeed had removed all the hair from their faces, but many of their companions had retained at least moustaches. And they wore velvet breeches and cambric shirts. One or two sported coats and one hardy soul even insisted on wearing a breastplate, despite the heat. Their heads were bare, the occasional one bound up in a brightly coloured bandanna; their feet were also bare. But they had armed themselves well, and no one could possibly mistake them for anything less than fighting men.

Nor were the two visitors likely to make any mistakes in their judgements. First in the gangway was a small man, with narrow features, a perpetual frown to suggest that he was shortsighted, but none the less with piercing, inquisitive eyes. He did not uncover as he gained the deck, but instead stared aft and then up at the rigging, seeking a flag and finding none. He wore a broad-brimmed hat, blue with a gold trim, and his coat was also dark blue, edged with gold lace. His breeches were white buckskin, which made a startling contrast. His stockings were also white, and his shoes black leather. But most amazing of all, he was unarmed and carried only a cane similar to the one Kit remembered in the possession of Philip Warner.

'By God,' he remarked. 'As villainous a collection as even I have ever seen. My name is Thomas Modyford, and I am His Majesty's Governor of Jamaica. Who is master of this ship?'

Bart stepped forward, looking unusually nervous. 'I have that privilege, sir.'

'A *boucanier*,' Modyford said, in tones of contempt.

'As are my followers, monsieur.'

'And whence came you by this ship?' The question was asked by the second man, who now appeared at the top of the ladder. He was altogether bigger than his companion, although not tall, heavy-set with powerful shoulders and wide thighs, suggesting an enormous physical strength. His face was round, with full cheeks and a big chin, decorated by a carefully trimmed wisp of brown beard, as his moustache was also carefully combed and curled. The marks of the dandy extended to his clothes; his coat was of gold-coloured cloth, and open, to show the lace in his shirt front, and his red breeches vanished into cavalier boots which clumped on the deck. His sword was a Spanish rapier, hanging from a wide, crimson velvet baldric, and he wore a leather belt at his waist, ostensibly to carry two pistols, but more, Kit thought, to pull in his belly. He sported a diamond ring on each of the fingers of his left hand, and smelt of pomade. He might easily have been mistaken for a fop. But there was a habit of command in his voice, and his brown eyes, disarmingly mild, flickered from right to left with total certainty as he established the capabilities of the ship.

'We took her, monsieur,' Bart said. 'Off the coast of Hispaniola. Not two days gone.'

'Took her, by God,' Modyford said. 'With this band of butchers?'

Bart grinned. 'It was butchery we needed, Your Excellency.'

'You've a cabin?' asked the big man.

Bart indicated the companion-way. Modyford stepped past the waiting men, but his companion checked before Kit, frowning. 'I know your face, boy,' he said. 'Have you sailed with me before?'

Kit's heart started to pound. The voice had a Welsh lilt to it.

'No, sir,' he said. 'Perhaps you knew my father. My name is Christopher Hilton.'

'Tony Hilton's boy?'

'His grandson, sir.'

'Then you're a rascal, by Christ. I've known no greater scoundrel than Tony Hilton, and I'm no stranger to villainy.'

Kit felt his cheeks burn. But mainly with anger. His name, and Susan's memory, were his only worthwhile possessions. 'You'll acknowledge he was also a man of courage and ability, sir.'

'What, Tony Hilton?'

'Or must I make you,' Kit shouted, his hand dropping to his sword hilt.

'Draw on your betters, would you?' Modyford cried.

'Kit, be careful,' Jean begged.

But the big man laughed. 'Tony Hilton's grandson, by Christ. You've the manner more than the appearance. When first I came to these accursed islands I sailed with Tony Hilton. Aye, he had courage, and ability, and he was my friend. As will you be. Give me your hand, boy. My name is Henry Morgan.'

Kit had his fingers crushed.

'Christopher Hilton.' Modyford was frowning. 'You're from Tortuga?'

"Some time ago, sir,' Kit said.

'Aye. Your name was mentioned to me but a few months back, as I recall. Why, 'tis a small world, to be sure.'

'My name, sir?' Kit was incredulous.

'In St John's, it was. I've estates in Barbados, you understand, and was on my way home to Jamaica from a tour of inspection, when a contrary wind blew me into Antigua. There I was the guest of the Deputy Governor, Colonel Philip Warner.'

'And *he* asked after *me*, sir?'

'He mentioned your name, Master Hilton, but in no very complimentary terms, I am sorry to say. I spoke of the projects planned by my friend here, Admiral Morgan, and Colonel Warner wondered that we did not recruit in Tortuga. A den of cut-throats, was his description of the place. Of whom, he said, the Hiltons are the worst. There are but two left, thank God, he said, the old whore and her pirate grandson.'

'My grandmother is dead, sir.'

'Then you've my sympathy.' Modyford's face relaxed into a smile; his eyes remained cold. 'But you're not without a friend in the Warner household, lad, if it's any solace to you. The Governor's daughter, young Mrs Templeton, took me aside and asked if indeed we planned to visit Tortuga. They were then unaware that it had been taken by the Dons.'

'Mrs Templeton?' Kit's heart pounded more than when he had boarded the coaster. 'Would her name be Marguerite?'

'Aye. The most beautiful creature I have ever seen. There's the truth. And married to a man four times her age. A sad waste.'

Sad? And Marguerite had asked after him? Marguerite, whom he had all but forgotten? Marguerite, whom he had caused to hate him, he was sure. 'But, sir,' he cried, as Modyford would have turned away again. 'What did she say?'

Again the frosty smile. 'Why, I forget most of it, indeed I do. Something about giving you her regards, as she had decided to forgive you. And I did not even find out what you had done to the gorgeous creature. But I formed the impression, as much from her father's dislike as from her own consideration, that you were a man of parts. The lad is your sailing master, no doubt,' he remarked to Bart.

'Eh? Oh, yes, indeed, sir,' Bart agreed. 'He is that. And a devil when it comes to action. Why, that is what we call him, amongst ourselves. The devil's own spawn.'

'The devil's own,' Morgan said, and laughed again. 'Aye, a good name for a Hilton. A good name for you, boyo.'

'She remembers me,' Kit said to Jean, ignoring the men. 'By God. After all these years, she remembers me.'

'And perhaps me also,' Jean said with a smile. 'Will you not allow me to meet these gentlemen?'

'Oh, forgive me, dear friend. I am quite overwhelmed. Quite . . . allow me to present my friend, Jean Du-Casse, Captain Morgan.'

Morgan frowned through his smile. 'Admiral, Kit. You'll call me Admiral. The pleasure is mine, Monsieur DuCasse. You've wine on board this ship?'

'Oh, indeed, monsieur,' Bart said, and led the way into the great cabin.

'A Spanish merchantman.' Modyford sat at the table, still without removing his hat. 'And taken by a handful of *boucaniers*, by God.'

'You came in through the stern, there.' Morgan did remove his hat, placing it carefully beside him. He had found the bullet marks on the deck-head, while the stain on the table was clearly blood.

'Kit led the way,' Bart said. 'Why, he'd have taken her single-handed if we'd lagged behind.'

'Tony Hilton's grandson,' Morgan said again, smiling at the boy. 'Your grandfather had a gift of command, Kit, lad. You'd do well to follow in his footsteps. He might have made a great name for himself, but his interests lay at home, with that magnificent woman of his. She's dead, you say?'

'She was hanged by the Dons when they took Tortuga.'

'By God,' Morgan said. 'Hanged, by God.'

'So you've a score to settle,' Modyford said.

Kit stared at him. The thought of Marguerite remembering him had quite driven every other concept, even his reason for being here, from his mind. But how could *he* remember *her*, without also remembering everything else. 'Aye, sir,' he said, 'I've a score.'

THE DEVIL'S OWN 49

'You all have, Mr Hilton', Modyford said. 'As you were *boucaniers*. First thing, you'll hoist the English flag.'

'I am a Frenchman, sir,' Bart said. 'And so are all my crew, saving only Kit.'

'If you sail with me,' Morgan said. 'It is as Englishmen.'

'And do we sail with you, Admiral?' Jean asked.

'These ships are not here to rest,' Morgan said. 'I've accumulated them all the year. This ship of yours will carry a hundred men.'

'She'll sail, and fight, better with forty,' Kit said.

'Spoken like a seaman, Kit. But I need men. Men are even more important than ships. The ships must carry them without sinking. Nothing more.'

'Carry them where, Admiral?' Bart asked.

Morgan smiled at him. 'Where Henry Morgan sails is known to Henry Morgan alone,' he said. 'Saving my good friend Governor Modyford here. But I'll promise you all the riches in the world, Captain Le Grand. Ask those who were with me at Porto Bello, or Maracaibo.'

Bart glanced at the two boys. ' 'Tis what we came for.'

'Aye,' Kit said. 'We'll sail with you to hell itself, Admiral Morgan.'

Still Morgan smiled. 'It may well come to that, Mr Hilton. And you will, indeed, sail with me.' He caught the expression on Kit's face. 'And your friend, Monsieur DuCasse. We'll find you another sailing master, Captain Le Grand. These two young men are my special charge. Why, the very name of Hilton will inspire the fleet.'

Because it was, after all, a fleet. There were more than a score of ships, led by the two galleons, but dwindling down to little ten-man cockleshells, wallowing in the long Caribbean swell. A fleet, carrying him to fame and wealth? Morgan promised him no less. And what would he do then? How the mention of her had indeed brought memory flooding back, every gesture, every movement, every change in her tone. Married to a man four times her age. And a mother? He did not know. But thinking of an episode from her past. Suppose, then, he did reappear, famous and wealthy?

Supposing it were possible. He stood on the poopdeck of the *Monarch*, the larger of the two galleons, and watched the rest through his glass. They had been at sea for over a week, making ever south-west across an empty ocean, and throughout that time they had been favoured with a light beam wind. Yet on nearly all the ships the pumps had clacked ceaselessly, and streams of dirty brown water poured over the sides; leave vessels as rotten as these for twenty-four hours and they took six feet of water in the hold. How they were ever manoeuvred or fought, what would happen were the slightest wind to spring up . . .

'It does not bear thinking about.' Morgan stood beside him. Now that they were at sea he had discarded the coat and the rings and the rapier, and wore only an open-necked shirt and breeches, with a cutlass hanging from the belt at his waist. Yet his hair was as carefully dressed as ever; he had his surgeon attend to it every morning.

'You're a mind-reader, sir,' Kit said.

'Faith, 'tis not difficult to read your mind, Kit. You spend more time on the helm, more time staring at the charts and studying the set of the sails, more time watching those other ships, than you do sleeping. The sea is in your blood.'

'And is it not in yours, sir?'

'By God, the very sight of it turns my stomach. My people were farmers. Good farmers, lad. You've a knowledge of Wales?'

'I've a knowledge of no land save Tortuga and Hispaniola, sir.'

Morgan nodded. 'What will you do, where will you go, when you've pockets full of gold?'

'You speak as if this is to be your last venture, sir.'

'Every venture is my last, boyo. Until I am sure I'm alive at the end of it. But this one . . . I pursue a dream. 'Tis a thought I have had for years. Where do you think we are headed? Look through your glass. Forward for a change.'

Kit peered at the dark line of trees, fringed with surf, which suddenly filled the horizon. ' 'Tis a large island, to be sure.'

' 'Tis the Main, boy.'

Kit brought up the glass again. The very thought made his heart pound. 'Then it is Porto Bello we seek, Admiral? I would have thought, after the attention paid it by Drake, and yourself, and God knows how many in between, that it was scarce worth sacking.'

'Porto Bello is not worth sacking,' Morgan said. 'And there is fever. Oh, 'tis an unwholesome coast. I seek more. That bay opening to port is the mouth of the River Chagres. We will anchor there. I know the place well; I reconnoitred it three years ago, which is when this plan first came to me.

I have arranged with the Indians who inhabit this coast to supply us with canoes, and we shall make our way up the river. It is quite practical at this season. When the rains come, then it is a violent torrent. But now it will be calm and quiet.'

'You mean to go inland?'

'There is a lake from whence this river rises. That is our first destination. You'll command a canoe, Kit. But mark me well. This venture, like all such ventures, will be a perilous business. Keep your wits about you, and even more, stay close to my pennant. Bear that in mind, boy. Now, and afterwards. Now see to your gear. Take your friend with you.'

For the land was opening fast, and a few hours later the *Monarch* was slowly entering the bay, sail shortened to mere scraps of canvas, leadsman hanging in the bows to call the depths, while the deep blue shaded to a deep green, and then to pale green, so clear that they could pick out every rock and every patch of seaweed below the surface, before suddenly changing to an opaque brown as they entered the discharge from the river.

Kit stared at the shore through his glass; the beach seemed to stretch interminably in either direction, broken only by the gush of slow-moving brown water. But there were also people on the beach, just visible against the crowding trees. He had never seen an Indian, although Grandmama had told him sufficient tales of the Caribs who infested the islands south of Antigua, and against whom the Warners had waged an unceasing war of survival, despite the love shared by old Sir Thomas and the Princess Yarico. Or was the enmity because of that love, and its result, the legendary Indian Tom Warner?

But these would not be Caribs, on the mainland. Indeed, they did not look very warlike, being small, squat, brown-skinned men, wearing only breech-clouts, carrying wooden spears and bows and arrows, surrounded by dogs, and by naked children. There were women, too, gathered behind them, some entirely naked, others wearing little aprons; they would be the married ones. But if he had hoped to be excited or even interested by them, he was again disappointed. Shorter than their menfolk, with protruding bellies and sagging breasts, with flat, ugly features and dank black hair lying below their shoulders, he thought them repulsive. Or would he find any woman so, at this moment?

'The Admiral wishes us to disembark,' Jean said, and at

that moment the order was given and the huge rusting anchor plunged through the suddenly dirty water to disappear into the mud of the bottom. Jean's eyes gleamed, and he was clearly excited. Like Kit, he had stripped to the waist, and wore only a pair of breeches, and the belt from which hung his pistols and his cutlass and his powderhorn, while he carried a musket across his shoulder. He was prepared for war.

Kit went to the gunwale where the twelve men who were to form his section waited. As villianous a group of cutthroats as he had ever seen, scarred and vicious. Without exception they reminded him of Bale, the villain who had dogged Grandmama with pathetic adoration, and who had no doubt long since found himself at the end of a Spanish pike. Yet all were prepared to accept a boy as their commander, because the Admiral had said they must, and because the boy's name was Hilton. He had never anticipated this kind of fame, in all his dreams of power.

But the fame of a Morgan, now, there *was* something to be dreamed of. A farmer, from the hills of Llanrhymny, who could snap his fingers and have every villain in the New World dancing to his tune. Because he carried the aura of success. He let no obstacles stop him. At Porto Bello he had driven priests and nuns in front of his men to receive the fire of the Spanish soldiery, and won. At Maracaibo he had taken the town without difficulty, only to find himself bottled up by a Spanish fleet and by a fort which had so fortuitously seemed abandoned when the buccaneers had entered the lagoon. He had scattered the enemy vessels with fireships and avoided the guns of the fort by a splendid piece of subterfuge, and extracted his men and himself with all their gold and hardly a casualty. And when, soon afterwards, the magazine of his ship had exploded while he was entertaining his captains to dinner, and sent them all to perdition, he had been the sole survivor, merely blown overboard. So these cut-throats would indeed follow him to hell, confident that he would lead them back again.

Or did it merely mean that to be one of Morgan's captains was a highly dangerous business? Because clearly he had been marked for such a distinction, Kit thought.

Now the rest of the fleet was bringing up; anchors rattled through their hawse pipes as sails were furled, and the ships swung to the gentle breeze while boats were lowered. The Admiral's barge was already at the beach, and Morgan was haranguing the Indians who clustered forward to receive the

THE DEVIL'S OWN

handfuls of beads and the few rusty muskets which they valued more than all the gold in America. Meanwhile a coxswain had planted the huge staff from which flew the Cross of St George, as a rallying point for the boat commanders, and these, as soon as the various pinnaces had disgorged the landing parties, were gathered beneath the flapping cloth. Kit and Jean hurried to join them, to stand in the company of all the weather-beaten hell-hounds who had sent more Spaniards to their deaths than he had ever seen in his life. He felt suitably humbled, but more exhilarated. Gone were his doubts. Why, there must be nearly two thousand men on this beach. Two thousand of the toughest scoundrels on the face of the earth. And they waited only for the word from their Admiral.

Morgan came towards them, his boots crunching on the sand. The chieftain walked at his side, peering down the muzzle of the musket he had been given.

Morgan stopped before the three score men he had selected to lead his cohorts. He grinned at them, while the sweat stained the shoulders and armpits of his shirt.

'The chief has found us one hundred and forty canoes,' he said. 'And to do that he has scoured the entire country. Each canoe will take ten men. That means we march with fourteen hundred. I'd have liked more, but beggars can't be choosers. And it means we leave a sizeable force to guard the ships and this bay. For we must come back the way we go.'

'Up that river?' someone demanded.

Morgan drew his cutlass, began to make marks upon the sand. 'Fifteen miles to the lake. There'll be no problem up to there. Then the lake itself stretches for some ten. But after that it's walking. Through that.' He pointed with his cutlass at the wall of green jungle, matted and intertwined, which lay only a few feet away. 'I'd have no man be under any misapprehension as to what he's at.'

'Begging your pardon, Admiral Morgan,' Captain Jackman said. 'But are we not being over-elaborate? You may be sure that by now the Dons know there is a buccaneer fleet on this coast, and they will also know, by simple arithmetic, that we can mean one of only three places. Porto Bello and Nombre de Dios are plucked bones. As we must head for Nicaragua, why not let us do it direct? To ascend the Chagres can only add several days to our journey, and as it will mislead nobody, it seems to me to be no more than a waste of time and energy.'

Morgan stared at him, his mouth still forming the smile.

'So we are marching on Nicaragua City,' he said. 'That is what the Dons will think, in your opinion.'

'There is nowhere else worthy of such an expedition.'

'Nowhere?' Morgan threw back his head and laughed. 'And is not Nicaragua City also a plucked bone? Did not John Davis ascend there but two years gone, and storm the walls? Is there anything there worth having, from a woman's hole to a single pot of gold, now? Think you I would lead fourteen hundred men to such a limited feast?' He dug his sword once again into the sand. 'From the lake we descend. There is a trail, but in any event this good fellow has promised to lead us. He asks only a Spanish sword in payment, and by God he shall have mine when he delivers us upon the shores of the Pacific.'

There was a moment's stunned silence.

'The Pacific?' Bartholomew Le Grand whispered.

'In the steps of Drake and Oxenham, by God,' said Captain Sharp. 'What will we do, Admiral? Seize ships and prey upon the Spanish trade with Peru?'

'Faith, that were a slow business,' said Captain Tew. 'It would make more sense to sail our own ships around the Horn.'

'Excepting that they would sink before you breasted Brazil,' Kit said.

Morgan laughed again. 'Ships?' he shouted. 'Piracy? Ships are for transport. And piracy is for those who fear to prosper. No, no, my friends. My *matelots*. I will open for you the gates of the most wealthy city in the world. For where does the gold of Peru, and the riches of the East Indies come ashore, my friends? Where is the entrepot for the entire trade of Spanish America? Babylon had nothing to offer when compared with Panama City.'

This time the silence was longer.

'You'd assault Panama City?' Jackman asked at last.

' 'Tis defended by an army,' Tew whispered.

'For that purpose,' Morgan said, 'I have brought an army to this beach. I tell you this: be the walls the highest and the thickest in the world, and they are that; be it defended by an army of Spanish soldiery, and it is that; and be it also a place of gold and silver, and plate, and fine clothes, and women, my friends, the most beautiful women in the world, and it is that; and be it the safest place in the world, as it is claimed, we shall take it, or you shall bury Henry Morgan in this mud.'

3

The Scum of the Earth

A shot rang out, and then another; a ripple of fire rolled along the bank of the river, and in one of the leading canoes a man screamed with pain, and slumped over his paddle. For the rest, the bullets merely splattered the unending brown of the water.

'You and you and you,' Morgan bellowed from his boat, which led the van. 'Flush out those bastards.'

Kit cursed, but swung his canoe out of the column. On his left Jean did the same, and on his right Bart's men followed their example. This was the seventh time in two days they had been ordered to clear the banks.

'Give way,' he shouted. 'Give way.' The buccaneers obeyed, faces mouthing oaths, arms shedding sweat; they were stripped to the waist, had shaved their heads and bound them up in bright coloured kerchiefs; their feet were bare and their breeches were stained with mud and sweat. But their cutlasses were bright; Morgan's orders had made them polish the blades every evening.

Cutlasses were essential for cutting back the ever present jungle. Surely not for cutting down Spaniards. For while the jungle never ceased its presence, the Spaniards came and went, filtering along the banks of this interminable river, delivering their volleys and disappearing again. Morgan's boast that every Indian in the isthmus would fight against the Dons had been proved false; no soldiers could move through these forests without Indian guides.

The prow of the canoe drove into the bushes which drooped over the brown water. The leading buccaneer seized the branches to push them aside, and shrank back in horror as a snake slid down the tree and wriggled into the undergrowth. For a moment the entire company hesitated, and then Kit himself went forward.

'What are you?' he demanded. 'Men or girls?' He grasped the bushes and swung himself ashore. But even as his feet left the boat he shuddered; no one knew for sure what hell might be lying immediately beneath him. There was that man the day before yesterday who had stumbled into a teeming ants' nest and lost most of his flesh before he could be dragged clear. There was that canoe which had overturned, and amongst whose crew leather-backed brown monsters called caiman by the Indians had swarmed with savage destruction before anyone could attempt their rescue. And there were the four men who had already been bitten by snakes, and had died in seconds. Beside all of those horrors, which clung to the brown water and the green banks with unceasing determination, what were a handful of Spanish soldiers?

His feet stamped through the soft earth, found the hard. He drew his cutlass, waved his arm. He could hear the shouts of Jean's men and Bart's, a little farther up the river. And he could see, too, the shattered branches and the imprints on the earth where the Spaniards had rested their muskets. But the men were gone. They were pursuing a war of attrition, knowing they could not concentrate a sufficient force in the jungle to meet the buccaneers head on.

And they were pursuing it successfully.

Bart shouldered his way through the trees. 'Christ,' he said. 'What would I give for a stretch of open ground. I'd even settle for Hispaniola again.'

'So long as we would be doing the hunting there as well,' Jean said. 'Let us regain our canoes. The Admiral has said that we shall certainly meet with resistance at Cruces, and it cannot be more than a day away now.'

'And that will be long enough,' Bart grumbled. 'My men are down to their last mouthfuls of meat.'

Kit re-embarked his crew, took his place in the stern. They had wasted half an hour in that futile action, but as yet even the centre of the long column of canoes had not passed their landing. And now, by this natural leap-frogging process, their places in the van had been taken by another three canoes, and they could allow themselves to relax. Until Cruces. For Morgan had indeed told them about this town, an important resting place on the gold road from Panama to Nombre de Dios, situated on the shore of the lake. The Spaniards would certainly fight for Cruces, and the town was fortified. There would the mettle of these men be tested. As if it had not been tested many times before. Perhaps it was his own mettle he questioned. But had he not led

THE DEVIL'S OWN

the assault on the Spanish brig? He had known no fear then. Only an anxious anger. So now was a strange time to start doubting himself.

Or perhaps he did not doubt himself, but only the horrors that would come afterwards. For now he had two memories to haunt his midnight hours; the priest had joined Grandmama.

'The lake,' someone shouted from the canoe in front of him. The word had been passed down the command. 'The lake,' one of his own crew shouted. He turned, and cupped his hands to call the glad news. 'The lake,' he bellowed at those behind him, and listened to the word rippling down the column like a *feu de joie*.

But was it a lake? Or had they in some fantastic fashion managed to cross the isthmus in four days? For the banks of the river were widening, and even disappearing from sight; he could see no land ahead, only the swarm of canoes, spreading out like a cavalry charge as they reached the open water, after the constant effort of pulling against the current over the previous days. Now they entered a world of light and air, compared with the oppression of the huge trees. Flocks of wild duck rose from the reeds on either hand, and scattered towards the sky, eagerly watched by the men, who were already weary of a diet of rotting beef. Reeds were everywhere, emerging in patches above the surface and then disappearing again. Now indeed they needed the Indian guides, or they might row round and round in circles for the rest of their lives. But the Admiral's canoe, painted a bright red so that there could be no mistakes in identification, rowed steadily forward, bearing just west of south, until even the reed-beds and the flanking forest had disappeared, and they followed an open expanse.

And now he could see land again. The morning sun reflected from the walls. Cruces. Filled with armed Spaniards determined to halt this expedition here and now. How would Morgan command the assault? Would he merely point his sword at those battlements, and leave it to the desperate valour of his buccaneers? Kit rather suspected that would be the case, and felt relieved that there were close on fifty canoes between his own and the front. He would not have to be a forlorn hope on this occasion.

Morgan's boat headed straight for the beach beneath the walls; the roofs of the town, dominated by the church, were now clearly in view. But the Spaniards were wasting no powder. The loopholes remained silent, staring at the canoes.

'Give way,' Kit shouted. 'Make haste. Paddle you devils. Paddle.'

For the exhilaration of battle was once again seizing hold of him, and he no longer wanted to lag behind. He wished to be up there with the leaders, with the Admiral and with the van. But each of the hundred and forty canoes had increased its speed, and the whole little armada surged at the walls. Yet still there was no fire, and now he saw that the main gate was open, swinging to and fro on its hinges.

'By Christ,' he whispered. Morgan had seen it too. The lead canoes were already beached, and the buccaneers were pouring ashore and up the beach, their bandannas forming a brightly coloured pattern of bouncing balls, and led by the Admiral himself; Morgan had retained his broad-brimmed black hat, although like them he had shaved his head.

'Hurry,' Kit begged his men. 'Hurry, you bastards.'

The bottom grated and they dropped their paddles. Kit was already over the side, splashing through knee-deep water as he gained the beach, to join the mob which flooded through the open gates, to debouch into the single street of the town, to stop, and stare at the empty houses, the open doors. To listen to the silence which gradually overcame even the cries of the invaders.

They huddled, insensibly, and looked towards the church. Morgan had entered there, and now he stood on the steps and faced them. 'They've gone,' he shouted. 'Run like the curs they are. They'll not have left much behind them, lads, but what they have we must find. Or we'll go hungry for the next couple of days, eh? Scatter now, and discover what you may. Kill me every Spaniard you find. We'll have no quarter. Remember that. And find food, lads. But reassemble on the note of the bugle. Forget that, and you are dead men.'

The buccaneers gave a tremendous whoop, and tore at the houses on either side. Empty, stripped of anything valuable. And yet containing enough for destruction. Beds and articles of furniture were slashed and cut and pounded into rubble; doors were torn from their hinges, windows poked out. Cellars were tumbled. But no article of food was found, much less any of gold. Tempers began to run high, curses and oaths mingled with the sweat and the clash of arms to disturb the still air.

Until a roar of joy sent them back to the street, and milling into the square. Bart's men had forced the great doors

THE DEVIL'S OWN

to the church cellars. Here too there were no men. But here there were casks of wine, row upon row of them.

'They'll be fit for naught for days,' Kit muttered. He stood close by the Admiral.

'Aye,' Morgan said. 'But there's none of us here will restrain them from that liquor.'

They were already stoving in the casks, holding out mugs and even hands for a first taste of the flowing red liquid. And now the first cup was filled, and the man who had thrust the first bung raised it high. 'Here's to ye, Admiral Morgan,' he bellowed, and gulped at the wine, allowing it to flow out of his mouth and down his cheeks, cascade over his shoulders. 'By Christ, but that was good. And another, lads.' He bent to refill his mug, and gave a shriek of agony, which was echoed by the man beside him, who had also finished a mug.

Cups dropped, and the men crowding round the barrels reeled backwards. Three of them lay on the floor of the cellar, gasping and writhing.

'Poisoned, by Christ,' Morgan said. 'We should have known. By God, lads, we had better be on our way. You'll know what to do to those Dons when we catch up with them.'

'But what will we eat?' asked a voice.

Morgan stared at them. 'You'll eat in Panama City,' he shouted. 'What are you, then, afraid of going hungry for a day or two? The sooner you get back to the trail, the sonner we'll be there.'

In the square the first drops of rain began to fall.

* * *

A bugle blast wailed through the forest, and the weary men stopped moving. Many immediately sank to their knees and then on to their bellies, regardless of the soaking leaves or the inches-deep mud stirred up by those who had gone before. And where they fell, they lay. There was no point in calling them to stack arms, in commanding them to pitch tents. They possessed neither food nor cover. At least half of them shook with fever. But they marched, and would continue to march, through the endless jungle. Because to stop meant death.

Kit pushed his way past the wet branches, and found Jean. The Frenchman sat on a fallen log, and had taken off his belt, already half chewed into strands.

'That is worse,' Kit said. 'It but makes the juices flow.'

'Aye. But my belly is filled with gripes and wind. I explode as I walk,' Jean said. 'Think you these men will have the strength to fight, when we reach the ocean? How does the Admiral know he can trust these Indians? How do we know we are not being led round in circles?'

'Because we are seamen, and are following the course of the sun,' Kit reminded him. 'So, eventually, we must again come to the sea. We know it is there.'

'I wish I possessed your confidence,' Jean grumbled.

'Whisht.'

Something had moved in the bushes close by. Kit turned, slowly. Behind them the army was still settling, with an enormous rustle of sound, but muted; there was no laughter and no shouting, there was no reason for either. There were only sighs and curses. And in the jungle something had moved, not twenty feet away.

'A Spanish scout, you think?' Jean whispered.

'I doubt it. They can have no doubts where we are and in which direction we are headed.' Kit dropped to his knees, cautiously parted the bushes to make his way forward. 'By Christ.'

Jean was at his side, peering into the gloom. And drawing his breath sharply. In front of them was a large bird, with brightly coloured wings, one of which seemed broken, for it could do no more than drag itself through the bushes.

'What is it?' Jean whispered.

'Some kind of pheasant, perhaps,' Kit said.

'But it will be good to eat.'

'Aye. You go that way.' Cautiously he wormed his way through the grass behind the bird, his knife in his hand. His powder was too damp to fire, and in any event, he had no wish to alert anyone else to his prize. His mind was entirely caught up with the problems of his own belly.

The bird had heard him coming. It turned and scuttled through the trees, away from Jean as well, moving much faster than they could. He rose to his feet in frustration, threw himself full length, missed the tail feathers by inches, and listened to the squawk of terror. He reared back on his heels, and gazed at the black man. He had seen him before, marked him for his size and his demeanour, for he was about the biggest man he had ever seen, and carried himself with a studied dignity. His face was long, and the colour of midnight, which he accentuated by wearing a white bandanna. His expression was bland and disinterested, even now, as he held the fluttering bird in his hands. Like everyone else, he wore only a pair of breeches and his feet were bare. Unlike most of the others, however, his only weapon was his cutlass. Perhaps he knew sufficient about tropical forests to understand that powder was not a reliable commodity in these conditions.

Now he grinned at the two young men, and with a sudden twist of his wrists ended the pheasant's life.

'We saw him first,' Jean muttered, rising from the bushes to the left.

The giant continued to smile. 'We saw him together, Monsieur DuCasse," he said, his voice quiet. 'But we will have to share him raw.'

Kit frowned at him. 'You do not claim him as your own?'

'I will share him with you two gentlemen, Master Hilton,' he said. 'But no others.' He squatted, was already plucking at the feathers.

'How are you called?' Jean asked.

The Negro shrugged. 'I no longer have a name of my own, sir. I was given a title by my late owner. Marcus Vipsanius Agrippa. How does that sound, sir?'

'By God,' Kit said. 'He had a sense of humour, your owner.'

Agrippa shrugged again, and tore off a wing, which he offered to Kit. 'He was a devil, Master Hilton. You will still find the marks of his whip on my back.'

'Where was this?'

'Barbados, sir.'

Now Jean was also eating, the blood rolling down his chin. 'And you made your way from Barbados to Port Royal?'

'Indeed, sir. After being a slave, and having escaped, all other aspects of life come easy.'

Kit stared at the man. There had been no slaves on Tortuga; there had been no reason for them. And the knowledge that they were employed in the islands farther south, and in Jamaica as well, for that matter, had never really meant much to him before. He had put them down as a people apart, black people. But here was a black man speaking with a more educated choice of words than anyone in the fleet.

Agrippa was smiling at him. 'Because I was a slave, Master Hilton, does not mean that I am a mindless savage. I do not come from the great river, from the great bay. My lands are farther north. I am a Mandingo, sir. There is Arab blood in my veins.'

'And where did you learn such good English?'

My master taught me. He was an intelligent man, and he perceived my own intelligence, and so taught me more.'

'And yet scarred your back,' Jean observed.

'Have you not observed, Monsieur DuCasse, that it is the most intelligent people who are the most cruel? As perhaps they think more quickly than stupid people, so they have more time to think, but no more subjects to think about, and so they must fill the empty spaces with their desires. And deep down inside all of us there is a desire to hurt, to be cruel.'

'My God,' Jean said. 'A Negro philosopher.'

'There were philosophers in North Africa long before any were discovered in France, Monsieur DuCasse.'

Jean frowned, and then smiled. 'Why, I suppose you are right, Master Agrippa. And I thank you for securing our bird for us. Now I must rejoin my men.'

'And I also.' Kit stood up, and hesitated, then thrust out his hand. ' 'Tis strange, how people meet, Master Agrippa. My thanks.'

The Negro hesitated in turn, and then closed his fingers over those of the boy. 'I have never shaken hands with a white man.'

Kit was embarrassed. 'I'd have you march with my section. I'll speak with the Admiral.'

Agrippa's grin had returned. 'I march with my own section, Master Hilton. At its head.'

'You?'

'Why not? Admiral Morgan wishes only the strength in a man's mind, the strength in his arm. He shows no interest in the colour of his skin.'

'Aye. He has the hallmarks of greatness.'

'Which is why we follow him, Master Hilton. For be sure that many of us will die, before we regain the mouth of the Chagres. Now I bid you farewell. I will see you in Panama.'

A strange meeting, with a strange man. But a most valuable one, if only because it had taken some of the griping pain from his belly, Kit thought. Next day he looked for the big man, but did not find him. The army straggled now, a long column of sweating and cursing and starving men. At least the rain had ceased two days ago, and the forest was again dry. And now they were descending, and walking was easier. But it was distressing to hear the wind growling in his

THE DEVIL'S OWN

belly, and to listen to the grunts and farts of the men around him, to watch them chewing at their belts, and tearing leaves from the trees to cram into their mouths. Now they all suffered from leaking bellies as well, the more nauseating because they could excrete only liquid. Within a week they would be too weak to raise a weapon, much less force their way through the jungle.

Within a week. He had lost track of days. They came and they went. They had paddled up the River Chagres for nearly a week; they had left their canoes at Cruces, and they had marched through the forest for nearly a week. And now it was again night, and the men groaned and cursed and snored around him. And yet there had been no suggestion of mutiny. Was it because they knew that they could only go on, or die? Or was it because they trusted their Admiral? He had led them into hell before. Surely he would lead them out the other side, this time again.

'Whisht.' Portuguese Bart, crawling through the darkness. But a darkness already tinged with grey.

Kit sat up. 'What is it?'

'The Admiral summons his commanders to a conference.' Bart whispered. 'Come quietly.'

Kit picked up his cutlass, it was second nature now, whether he needed it to slash at a jungle creeper or to protect himself from snake or spider, and made his way along the column, past the line of sleeping men, lying as they had fallen from yet another endless march through the forest. It took him half an hour to reach the head, and by then the dawn chill was already spreading through his bones, and the first light was commencing to shroud a grey mist across the trees.

They crossed a sudden open space, and came once again to the trees. Here they grouped, near a hundred of them, the men who would be responsible for making the buccaneers fight, when it came to that.

And in their centre was the Admiral. 'Hush,' Morgan said. 'Listen.'

Across the suggestion of dawn a bell tolled, gently in the distance. They stared through the trees, but could see nothing; the mist blanketed the forest in front of them.

'A mule train, you think?' Jackman whispered.

'How can that be?' Sharp demanded. 'There is not a Spaniard in all America but knows we are in this forest.'

'That bell is the cathedral in Panama City,' Morgan said, grinning at them. 'We have arrived, my bravos. Awake your men, and bring them forward. We will leave the forest under cover of this mist, and be in position before the city awakes.' He drew his cutlass, and raised it above his head. 'This day we unlock the doors to more wealth than any man here has ever dreamed of, let alone seen. Today we make ourselves immortals, lads. This day Henry Morgan comes to Panama.'

Supposing they lived to tell of it. For now the mist would lift. Kit knew the signs too well, from his years in Hispaniola. There was the sudden increase in heat, the sudden closeness of the air, the sudden change in the colour of the vapour around them, from white to yellow. And where were they, in relation to their goal? He doubted even the Admiral knew that. The bell had ceased to toll some time before, or its knell had been lost in the clank and rustle of twelve hundred men tramping across the ground.

Certainly they had left the forest, some time ago, and now followed a well-defined path down the hillside, but even the path was flattening out. And was this path not the Gold Road, which led straight through the main gate of Panama City itself? Would they not see the enemy until they banged on those iron-bound portals?

Or could Panama also have been abandoned? There was a dream, born of fear, of the nagging, grinding pain in his belly, a pain induced as much by fear as by hunger. Now he marched on the Spaniards, as they had once marched on him. He had been less afraid, then. He had known less of what life and death were about.

The mist cleared. The sun drew it from the ground as a woman might whisk the sheet from the bed she would remake. And the buccaneer army stopped, and stared, while a rumble of amazed murmur rose from their ranks. They had almost arrived at the foot of the empty hillside, worn free of trees and most of its grass by the fall of how many hundreds of thousands of feet, down which the Gold Road flowed? The road itself continued in front of them, skirting the plain to arrive at the gates of the city, huge timber erections studded with iron, which filled the open spaces in the high stone walls, while beyond the walls there could be no doubt that here was a city; the rooftops and the balconies rose above the battlements, and above even the rooftops there rose the towers of the four cathedrals. These towers now once again gave off a peal of bells, summoning the people of Panama to arms.

Panama promised wealth; the district around it already provided beauty. To their right the plain undulated towards the sea, clearly not the parade ground they had first supposed it, but rather a rabbit warren of bushes and ravines, not deep, but sufficient to hide a man. Or men. And beyond it the eternal surf played on the endless beach, guardians of an ocean which stretched half-way round the world to the kingdoms of the Great Khan, and the Mikado of Japan. The sun, rising from out of the forest behind them, sent a long swathe of glowing gold across that fathomless sea, suggestive of the prize they sought, if they had the courage, and the stamina, and the ability.

For Panama was awake. The gates were open, and out there came squadron after squadron of lancers, dressed in bright uniforms, with brighter pennants flying from their spearheads, yellow and red. Kit looked around, and found Jean and Bart Le Grand staring with him. How many men present had a long score to settle with the Spanish lancers?

Behind the lancers there came the tramp of infantry, displacing as much dust as even the horses, an immense mass of men in breastplates and helmets, pikes or muskets at their shoulders, every step matching every other. This was the Spanish *tercio*, the infantry division which had conquered the world with the same ease as it had conquered Europe.

'By Christ,' someone muttered. 'But there are thousands of them.'

The buccaneers watched the enemy form line, the infantry in the centre in a solid body, the horsemen milling about on each wing. Nor apparently were the Spaniards yet finished summoning their army; a real cloud of dust rose from close by the city gates. More cavalry? Morgan stared through his telscope, his whole face a frown. 'Cattle, by God. They mean to rout us with cattle.' He closed the glass with a snap, turned to face his army. 'You'll run, God damn you. Make for the plain, and take shelter in the ravines. But stay close.'

The buccaneer army debouched from the road without any further hesitation, making little noise beyond pants and grunts as they staggered for the plain. From the Spanish ranks there rose a cheer, as they assumed their enemies to be already defeated.

'Kit Hilton,' Morgan bellowed. 'Bart Le Grand. Jean DuCasse. All you men who were *boucaniers*. Assemble here, by God.'

Kit left the men who had crewed the canoe with him, ran to Morgan's side, trailing his heavy musket. Soon there were two dozen of them.

'We've a hard day ahead of us, lads,' Morgan said. 'They outnumber us, and they're regular troops. Our boyos are weak with hunger, and they'll need all their strength. So isn't it a good thing the commandant has done, driving those beef cattle towards us?'

The herd was contining to approach at a gallop, the hammer of their hooves making the earth shake, while the dust cloud eddied above them.

'You leave it to us,' Bart said. 'We'll not waste a ball, Admiral. Come on, my bravos. To that ridge.'

Kit followed him across the uneven turf. Outnumbered, two to one, by regulars. His belly rose to meet his heart, and his heart sank to meet his belly. What hope had they? But perhaps, after they had slaughtered some of the cattle, Morgan would lead them back into the forest and safety.

Except that what safety could there be for a defeated band of buccaneers, fifty miles and incredible hardships away from their ships, who had even lost faith in their general?

Supposing they survived the cattle. He lay on his belly on the already dry earth, and watched the tossing horns, the scorching hooves, the seething dust pounding towards him. Nothing would stop them now. His throat tightened.

'That big black bull,' Bart growled. 'And those on either side. We must drop them together, friends, or they will trample us to death. Take your sights. But wait for my command.'

Kit licked his lips, and found he had no saliva. But his breeches were wet. Christ, how frightened he was. The stampeding cows were not more than a hundred yards away. Would Bart ever give the command? Would there be time even to squeeze the trigger? And suppose the flint misfired?

'Fire,' Bart shouted, and the muskets rippled flame and sent black smoke up to join the dust.

'Load,' Bart shrieked. 'Load, you miserable sons of whores. Load.'

Desperately Kit crammed a ball into the muzzle of his gun, and rammed it down. There were cows all around him now, hurtling past, lowing and roaring, but separated by the wall of flame which had been hurled at them as much as by the dozen which had collapsed to form a mound immediately before the score of crouching men. And now the muskets were sounding again, driving the herd of cattle into two ever-divergent streams; at this range not even a musket could miss.

The sound lessened, although the dust continued to whirl and make them cough and choke. And now it was replaced by a tremendous whoop as Morgan led the main body forward. Men swarmed around Kit, tearing at the still breathing cows, slicing through quivering limbs and stripping the tough hide away from the warm red meat beneath. Some were already lighting fires to roast their breakfast; the main part just crammed the raw meat into their mouths.

'Kit. Kit. Where are you, Kit?'

Jean carried a beefsteak in each hand. They had been charcoal broiled, so that the outsides were black but blood still oozed.

'Eat one of these,' Jean commanded. 'And feel the strength flow back into your limbs.'

The meat was hard and tasteless, but to teeth which had chewed nothing but leather belts for three days it was like eating the tenderest of sucking pigs. Saliva mingled with the blood which filled his mouth.

'You shoot good, Master Hilton,' Agrippa tore at a rib. 'Now we must all fight good, eh?'

The dust had cleared, and the Spanish army lay in front of them, amazingly still, whereas surely, Kit thought, had they but launched an attack while the buccaneers were feeding, the victory would immediately have been theirs. No doubt they counted the victory secure in any event. And the moment was already past, for the bugle was sounding again, and the men were reluctantly scrambling to their feet, many tucking meaty ribs and lumps of steak into their belts.

Morgan had moved to the front. 'Musketeers,' he bellowed. 'Bart Le Grand, take the right flank with a hundred men. Kit Hilton, take the left. Not sharpshooters only, now. Any man who can fire a musket quickly and knows how to aim. The rest follow us.'

'You'll march with me, Jean,' Kit said.

'I would like that privilege also, Master Hilton,' Agrippa said.

'And you shall have it, by God. Come, load those pieces.'

The main body was already moving forward; Morgan's captain had unfurled a tremendous Cross of St George at the head of the column, flying from a long spar.

'You and you and you,' Kit bellowed, singling out men with clean-looking firepieces. 'To me on the flank. Come on, now. Make haste.'

For he could see what Morgan feared. As the buccaneer army advanced across the plain, the two bodies of lancers had also moved forward, trotting from their positions in line with the *tercio*, and obviously meaning to charge the flanks of the attacking army. The cattle still stampeded aimlessly across the open ground beneath their banner of eddying dust, and behind them also now were the steaming carcasses and smouldering fires of half an hour ago. And now the thudding of the hooves was growing loud again as the horsemen approached, gradually fanning out into a line as they drew parallel with the buccaneers.

The bugle sounded, and the flagstaff was placed in the ground; they were still out of range of the infantry, at a quarter of a mile distance.

'I think we are opposed by a fool,' Agrippa muttered, settling the stock of his firepiece into his shoulder.

'Hold your fire,' Kit commanded, remembering how Bart had controlled them against the cattle. He walked up and down the line of half-naked, bearded, sweating savages he had been asked to lead. 'Hold your fire.' He took his place at one end of the line, and heard the rattle of cutlasses behind him. The cavalry were lowering their lances, and the trot was becoming a canter. He estimated there were just over a hundred of them on each flank.

'Remember Hispaniola,' Portuguese Bart yelled, and the cry was taken up. 'Remember Hispaniola.'

'Fire,' Kit shouted, as the range closed, and the muskets rippled with explosion and smoke. The lancers did not check but a good score of their number fell, and the collapsing horses brought down several more.

'Load,' Kit yelled. 'Load, make haste. Load.'

But there was not time. The horsemen were coming on again.

'Pistols,' he bellowed. 'Pistols and cutlasses. Steady now.' He drew his own weapon, braced his feet as if he would fight a duel, and fired; a horse in front of him reared and whinnied, throwing its rider and falling backwards on to him. And then the noise of the immediate conflict was drowned in a tremendous roar, and he looked over his shoulder. Morgan had deemed the safety of his wings in good hands, and had given the order to charge. With a howl of contempt and fury a thousand buccaneers launched themselves in a small tight body against the very centre of the imposing force in front of them.

But for the time being Kit and his musketeers were fully engaged with the horsemen. Now the mêlée became general, and in the first rush three of the buccaneers went down with spears in their bellies. But at close quarters the spears could only be used once, and long before the horsemen could control their mounts or drag their swords free they were seized and jerked from their saddles, and butchered on the ground. Cutlasses rose and fell, blood splattered and stained the brilliant steel, men howled, with pain and despair and with exultation, horses neighed with utter terror and added to the confusion as they raced to and fro.

But this fight was won. 'To me,' Kit bellowed, his voice hoarse and sweat running down his cheeks. 'To me. Follow me. Jean. Agrippa.'

'We are here,' Jean shouted. And so were still seventy others. Kit pointed his cutlass in the direction of the city, and advanced at a run, and checked in amazement. For now the dust again cleared, and in front of him the much-vaunted Spanish infantry were fleeing in every direction, some seeking the seashore and the boats which waited there, others running with desperate fear for the terrible safety of the forest. Morgan's charge had won the day, and already the buccaneers were battering at the gates of the city itself.

Had ever a day been so hot, and it was still early in the morning? Had such a day ever been seen, in all the brief history of America? For had such a city ever fallen to so few men, and to such men? They ran through the streets, no longer fearing opposition where there was none. The houses were shuttered and silent, and perhaps empty. They reached the central square, and gazed in amazement at the immensity of the cathedral, rising up and up and up, its square tower the one they had seen from the forest. Then they gave a whoop, and ran for the great barred doors.

Others had found the city hall, and beneath it, the dungeons. Here there were shouts and screams, and the buccaneers seized glaring torches and made their way down the noisome corridors, bursting open the doors of the cells to release the things that lay within. For these were surely not men. Some had lost one eye, some both; the marks of the fire still clung to their temples and foreheads. Others had lost ears and fingers and toes, and others whole limbs. More than one had been castrated. And all had been whipped so savagely their backs were masses of festering sores, while all showed the bones and paper-thin skin of men who had been starved as a matter of course. And these were the lucky ones, whom the Inquisition had not yet burned.

'By God,' Morgan said. 'By God. We'll have a Spanish life for every mark on every body. What say you, boys?'

The roar of angry lust filled the gaol.

'Make them scream, boyos,' Morgan shouted. 'And make them yield every last drop of wealth they possess. Tear it from their living bellies if you have to. And bring it to the square in front of the cathedral. For mark my words; we share and share alike, according to the articles under which we sail. The man who forgets that hangs.'

They uttered another scream and poured into the square once again, their yells mingling with those already issuing from the cathedral, where some of the buccaneers were dragging out the great gold services and tearing down the crosses from the walls, while others had invaded the offices at the back of the building, and the cellars below, and reached the hiding nuns.

That was too terrible to contemplate. Kit found himself in the midst of a band rampaging down a side street, ignoring promising shops and smaller dwellings as they searched for bigger game, and finding a mansion at the end of the street, set back from the road behind wrought-iron railings and a huge, locked gate. But these were seamen. They swarmed over the wall in a matter of seconds, advanced across the splendid garden, kicking aside rose bushes and flowering oleander, their sweat and the blood on their arms drenching even the odour of the jasmine.

A dog barked, and two ran from the rear of the building. They were met by swinging cutlasses and stretched lifeless on the patio before the front entrance. Now, Kit thought, this day, we avenge your death, Grandmama. Fully. But he felt sick.

The door was barred, but had never been intended to resist so tumultuous an assault. Muscular shoulders were hurled against it, regardless of bruised flesh or broken skin, and it flew open. Kit was one of the first through, scattering across a parquet floor beneath a high, painted ceiling, to come to rest against a mahogany dresser, to stare at the huge vases in front of him, filled with bright flowers.

'By Christ,' someone said. 'Solid silver.'

'There'll be more,' another said, and ran into the inner room. Here double doors opened on to the centre courtyard, a place of peace and more flowers, where a fountain played. ' 'Tis a palace.'

'And empty?' someone demanded.

'There'll be cellars.' The first speaker, whose name was Scotch Mack, had taken command. 'We'll to them first. Come on, lads.'

They flooded across the courtyard to the kitchen, where the fires still glowed in the huge ovens; it was so early the family had not yet even had time to breakfast before the disaster had fallen on their city. A pan of cooking fat simmered gently, giving its tang to the already rancid air. And there, sure enough, was the door leading down to the cellars. This too was barred, and this too was torn from its hinges in a matter of seconds. They tumbled down the staircase to find themselves in the midst of endless rows of bottles.

'French wine, by God,' Mack shouted, and seized one, to snap off the neck against a pillar and upend it over his face. They all followed his example. Warm liquid splashed on to Kit's cheeks and flooded down his neck; some found its way into his mouth and helped to calm his tumbling nerves.

But already the buccaneers were battering against an inner door, and a moment later they gazed at the people inside. A man, well past middle age, tall and with some dignity in his face to offset his obvious fear. A woman, no doubt the man's wife, for she was of an age with him, like him wearing an undressing-robe over her nightclothes, thin and pale, with white hair loose on her shoulders. Two Negro women, dressed, and wearing aprons. And another woman, younger than the couple, although considerably older than any of the buccaneers. Their daughter, Kit estimated. She was tall and plump; her hair was a rich brown and her face had the aquiline splendour of a woman accustomed to rule. Now she stood in front of her parents and her servants, her hands clasped. She wore a deep blue robe which brushed the floor, and her hair was also loose, gathered in a long strand over one shoulder.

'By God,' someone grumbled. 'They're old.'

'They'll have children,' Mack promised. 'And gold, buried.' He seized the younger woman by the hair, dragged her against him. She gasped for breath, and tried to maintain her dignity as he brought her close. 'Gold,' Mack shouted into her face, and she gagged on his breath. 'Where have ye buried your gold?'

She tried to shake her head, but that was impossible.

Her father spoke, in a thin voice which trembled. 'We have no gold buried, monsieurs,' he said in French. 'What we own you see about you. You are welcome to it. Leave us only our lives, I beg of you.'

Mack stared at him for a moment, and then thrust out the hand holding his cutlass. The old man swayed backwards, but the thrust none the less split his undressing-robe and nightshirt, and slashed his chest. He stared down at the blood in horror.

'Bring them,' Mack shouted, and started up the stairs, still holding the woman's hair, so that she had to run behind him, her body dragged forward. She struck at him with her fists, and another of the buccaneers swept her legs from the floor. The pair of them carried her up the stairs, and deposited her on the kitchen table. The rest brought the other four people. Kit found himself holding the old woman by the arms as he pushed her forward. She glanced over her shoulder at him, and whispered in French, 'But you are only a boy.'

The sickness in his belly grew, into a huge solid mass which threatened to erupt at any moment.

Mack was shaking the younger woman to and fro by the hair, in front of the old man. 'Gold,' he repeated. 'Tell us where you have hidden your gold.'

The old man fell to his knees, still clutching the blood seeping from the wound in his chest. 'Oh, God,' he begged. 'Oh, God.'

The two Negresses cowered against the wall; the woman Kit was holding also sank to her knees, and he let her go. The younger woman said something in Spanish, her face twisted with pain as Mack dragged on her hair.

'We'll make ye squeal,' he growled. He looked around him, quickly, searching the kitchen with his gaze. The woman's eyes followed his, rolling. And then he smiled; he had seen the pan of cooking fat. 'Heat that up,' he said.

One of the men gave a whoop, and thrust the pan over the flames. Immediately it began to sizzle, and the aroma drifted through the kitchen. Mack let go of the woman long enough to grasp the front of her undressing-robe and tear it free. Underneath was a white nightgown, and this too was torn away, to reveal large, sagging breasts, nipples hard with terror, flesh white and filled with pumping blue blood-vessels.

THE DEVIL'S OWN

'Over here,' Mack said. 'We'll cook ourselves some breakfast.'

The woman screamed, a shriek of real terror as she understood what was going to happen to her. Kit ran from the kitchen and up the stairs. So she was a member of the nation which had murdered Grandmama. Against whom his family had fought all of their lives. Against whom he must fight all of his life and against whom he had sworn eternal vengeance. But in such a bestial fashion?

He paused, at the top of the huge staircase, facing a gallery of empty doorways, and listened to another scream, while the smell of cooking flesh came seeping upwards. He hurled himself forward, through the first doorway, found himself in a bed-chamber, a wide expanse of costly drapes and highly polished wooden floors, dominated by the immense tent-bed in the centre of the room. He flung himself on this, pulled the pillows over his head, stuffed them into his ears as shriek after shriek, now accompanied by roars of laughter, came howling upwards through the house.

And heard another sound, closer at hand. He sat up, right hand instinctively snatching the cutlass from his side. The room was empty, but a door had opened, and then closed. And now he saw the door, a small one clearly giving access to a dressing-room. He tiptoed across the floor, seized the handle, pulled the door wide, gazed at the two girls, huddled against the far wall from whence they had been dragged by their mother's screams. Because clearly they were her daughters. One was perhaps fourteen, the other a year or two younger; each possessed the statuesque dignity of their parent, if that still existed, the strong features, the rich brown hair, the tall bodies, hardly concealed beneath their nightdresses. No doubt their father had fallen on the plain. Or had he run like a coward to the shelter of the forest, leaving his women to suffer?

'Oh, Christ,' Kit said. Because here was what those monsters downstairs really sought. The gold would keep, but not their lust.

The girls stared at him. The woman downstairs had stopped screaming, and the only sound was the terrible laughter.

Kit ran back across the room, closed and bolted the bedroom door. The girls watched him. They held hands, but had said nothing. 'Listen,' he said. 'I claim you as my prisoners. My slaves, eh? Be that, and you will be safe.' He spoke in French, and watched the older girl's eyes flicker. 'You understand me,' he said. 'What is your name?'

'Isabella.' The voice was low. Perhaps she was not afraid. Perhaps she did not know what might soon be happening to her.

Kit sat on the bed. Suddenly he was exhausted. And afraid. Of himself. 'Isabella,' he said. 'You understand what is happening?'

She nodded, and her sister's fingers tightened on her arm.

'Come here,' he said.

She looked down at her sister, and then gently freed her hand and walked across the room to stand in front of him. The nightdress became filled with light as she stood between him and the window; he could trace the curve of her thigh, the long line of slender leg beneath. Was he then no different to those abominations downstairs?

But she was close enough to touch. She humoured him, perhaps in an attempt to save her sister. There was courage here, and resolution. Perhaps even curiosity. Or was he no more than hoping for these things? Because he could not save her now. It had been too long. It had been forever, in fact, and here was no whore, but something young, and fresh, and totally innocent. Something beyond his experience, beyond his wildest dream. His hands stroked through her hair, and drifted across her shoulders and she understood her fate. He held her close and buried his face in the front of her nightdress, and found softness there too. She was Marguerite Warner, come to life, here in his arms, passive and non-resisting. She was a dream, suddenly walking. Yet he did not wish to hurt her. He prayed she would not resist, as his hands slipped down her back and raised the nightdress over her thighs. Her legs were better than he could have hoped; the down on her belly came as a surprise, but one which only increased her desirability. He lost his face in that dry forest, and realized that he was afraid to raise his head, afraid to look into her face. But this had to be done, as he laid her on the bed beside him, and found to his amazement that her mouth was open. With passion? Or with prayer? Tears rolled out from her eyes, but he felt her fingers biting into his shoulders as his body crashed on to hers, and again. It took no more than seconds, such was the urgency of his passion. She moaned once, and then lay still, as did he for some seconds, before slipping from her body and from the bed, to kneel beside her.

'May God forgive me,' he whispered. 'May you forgive me, Isabella. May God have mercy on me. I swear, I will protect you. I will marry you, Isabella. This I swear. I will look after you and honour you, always, Isabella. And I shall protect your sister. This I swear, Isabella. Say that you understand me. Say that you believe me.'

Now he wept as well, and the girl had ceased crying. She stared at him, her forehead gathered into faint wrinkles. A voice shouted outside, calling his name in the rolling tones of Agrippa.

He went to the door, unlocked it. 'They said you were up here,' Agrippa said. 'I feared for you, Master Hilton. I fear for us all; this army has gone mad. And now the town burns.'

Kit inhaled, and smelt the tang of smouldering wood. 'Aye,' he said. ' 'Tis not a day I shall want to remember. But . . .' he saw the expression on Agrippa's face, and turned, as the pistol exploded. He gazed at the figure of the younger girl, falling forward to her knees as a gush of blood exploded from the white front of her nightdress. 'Oh, Christ,' he cried.

But there were two pistols in the belt he had so carelessly thrown on the floor. The girl Isabella had turned to face them, and as they watched she dropped the weapon she had just fired and drew the other. Her face remained as impassive as earlier when she had been raped; only the dark eyes suggested the torment that was burning in her brain.

'Duck, man,' Agrippa yelled, seizing Kit's shoulder and throwing him to one side. But Kit knew the bullet was not meant for him. She had already reversed the pistol and placed the muzzle inside her own mouth.

Song and laughter filled the forest, scattered outwards from the river, accompanied the splashes of the paddles. But even paddling was no labour, on this journey; the boats flowed with the stream. And besides, they followed the lead canoes, on which the gold was stacked, as a pack of dogs might follow a butcher's van. They homed, on the beach at Chagres, where everything they had ever dreamed of would be granted to them.

As if they had not already accomplished their wildest dreams. There was scarce a sober man in the army, and they had brought enough wine to float their fleet with them. They had brought captives, too, women and young girls and boys, and those who did not work the paddles continued a week-old orgy in the bilges of the canoes. They sang, and laughed, and belched, and fornicated, and crammed their mouths with sweetmeats and fine cheeses, and relieved themselves where they sat. They were men who had scaled the heights, and taken the untakable. A vast stench accompanied the fleet. Port Royal might have transferred itself bodily to the Panamanian jungle.

'A ship.' Jean DuCasse lay in the stern of the canoe and waved at the branches which occasionally passed overhead. 'I shall buy a ship. Twenty guns to a broadside. Sakers fore and aft. I will put a copper sheath on her bottom. No worm for Jean DuCasse. With that ship, I will conquer the world. You'll sail with me, Agrippa?'

The Negro smiled, but his smile was sad. 'What of Master Hilton?'

'Christ.' Jean stuck out a foot, prodded a toe into Kit's thigh. 'He is a melancholy fellow, for a devil from hell. I know not what will become of him, Kit, Kit. They were but bits of flesh. Had you not taken the girl, someone else would, and much less gently.'

Kit turned. 'We are all bits of flesh, Jean. We are but arrogant if we assume that God could ever have created *us* in His likeness.'

'Listen.' Jean stared at the bottle, and threw it over the side. 'Listen. Those were Spaniards. They hanged your grandmother. Whatever they suffered was yet too good for them.'

'What we will suffer will surely be too good for us,' Kit said. 'There were no men at Panama, Jean. There are no men here. Does it make you proud to belong to a pack of wild animals?'

'For Christ's sake,' Jean shouted. 'What would you do? Fight for the Dons, then?'

Kit sighed. 'Had I a flaming sword I would destroy us all,' he said. 'Dons and buccaneers, and leave these blessed islands to the Indians, as I have no doubt was originally intended.'

'Bah,' Jean declared. 'Did not the Indians kill one another? Are not the Caribs cannibals? Now, how much worse can you get than that? Did you see any Spaniards eaten alive, back there?'

'Is that the worst fate which can befall a man?' Kit demanded. 'I tell you this, I have done with it. May Heaven strike me dead if I ever seek to take a human life again, save in defence of my own.'

'There speaks a unique buccaneer,' Jean said. 'What say you, Master Agrippa?'

The Negro continued to stare at Kit. 'That Master Hilton is right, Monsieur DuCasse. Supposing such a thing is possible. I had thought there could be no man more vicious than a Barbadian planter. Now I know better.'

'God's truth,' Jean said. 'You are a right pair. What will you do, then? Become priests?'

Kit stared at the blue vault of the heavens; they were close to the beach. 'What do you estimate each share in this victory will be worth?'

'You mean you will dirty your hands with such blood-stained money?' Jean asked. 'You amaze me.'

'If I can put it to good use,' Kit said. 'Tell me its worth.'

Jean shrugged. 'They are speaking of a thousand pieces of eight to the lowest deckhand, and each of us commanded a section.'

'Then say five thousand pieces of eight.'

'But you also commanded a squad of musketeers,' Agrippa said. 'Which indeed played a decisive part in the battle.'

'Ten thousand pieces of eight, Kit,' Jean said. 'I would estimate that to be your share. There is a fortune, if you like.'

'In gold,' Kit said. 'There will be few people can have seen that much money before. Not in the Leewards, to be sure. I'll to Antigua, by God. And buy myself a plantation. Will you come with me, Agrippa?'

'I'd know your purpose.'

'No slavery. You have my word. A plantation on which men will work for a decent wage, and hold their heads high, because they are free. What say you to that, black man?'

Jean laughed again. 'Faith, the noise of battle has addled your brain, Kit. Slavery is a natural condition of man, unless he be strong enough to fend for himself. Besides, your fellow planters would stone you in the street.'

'That pack of curs? I'd have their tongues out of their throats before they could spit.'

'And what of your oath, not to spill blood save in self-defence?'

Kit flushed; he had already forgotten those hasty words. 'I meant, save in a worthwhile cause.'

'Now you are being specious. What you should say is that

you fell in love with a pair of Spanish thighs, and were saddened to see them disappear. But what would you have done with them, Kit, once they were yours? They could never have done other than hate you. Come now, own the truth of what I say.'

'I'll have no more of this,' Kit said. 'There is a new oath. I'm to Antigua, and a better life. By God, I'll make sure of that.'

'Then I'll come with you, Master Hilton,' Agrippa declared. 'Add my share to yours, and we'll be doubly sure of that plantation. 'Tis a dream I have had. Make it come true, and I'll never leave your side. That *I* swear.'

'And here's my hand on it.' Kit felt the firm grip of the huge black.

'And there's the beach,' Jean said. 'So you can set about making your dreams come true. But what's that?'

They sat up to stare forward. The river was widening before opening into the bay where the ships lay at anchor, and beyond was the blue water of the Caribbean Sea. Each was a most welcome sight. But not apparently to all. The first men to reach the beach and scramble from their canoes were yelling and gesticulating, and now they were rounding the last bend they could see that the *Monarch* had already put to sea, and was in fact nearly hull down as she made her way towards Jamaica.

'But what is the matter?' Jean led them ashore. 'Bart. Bart? Give us a reason for this hullabaloo.'

'Reason?' Bart bellowed, his face red with rage. 'Reason? Why, did not that foul wretch Morgan promise that the money would be divided here on the beach at Chagres? And to make the division easier did he not command that all the goods we assembled were to be shipped in the lead canoes?'

'So he did,' Kit agreed.

'Well, sir, you may be interested to know that this villain, whom you are proud to call friend, travelled down with those canoes, ever urging his men to greater efforts so as to draw away from the rest of us, and on reaching the beach he loaded every last penny on board that ship of his and put to sea.'

'But . . .' Jean stared at the angry faces, gathering in ever increasing numbers on the edge of the water to stare after the departing flagship, demanding explanation from the crews they had left behind, who could only say that they had

THE DEVIL'S OWN

known of no arrangements made in Panama, as they had not been present. In loading the Admiral's ship they had done no more than obey orders, as they had always obeyed the Admiral.

'What must we do?' Jean asked, staring at Kit.

Kit began to laugh.

But that was long ago. How long? Since the beach at Chagres? Or since he had laughed?

Or since he had lain upon the girl Isabella, and known a moment's paradise before stepping down into hell?

And would he ever laugh again? He sat on the beach and gazed at the empty harbour. Empty compared with the crowded activity they had seen on their first arrival here, more than a year gone. It had been full once more, when the fleet had come storming back from the Chagres, searching for their Admiral. But the Admiral had gone, stopping at Port Royal long enough to pick up his friend Tom Modyford. Some said they had had no choice; peace had been signed between England and Spain on about the day Morgan had disembarked his army, and so for all the Cross of St George under which they had marched, they had committed piracy and robbery, murder and rape—not an act of war. Morgan and Modyford had gone home to explain, and attempt to avoid the hangman. And they had taken the money with them. Perhaps to bribe the King. Who could be sure? Certain it was that none was left in Jamaica.

Kit had supposed then that he would witness another sack, another horror to equal that of Panama. But was Port Royal worth sacking, when they could have anything of value there for the asking? And for the main they were English, and this was a part of England. They would be murdering their own kind, and not all of them were prepared to go as far as that. He had played a part in averting that disaster, and was proud of it. The result was that the French had left immediately, angrily declaring that they would never again sail with the English. Bart had gone amongst the first, and Jean had gone with him. He had made a last effort to persuade Kit to accompany him. They had been friends all their lives; they had watched their only relatives die together. They had fought for each other for two years in Hispaniola, and they had shared everything in life worth having.

Kit had refused. Then, he had still been gripped by the tragedy in which he had participated. He had been as confused and as disappointed as any of them. He had both liked and admired Morgan, as he had respected the Welshman's courage and ability. He had thought that they might become friends, that he himself had been marked out for advancement by the buccaneer Admiral. He remembered the words Morgan had used before they had landed. 'Stay close to me,' the Admiral had said. At the time that had meant nothing more than that Morgan wanted his section commanders close within earshot. But had he even then been planning to desert his men? Had he led them through that frightful forest, won for them that fantastic victory over a Spanish army, and then loosed them in that abominable sack, all the time only waiting for the business to be completed so that he could steal the fruits of their valour?

If that were so, and who could doubt it, then what remained in life worth having? That had been no act of revenge against the Spaniards, no act of war, even, in defence of the British colonies in the Caribbean; rather had it been a calculated robbery of the very men who had followed him to hell and back. Kit's personal anger at having participated in such a crime and in such a dupe redoubled every time he thought of it. As his own resolution, his very manhood, had dwindled every time he thought of it. So he had stayed, waiting in Port Royal, perhaps for Morgan to come back, perhaps for the memory of that dreadful day in Panama, which obscured even all those other dreadful days before, to fade.

He had become a beachcomber, in a society of thieves and whores. He was not the only beachcomber. How had he despised those gaunt and dead-eyed men in the tattered breeches who had kicked the stones along the Tortuga shore? How he had thought Bale too low even to be considered human. He had thought, had any man the right so to misuse the gift of life? But had not all those men, even Bale, something similarly terrible of which they dared not think, and of which they dared not risk a repetition?

And Morgan had not come back. There were rumours that he had been convicted, and would be hanged, and others, that he had amused the King, and so would be acquitted, and returned in triumph. To face the men he had deserted? There would be an act of courage.

Footsteps. He did not turn his head, because these he recognized. He was not alone. Perhaps Agrippa, in that huge black brain of his, locked behind those sombre dark eyes, had also found Panama beyond the reaches of his stomach. Or was Agrippa also waiting to have his revenge on the Admiral? How many were there like that?

'A bottle of wine,' Agrippa said. 'And this fish. Roasted, fresh.'

The snapper was still hot.

'Now, where did you get that?' Kit asked.

'A bet,' Agrippa said carelessly. 'That I could not balance my cutlass on the end of my chin.' He grinned. 'There are always people who will bet me that. This one is a dandy.'

He pointed at the only ship in the harbour which looked capable of going to sea in safety, a trim two-masted schooner which had dropped anchor but two days previously.

'A dandy, in Port Royal?' Kit chewed, slowly. They did not eat this well every day; they did not even eat every day.

'A sight-seeing Virginian,' Agrippa said. 'Do they have slaves in Virginia, Kit?'

'Now that I cannot say. Why, had you thought of shipping with this man?'

'Him, no,' Agrippa said. 'He is a shade too tart for me, and besides, there is a wildness in his eye. But it is a fact that every day we spend here we grow less fit to spend any days at all anywhere else. We must do something, Kit.'

'I make no claim on your company.'

'While you sit here and rot? By God, I will soon think that Monsieur DuCasse was right, and that you pine after that girl. No man should brood for so many empty months. What of those dreams you spoke of?'

'Like most dreams, they were overly dependent upon money,' Kit said.

'And can we not earn some more?'

'By pirating? The thought still turns my stomach.'

'By shipping as seamen, then.'

'By Christ, but you are a simple soul. Do seamen exist any better than sitting here? Except that they must work and be flogged for their pains. I'll hear no more.'

He got up and walked away from his friend, into the acrid stench of the town. He was at least safe from molestation. Most people here knew Kit Hilton, and all had heard of his grandfather. They knew he could handle his cutlass better than most, and they knew he had commanded the musketeers before Panama. If he chose to waste his life on the beach, there was no one in Port Royal disposed to make an issue of it; rather did they still remain anxious to greet him, to receive a nod or even a glance from so famous a buccaneer.

But this day he walked with more purpose than usual. A man with a wildness in his eye. A tantalizing phrase. He would see for himself, and if the stranger was indeed a gentleman, he should not be hard to find, in these surroundings. Besides, he knew where to look. The tavern lay at the end of the street, and even on a hot afternoon would be filled with thirsty seamen, and acquisitive whores, and the hangers-on to both, the pimps and the men who were handy with a pair of dice, and equally with their knives when the dice would not roll true.

Today the tavern was more crowded than usual. Men overflowed through the door on to the street, scuffling and muttering amongst themselves as they fought for a better position, while the effluvium of their unwashed bodies surrounded them like a miasma. Kit elbowed his way through them, reached the doorway, gazed into the termite-eaten timbers of the room, at the long board set upon two empty barrels which served as a pot-table, littered with bottles and jars, for most of the liquor sold in this establishment was home-brewed and the more potent for that. Beyond the trestle, the space that was normally crowded with drinking, lecherous seamen had been cleared; here three men crouched on the floor and rolled dice. Two of them Kit knew well enough; he had been with Captain Jackman on the march to Panama, and had often enough been offered a berth on his ship since returning. And John Relain was an officer in the garrison; his face was deeply pock-marked, and he moved stiffly, as if the habits of discipline and drill had entered his very bones. Except when rolling dice; then his lean face came alive and his shoulders quivered with excitement.

But it was the stranger he had come to watch. He and everyone else. A gentleman, certainly. He had discarded his blue coat, and his shirt was cambric, and freshly laundered; Kit had forgotten that clothes could be so white. His breeches, too, were of best broadcloth, in pale blue, and his stockings had a whiteness to match his shirt. But his clothes were irrelevant, merely a showcase for the man himself. He knelt, but Kit estimated that he was tall enough, and he had a good pair of shoulders. Above which, at the top of a somewhat long neck, was a singular face, with features that were large but splendidly proportioned, to form an impressive whole, dominated by the straight nose and even more by the sparkle in the grey eyes. Expressions flitted across his face with rapidity and completeness, changing in less than a wink from a frown of pure venom as the dice disobeyed his whim to a smile of a quite dramatically winning quality when he saw the game was his. He was bareheaded, and wore no wig, although his hair was cropped sufficiently short to suggest that he was no stranger to one.

And the dice was rolling his way often enough to keep that winning smile more in evidence than the disturbing frown. That much was testified to by the pile of coins beside his elbow. And that was what the onlookers wished to see. Captain Jackman was a bad man from whom to take too much. Already his face was red and his great, shaven scalp glowed.

The strange young man was rolling once more. 'Seven it is,' he said, triumphantly. 'My stake, sir. You'll bet again?'

'And your dice, by Christ,' Jackman growled. 'We'll have another pair.'

The young man frowned. 'Do you seek to question my honour, sir?'

' 'Tis too steady a winner you are. What say you, Master Relain?'

'Aye,' the soldier agreed. 'We'll have them changed.'

'Then, sir,' the young man declared, 'I withdraw from the game.'

'You'll not, by God,' Jackman said. 'You've my money there.'

'You mistake the situation, sir.' The young man scooped the money into his hat, and stood up. 'It is my money, now.'

'A cutpurse, by Christ, Jackman said, and also got to his feet, drawing his cutlass as he did so. The American stepped back, laid the hat on the table with a resounding tinkle, and found his own discarded swordbelt. But he wore nothing heavier than a rapier, a wisplike gleam of steel, hardly calculated to face a cutlass, especially when wielded by such an old hand as Ben Jackman.

As the onlookers knew. 'Cut his whistle for him, Ben,' they bawled. 'Take off his ears.'

Jackman grinned, and whipped the cutlass to and fro. The young man watched him come, no longer smiling, but not obviously concerned, either, his right leg and his right arm alike thrust forward, his left arm free behind him and pointing at the ceiling; clearly he had been taught swordsmanship in a good school. But this was no school at all. Jackman leapt forward, and the two blades clashed for a moment; the young man sought to parry and then riposte, and saw his blade beaten aside by the sheer force of the onslaught. He recovered quickly enough, and was again in position to parry the next sweep, but this was travelling with such tremendous violence that it swept the slender sword from his hand, to send it clattering against the wall, while the onlookers howled their glee.

The young man glanced after his weapon. His face was pale, and he breathed a trifle heavily, but he remained apparently unafraid.

'His ears, Ben,' the crowd shouted. 'Off with his ears.'

'Aye,' Jackman said, advancing. 'I'll have them, and my money too.'

The revulsion against these men, against himself for being one of them, against the heat and the stink and the avarice with which he was surrounded, welled up into Kit's throat. Before he had stopped to weigh the consequences he had drawn his own cutlass, reversed it, and thrown it across the room. 'Try stronger metal, Virginian,' he suggested.

There was a lull in the tumult, as heads turned, amongst them Jackman's. The young man hastily reached forward, stooping to pick up the cutlass and ducking under Jackman's arm in the same instant, and turned, his right arm snaking forward. He may never have been taught the use of a cutlass, but he clearly knew weapons; the broad, sharp blade was already waving menacingly, and now he smiled, and it was Jackman's turn to frown.

'By Christ,' Relain muttered, and drew his sword.

'Avast there.' Kit moved against the wall, and levelled his pistol.

'By Christ, Kit Hilton. You'd take a sharper's side?'

' 'Tis yet to be proved that he has cheated,' Kit said. ' 'Tis more likely your luck has run low.'

'By Christ,' Jackman said, still watching the American, but making no move to advance. 'You'd turn this into a mêlée, Kit? You'll find too many against you.'

'You'll need men with stomach, Captain Jackman.' Agrippa's bulk filled the doorway. He had not yet drawn his cutlass, but his hand rested on the hilt. The spectators muttered amongst themselves, but even Jackman's crew were reluctant to become involved in a fracas which must cost some of their blood to no obvious profit.

'Ah, bah,' Jackman said. He slid his blade into its scabbard, and picked up his hat to cram it on his head. ' 'Tis only money, by God. There is plenty more where that came from.' He stepped past the motionless American, followed by the soldier, and pushed his way into the crowd.

'Faith, sir,' the young man said. 'I owe you my ears, it seems. And maybe more.' He made one or two passes with the cutlass, and then reversed it as he held it out. 'You'll find that I understand a debt, sir. And this weapon it seems I must learn to use. They call you Kit Hilton, sir. 'Tis a name I have heard. Daniel Parke, of Virginia, at your service.'

'And this is Marcus Vipsanius Agrippa,' Kit said.

Parke already holding out his hand, checked and half turned. 'Indeed, we have already met, when his dexterity cost me a gold coin. He is a good servant, I have no doubt.'

'You mistake the situation, Mr Parke,' Kit explained. 'Agrippa is my friend, not my servant.' He found the American's fingers dry and firm, despite his exertion. But Parke did not offer to shake hands with the black man.

'Then is he a good friend also,' he said. 'I would depart this place, gentlemen. I have a ship, at anchor in the bay. Perhaps you would join me on board for a glass of wine.'

'That would be most pleasant, sir,' Kit agreed, and accompanied him out of the tavern, Agrippa following behind. 'Did you say the ship was yours?'

'A charter, you understand. It is my father's wish that I visit the Caribee Isles, to understand something of this sugar cane which is on everyone's lips. Perhaps it can be planted with profit in Virginia.'

'And for that he chartered a ship?' Kit wondered. 'By God, sir, gambling for that you can surely be nothing more than a pleasure. But you'll find little cane in Jamaica.'

'So I have discovered,' Parke said. 'And to say truth, it was not my father's intention that I come here. But, visit the West Indies and not see Port Royal? I could as well sail the Atlantic and not pay my court to His Majesty. Although, had you not happened on the scene my stay here might have been a miserable one. Again, my thanks, sir. You have but to name your wish, and I shall grant it, if I can.'

'I wish no reward, Master Parke,' Kit said.

'To you, Kit, my name is Daniel. I'd not have you forget that.' They were at the shore now, and a boat was pulling from the schooner. Parke halted, and looked Kit up and down. 'I said I heard your name; now it comes to me. Your father was Governor of Tortuga a while back.'

'My grandfather,' Kit said.

'No matter. You are cast in his mould. And you are a buccaneer. A compatriot of these people, I have no doubt.'

'I was with Jackman, and Morgan, at Panama,' Kit said. 'As was Agrippa.'

'The devil,' Parke said. 'I envy you, sir.'

'As I envy you, Daniel, for having not yet discovered the beast in man.'

'Ah. And so you turn against your fellows. And yet would remain here in their company? Be sure, that even with this gigantic fellow to guard your back, they will find a way to slip a knife between your ribs. At least let me offer you a passage to some more congenial clime.'

'You are returning to Jamestown?'

'Not for a while. I must first pursue this stalk which has become so valuable. I am bound for the Leewards. St Kitts and then Antigua. I have letters of introduction to Sir William Stapleton and Colonel Philip Warner.'

'Warner,' Kit muttered. How painfully his heart pounded, and he had thought to forget that name, with all his other memories.

'You know Colonel Warner? His family is the oldest and most famous in these islands, so I am told.'

'With mine, Daniel. Together they founded these colonies.'

'Indeed? But you have not answered my question.'

'We have met, Colonel Warner and I.'

Parke gazed at him, frowning, and then smiled that tremendous smile. 'Then meet him again, Kit. As my guest. I promise you he shall sing a different tune.'

Kit glanced at Agrippa. 'What say you, Agrippa? 'Twas our first idea.'

'You have but to decide, Kit.' The Negro's voice was as calm and as deep as ever.

'Then we accept, Daniel,' Kit said. 'And here is my hand on it.'

'And mine,' Parke cried. 'I am honoured by your company, sir. Here is my boat. Unless you have gear to gather, we can weigh anchor this evening.'

'No gear,' Kit said. 'And to say truth, I shall not even cast a glance over my shoulder.'

The boat was at the beach, and Parke ushered his new friends on board. He sat beside them in the stern, took the two dice from his pocket of his coat, and dropped them over the side, watched them drifting downwards through the translucent depths. ' 'Tis certain they will bring me no more fortune than they have already achieved.'

Kit smiled. 'You flatter us, Daniel. Now tell me straight, *were* they loaded?'

Parke's laughter filled the afternoon. 'But of course. How else may a gentleman be sure of winning?'

4

The Lady of Green Grove

'By God, but 'tis a thriving place.' Daniel Parke clung to the rigging as the schooner brought up into the wind and dropped her anchor. 'They tell no lies when they speak of the prosperity of Antigua.'

Kit could not quarrel with that judgement. St John's nestled beneath the gentle hills which surrounded it, in strong contrast to the more rugged outlines of St Kitts, which they had left at dawn. And it prospered; the steeples of the churches, the fresh paint on the houses, the bustle on the waterfront and even more important, the activity in the harbour itself, where two ships were being warped away from the quayside to allow two more to take their places, were sufficient evidence of this. But for a week now he had known the nostalgia of being amongst these islands, where it had all begun, where Tony Hilton and Edward Warner, and Susan Hilton as well, had fought side by side to establish themselves, where they had slept under the sky often enough, with no change of clothing and no certainty where they would obtain their next meal. How Susan would have stared at this metropolis.

And how inadequate did he suddenly feel. For had he a change of clothing? Daniel had done his best, and they were much of a likeness in build. But Daniel's clothes had been made by the best tailor in all Virginia; they were magnificently cut, and cut from magnificent cloth—and they had been intended to cling to Daniel's frame like a second skin. Too obviously they had not been so created for Kit Hilton. And these haughty planters would know that.

'There's a boat waiting, Mr Parke,' said the captain of the schooner. 'I know you're in haste to be ashore. Your baggage can follow later.'

Daniel Parke stepped down from the rigging, and preened himself. He wore a mauve velvet coat with gold buttons, and in honour of the occasion had donned a grey periwig beneath his black tricorne. His cravat was white, and edged with lace; his shoes black leather, with red heels and metal buckles; his stockings were grey. He did not deign to carry a sword at all, but preferred a gold-handled cane. 'Do you think I will stand out well amongst these islanders, Kit?'

'You'll have them bowing,' Kit observed, and straightened his own hat, a plain brown tricorne. He wore no wig, and his coat was open over his white shirt. And he carried a cutlass, hanging from a leather baldric. He had no wish to rival his friend, even if that had been possible. But Christ that he would stop sweating from fear.

Fear of what? Of stepping ashore amongst civilized people, knowing what he was? Or fear of seeing the Warners again, and one Warner in particular? Again, knowing what he was.

'Let us assault this shore,' Parke decided, descending the ladder to the boat. For this, Kit was coming to realize, was how his new friend looked at life. There could be nothing ordinary, nothing dull, nothing even peaceful, around Daniel Parke. Life was a military exercise, a continual battleground, with Marshal Parke ever eager to tilt at whatever windmills he could find.

'And Agrippa?'

'Oh, bring the big buck, by all means,' Parke said. 'We may have need of his muscle.'

Agrippa took his place in the bows, while Kit sat aft with Parke, and the boat pulled for the shore. It was early afternoon, and the sun was starting to drop, but it remained close and hot, although a breeze entered the harbour from the Atlantic, separated from them by the other myriad islands they had seen from the ship as they rounded the headland. But there were no other islands, once one made the acquaintance of Antigua. None which mattered, at any rate. Soon they were in the midst of the bumboats and the jollys, which were making their way out to the new arrival, handled by sweating white men in garb hardly superior to any to be found in Port Royal, Kit discovered to his relief, but in the main cheerful, happy, and more important, healthy-looking men. For he had heard sufficient tales of the debilitating fevers which could ruin a man's health in the southerly islands, and he had seen enough of it in the march to and from Panama.

The boat nosed its way alongside stone steps, and the oars were shipped. Agrippa took the painter ashore, and Kit and Parke followed him on to the crowded jetty where the stevedores, mostly Negroes these, stopped to stare at the new arrivals, and a few white men also gaped. 'By God,' someone said. 'A gentleman. A regular marcaroni.'

Parke tapped the fellow on the shoulder with his cane, and the suggestion of laughter died as he took a closer look at the American's face, and eyes. 'Aye,' Parke said. 'I am a gentleman, and you'd do well to remember that, before I have my friends here set about breaking your heads. Buccaneers, my bravos. Morgan's men.'

The onlookers, now fast forming a crowd, gaped some more, and Kit and Agrippa exchanged glances. Parke had made them relate their adventures in Panama often enough after dinner on board ship, but that he would shout their erstwhile activities from the rooftops had not crossed their minds.

Certainly he was pleased with the effect of his words. 'You'll not have seen their like in this backwater, I'll wager. Now, you, I have letters for the Deputy Governor. You'll direct us to his estate. Quickly.'

'Sure, and Colonel Warner's estate is a tidy drive from town,' someone said. 'Ye'd do better to try the Ice House, your honour. 'Tis certain ye'll find him there.'

'The Ice House?' Parke queried. 'There's a strange name. Can you tell me what they store there?'

'Why, ice, your honour. Brought all the way from the Arctic, it is. Ye'd not have a gentleman's drink warm for lack of a drop of ice, now, would ye? 'Tis the big house on yonder corner.'

'Ice,' Parke said. 'Brought all the way from the Arctic, by God. To cool the drinks.'

'Does it not melt before ever it reaches this far south?' Kit asked.

'Oh, no, sir,' explained the foreman. 'The ships are specially constructed, ye understand, the holds lined with metal covered in sawdust, to keep down the temperatures. And fast they are. 'Tis scarce a fortnight's voyage, for them.'

'Special ships to cool a man's drink,' Parke said, in continuing wonderment. 'And all financed by sugar. By God, sirs, 'tis an economic revolution we are witnessing. I think we shall investigate this fabulous house.' He led them up the street, cane slapping against his stockinged legs as if he would encourage himself. Now they left the bustle of the docks and found themselves on a wide and pleasant road, no more than rutted dust, to be sure, but lined with enormous trees, each a mass of brilliant red flowers, and backed by shops and houses, in a profusion and state of repair Kit had seen nowhere save in Panama itself.

'What a splendid sight,' Parke cried, pausing at the corner.

'The trees are called poincianas,' Kit said. 'And are named after an erstwhile governor of French St Kitts, the Sieur de Poincy, who was something of a botanist.'

'By God, Kit, but you're a mine of information.'

Kit flushed. 'My grandmother was acquainted with the gentleman.'

'Was she now? But it was less the flowers I was admiring, magnificent as they are, than the evidence that even the humans in this delightful place are worthy of closer inspection.' He pointed with his cane, and the two white girls on the far side of the street giggled and darted away. Their faces were concealed by the shade of enormous straw hats, but their figures were indeed eye-catching, especially as they appeared to be wearing but a single petticoat beneath their muslin gowns. Parke glanced at his companion. 'But you, I observe, show no great interest in nubile females.'

'Perhaps I have seen sufficient such as they are reduced to the last extremity by lustful fingers,' Kit remarked. 'Amongst them my own.'

'By God, sir, but on occasion you are an uncommonly solemn fellow. So you once forced a Spanish hymen. You may be sure that in taking her own life, and that of her sister, she committed by far the more serious crime by the lights of her religion. This seems to be the right place.'

They had paused before a large doorway set into the highest building on the street, which appeared like a gigantic warehouse, for it stretched back a considerable distance as well. Parke rapped on the door with the head of his cane, and after a moment it was opened by a Negro wearing white breeches and stockings beneath a blue coat, with a white wig on his head and black leather shoes on his feet. 'Your pleasure, sir?' he inquired.

'By God,' Parke said. 'By God. You'd do well in Jamestown, by God. We seek your Governor, Colonel Philip Warner.'

'Colonel Warner is within, sir. Will you enter?' The doorman's gaze flickered to Kit, and he hesitated, and then bowed again.

'Thank you, fellow,' Parke said. 'Make way there. Make way.'

For the majordomo had straightened and was blocking Agrippa's way. 'No slaves are permitted, unless they are employed by the House.'

'Slaves?' Parke said. 'Who spoke of slaves? This man is my friend.'

'I should have said, sir, no man with a black skin is allowed within, unless he is employed by the House.'

'I'll have you whipped, you insolent dog,' Parke shouted. 'By God. Kit, cut me this fellow's ears.'

'In truth, Mr Parke, I'll not be the cause of a riot,' Agrippa said. 'I'd as soon explore this pretty little town.'

'By God,' Parke said. 'You'll go where I go, by God, if I so choose. Stand aside, fellow.'

Suddenly the street was crowded, with white people and black, issuing from stores and behind trees from whence they had been surreptitiously watching the strangers. It occurred to Kit that they might well have a riot after all. For the majordomo was showing no signs of yielding.

And Daniel Parke was going red in the face. 'By God,' he shouted. 'Kit, draw your sword. Draw it, by God, and clear me a path.'

Kit chewed his lip, uncertain what would be best, when a voice inquired, quietly enough, 'What seems to be the trouble, John?'

The majordomo sighed with relief. 'These gentlemen, Colonel Warner, sir, wish to bring a black man into the Ice House.'

As if Kit could ever really have forgotten that voice, that strut. And yet, to his surprise, Philip Warner this afternoon wore none of the finery he had sported in Tortuga, but preferred a plain coat and an unrufled shirt, with loose trousers rather than breeches, hanging over riding boots. He did not carry a sword, and did not wear a wig, but instead a black tricorne. Nor were any of the men crowding behind him better dressed.

'Strangers,' he observed, gazing at Parke with a frown. 'And you would begin by changing our laws? I'll have your name, sir.' But before Parke could reply, his gaze had flickered across to Kit. 'By God,' he said. ' 'Tis the buccaneer himself.'

'I sailed with Morgan, Colonel Warner, certainly,' Kit confessed. 'But that was in my heritage, would you not agree? Now I have given up the life in a search for something better.'

'Morgan? Morgan, did you say?' The other planters pushed forward. 'Were you at Panama?'

'I had that misfortune, sir,' Kit replied to the man who had asked the question.

'Fear not, gentlemen,' Colonel Warner said. 'The lad is an old acquaintance of mine. Kit Hilton. You'll have heard the name. His people were in the employ of my family when first we came to these islands'

'Why, sir, I . . .' Kit bit off the words. He had no wish to brawl with the Deputy Governor, at this moment.

Warner smiled at him. 'And faith, lad, you look the part. What of your friend?'

'By God, sir,' Parke declared. 'I had supposed you had forgotten my existence. Daniel Parke, of Virginia, at your service.'

'Parke?' Warner extended his hand. 'Why, sir, a thousand apologies. I received a letter but a fortnight gone, from your father, informing me of your impending visit. Why, sir, I but wish you had established yourself sooner. Now my manners stand shot to pieces, with only patchwork left to be accomplished. But I had not expected to find you in such company.'

'Kit is my good friend, Colonel Warner.'

Warner continued to smile. 'And mine. Why, when last was it we had the pleasure of meeting, Kit? Two, three years?'

'More than four, Colonel,' Kit said.

'And since then much has happened. Yes, indeed. You'll take a drink of rum punch with me, gentlemen. Not your servant, Kit. Our laws are meant to be obeyed.'

'My . . .'

But Agrippa interrupted him. 'I will look at the town, sir,' he said, gravely.

'A likely fellow,' Warner said. 'You must tell me how you came by him. But first of all, the punch. Back, gentlemen, let us show our visitors true Antiguan hospitality.'

'Punch?' Parke demanded, as he was escorted from the

lobby into a large room, distinctly cool as opposed to the heat of the street, but remarkably lacking in furniture; the bare wooden floor was scattered with sawdust, and there were only some tables against the far wall, behind which Negro servants, as liveried as the doorman, were handling mugs while others came through from the back door with enormous blocks of ice set in wooden tubs, which they proceeded to assault with hammer and spike rather in the fashion of marauding artillerymen.

'The sweetest drink in all the world.' Warner assured him. 'And made from our own good sugar. The liquid molasses, you understand, suitably thinned and fermented. There you have the rum. Add some lime juice, to keep out the scurvy, and some sugar, to sweeten it up again, and a good deal of ice, for fear the strong liquor lays you flat in a single blow, and you have nectar, Mr Parke. Sheer nectar.'

'Knock me flat?' Parke grumbled, raising his mug. He drank, with a lusty sigh, and stepped back. 'By God.' He blinked. ' 'Tis certainly stronger than wine.'

Kit, who had made the acquaintance of rumbullion on board Morgan's ship, sipped his punch more cautiously, very aware that he was being scrutinized by every man in the room. Perhaps he was the first real-life buccaneer any of them had ever seen. It certainly behoved him to tread warily in this society. But already questions were bubbling into his brain, if he dared ask them.

'Aye,' Philip Warner said. 'We had heard of the fate of Tortuga in the recent war. But you cannot say I did not warn you, Master Hilton. I trust your grandmother made her escape in time?'

'My grandmother was hanged by the Dons,' Kit said.

'The devil,' Philip muttered, and a murmur of outrage went round the room. 'And so you sailed with Morgan. By God, I cannot altogether blame you. And as you pointed out, it is in your blood. And so what brings you to Antigua? You're no cane-planter, I'll be bound.'

Kit glanced at Parke, who promptly came to his rescue.

'No, sir, he is not. But he has sworn to turn his back upon villainy and bloodshed, having had a bellyful in Panama. Kit seeks employment, Colonel Warner. And be sure you will find no stouter seafarer in all these islands. I give you my word on that.'

'Employment?' Philip Warner stared at Kit. 'You came to Antigua for employment?'

Kit was flushing with embarrassment and even anger at Parke's latest pronunciamento. 'No, sir, I did not. Having made Mr Parke's acquaintance, I agreed to accompany him on a tour of these islands.'

'Oh, come now, Kit,' Parke said. 'Do not dissemble before these gentlemen. Would you not make your future here amongst your own kind, rather than come with me to America, a nameless vagabond?'

'I do assure you, Daniel,' Kit began, but Parke was already bounding off on another, more vital subject.'

'I wonder, Colonel Warner, if I might ask after your daughter, Marguerite? I have heard that she is the most beautiful charmer in all the world.'

Philip Warner's gaze was cold. 'In Virginia, sir? In any event, my daughter is lately widowed, of Harry Templeton, may God rest his soul in peace, and is not at this moment receiving.'

Marguerite, a widow? Now why, Kit wondered, did that set his heart pounding? They had met but once, and four years in the past, yet suddenly her memory came clouding back with a clarity he had thought to have lost forever. And if Modyford was to be believed, she might also remember him.

'Then I apologize,' Parke said, without a hint of embarrassment. 'Now, tell me, can the Deputy Governor of Antigua not find a suitable post for a man of Kit's talents? Especially as he is an old friend.'

Warner pinched his lip, and glanced at his companions.

'I seek no charity, sir,' Kit insisted. 'Nor will I accept any, even from you, Daniel. If my passage irks you, be sure that I am prepared to work it, from here to Barbados.'

'And what would you do there that you cannot do here?' Parke inquired. 'If only you would understand that I seek to help you, dear Kit. The Leewards are the future of this hemisphere, sir, nay, of this entire empire, So it is loudly said, and what I have seen here today but convinces me of the truth of that statement. I have heard a respectable merchant, a man with much knowledge of trade and affairs, declare that within fifty years an ounce of good sugar will be worth more than an ounce of pure gold. I will not dispute that point, sir. I but suggest that you remain in close proximity to such a bottomless mine, for be sure that wealth will filter.'

'An admirable sentiment, and prognostication which agrees

THE DEVIL'S OWN

with my own,' Philip Warner said. 'But to find a suitable post for Hilton . . .'

'The sloop,' said the man who had first addressed Kit, a heavy-set fellow with a shock of red hair, and not much older than himself, Kit estimated.

'Edward Chester,' Philip said offhandedly. 'One of my associates. You have a solution to this problem, Edward?'

'Indeed, sir. Do we not at this moment need a master for the *Bonaventure*, and is not Mr Hilton a seafaring man, who comes from a line of seafaring men? And a man of spirit, too. Why, he could be the answer to a prayer.'

Warner was frowning as he gazed at Kit, while Kit's heart was bounding with excitement. A ship, of his own? Even if it was only a trading sloop? And based on St John's. Where surely a chance meeting could be arranged.

'These are treacherous waters,' Warner said.

'None a seaman might not navigate,' Chester insisted.

'And treacherous times.'

'For a man who sailed with Morgan?'

'Tell us of this sloop,' Parke said. 'I do assure you that Kit will handle her as I might handle my horse, and there is no better horseman in all America.'

'Indeed?' Philip asked, somewhat drily. 'Perhaps I doubt that it will be sufficiently interesting for Mr Hilton. We speak of a sloop, you understand, which is jointly owned by a consortium of planters here and which trades with St Eustatius.'

Kit frowned. 'Is that not a Dutch colony?'

'Indeed, sir, so it is,' Chester explained. 'And as the meinheers, very generously, do not charge any duties upon their imports to that island, we find it convenient to import most of our European goods through their warehouses, and then bring them here privily.'

'Smuggling, by God,' Parke shouted, and burst into laughter. 'I like the sound of that.'

'We prefer to call it customs avoidance,' Philip Warner said.

'But . . .' Kit stared at them in horror. 'Are we not at war with Holland? And what of the Navigation Acts? Are we not specifically forbidden to carry any goods to or from English soil except in English bottoms, and equally forbidden to trade with any country save England herself, or our sister colonies?'

'By God,' someone in the crowd said. 'And this man sailed with Morgan?'

Kit rounded on them. 'However mistaken he may have been, sir, in his knowledge of current politics, Admiral Morgan considered he was carrying on legitimate warfare against the flag of Spain, when he landed at Chagres. Now, were you to offer me a command *against* St Eustatius . . .'

'By God,' Chester said. 'What a bloodthirsty fellow you are, Mr Hilton. And did you not just claim to have turned your back on violence? Why should we fight the Dutch merely because some trumped-up ass in Whitehall suggests it? Those Hollanders are far more our people than any of the mountebanks who surround the King.

'Treason,' Kit said. 'You speak treason, sir. And before the Deputy Governor.'

The assembly looked at the smiling Philip Warner. 'It seems that you require a simple lesson in West Indian politics, Kit,' he said. 'To be sure, Sir William Stapleton would call what we have just heard, treason. But Stapleton, fortunately for us all, is in St Kitts, and that is hull down on the horizon. And he is not a planter, sir, not one of us. He is merely an ambitious soldier with a reputation to make or lose. We, sir, cultivated these islands before the gentlemen in Whitehall knew of their existence. Your grandfather was involved in that venture. And when Whitehall discovered that we could make a living here, their one thought was to tax us as heavily as they might. And in those days we grew tobacco. When we, not they, discerned the additional value to be gained from sugar, they had no desire to advance us the money or provide us with the slaves we needed; we might have starved, but for our friends the Hollanders. And now that we are again prosperous, more prosperous than ever before, in fact, thanks to the men of Amsterdam, Whitehall would slap yet heavier taxes upon us. Sir, I am often sickened at the thought of being an Englishman. Indeed, I am not. I am an Antiguan. As are these gentlemen. As must you be, if you would remain here. We lack the power, at present, openly to defy the Government, but I'll be damned if we'll pay them more than lip service. Do I speak for us all?'

There was a roar of approbation.

'By God,' Parke said. ' 'Tis a spirit I cannot help but admire, even if I doubt it would be well received in Jamestown. Methinks, Kit, you'd do well to go along with these gentlemen. This is a small world, which can only grow bigger. Be

THE DEVIL'S OWN 97

sure that every man who takes his place at the beginning of the process must also, by the very nature of things, grow to a similar size.' He burst out laughing again at the confusion on Kit's face. 'I tell you what I shall do to help you settle your mind, old friend. I will sail upon your first venture. As supernumerary. For I was never yet involved in a business which did not yield a handsome profit.'

'By God.' Daniel Parke levelled his telescope. 'Are there houses, too?'

It was an hour past dawn, and the sun still hung low in the eastern sky, promising a day of invariable brilliance. They had left Antigua the previous night, making north with the trade wind on the beam, under cover of darkness to avoid any chance encounter with the revenue frigate from St Kitts. At midnight Kit had altered course to run down on the little island of St Eustatius, and there it was, three miles to port, hardly more than a rock sticking up out of the Saba bank, but containing a town as large as St John's, and one which as Daniel had just commented, seemed to contain nothing more than an endless bank of enormous warehouses, crowding the waterfront. Which was itself crowded, with shipping, flying the French and English flags, as well as the Dutch.

'A free port,' Parke murmured, sliding down to the deck. 'Why, 'tis a fabulous conception, Kit. What right has any government to tax a man's necessities?' He gave a peal of that winning laughter. 'Or his luxuries, by God.'

Kit was preoccupied with conning the entrance to the harbour. 'We'll have that mainsail down, Agrippa,' he shouted. 'And bring up under jib alone. Smartly now.'

Because it was exhilarating, there could be no doubt about that. It had been exhilarating just to step on board, and know that the *Bonaventure* was his to command. A smuggler. But a trim, fast craft. Well, she had to be, to be successful at her trade. And she had teeth: four cannon. He prayed they would never be fired in anger.

And now they had arrived. Under foresail alone, and under the blanket of a single hill which made the tiny island, the sloop slipped gently up to a gap in the line of moored vessels, and the anchor plunged into the clear green water.

'Nicely done, Captain,' Parke cried, and slapped him on the shoulder. 'I'm for the shore. Look there, man, do I not know that vessel?'

Kit followed his gaze through the forest of masts. 'None I recognize.'

'A Jamestown schooner, by God. I'll across and pass the time of day. And maybe take a glass of this killdevil which clouds a man's brain. You'll accompany me?'

'I think I had best be about my duties,' Kit said. 'We are to sail at dusk again, and I suspect this is our bondman now.'

A lugger approached under shortened sail; her decks were crowded with bales and boxes, and with people as well.

'Then I'll leave you to it,' Parke said. 'If you will permit me the use of your jolly boat.'

'Gladly,' Kit said. 'But be sure you are back by five of the clock.' He went to the rail, hailed the boat which was bringing up alongside. 'Do you speak English?'

'But of course, Captain,' said the man on the tiller, a large, fair, red-faced fellow. 'You are new to us.'

'I master the *Bonaventure*, sir,' Kit said. 'And I have the necessary papers in my cabin.'

'I never doubted that.' The Dutchman swung himself up the shrouds. 'Pieter Lenzing, at your service, Captain.'

'Christopher Hilton.'

'Hilton,' Lenzing mused. 'Hilton. I have heard the name.'

'My grandfather was Governor of Tortuga.'

'And before that I have a notion he sailed with Piet Heyn.' Lenzing squeezed Kit's hand. 'I had not supposed that such a privilege could ever be mine, Captain Hilton. We'll to your cabin, if I may. But I can give the order to start loading now.'

'Then do so,' Kit agreed.

'And may Meinheer Christianssen come on board?'

Kit frowned. 'You have the advantage of me, Meinheer.

'Dag Christianssen,' Lenzing explained. 'He has spent a week here, purchasing goods, and now wishes to return home.'

'To St John's?'

'That is his home, certainly. But of course, you are new to Antigua. Dag owns the central warehouse there.' Lenzing laid his finger alongside his nose. 'A Quaker, you understand, Captain, like so many of the Danes who come to these islands. But there are advantages . . .'

Kit returned to the rail, looked down at the man and the woman. Dag Christianssen could have passed for a Dutchman, a burly man with a florid face and a mass of golden hair, which he apparently seldom cut and never shaved, for it flowed from his chin and around his ears like a waterfall. He might even have been a *boucanier* but for the cleanliness and severity of his dress, for despite the heat he wore a long black coat, and black stockings, while his cravat, if white, was not more than a glimmer at his throat, entirely lacking in lace. His hat was a plain black beaver, such as had been popular in England under the Commonwealth.

But the woman. Surely she was his daughter, for she could not be more than a third of his age, although she possessed his height and colouring, a tall stem of golden beauty. Perhaps. Her face was long, and too serious. Nose and chin were straight and well-shaped, and separated by a mouth wide enough for generosity, and flat enough for determination, as well. As she also wore a wide hat, in grey, Kit could not see her eyes, nor was it easy to decide on her figure, for she was totally concealed beneath a shapeless grey gown, high-necked with a wide white collar, and only slightly pulled in at her waist by a belt. But her height and obvious slenderness promised well, and she moved well, too, with an easy grace.

'Quickly,' he bellowed at Agrippa. 'Assist the lady.'

The big man grinned, and swung his leg over the gunwale to give her his hand.

Her father came up unaided. 'I have not had the pleasure of your acquaintance, Captain, but it is glad I am to see you. The previous master of this vessel was an unmitigated scoundrel, and no seaman into the bargain.'

'So any change must be for the better,' Lenzing smiled.

'Aye,' Kit said. 'It is to be hoped so. But I make no claims to virtue, Mr Christianssen. My name is Christopher Hilton.'

'Hilton?' The merchant frowned. 'A familiar name.'

'Indeed it is,' Lenzing agreed. 'His father and grandfather were buccaneers, men of action, Mr Christianssen. As is this young man, I'll be bound. Come below, Captain, and we'll take a glass and itemize the manifest.'

He headed for the cabin, obviously familiar with the ship. Kit hesitated, watching the young woman straightening her skirts as she reached the deck.

Christianssen followed his gaze. 'My daughter, Lillan, Captain Hilton. Our new master is a buccaneer, it seems, my dear.'

She gave Kit her hand. The firm quality of her features increased with a closer inspection, and her eyes were a magnificent clear blue. 'I trust we are safe in your company, sir.'

'Your father omitted to finish his tale, Miss Christianssen,' Kit said, with some embarrassment. 'I have seen sufficient piracy to understand that it is not for me, God willing.'

'Then there is yet hope for your soul, Captain,' she said. 'But you should be about your business.'

'Will you not join us, sir, and your daughter?' Kit asked the tradesman. 'Surely, if you own the St John's warehouse, the goods I import from this place are of interest to you?'

'Indeed they are, Captain,' Christianssen agreed. 'And more than half of them are destined for my cellars, to be sure. But I prefer not to indulge in spirituous liquors, you understand, and I would not interfere with either your or Mr Lenzing's pleasure. So you attend to your manifest, and I will attend to my business, no doubt to our mutual profit.' He turned back to the rail to supervise the loading.

Kit continued to hesitate, standing beside Lillan. Now why, he wondered. Was he not working for Philip Warner only in the hope of once again meeting Marguerite? All other women could be nothing more than distractions. And in any event, would Lillan not shrink away from his side had she the slightest understanding of what he really was, of what he had really done, with his life?

'Pray do not let us detain you from your affairs, sir,' she said.

'You may believe, Miss Christianssen,' he said, 'that I would far rather be detained here by you than either drink a glass of rum or scrutinize a manifest with Meinheer Lenzing. I am also concerned that this vessel lacks proper accommodation for ladies.'

'Then please cease to be, sir,' she said. 'In the first place, it is a journey of only a few hours, and in this pleasant climate it is no hardship at all for me to remain on deck throughout the night, and in the second place it is a voyage I have made several times before.'

'I stand corrected,' Kit acknowledged. 'Yet I hope, if you will permit me, and if you do intend to spend the night on deck, that you will not turn your back on my company, as I also must be on duty throughout the voyage.'

She glanced at him, her face severely composed. 'I should be delighted to talk with you, Captain Hilton,' she said. 'If you can spare the time from your duties.'

'Now, sir, Captain Hilton,' said Barnee the tailor. 'If you will stand as straight as if you were about to engage in a duel, and take a deep breath, I should be entirely reassured concerning this coat.'

'I already am standing straight, Barnee,' Kit said, and cast an embarrassed glance through the open door of the shop on to the street; there was hardly a more public place in all St John's than Barnee's shop. But he did as he was bid. The coat was of blue broadcloth, and cut with splendid accuracy, to fit every contour of his body. 'What do you think, Dan?'

Parke, whose every coat fitted in just such a fashion, leaned against the wall of the shop with folded arms. 'I had not suspected my bold buccaneer was at heart a dandy,' he said. 'Or is this expensive purchase designed to catch the eye of a lady?'

'Better that than for my own pleasure,' Kit said, turning this way and that to look at himself in the mirror.

'Aha,' Parke said. 'Believe me, friend, I have watched you closely this past month, and you could do worse, saving that I would wish no man to become enamoured of a Quaker.'

'A Quaker?' Kit turned, and frowned, and laughed. 'Oh, you mean Lillan. Why, I doubt not that she would utter similar words, only with a reversed sentiment. You mistake the situation entirely.'

'Another? Faith, you are a secretive fellow.' Parke sighed. 'But I suppose I have spent too much of my time buried deep in the sugar factories to appreciate the society of this island. Yet it grieves me, dear friend, to take my leave without meeting this charmer of yours.'

'Then dally a while longer,' Kit suggested. 'I cannot see that there is so great a haste about visiting Barbados. I had supposed you to consider Antigua a perfect paradise.'

'Indeed I do. But letters from my father keep reminding me that there are other islands, other sugar factories, even other handsome young women, to be investigated.'

The tailor at last stood back and clapped his hands. 'A perfect fit, a perfect cut, Captain Hilton, if I do say so myself. Now, what that coat wants is a matched pair of breeches to go underneath, and why, sir, you'd look fit to walk through Hyde Park itself.'

'I am extremely unlikely ever to walk through Hyde Park, Mr Barnee,' Kit pointed out. 'And I think the breeches should wait until I have managed to pay for the coat, don't you?'

'Oh, fie upon you, sir,' Barnee declared. 'Did you suppose I'd come running behind you for payment? You are employed by Colonel Warner, and that is sufficient for me. Now, as to the breeches . . .'

'I'll run up no debts, Mr Barnee. Colonel Warner owes me a month's wages, which are due this day, and by God, sir, the first person I shall settle is yourself.'

'And speak of the devil.' Parke removed his tricorne with a flourish. 'Good day to you, Colonel.'

Philip Warner stepped into the tailor's shop, kicking dust from his boots. He did not trouble to uncover. 'What, Barnee? What? Dandifying Captain Hilton? Was I invited to a fitting?'

'A man needs a new coat, Colonel Warner,' Barnee said primly.

'And right glad am I to see you, Colonel,' Kit said. 'Mr Barnee has been good enough to trust me while making this splendid garment, and I would not like him to have to wait much longer for his money.'

'Money? Money?' Philip Warner burst out laughing. 'Now, what gives you the impression that I propose to pay you money?'

Kit flushed. 'I have commanded your sloop for a month, sir, as we agreed. In that time we have made twelve voyages to St Eustatius, and every one of them we have returned with our holds full of smuggled merchandise. I'd have thought you'd be more than satisfied.'

'Kit, Kit,' Warner said. 'I am more than satisfied. Much more. Compared with that fellow Longstreet you are a treasure. I came down here today, not merely to settle with you, but to insist that you remain in my employ. And to offer you a bonus in addition.'

'Faith, sir,' Kit said, frowning. 'I do not take your meaning. You said not a minute ago . . .'

'That I have not a penny with which to pay you. Tell us, Barnee, when last were you paid in coin?'

'Well, sir . . .'

'There you are, lad. Coin is scarce, and not to be wasted. And what would you do with it, save gamble it away overnight? I know you buccaneers, by God. Now, sir, here is my statement. I promised you ten pounds for the month, and here, I have written down that I owe you ten pounds. But more, so much profit have you brought into my warehouses that I have added another ten in reward. So there you have, twenty pounds, over my signature.'

Kit took the piece of paper, slowly, stared at the figures. 'But what am I supposed to do with this, Colonel?'

'Use it, to your heart's content. It is a charge against my credit, and will in turn establish yours. Now, for instance, what is this rogue Barnee charging you for this suit?'

'It is but a coat, Colonel,' Barnee protested. 'And I am making no profit at two pounds.'

'I repeat, you are a rogue. But none the less, Kit, if pay him you must, write him a cheque for two pounds, over your signature, and let him certify that it is so paid on my bill in turn. Or if not, just show him my bill and let him be sure that you have the credit.'

Kit scratched his head. 'Except that I do not have the money.'

'By God, lad, but you are a primitive soul. Credit is worth far more than money, as the only person who can take away your credit is you yourself, by your extravagance. And the proof of a pudding is in the eating, is it not? Ask Barnee whether he will not be satisfied with a bill of yours, whether he has any doubt that he may exchange it anywhere on the island for goods.'

'Indeed, sir,' Barnee said. 'If your credit is backed by that of Colonel Warner's, then you will have no problem. I attempted to explain that much to you just now.'

'Except that every bill must be redeemed eventually,' Kit said. 'Must it not?'

'Why of course,' Philip said. 'Every year, when we have finished grinding the crop and our sugar is ready to be shipped, my bills are collected and set against the value of my shipment. It is all done by my agents.'

Kit scratched his head. 'But how do you know where you stand, Colonel?'

'Where I stand, Kit? Where I stand? I know where I stand every morning when I ride through my fields. Now then, I must along to the warehouse and see what you have brought in this last time.'

'Then you will require my presence, sir.'

'Not in the least,' Warner smiled at him. 'I never saw a man yet invest in a new coat of such splendour who wished to discuss business. You take your Danish lady-friend out for the walk you intend, and take my blessings with her. For I tell you straight, Kit, if I had my doubts about employing you when you first landed here, in view of your antecedents and your reputation, why, I admit myself to be mistaken. You are a steady lad, sir, a steady lad. And the Quaker will make you steadier yet. You'll retain command of the *Bonaventure*?'

'Well, sir, I must say . . .'

'Good, good, then it is settled. My associates will be more than pleased. Good day to you, Barnee. Daniel, you'll join me for dinner?'

Parke hesitated, and then nodded. 'With pleasure, Philip. A farewell feast.'

'And never will a guest be more sorely missed. Good day to you, gentlemen.'

He bustled across the street to the Ice House, and Kit scratched his head some more. 'He leaves me breathless. Do you know, when first we met, I had thought him a pompous boor. But he can be a very pleasant fellow. Certainly I could not have asked more of him. And I owe it to you, I am sure.'

Parke was frowning as he gazed at the street. 'Oh, indeed, he is a pleasant fellow, Kit. And yet, I sometimes wonder whether I have done you any favour in bringing you here.'

'Well, I have no doubts on that score.'

'You think so? Has it occurred to you that while I am entertained most royally at Colonel Warner's plantation, you have never even been invited there? Have you ever met Mistress Warner?'

'Well, no. But I am happy enough on my ship and in my station. I glory in every minute I spend at sea. And then, Daniel, however much of a friend you are to me, there *is* a difference in our station. Your father owns a cotton plantation larger than Colonel Warner's, and his father founded these colonies. Mine was a buccaneer.'

'A friend of Thomas Warner's, though. At least, your grandfather was. And none of your brothers or uncles are cannibal kings, at any rate. I think you set too low a claim upon yourself, dear Kit. The other criticism that I have to make of your situation is somewhat more serious, I think. You are now a man of substance, are you not, with a bill for twenty English pounds neatly folded in your pocket.'

'And right comforting it is too, I can tell you,' Kit said. 'I have never owned so much in my life before.'

'But it is dependent upon Colonel Warner's credit, is it not?'

THE DEVIL'S OWN

'Do you doubt *that*?'

'Not in the least. Having ridden every corner of his plantation, I have no doubt that he does understand his worth whenever he looks out of a window. But yours exists only as long as he supports it. Bear that in mind, Kit. There are other forms of slavery than the handcuffs and the whip. But perhaps I have already said too much. You will make your home here, and marry your Quaker, and be happy. And I must take myself back to the hurly-burly of Virginian society, compared with which these islands seem like untroubled paradises.' He seized Kit's hand. 'But I would not have missed this voyage for the world, especially as it brought me your acquaintance. I trust we shall meet again, some day.'

'Oh, we shall,' Kit cried, suddenly aghast at the idea of his friend's departure. 'And you shall not find me changed. Believe me. As to why you, and Colonel Warner, and everyone else, it seems, should suppose that I am enamoured of Lillan Christianssen, or if I were, that she would consider betrothing herself to a buccaneer, a man of violence and with intolerable crimes staining his soul, why, the idea is preposterous.'

'Is it?' Parke inquired. 'Then tell me why she smiles whenever she sees you? And tell me what you talk of when you walk together of an evening?'

'Can two people of opposite sexes not be friends?' Kit demanded. 'As to our conversation, it mostly concerns Master Fox, for whom she has a reverence almost amounting to worship, and in whom she would also interest me.'

'So, then, we shall find you a Quaker yet. And in any event, Kit, you betray yourself in this coat. Now I must go. Adieu, dear friend. A thousand times adieu. But we shall meet again. I make that resolution, and Daniel Parke is a man of his word.'

He hurried off, patently upset at having to say farewell. And Kit let him go, because even Daniel's departure loomed small by the standards of this afternoon's adventure. As during his month on Antigua the widow Templeton had not visited St John's, then would he visit the widow Templeton. This coat had been designed for just that purpose. So what of Daniel's words? Did Philip Warner seek to make a slave of him? As if a white man could make a slave of another white man. And did it matter if he placed himself in Philip's power, for a while, as long as he could enjoy Marguerite's company, from time to time?

He left the shop, stood for a moment on the sidewalk, enjoying the knowledge that he was, for the first time in his life, truly well-dressed.

'Why, Kit, how splendid you look.' Lillan smiled at him, and then frowned. 'The rumour is true.'

His turn to frown. 'What rumour?'

'That you are to leave Antigua.'

'I? Leave Antigua? Now, wherever did you learn that?'

She flushed. 'Mr Parke and the master of his schooner were at the warehouse yesterday, completing their stock and settling with Papa. In coin, too. He knows not what to do with it. And as you came to St John's in the company of Mr Parke . . .'

'It seemed natural to you that I should also leave in his company. Not I, Lillan. My past is too firmly set in these islands. I should feel a stranger anywhere else.'

'And you will never be a stranger here, Kit.' Her flush deepened, but she smiled through it. 'Then will you come to supper? Mama would be so pleased.'

Kit Hilton, dining at the merchant's, on fish and water and grave talk, while Daniel Parke dined at Colonel Warner's Goodwood, on wine and meat and gay laughter and gayer gossip, with dice to follow. There was a salutary lesson in relative society, he thought.

'Alas, Lillan, I cannot, this night,' he said. 'Believe me, I am sorry. But I shall call. Tomorrow.'

'I'm sure Papa will be glad to see you,' she said, and gazed at his coat once more. 'I had best not detain you. Until tomorrow, Kit.'

She walked down the street with the graceful flutter of skirts; but what skirts, how drab and formless. And the flat grey hat, tied so securely under her chin, allowed but a wisp of the golden hair to trickle on to her back. Lillan Christianssen? What rubbish. A Quaker? A woman who thought life should be a vast realm of goodness, when anyone could have told her different? But Lillan was, in any event, only a girl.

Agrippa approached, leading the hired horse. 'He's quiet enough, Kit,' the big man said. 'I wish I could be as sure of his rider.'

'I can sit a horse.' Kit mounted. 'There. Do I not look splendid?'

'You'd turn the heart of any girl, Kit.' Agrippa retained the bridle. 'You're sure of what you do?'

'You do not understand, dear friend. This girl and I have known each other for years. At least, we met as children, and I have carried her image in my heart ever since. Why do you think I came to Antigua?'

'I thought you sought a plantation, where there'd be no slavery, where there'd be no unhappiness, where all would share in the common profit.'

'And is not Green Grove a plantation? The largest in the Leewards, so it is said.'

'Scarce the sort of place to suit you, Kit. And if this Mistress Templeton is such an old friend, I'd have thought she'd have come to see you, before now.'

'Oh, God Almighty,' Kit shouted. 'She is but recently a widow. She has gone nowhere, these last four months. Why should she make an exception for me? But now, I will call upon her, and pay my respects. And who knows what may follow? You are right, Agrippa; I spoke of owning a plantation. So tell me how it should be done? By sailing Philip Warner's sloop to and from St Eustatius until we are caught by the revenue frigate and hanged? By God, in our situation, there is but one way to own a plantation, and 'tis a way I have always meant to follow. Now stand aside.'

Agrippa hesitated, and then obeyed, and Kit kicked the horse forward, clutching the reins for dear life. Fifteen minutes later he was through the town, and upon the high road which led south, to the sheltered harbours of English and Falmouth, where Edward Warner had first landed with his handful of colonists, from where Aline Warner had been kidnapped by the savage Caribs, and to where Edward had returned with his beautiful French bride, after his successful expedition of vengeance. There had been men about in those days. Edward had wooed Aline, as a slave wooing the daughter of a wealthy planter. He had faced every odd, as Tony Hilton had faced them, and won. So men might have diminished, to Grandmama's cost. But the Hilton blood had not diminished. Kit Hilton would similarly carve, or woo, himself an empire from this fertile land.

Thus he sought to delude himself, that he had come to Antigua with a purpose, with all the cold determination of a DuCasse or a Morgan, and had humbled himself to Philip Warner, for that purpose. As if he had not clutched at the straw that had been Daniel Parke, to raise himself from the Port Royal beach. As if he had ever done more than dream, of Marguerite Warner. As if he sought, this day, anything more than a smile, if only of recognition.

Yet it was a fertile land. No high mountains, as in almost all the other islands. No rushing rivers; water was as much of a problem here as in Tortuga. No teeming jungle, in which a man might hide, or become lost. Antigua was a place of gentle, rolling hills, and green fields separated by the endless ribbons of white dust road, with only an occasional great house or a towering sugar mill to break the skyline. And soon enough not even those. But these fields were green, and the green was all waving stalks of sugar, reaching six, eight, ten feet into the air, bending before the trade wind, each stalk worth its volume in solid gold. A growing wealth in every way.

He reined his horse as a file of Negroes approached him, walking in front of a black man who carried a whip. And what a whip. No cat of nine tails here, but a single long piece of plaited leather, with a gleaming steel tip. They did not more than glance at the rider.

'Holloa, there,' Kit shouted. 'I am looking for Green Grove Plantation. Can you direct me?'

The file stopped, because the foreman had stopped. 'Green Grove, mistuh?' he inquired. 'You been riding Green Grove this last hour.'

'By God,' Kit said. 'I thank you.' He kicked his horse, and moved down the path. This past hour. They had not exaggerated, then, when they had told him that Harry Templeton had been the biggest planter on the island. Perhaps in the Leewards. And it all now belonged to his widow. But of her they would not speak. Because she was the Deputy Governor's daughter, and therefore above gossip?

And now he reached the brow of a shallow hill, and looked, in the far distance, at the sea. But between himself and the sea were more endless acres of green cane, separated by perhaps a mile from what appeared to be a small town. He identified the Negro village, with its orderly rows of barracoons, and the trim, low stone walls which surrounded the white man's compound, with the houses of the overseers and the book-keepers, and beyond that, the bulk of the boiling house, the factory, placed downwind of the houses themselves. Even farther back, and dominating the whole, was the Great House, a massive four-square structure, built upon solid stone cellars, loopholed for defence, with the ground floor entirely surrounded by deep verandahs, each side reached by a flight of wide, shallow steps, and with the upper floor lighted by enormous jalousied windows, although each window mounted its heavy wooden shutter as a protection against either hurricane wind or rampaging slave rebellion. The roof sloped deeply, to throw off water, and was made of green shingles, and, to his surprise, from the back of the roof there arose a great stone chimney. As that surely could not be needed for heat in this climate, it suggested a table to match the house.

But the plantation did not even end with the beach and the sea, for off the shore there was yet another little island, perhaps half a mile across the water, as green and as fertile in appearance as its larger neighbour; although there was no evidence of cane growing there, there were certainly people in residence—he could see a wisp of smoke rising from admist the trees.

His heart pounded as he rode down the slope towards the gate. It was nearly five years now, and much had happened in that time. They were both older, and no doubt wiser. And she would know by now that he was living in St John's. Her father would have told her, if no one else. So the widow Templeton never left her estate; how had he waited for the mourning period to end. But she would expect Kit Hilton to call. His only fear was that Barnee had been too long in making the coat.

And how he wanted to see her again.

The gate was closed, and a white man lounged beside it. 'Halt there,' he shouted. 'What business have you with Green Grove, Captain Hilton?'

He was an unprepossessing fellow, whom Kit had met often enough in town. 'No business, Dutton,' he said. 'I am here to call on Mrs Templeton.'

'Mrs Templeton receives no visitors,' Dutton pointed out. 'Unless their names be on this list.' He flourished a length of scroll. 'Yours is not, Captain.'

'No doubt because your list has not been revised recently enough,' Kit said. 'Carry my name to your mistress and I will be admitted. I do assure you of that.'

Dutton shook his head. 'My mistress knows of your presence on this island well enough, Captain. She has given me no orders about admitting you. Now turn your horse and get you gone, or I'll set the dogs on you.'

'You'll do what? Why, by God . . .' Kit instinctively

reached for his cutlass, and found nothing; he had deliberately left all weapons behind, for this visit.

Dutton grinned, and brought up a wide-muzzled blunderbuss. 'Or better yet, I'll pepper your horse and have us discover just how safe you sit there, Captain.'

Kit stared at the man. 'You'll find I'm not an easy enemy, Dutton.'

Dutton shrugged. 'We of Green Grove have many enemies, Captain. One more will not frighten us.'

Kit raised his head, to gaze at the house. There was a woman on the verandah. That he could tell from the flutter of her skirt. But nothing more at this distance, save that he could decide she was at once short and slender, a drop of precious femininity. But not to him. She had stood there throughout the conversation, no doubt intending to make sure her instructions were obeyed.

He pulled the horse around, and rode back the way he had come.

She had chosen not to forgive, after all. Was that unreasonable? Was there a single reason why the mistress of Green Grove, now the wealthiest widow in all the Caribbean, should deign to look at an ex-buccaneer, who was in the employment of her father, and at a very nefarious game?

But why, then, was he in the employment of her father at all, breaking the law three nights a week? He stood at the taffrail of the *Bonaventure,* and watched the sun come peeping above the island of Barbuda, hull down on the eastern horizon. By now he knew every ripple of these waters. He had sailed them too often. And always at night. Always the view was the same, at dawn, St Eustatius on the outward journey, Antigua on the homeward, after the long sweep north. Now they were once again coming home, close-hauled to beat down against the unfailing trades, their hold filled with French wines and sweet meats, with Dutch powder and cloth, at a fraction of the price Philip Warner would have had to pay to import it from England, and all obtained on that never-ending credit which was the mainspring of West Indian prosperity.

But the risk was not Philip Warner's. It was Kit Hilton's. And one day . . .

He frowned, into the gradually lightening sky. Sooner than he had supposed, by God.

THE DEVIL'S OWN

Agrippa came scrambling up the ladder. 'You see that fellow, Kit?'

'Aye.' Kit levelled his glass. 'The revenue frigate, and up wind of us.'

'We'd best run back for St Eustatius.'

'No chance of that,' Kit muttered. 'With the weather gauge they'll hold us off and we'll find ourselves on a reef in the Virgins before we know it. If they didn't catch us up long before. We've a foul hull, and you can bet your last penny theirs is clean enough.'

'But man . . .'

Kit chewed his lip. 'With that square rig, she'll not beat to any purpose, Agrippa, clean or foul.'

'Yeah, man, but it is we who are doing the beating. She's coming fair and free.'

'And should we pass her? We'll show her an empty stern, then.'

Agrippa scratched the bandanna which covered his head. 'Man, Kit, how are you going to pass her without exchanging fire? And that is a warship. We will hang by breakfast.'

'So we'll breakfast now,' Kit said. 'And then load the guns. One exchange and we're through. It'll be worth it, Agrippa.' He glanced at his friend. 'You've not lost your stomach for a fight?'

'It is you I'm thinking about, Kit. You'd fire on the English Navy?'

'I never claimed I'd not fight in self-defence. And we'll do no harm, Agrippa. Elevate the guns as high as you may, it will be easy with us on the larboard tack. We want to slow her up, not kill anybody. And to make sure she cannot prove it was us, afterwards, hang your spare canvas over our name plates and wrap the figurehead as well. There are sufficient small craft sailing these waters to leave them in some doubt.'

Agrippa hesitated, and then shrugged and went down to the main deck, where he set about explaining to an incredulous crew that they meant to shoot their way past the warship.

Kit dismissed the helmsman, and himself took the tiller. This was a time for no hesitation, for no delay in carrying out a decision. He looked up at the sails; every one was filling, and the sheets were straining. He could get the sloop no closer to the fresh wind. And now the gap was rapidly closing as the warship bore down on them. There was no question of parleying; there were no English islands north of their position, and they were clearly not on passage from the open Atlantic, nor was it likely that a ship this small would have come down from the American mainland. His first problem was to stop the frigate from approaching close enough to identify them.

He watched the activity on the warship's deck. For the moment they were confused by the rapid approach of the stranger. But they were running out the bow-chaser, preparing to send a shot in front of him.

'Light your matches,' he called down into the waist.

Almost as if he had commanded the frigate there was a flash of light and a puff of black smoke from the bluff bows which were not pointing directly at him. The ball was well aimed, and splashed into the sea about a quarter of a mile ahead.

'Aim your pieces,' Kit yelled. 'And fire as they bear.' The whole ship trembled, and rolled farther to starboard as the two cannon exploded together. The gunners dropped their linstocks and ran to the rail, to peer into the morning. And utter a gigantic cheer as one of the balls struck home, smashing into the base of the long bowsprit, and sending all the jibs whipping away as their halliards were severed. Coming downwind the loss of her headsails made no difference to the frigate's speed, but her already limited capacity for windward work would be reduced to nothing. Hastily she put her helm up to bring her broadside guns to bear, but Kit had already altered course, and the *Bonaventure* streaked away on a board reach, gathering speed with every second, white water foaming away from her bows. Antigua now rising from the ocean on her port bow.

Behind them the day trembled, and the frigate was enveloped in black smoke; but the flying ball plunged harmlessly into the sea.

Agrippa climbed the ladder. 'We'll not get back up to St John's.'

'Nor should we, as that is where she'll look for us first,' Kit said. 'We'll make for Falmouth. We can be unloaded there, and then let them decide which one was us, from all the dozens of sloops in these waters.'

'Well, then,' Agrippa said. 'You are to be congratulated, Captain Hilton, on a successful action. Colonel Warner should be pleased. I have no doubt that he will present you with another bonus.'

Kit glanced at his friend. 'I know your meaning, Agrippa.

THE DEVIL'S OWN

By God, I saved our necks, nothing more. We'll sail no more for that scoundrel Warner.'

'Now there is a word I have been waiting to hear,' Agrippa said. 'So why have us returned at all? You'll have heard that Morgan is returned to Jamaica? Sir Henry, by God, and Deputy Governor to boot.'

Kit shook his head. 'I'll not sail for that scoundrel, either. And you'll have heard, old friend, that he is also hanging every one of his old acquaintances he can discover. No, by God, we'll act straight up. You may leave the matter to me. Just find me a horse the moment we anchor.'

The exhilaration was passed, and in its place was growing a deep anger, against himself for firing upon the English flag, against Philip Warner for placing him in this position. But against all the Warners, perhaps, for treating him as an inferior being, for so many things. For an understanding perhaps that Daniel had been right all along, that to Philip he was just a useful piece of humanity, to be enslaved and dominated as if he were, indeed, a slave.

While to Marguerite he did not exist.

The anger sustained him after the anchor was dropped, after he had mounted the hired horse and made his way inland. The last time he had taken these roads it had been with a lilt in his heart. Now it was with grim anger bubbling throughout his system. And once again he was exploring fresh ground, because he had never been to the Warner plantation. He had never been invited, in two months. How all of Daniel's strictures came bubbling back to him in endless outrage.

A replica of Green Grove, although on a smaller scale. No doubt each plantation had been copied from the others, once a suitable design had been discovered. And once again a closed gate, with a man waiting beside it. But this one looked friendly enough. 'Good morning to you, Captain Hilton,' he said. 'What brings you to Goodwood?'

'I'd speak with the Colonel,' Kit said. 'The matter is urgent.'

The man nodded, and released the bolts on the gate. 'He's at the house, Captain. You'll find he has just returned from aback.'

Kit urged his horse up the drive, past the overseer's houses, watched from the little porches by the women and children, the poor whites, prevented from lack of credit and lack of opportunity from sharing the enormous luxury of the planters, doomed to a lifetime of servility and poverty, with only the pleasure of taking out their spite on the even more unfortunate Negroes beneath them.

Was that, then, to be the eventual fate of Kit Hilton? By God, he *would* turn back to piracy, first.

He dismounted at the foot of the steps to the Great House, and a slave immediately ran forward to take his bridle. Philip Warner sat on the verandah, eating the late breakfast in which most of the planters indulged after spending the cool dawn hours in the fields, supervising the day's work plan, before the heat of the sun made such exposure prohibitive for Europeans. With him were his three senior overseers.

'Kit?' Philip asked. 'What brings you to Goodwood? Not trouble, I hope?'

'Trouble,' Kit said. 'We encountered the government frigate from St Kitts.'

'By God,' Philip said. 'And gave her the slip, I see?'

'We exchanged fire to do so.'

'You fired on the man of war?' demanded one of the overseers.

'It was that, Mr Haley, or a rope around our necks.'

'By God,' Philip said. 'But she'll not identify you?'

'I trust not, Colonel Warner. The sloop is in Falmouth now, and I have given orders for her to be unloaded as rapidly as possible. The warship will not make here before she has repaired the damage.'

'If she bothers to come at all, in the circumstances,' Philip mused. 'You're a man of spirit, Kit, I never doubted that. But we'd best lie low for a while.'

'And find yourself a new captain while you are about it, sir,' Kit said. 'I'll have no more part in this business. I'd not anticipated having to go to war with the Navy.'

'What? What?' Warner demanded, getting up. 'You knew the risks.'

'Maybe I had not weighed them properly. My mind is made up, sir. I shall seek employment elsewhere.'

'Not on this island,' Philip shouted.

'Well, then, I shall leave this island,' Kit said, keeping his temper under control with difficulty. 'By God, sir, I'll tell you what I will do. I'll take myself to Sandy Point, and ask Sir William Stapleton for a position. I'll sail *on* the revenue frigate, sir, not against it. Then we'll see how your smuggling ventures fare.'

'By God,' Warner said. 'A Hilton who is at once a coward

and a turncoat. Aye, your family was ever a scurvy lot, you bitch's bastard. And frightened with it. You can see the yellow bubbling through the white.'

'You'll take back those words, sir,' Kit demanded.

'Will I? Or you'll make me?'

'By God, sir, I will, even if I doubt it will be worth wasting time on a cur such as you. You seek to impugn my family, sir? What of your own, with your treacheries and your feuds, and your cannibal brother?'

'Take him,' Philip shouted, and a heavy stick crashed across the back of Kit's head. Yet it did no more than stun him. He found himself on his hands and knees, turned, dragging his sword from its scabbard, and was met by a kick in the face which sent him rolling down the steps. He gazed up at a crowd of black men, all armed with staves, and realized that he had lost his sword and was in some danger of being beaten to death. He threw up his hands to protect himself and was struck a sickening blow on the arm which left it paralysed. He attempted to roll on to his face to protect his groin and belly, and felt a succession of blows crashing into his back and legs. Dimly he heard voices shouting, women's voices as well as men's, and the beating stopped. But he could not move, he could feel nothing but the surging pain which ran through his body like a continuous thread, above the blood which kept surging into his mouth. I am dying, he thought. Oh, God, I am dying.

Hands gripped his legs and arms, and he attempted to scream with pain, but only blood ran out of his mouth. Then he was thrown down in another excruciating jolt, on to wood, which immediately commenced a whole series of jolts, each one sending his tortured brain screaming away into the recesses of consciousness, but never so far as to bring merciful oblivion.

Time no longer had meaning. The jolting was never-ending, he was taking a journey down to hell. Perhaps that was how all men went to hell, bouncing in the back of a cart. Until without warning it stopped, and the hands seized him again. For a moment he hung in the air, then the ground rose up to meet him with another mind-shattering impact, and he rolled, arms and legs flopping helplessly and painfully, until he came to rest. His face and eyes and ears and nose and mouth filled with dust to coagulate the blood, and he coughed and spat, supposing he would choke. Then he lay still, knowing only the pain which gripped him like a living enemy, tearing at his legs, his arms, his bowels, his head. Movement was impossible, nor did he see how it would ever become possible again. He was lost, at the bottom of a pit of agony, an eternity of misfortune which had been his since time began.

And was not yet over. For there was a voice, a voice he had heard before, and movement around him, and hands once again touching his body and bringing moans of agony to his lips. But these hands were strangely gentle and made more so by the insistent voice, commanding and instructing. With a tremendous effort Kit forced open his eyes, gazed at the morning through a welter of blood, at more black men; he could not tell if they were the same as those who had first beaten him into the ground.

And then at a white face, strangely pale, inexpressibly beautiful, set in a framework of straight, long, dark brown hair, undressed save for the bows which secured the strands.

The face which, angry or smiling, had lured him onwards for so long. Marguerite Warner.

5

The Devil's Honeymoon

Now at last did consciousness depart. Or did it? He could never be sure. He seemed to exist in a world of dreams, in which pain dominated, certainly, but in which there was also light and pleasant voices, and occasionally even laughter, and sweet scents and quiet, and acres of softness. He found it confusing, and chose to focus on the essentials, on the pain itself, on one voice more than any other, because of its familiarity, and on one physical object, a vast glow which seemed to hover in the sky, a million miles away.

The bright object gradually came to replace all else, even the soft voice and the gentle hands. He tried to reach it, and watched it take shape, slowly and indefinitely, but with gradually sharpening edges. It hung, at the foot of the bed. The bed? He turned his head, from side to side, amazed at the effort it cost.

And amazed, too, at his surroundings. For he lay in the centre of a vast tent-bed, beneath linen sheets of a whiteness he had not suspected to be possible. The mattress scarce seemed to exist below him; it and his pillows were stuffed with feathers.

The bed occupied the centre of an equally vast room, at once wide and square and high-ceilinged. And the bright object was a chandelier, just visible beneath the roof of the tent, a mass of gleaming facets of light although none of the candles were lit. What miracle was this? But then he saw the windows, huge open doors of glass, through which there drifted at once a cooling breeze and the morning sunlight, playing on the chandelier, having the effect of a flaming signal.

And through the window there came the smell of sweetness. Or was it all around him? Certainly it seemed to soak the bed on which he lay, the nightshirt in which he was dressed ... the nightshirt? Another magnificent cambric garment, as softly limp as the sheet, and as clean.

The scent made him drowsy. The scent, and the breeze, playing gently on his face, and the silence. A strange silence, because his instincts told him that he was surrounded by sound, that he could even hear it, if he tried hard enough to listen. If he could summon the energy. But why should he do that? Why should he do anything, except lie here, in the softness and the breeze, and the quiet? If he had died, and this was heaven, then he was truly content.

Except that there was no possibility of Kit Hilton, the man who had been at Panama, ever attaining heaven.

The door opened, and he turned his head again, more easily this time. A black face stared at him, smiling, and then came across the room to look more closely. She was a young girl and wore a white dress; her hair was concealed beneath a cap.

'Where am I?' Kit asked. How thin and soft his voice; it seemed no more than a whisper.

'Well, glory be,' she said. 'You's awake. Now you wait so, Captin. I got food for you.'

She disappeared. Kit tried to push himself up, and found that he could not. He raised his right hand, with a tremendous effort, gazed at it in horror. That hand, which had grasped a cutlass or a musket to such terrible effect, which had been feared even when he had been beachcombing in

Port Royal, was no more than a mass of bones and veins, held together by a bag of thin skin.

The door was opening again, and now there were several girls, but led on this occasion by a tall and dignified black man, who wore a deep crimson coat over white breeches, and carried himself with an air of authority. The girls each bore a tray, and these in turn were placed on the table next to his bed. Here were morsels of broiled tuna, cups of soft green avocado, broth made from the pulpy okra, and a glowing dark red liquid in which floated lumps of ice.

The butler bent over the bed. 'You must allow me, Captin.' He raised Kit's shoulders, and one of the girls pushed a mass of pillows under his back, while another held the cup to his lips. It seemed to him as the liquid reached his parched throat that he was tasting pure nectar. It reminded him of that first gulp from the stream in Hispaniola, how many centuries ago. He swallowed, and smiled at the girl, and sighed. 'What is it called?'

'Sangaree, Captin,' the butler said. 'Red wine, with some brandy, and fruits, and ice added. Now you must eat. You must put the strength back into those muscles.'

The food tasted scarcely less pleasant than the drink. But Kit was too tired to consume very much, and after a few mouthfuls he sank back on the pillow.

'Enough,' said the butler, and the girls hastily carried the trays from the room. 'There will be more when you are ready.'

'Where am I?' Kit asked again.

'Plantation Green Grove, Captin.'

'Green Grove. Green Grove? Then where is . . .'

'The mistress is aback, Captin. But she will return at eleven of the clock. Now you must rest. I will tell she that you is awake.'

He withdrew, closing the door, but leaving Kit propped up on the pillows. The mistress. Now memory came flooding back, of the faces standing above him when he had been picked from the ditch. Marguerite? Marguerite Warner? No. Marguerite Templeton, now. Rescuing him from the anger of her father? That was unbelievable. It was also magnificent. It made him tremble, brought tears to his eyes. It made him want to get out of bed, and make his way to the window, and see if he could find her in the canefields. But that was impossible. So he must lie here, and wait. Marguerite. For

THE DEVIL'S OWN

how long had his life been devoted to just that object? Marguerite.

He dozed, and the food and the wine stretched out from his belly to dull his brain, to send him back into his dream world. Only this time he did not dream. Now he was to awake, from all the dreams, and from all the nightmares, too. So perhaps buccaneers did, after all, attain heaven.

Voices, outside his bedroom door, and one raised in protest. Now he must strain his ears to hear the muted sounds of the house. It was nearly noon. He could tell that because the sun no longer played on the chandelier, and the very breeze, which had not abated, was hot as it stroked his face and arms.

'Ridiculous, Mrs Templeton?' demanded the man. 'When I heard, why . . .'

'Tell me, Mr Spalding, when last did you visit me?' Marguerite. He would have remembered that quiet tone anywhere.

'Why, I . . . I had gained the impression I was not welcome here.'

'Oh, indeed you were right, Mr Spalding. I detest criticism in any form. Of myself, of my plantation, of the way I operate my plantation, or of my habits, which seem to be your present occupation.'

'Why . . . why . . . really, Mrs Templeton.' Spalding would be going red in the face. Kit remembered he was the vicar of the St John's Anglican Church, a man who avoided him; Spalding always crossed the street to walk on the other side when he saw Kit Hilton coming. 'I felt it my duty. This man is a pirate, madam. He has murdered people with his own hands. Far worse. He was at Panama. Can you imagine what he must have done there? Women, girls, why, madam, the imagination boggles.'

'And your voice sounds positively envious,' Marguerite said.

'He is also known as a friend of black people and Quakers,' the parson said, dropping his voice so that Kit could hardly hear it.

Marguerite laughed, a sound as softly contemptuous as her voice. 'A far more serious crime, I do agree, reverend. Would you like to leave now, or will you attend me in my bath?'

'You . . . you astound me, madam. Be sure that I shall be to Colonel Warner this morning, with this sad news.'

'Then I should certainly hurry, if I were you. Maurice Peter, will you show Mr Spalding to his horse?'

There was a short silence, while Kit stared at the door, and then at last it opened. She had removed her hat, and was untying her hair, so that it fell straight to her shoulders. She wore a pale green riding habit, but had unbuttoned the long, masculine coat to reveal the cambric shirt beneath, tucked into the divided green skirt. And beneath that? His eyes were too weak to be sure, but he would have said nothing. Christ, what a thought for an invalid with too many crimes of lust already on his shoulders.

She moved quietly; she had taken off her boots and thrust her bare feet into slippers. She looked as far removed from the splendid lady who had climbed the hill in Tortuga as it was possible to imagine. And now she paused, six feet from the bed, and gazed at him, her face breaking into a smile. She had not smiled in Tortuga, and he had found her entrancing. But entrancing was nothing, when considered against the context of her face smiling. The small mouth became large, and the firm chin softened, and the green eyes glowed with little facets of light, almost like her chandelier. 'Kit Hilton,' she said. 'There were times when I thought I would have to bury you. And then I remembered, he has crossed Panama. He will survive a beating.'

She came closer. Her hair was free, and now she took off the coat. The sweat-wet cambric clung to her shoulders, as it stuck itself to the high breasts and outlined the dark aureoles. A lady, sweating. That surely reduced her to no more than a woman. There was sweat on her face, beading her forehead and her upper lip. And surely, therefore, there was sweat in other places as well.

'They told me you were able to speak,' she said, standing beside him.

'How long have I been here?'

'You are at least direct, Kit. A week. Do you remember what happened?'

'I quarrelled with your father.'

She nodded. 'And he set his slaves on you. Do you hate him?'

'Perhaps I was hasty.'

Her eyebrows raised. 'Hardly a piratical sentiment. You'd do well to hate him. You may be sure he hates you. And will hate you more when Spalding reaches Goodwood.'

'Then why did you bring me here?' His hand moved, and

touched hers as it lay on the coverlet. 'You refused me admittance, but a week gone.'

'It had taken you three weeks to call upon me,' she reminded him. 'Besides, should a lady succumb to the first advance made by a gentleman?' Her smile was back. 'And you are not even a gentleman, as I am reminded time and again.' She half turned her head as there came a gentle knock on the door. 'My bath is ready. Now you must lie there, quietly, until I return.'

She moved to the door.

'I thought *you* hated me,' he said to her back.

She paused, but did not turn her head, then continued through the doorway.

Christ, how slowly the afternoon passed. How frustrating to lie in bed, unable to move, to know that that beauty, that smile, that confidence, was in the house with him. Being bathed. His brain was filled with the sweat-soaked shirt, with the beads of sweat on her lips—he had wanted to kiss them all away, one after the other. And for all the sweat, she had moved in the middle of that aura of sweet-scented perfume.

Marguerite Warner. Marguerite Templeton. By Christ, he had to be dreaming, after all.

She wore a crimson undressing-robe, secured at her waist by a wide pink sash. She filled the room like an explosion. And she no longer sweated. Her skin glowed, from the bath, and she looked rested. Her hair had been piled on top of her head, to leave her face exposed, and beautiful.

'They hanged your grandmother,' she said, looking down at him. 'I doubt I could ever have liked her, but it was not the fate for a woman. And so you took to piracy, so unsuccessfully that you finished working for my father.' She smiled, and shook her head. 'You will have to practise success, if you are to remain at Green Grove.'

He licked his lips. 'And am I, to remain at Green Grove?'

'Perhaps you would rather be handed over to the Quakers?'

So she was, after all, no more than a woman, and given to jealousy. But, Marguerite Templeton, jealous of Lillan Christianssen? Over Kit Hilton? That seemed incredible.

'I had supposed *you* hated *me*,' he said.

Marguerite moved away from the bed, and four maidservants entered. Two carried enormous towels, a third a huge basin, and a fourth a pitcher of steaming water. The butler came behind, and he placed the rocking chair for Marguerite to sit down, close to the bed, but far enough away so as not to interfere with the girls.

'What is to happen?' Kit asked.

'You are going to be bathed. I demand cleanliness, at Green Grove.'

'To be bathed? But...'

'These same girls have bathed you every day since your arrival,' she pointed out. 'And I have sat here and watched them do it. They are slaves, and of no account; I am a widow, and perfectly accustomed to the male body. So pray stop twitching and rolling your eyes. Although,' she added with a smile, 'it is a relief to find that you are rediscovering your manhood.'

For the sheet was already removed and so was his nightshirt, all by the softest and most gentle hands he had ever felt.

Marguerite rocked, gently, to and fro. Her gaze never left his body. But how thin and pitiful he was, with bones jutting out from every pouch of skin.

'You'll fill out,' she told him. 'It will be my charge. I did hate you, Kit. When I got out of that water butt. I hated you all the way back to the ship. In many ways you owe a great deal to my father. For when I continued to curse you as I changed my clothes, he interrupted me to point out that you had acted as you did because you had fallen in love with me at first sight. And when I looked back upon it, it seemed obvious.'

The towels were spread under his raised body, to protect the sheets, and now the hands were gently washing him, while the water itself seemed filled with Marguerite's perfume.

'But you did not come back,' he said. Dreaming. There could be no other answer, for him to be lying here, in the midst of five women, one of whom had filled every dream for five years.

'Why should I?' she asked. 'You certainly deserved to be punished. Besides, I had more important things on my mind. My marriage. It took place almost as soon as I returned to Antigua. I was seventeen. It took five months to consummate the event. Harry was seventy-two. Believe me, Kit, in producing in him a condition which would make me a woman, I learned more about male anatomy than you know, I'd wager.'

'You've an uncommonly vulgar tongue.' He was surprised by his own anger.

'Which you must learn to live with. Everyone else has had to do so.' She ceased rocking and got up, to stand next to the bed as the towels were folded over him and the soft fingers gently dried him. 'I only say what I wish to say, and hide nothing. It is the only way to live.'

'And you care not whom you offend.'

'That will do,' she told the girls. A clean nightshirt was produced and dropped over his shoulders, and she herself saw that it was neatly settled. Then she lifted the sheets over his body. By now the last of the girls had left, and the door was closed. 'I care not whom I offend,' she said. 'Harry did me but one honest service in his entire life. He managed to remain alive until my twenty-first birthday. So now, you see, I am at once the most beautiful and the most wealthy woman in all the Leeward Islands. That combination also makes me the most powerful and the most independent.' She smoothed the sheet, and then sat beside him. 'I made but one resolution, which I propose to keep; that when I married again it would be to a man who not only would warm my bed, successfully, but would also be fit to stand beside me on all other occasions.'

She was no longer smiling; her eyes seemed possessed of a life of their own, separated from her body, shrouding him.

'You are too straight for me,' Kit confessed. 'You have my brain in a whirl. And I doubt you know what you do. I marched with Morgan, on Panama.'

'So I have been reminded, endlessly. I would have thought that proved you at least a man.'

'Have you any idea what can happen, when a town is sacked, and when there is as much hatred as hangs on the very air in these West Indies? How can you, living in this wealth and splendour and security of which you boast.'

'You have been delirious, from time to time, this last week,' she said softly. 'What was her name? Isabella? I sometimes feel I know the child.' She picked up his hand and turned it over, looked at the palm. 'Perhaps hands that are guilty are those I seek.' She smiled at him. 'Am I not a shameless hussy? Oh, I had all but forgot you, Kit Hilton. Until the day you reappeared in St John's with that detestable Parke. So he was your friend. But he was none the less detestable. He called here with my father, and had the nerve to make advances to me.'

'He told me none of this.'

She got up, restlessly, her robe swirling to give a hint of bare shoulder underneath. 'Why should he, and arouse your jealousy? But he told me much of you, Kit. Or of your desire for me. He found it amusing. As well bring the earth and the sun into a common field, he said.'

'Like you,' Kit said, 'he is uncommonly straight. You'd have made a good pair.'

She stood before the window, gazing at her fields. 'I understood him to be speaking the truth. But come. You have been considered missing for a week. Now that Spalding has found you out, the news will be shouted from one end of the island to the other by nightfall. Is there anyone you wish informed of your whereabouts?'

'Agrippa.'

She turned, frowning. 'There is a strange relationship. I am not sure it is a healthy one.'

'Will you choose my friends, madam? I am grateful to you for saving my life, believe me. But I will not be ruled. Agrippa and I have seen much together.'

'He held the arms while you made free with the body,' she said, the contempt returning to her voice. 'Very well. I will have him informed. What of the Christianssens?'

'They also, if you would be so kind.'

She came back across the room, slowly. Her fingers played with the bow of her sash. 'Tell me about this girl, Lilian.'

'You are mistaken there, madam,' Kit said. 'She is only a girl, and she is also, as you keep reminding me, a Quaker. She knows naught of the feelings that can be created between a man and a woman, nor does she seek to learn, before her marriage. She regards me as a lost soul.'

'My question concerned your regard for her.'

'She is one of the few people who have shown me kindness, if that is what you mean.'

She stood by the bed, sucking her upper lip under her teeth in a peculiarly thoughtful gesture, a mixture of decision and apprehension, he thought. 'I shall tell her you are here, and close to regaining your health,' she said. 'I shall invite her to visit you, so that you may compare between us.'

'Your boast of straightness does you little credit, madam,' Kit said. 'By many that act would be considered treacherous.' Now why, he wondered, was he quarrelling with her? He worshipped the ground on which she walked, and she had saved his life, at the very least. But still her arrogance, her total assumption that what she desired would necessarily happen, was impossible to bear.

Her mouth relaxed, and she smiled. 'What is the business of living and loving, and dying, but inexpressibly treacherous?' She sat beside him again, seized his hands. 'I told you, I had forgotten your existence, until you reappeared. Until you became the talk of St John's. Kit Hilton, the buccaneer, the murderer and rapist and robber and pirate, the man who sailed with Morgan. Oh, you have set our delicate ears in a tizzy, Kit. I avoided you because I wanted you to come to me. I knew you would. And so I waited. For three long weeks. I would not see you when you came, and I would have made you wait even longer, but for your visit to Goodwood. I was there. Did you know that, Kit? I was visiting Aunt Celestine, when you came storming in. I watched you, from the upstairs window. And you never thought to look. Oh, you were splendid, in your anger, in your defiance of Papa. I had thought there was only one person in the whole world would ever do that: me. I knew then that you were what I wanted. That you were what I would have. I watched you being beaten insensible by those black bastards. There was naught I could do, then. I did not wish to reveal my intention, for fear that Papa would have you murdered before I could protect you. For he is that ruthless a man, you know, Kit. He is nearly as ruthless as I. But yet he is not, quite. And so I stood at the window, and exchanged pleasantries with my aunt, while you were savaged, and then stayed a while longer and took a cup of sangaree with Papa while your battered body was removed and thrown into a ditch, and only after a reasonable time did I leave, and pick you up, and bring you here.'

There were pink spots in her cheeks, and her whole personality glowed. A thought crossed his mind, that if, in possessing her love, he was experiencing the most tremendous emotion he had ever known, what must it be like to know her hate? 'And do you not fear his anger now?'

'On Green Grove?' She smiled, and he knew, what it would be like to feel her hate. Hell would be pleasant in comparison. 'On Green Grove, I fear nobody on the face of this earth, Kit. With you at my side, restored to health, I should fear nobody off Green Grove, either.' Her fingers tugged at the bow, and her robe fell apart. She wore nothing underneath. Once he had supposed she might possess the body of an athlete. Once he had done no more than dream.

But here was no dream. She possessed the body of an athlete, but of a woman athlete, not a girl; she had been brought to womanhood by a man old enough to be her grandfather, who had done no more than make her bloom, and then left her, in full flower. Waiting to be plucked. When she was ready. When he had the strength.

Dawn on Green Grove brought the sun flooding through the open french windows, picking out flashes of light from the crystal drops of the chandelier. Dawn was at once lazy and active, a time for reflection and a moment for testing a growing strength.

Kit rolled on his side, and the woman's head slipped from his shoulder. Her brown hair, so rich and so thick, was damp with sweat, and clung to her temples and her back. Her body was concealed beneath the sheets but was there for his hands, a treasure house of magnificent joy compared with which Panama City had been a hovel. He could caress her breasts; they were large, surprisingly so for so young a body, overflowing from his hands, soft and yet firm, with nipples which flared into life at his touch, even while she slept. He could search her waist, and count her ribs, for never was flesh so slenderly fine. He could spread over her thighs, and cup her glorious buttocks, more firm yet than her breasts, or slide round to explore the tropical forest which matted her groin with amazing luxuriance. And beyond, the ultimate paradise sought by man. As yet explored only by his fingers, although she had slept here for four nights. But each day, and each night, had seen an increase of strength, and soon . . . as her own fingers were now establishing. Her eyes were open, and her breath rushed against his face as she smiled.

'I must make haste,' she said. 'For I am determined you shall have no entry until we are wed. Am I not a prude?'

She laughed, as he would have searched further, and rolled away from him, and out of the bed, to stand for a moment, a glistening drop of marvellous womanhood that quite put the sun-gleaming chandelier to shame, while she listened to the bell tolling, bringing the slaves from their quarters, the overseers from their beds.

'I shall return early this day,' she said. 'And meanwhile,

the girls will dress you in your best.' She had sent to town for his clothes.

He frowned at her. 'You mean to marry me today?'

Again she laughed, a peal which echoed through the room. 'When I marry you, Christopher Hilton, it shall be an occasion not readily forgotten by Antigua. But today I shall declare my purpose. I have invited Papa for lunch, and if you can mount so hard and firm an assault at my gate you can certainly sit yourself for a meal. You are well again, Kit. Today we are betrothed.'

He raised himself on his elbow. Certainly this was easy enough. 'Philip Warner comes here, today?'

'I saw no alternative. It is near a week since Spalding will have carried him the news that you are here. And throughout that time he has ignored me. He considers that I am a lonely widow whose bed needs warming, and that I have chosen you to honour a passing fancy. We will surprise him, Kit.' She pulled on her undressing-robe as she went to the door, and there checked. 'But you will be polite. You are not yet strong enough to sustain the burden of a duel, nor would I have one between my father and my future husband. Leave the extravagant gestures to me, if you will. I request this especially of you, in case he arrives before I return from aback.'

'Then why go at all?'

'Because I am the mistress of Green Grove, darling Kit. I must be seen in the fields at least once in every day, as I must sit in judgement over my slaves at least once in every day, lest they forget that I am here, and that they fear me.' She smiled. 'Soon enough the responsibility will be yours, and be sure that I shall welcome the rest.'

The door closed, and he was left to wonder at just what the day would bring, although without apprehension. Apprehension was not a practicable emotion when in the dazzling company of Marguerite Templeton. And even wonder was clouded by memory, as he lay on the pillows and beneath the sheets still warm from the contact of her body, and still overhung with her scent.

And soon enough there was no time even for that, as the maidservants came to bathe him and help him dress, in his best blue coat, giggling and chattering amongst themselves, and all the while insisting that he make haste, for there were gentlemen waiting to see him.

'Already?' he demanded, and discovered he was sweating. But at last they pronounced him fit to be seen in public, and so for the first time he left the bedroom. And entered a world he had not supposed to exist. First of all he found himself on a wide, deep gallery, which circled the upper storey, allowing the stairwell in the center to descend to the lower floor. Off the gallery opened the doors of at least five bedchambers, all ajar, at the moment, while from the sound of cleaning and beating and rustling which emanated from every doorway he could not doubt that apart from his own four attendants there was an army of maids in each room, engaged upon putting it to rights, even if, so far as he knew, Marguerite and he alone slept in the house.

The gallery itself was floored with polished wood, and the walls were lined with paintings, of some quality, he estimated, mostly depicting scenes in and around Antigua. Most surprising of all, there was no ceiling to this centre of the house, but merely the rafters, beyond which the timbers of the roof could be seen, and above them the shingles, with four skylights controlled by great ropes on pulleys from the gallery itself. Certainly the amount of air made for coolness.

Then there was the staircase, circular as it rounded the gallery, down which he made his uncertain way, a girl supporting each arm and two more hovering beyond them, for his legs were still weak. At the bottom he faced the main door, which stood open to admit a view of the verandah and the drive beyond. Here the floor was parquet, and a similar surface stretched all around him. And here there waited Barnee the tailor and Agrippa. 'Kit,' said the black man, coming forward. 'By God, man, but it is good to see you. I thought you were dead.'

Kit took his hand. 'On the contrary, dear friend. And it is even better to see you, looking as well and as strong as ever. But I have been here so long, and you . . .'

'I have been well cared for, by the Christianssens, Kit.'

'And they too are in good health? Lillan?'

'They send you their best wishes.'

'But they have not come to see me?'

Agrippa looked embarrassed. 'Well, man, they think it is best not to. This Mistress Templeton, well, she is a strange woman. So it is said.'

'A strange woman?' Kit frowned, and then smiled. 'Why, I suppose she is. A most remarkable woman. Wait until you meet her. Barnee, what brings you here?'

THE DEVIL'S OWN

Barnee cleared his throat. 'Mistress Templeton commanded my presence, Captain. I am to make you some clothes.'

'The devil you are. But first, a glass of sangaree.' He turned to the maids. 'Do you know, this is the first time I have been downstairs in this house. Where should I take my guests? That way?'

He looked beyond the stairs to the left, at the enormous mahogany dining table with its twenty-four chairs, with its sideboard gleaming with silver decanters, with its chandelier hanging from the high ceiling.

'No, suh, Captin,' said one of the girls; her name was Martha Louise. 'You got for come this way.' She glanced at Agrippa. 'But the mistress ain't going want no black fellow in the drawing-room.'

'What nonsense,' Kit said. 'You'll bring us sangaree. Come with me, Agrippa. And you, Barnee.' He held his friend's arm as he turned to the right, to pause once again in astonishment. The parquet flooring seemed to stretch forever, but here there were chairs, and low tables, once again smothered with silver, ornaments rather than cutlery, and beyond, close by the wall, a spinet. 'Have you ever seen such splendour?'

'Now that I haven't,' Agrippa said. 'I was never allowed inside the Great House in Barbados.'

The girls were back, bearing the tray with its jug and the glasses. Kit sank into one of the chairs with a sigh; his head was swinging.

'Drink up,' he said. 'To our mutual healths. I'm assuming you do not have to take my measurements all over again, Barnee? I haven't changed that much.'

The men hesitated, their glasses in their hands. Boots were clumping on the verandah outside, and the girls were gathered in an anxious huddle by the stairs.

Kit forced himself to his feet again. 'Marguerite,' he said. 'You have not yet met my friend Agrippa, although you have heard me speak of him, often enough. Barnee you obviously know.'

Marguerite Templeton took off her tricorne as she entered the room; this day her hair was gathered in a single loose swathe. As usual was coat was open, and her shirt was wet with sweat. She carried a whip with which she flicked her boots. Philip Warner was at her shoulder, frowning at the men in front of him.

Marguerite came across the room, smiling. But she kept her hands at her sides. 'It is my pleasure, Agrippa,' she said. 'Any friend of Kit's is a friend of mine. But I should take it very kindly if you would finish your drink in the kitchen. The girls will show you. And Barnee. You understand, I am sure. I know Barnee does. The withdrawing-room is for my guests.'

'But . . .' Kit felt the blood rushing into his face.

'Agrippa understands my meaning, Kit,' Marguerite said, giving the black man her most dazzling smile. 'You told me that he has worked on a sugar plantation himself, and thus he understands more of the situation than you do, perhaps. I have five hundred slaves here, Kit, and I employ thirty white people. That is in fact below the legal requirement. My slaves have to be kept at my arm's length, and made to understand their place. This would be difficult were I to start entertaining black men in my withdrawing-room.'

'Why, I'll have no such thing,' Kit declared.

'The lady is right, Kit,' Agrippa said. 'And I would be the cause of no disturbance on a sugar estate. I but wished to assure myself that you were well. I look forward to seeing you in town.' He looked at the glass he held in his hand, then replaced it on the tray. 'You'll excuse me, Mistress Templeton.' He bowed, and left the room.

'By God,' Kit said.

'I'll be waiting in the pantry, Captain.' Barnee sidled round him.

'By God,' Philip Warner declared in turn. 'I think I came at an appropriate moment.'

'Your moments are always appropriate, dear Papa,' Marguerite said. 'Kit. It is good to see you standing up, and looking almost yourself. I met Papa on the drive. He has been spluttering all the way here.' She reached up and kissed him on the cheek.

'You had no right to treat Agrippa so,' Kit said. 'If I am to be here, then my friend must also be here.'

She held his arm, and she still smiled. 'If you wish Agrippa to live on my plantation, Kit, then I shall have a house built for him. You have my word. But he cannot come into *this* house except as what he is, a black man. I will explain it to you, when I have a moment. For the time being, I think we should entertain Papa. I am sure he would like to apologize to you.'

'Apologize?' Philip Warner shouted. 'Apologize, to that

THE DEVIL'S OWN

scoundrel? That murderer? That rapist? That nigger lover? Why by God, child, I've a mind to whip him again, here and now. As for having him in this house, I absolutely forbid it.'

Kit tried to move forward, but Marguerite retained her grip on his arm. And still she smiled, but suddenly the smile was the most terrible thing he had ever seen.

'Do be careful, Papa,' she said. 'Or Kit may have you thrown out.'

'Thrown out? That . . .'

'The future Master of Green Grove,' she said, very softly.

'The . . .' for a moment it really seemed possible that Philip Warner would have an apoplectic fit, so purple was his face.

'That is why we have invited you here.' She released Kit's arm, and poured two fresh glasses of sangaree, then held one out to her father. 'To drink our healths on the announcement of our betrothal.'

Warner stared at her in utter perplexity; he did not take the glass. 'I assume this is some sort of ghastly humour, Marguerite.'

'I was never more serious in my life, Papa. I have now managed this plantation for four years. Oh, yes, I was managing it within a week of my marriage to Harry. He was in his dotage and quite incompetent. I have restored it to its once great position, but the work has been hard, and lonely. I need the comfort and protection of a man. And it is the word man I wish to stress. I propose to marry Kit, in my chapel, in three weeks' time. I wish you to be the first to know. I will issue you an invitation in due course. And I would like you to give me away, Papa.'

'To that . . . that . . .'

'To my chosen husband. You selected my first, very wisely, Papa. Pray allow me the intelligence and experience to choose my second. I shall ride over some time next week to discuss my gown with Aunt Celestine.'

'And you expect to be welcomed?'

She smiled at him. 'Of course, Papa. Am I not your only daughter?'

He stared at her for some seconds, glanced at Kit, and turned and strode from the room.

Marguerite drew a long breath, and slowly released it again. 'Well,' she said. 'A more eventful day than I had expected. Who could have supposed they'd all arrive together?'

'Marguerite,' Kit said. 'I wish you to know that I honour your defence of me to your father, and will always respect you for it.'

'What strange words you use,' she said. 'I do not wish your respect, my darling. I wish your love. Only that. And you were going to continue and mention your friend Agrippa. Well, I honour your friendship for him, Kit, believe me. But as I will not thrust my father down your throat, Kit, so I hope and believe that you will not thrust your black friend down mine.'

She stood next to him. He could inhale her perfume, as he was close enough to touch the damp softness of her shirt. 'I was going to say that I feared you had estranged Mr Warner, on my behalf. He will never consent to attending our wedding. And what of your mother?'

Marguerite frowned, for just a moment. 'My mother is dead.'

'But...'

'Papa has a wife, of course. Aunt Celestine. She has always treated me as her own.' She laughed, a glorious explosion of confident sound. 'What, did you not know I am a bastard? Does that make me less desirable?'

'Sweetheart...'

'Then kiss me, and do not worry. Aunt Celestine will support my wish, and Papa will attend our wedding, Kit, because it will be the social event of the year, no, of the century, in Antigua. Have no fear on that score. Now come, Barnee is waiting to discuss your clothes.'

'And if I say so myself, Captain Hilton, sir,' Barnee said. 'It is a work of art.'

He stood back, and Kit surveyed himself in the full-length mirror. But was this really Christopher Hilton, buccaneer? He wore a black velvet coat, with gold braid and buttons, over a brocade waistcoat. His cravat was white, with fringed rather than laced ends; this had been Marguerite's decision, as so much had been Marguerite's decision. His breeches were also black velvet, as his stockings were black silk, and his shoes were black leather, with red heels and metal buckles. He carried no weapons, as befitted a bridegroom, but rather a cane, lacking a gold top, but embossed with leather from which hung a tassel. For when people are as wealthy as we, Marguerite had pointed out, where is the point in wearing jewellery?

And on his head, specially cropped for the occasion, was a brown periwig. Certainly he did not recognize himself.

'I swear I am a parson,' he declared.

'In velvet, Captain?' Barnee smiled. ''Tis hot, I have no doubt, but the quality . . . the quality, Captain Hilton. That sets you apart.' He raised his hand. 'Listen.'

The bell had started its chimes, a cascade of brilliant sound. And the bell, with its tower, had only arrived yesterday, transported bodily from St John's and erected in the yard outside the front verandah. As so many other things had been especially created or constructed for this one day in all their lives. The thought of the expense had him shuddering, but Marguerite apparently gave it not a thought. And now, with the bell, there came the rumbling of the carriages of the arriving guests; for there was not a soul in all Antigua granted an invitation to this event who was not appearing. From all the Leewards, in fact.

'So, now, sir, you must go down,' Barnee said. 'Your future awaits you. And may I offer you the first of the thousands of congratulations you will receive this day, Captain.'

'Be off with you, Barnee,' Kit growled. 'You are looking on me only as a future valuable customer.'

Barnee did not smile. 'You are already a valued customer, Captain Hilton. More. You are a liked and admired customer, and I will not pretend to feel so for all of my clients. If I had a single bequest to make, on this your wedding day, it would be that nothing, sir, nothing, either good or bad, happy or unhappy, should change the spirit and the demeanour I have grown to admire.'

Kit frowned at him. They had been in daily contact over the past three weeks as suit after suit had been fitted and completed. And in truth the tailor had been uncommonly serious most of the time, for a man who was in the process of making his fortune.

'I think you should explain that remark.'

Barnee flushed. 'I have already spoken too much, sir. It is the excitement of the occasion, if you will believe that. Now look, George Frederick awaits you.'

The footman, resplendent in pale blue and white, with a white powdered wig, was hovering in the doorway.

'Are the guests arrived, then?' Kit asked.

'Most of them, sir. But one uninvited, who asks for a word.'

'Agrippa.' Kit ran outside, hesitated on the gallery, glancing from the closed door behind which Marguerite was also no doubt making ready—he had not been allowed to see her all day—to the people who were stamping into the lobby at the foot of the great staircase, whispering and sweating, for it was only three of the afternoon and the sun was still high in the heavens, and who now looked up at the bridegroom to be, so soberly dressed in contrast to their reds and greens, pinks and whites, while the girls circulated amongst them, carrying trays laden with sangaree.

'The side stairs, sir,' George Frederick whispered, and Kit gave the assembly a hasty smile before running down the servants' staircase, which descended from an upstairs lobby between two of the bedrooms, and emerged in the pantry itself. Here was even more crowded, with the housemaids lining up in their best white gowns to be inspected by Maurice Peter the butler, with the tables covered in glasses and jugs of iced sangaree and rum punch, with plates of sweetmeats and cakes.

And here too, was Agrippa.

'I had to offer my congratulations, Kit. And perhaps say goodbye.'

'Goodbye, Agrippa?' Kit squeezed the hand, equally today, for his strength was all but returned. 'You're not leaving the island?'

'No, man,' Agrippa said. 'I work with Mr Christianssen, now. But I doubt we shall see much of each other in the future.'

'What nonsense,' Kit smiled. 'I must honeymoon. But I am well again, and be sure that I will be in town soon enough.'

'Aye, but hardly to the warehouse. That will be left to your overseers, Kit. Do you not understand? You are a planter, now. You belong with your fellows, in the Ice House.'

Kit frowned at him. 'There is something of the censor in your voice, old friend. Was this not always my dream?'

Agrippa sighed. 'A plantation, Kit. To be conducted as you saw fit. Not Green Grove. Now I must take my leave. I hear the music starting.'

For indeed the music of the spinet was beginning to drift up the hill from the chapel, whence it had been removed for this special occasion.

'Yet must you say more,' Kit insisted. 'I am surrounded by

THE DEVIL'S OWN

these hints and innuendoes. Now come, dear friend, explain your meaning. Be sure that I will not take offence.'

Agrippa hesitated. 'Why, Kit, they are only hints and innuendoes, in St John's. Have you not come to grips with the administration of your plantation?'

'Not mine, yet. Besides, I have scarce left this house, save for a quiet ride in the trap, since arriving. I have been treated as an invalid, royally, and then this last week there have been all the preparations, and the fittings, and the . . . you mean my bride is the subject of gossip, in town? Well, so she should be, I suppose. She has an individual cast of mind. But am I not the gainer by that? Be sure that there can be no kinder woman on the face of this earth.'

Agrippa gazed at him for some seconds. 'Aye,' he said at last. 'Of that I have no doubt at all, Kit, where kindness is concerned. Now I will leave. I'd not have you late for your wedding. But be sure my thoughts go with you, now and always.'

He had walked away before Kit could stop him, and a moment later was through the door. Where kindness is concerned. Now there was a strange remark.

'Captain Hilton. Captain Hilton, sir.' Passmore, the head overseer, a tall young man whose pretensions to good looks were spoiled by a squint, dressed in his best clothes, perspiring and anxious. 'It is time, sir.'

Kit followed him into the dining-room, and beyond, to the withdrawing-room, crowded with shuffling, whispering, sweating planters and their wives, with the plantation overseers and book-keepers, and their wives also, all wearing unaccustomed finery they could ill afford. Everyone in Antigua, Marguerite had promised. No, in the entire Leewards. Providing they possessed wealth or position, or were her employees. He feared for the safety of the floor, and smiled at them as he passed along, while they gazed at him and renewed their chattering; few had met him, but all had heard of him, of what he had been and of how he had come to be here.

'Captain Hilton. My word, sir, but you are looking your best today. As indeed you should be, sir.' The Reverend Spalding, wearing his best black surplice, and with a new wig. And being hypocritically charming, unaware that his conversation of six weeks ago had been overheard.

'Indeed, reverend,' Kit said. 'I also feel at my best.'

'Again as you should be, sir.' Spalding winked. 'I swear there is not a man in this congregation, nay, in the entire island, who is not heartily jealous of you at this moment, and will be more so as the evening goes on. But come, sir, I would have you meet your most important guest. Sir William Stapleton, Captain Christopher Hilton.'

The Governor of the Leeward Islands was a tall man with a red face and a martial air; he wore a red coat and a black periwig, and was one of the few gentlemen present to have retained his sword; but then he was a soldier pure and simple, who had made his reputation in the late war. Rumour had it that he was not popular with the planters; had he a touch of true patriotism in his soul Kit could well understand that.

'The buccaneer,' Stapleton's voice was dry. But he shook hands. 'You are to be congratulated, sir. Alone amongst the people here I claim no acquaintance of your famous grandfather. Had we met I should no doubt have been after hanging him from his own yardarm. But I am most heartily pleased at your own good fortune, sir.'

'My thanks, Your Excellency.' Kit wondered just what yardarm would be made available were the Governor ever to discover he had commanded the *Bonaventure* in its brush with the warship. Or was he, now being a member of the plantocracy, immune from such proceedings? It was a most delightful feeling.

'Kit, my dear fellow.' Edward Chester, his face as red as his hair. 'How good to see you again. You have not met my wife. Mary, this is the man himself.'

Mary Chester gave a little giggle of embarrassment, and half curtsied. She was hardly more than a girl, and plump and fair. 'You are the sole subject of conversation at our tea parties, Captain.'

'Which means your reputation has been torn to shreds, Kit,' Chester beamed. 'But I doubt that troubles you in the slightest. And dare I hope, once this happy affair is consummated, that we shall once again see darling Marguerite in society? The island has seemed a duller place these past few months.'

'I'm sure you should ask that question of Marguerite,' Kit said, and could not help but add, 'dear Edward,' just to watch the planter's eyes flicker. What a horde of hypocrites they were, to be sure.

A fan tapped him on the shoulder, and he hastily turned. This woman was almost as tall as himself, and middle-aged; her face was sun-browned and long, and unhappy, and her body angular. 'I think it is time,' she said, 'for you to take your place, and for us to meet. I am Celestine Warner.'

'Madam,' Kit said in confusion. 'Forgive my manners. I should have sought you out immediately. But I was not sure...'

'If we would attend? The marriage of our own...' she sighed, 'daughter? Who else do you think would give the bride away? Now come, I am sure these good people will have as much time as they need to gawp at you and pick your brains and whisper behind your back. For the moment, let us have you married.'

A woman to be liked. Because she alone was honest? Or because he could see the misery in her eyes; the strain of being Philip Warner's wife?

Passmore was waiting to escort him from the house, into the suddenly brilliant sunshine, and into, too, the cheers of the slaves, assembled in a vast mass half-way down the hill to applaud their master and mistress; for this day there had been no field labour. And how hot it was. As he smiled and waved at the Negroes he could feel sweat trickling down his arms. But he at least was fortunate; he was entering the chapel. How unlucky were those guests forced to remain outside; there was room within for only the twenty most distinguished.

The Reverend Spalding was already in place before the altar, almost obscured by the masses of flowers, and the spinet was gaining in volume. Kit heard the whisperings behind him, and the restless turning of heads and craning of necks. But he would not turn himself. He waited, until the soft footfalls sounded beside him, and then he allowed himself to smile at her, and was dazzled in return. She had elected to indulge her taste for colour, and wore a pink taffeta gown with gold stripes and a red lining, pulled back from a white silk underskirt which was edged with silver; her bows were of green velvet to complete a kaleidoscope of colour, magnificently set off by her hair, which was loose and brushed forward over her shoulders to lie against the brilliance of her gown, and was in turn illuminated by the high, white lace head-dress, which matched the white lace ruffles on her sleeves, while over her underskirt she wore a white linen apron, edged with lace. Her only jewellery was her pearl necklace, but her fan was ivory, and the whole was shrouded in the richness of her scent and illuminated by the splendour of her personality. She filled even the crowded chapel, and left it empty of competitors. Kit did not even notice Philip Warner, at his most resplendent, standing at her left shoulder.

And now her hand was in his, soft and damp, and the priest was beginning to speak.

'Gad, sir, but were I at sea on this night, and looking towards this shore, I would suppose this island to have suddenly discovered for itself a volcano such as St Lucia or Martinique.' Stapleton swayed, and tugged his cravat somewhat looser. The Governor had consumed a great deal of liquor. But then, who had not? And his observation was accurate enough, Kit thought, as he leaned against one of the verandah uprights, and looked out at the yard. There a gigantic bonfire had been lit, safe enough from the house for what breeze there was blew the sparks toward the canefields. And here the Negroes danced. And what a dance, for they had decked themselves out in a variety of fantastic garments and head-dresses, feathers and the masks of weird beasts, huge jaws and snapping teeth, great rolling eyes and long waving stalks of arms, some reaching as high as the second storey of the house itself, and they stamped and shuffled and swayed, brought their bodies close together, men and women, and separated again in long snaking lines. They had been given rum to drink on this most special occasion in their lives and they were celebrating the marriage of their mistress.

'Johnny Canoe,' George Frederick had said. 'They dance to the memory of Johnny Canoe.'

So then, was there nothing but pleasure in their sinuous movements? For Johnny Canoe was the English corruption of the name of the chieftain who had held his court in the Bight of Benin, and who had rounded up these unfortunates for sale to the Dutch slave traders. And if they were dancing to pull down a curse on his unhappy memory, might they not also, locked away in the secrets of their obeah, or magical religion, be bringing down curses on their mistress and their new master?

But they looked happy enough, and sounded more so. They exuded a quality of insidious sexuality, of abandon and gaiety, increased and accentuated by the throbbing drum which seeped upwards through the night, which reached out and encompassed the white people on the verandah. But certainly they too were in a mood to be titillated. They had

THE DEVIL'S OWN

drunk far too much, and they were gathered to celebrate a wedding, with all that entailed and promised; in the dark corners of the verandah men stroked and squeezed women they would normally pass by with a decorous bow, and women smiled and gasped, and sought this evening's temporary escape from the prison of their homes and their husbands. Why, Kit thought, given another hour, the entire crowd will be coupling on the floor.

Such was the power of the African drum. But it was not to be. Marguerite had drunk hardly at all, and she was on her feet, and at the sight of that dominant figure the drum stopped without warning, and the dancers too, and silence descended on the compound almost like a blanket dropped from the sky.

'Enough,' Marguerite said. 'I have been a widow for more than a year. My bed and my body alike have wilted in their loneliness. Would you keep me longer from my husband's manhood?'

A gale of cheering and laughter swept the night. The Negroes yelled and stamped and clapped their hands; but the drum remained silent. No one could doubt that the slaves at Green Grove were the best disciplined on the island.

But not the planters and their wives. Kit was seized by a forest of arms and rushed up the great staircase, a path along which Marguerite, laughing and protesting, had already been carried, and into one of the spare bedrooms, where his clothes were torn from his body with scant regard for Barnee's exquisite stitching, and replaced by an embroidered silk nightshirt, to the accompaniment of loud laughter and louder lewdity, and then hustled along the gallery, while the house servants and the more faint-hearted of the guests gathered in the hall below to clap and cheer their approbation of the coming events.

The great bedchamber was so crowded Kit doubted they would get through. But a space was cleared, and he was pushed between the laughing, cheering women, each of whom reached out to squeeze or kiss some portion of his anatomy. But at the least the enormous implications of everything that was happening were having the desired effect, and he was as hard and as anxious as any boy confronted with his first naked breast. God forbid that he should be anything less; he did not suppose this crowd would be satisfied with second hand news. Not on an evening of rum and sangaree.

Marguerite was already ensconced beneath the sheets in the huge four poster, the covers held primly to her neck, her hair spreading across the pillows. Her smile was a delicious indication of pleasure; this was her night, and clearly she felt not a drop of embarrassment, much less nervousness. Not even when the sheets were raised to allow him in, and the men gave a roar of approval as they caught a brief glimpse of her naked body.

And how warm she was. And damp. And eager.

'The thrust,' they shrieked. 'We'll see the first thrust, by God.'

Her breath was on his face, her smiling teeth but inches away. 'You'd best accommodate them, dear Kit,' she whispered. ' 'Tis certain they'll not leave us alone before.'

He drove his body downwards. Christ, what a memory that brought back, clouding up out of his unconscious to blanket his brain with despair. But there could be no despair here. There was no risk of this quivering body sliding away into a void of empty flesh. This was his, and again, and again, for as long and as often as he could wish or accomplish.

Her arms were tight on his back, and her voice continued to whisper in his ear. 'Stay,' she insisted. 'Stay, and thrust. Stay and thrust. And begone,' she shouted. 'It is done.'

The noise flowed around his head, filled his ears, clouded his senses. He thrust, and kissed her neck, her eyes, her nose and her mouth, and thrust again, and discerned the noise receding, driven by the sharp voice of Celestine Warner. The groom had proved himself a man, and the bride had revealed herself to be content. Now at last was the wedding completed, and now at last could they be left in peace.

And now at last was he exhausted, and prepared to sleep. But not to dream. A blanket descended on his mind, as he slipped from her warmth to lie on the cooler sheet, to lose himself in the oblivion of utter contentment, to awake, reluctantly, dragging his mind upwards through endless eons of drowsy sleep, to blink in the daylight, and marvel at the silence, although always there was that ripple of muted sound just beyond earshot, which told him that the plantation was also awake, and beginning its daily round.

The bed was empty. He sat up, pushing hair from his forehead, looking around him in sudden alarm. And finding Marguerite, fully dressed in her riding habit, standing at the

THE DEVIL'S OWN

window gazing out at the canefields somewhat pensively, but turning as she heard the movement.

'Sweetheart.' She came towards him, striking the small gong on the table as she did so. 'I would not disturb you earlier.'

'My darling.' He reached for her shoulders as she sat on the bed, explored her mouth.

A soft sound alerted them, and she released him as Martha Louise placed the tray on the table by the bed. 'Coconut milk,' Marguerite said. 'Cool and refreshing, and essential for a man on his honeymoon.'

He drank, and indeed it tasted delicious.

'And now,' she said. 'You must get dressed. For we must honeymoon as and when we may. There is a plantation to be managed, and I would have you play your part as soon as possible, that the people here may be in no doubt that they have a master again.'

'Of course.' He got out of bed. ' 'Tis a responsibility I have long anticipated sharing.'

'I will send the girls to you.' She turned, to face the still opened door as booted feet clumped on the stairs. 'Well?'

Passmore stood there, his face flushed, his hat held in both his hands. 'He had sought the beach, Mistress Templeton.'

Marguerite smiled. 'My name is Hilton, Passmore. I'd not have you forget that in the future. Aye, the beach. I had supposed him more intelligent. Which but proves how absurd it is to waste time in worrying. Very good, Passmore. Prepare the fire. I will attend shortly. As soon as Captain Hilton is dressed.'

Passmore bowed, and withdrew. Kit was already reaching for his pants. 'There has been a misadventure?'

'I had supposed so,' she said. 'But I was mistaken. I purchased a new batch of slaves but a month ago, and one of them, a buck about whom I will confess I had some doubts at the time, chose to make the excitement and the preoccupation of yesterday as an excuse to abscond from the plantation.'

'By God,' Kit said. 'A runaway.'

She buttoned his shirt for him. 'Every so often there is a new arrival who behaves in this fashion.'

'And you knew this, yesterday?' He held her shoulders. 'And did not tell me?'

'It was your wedding day.'

'Was it not yours?'

She smiled, and kissed him on the mouth. 'Slaves are a problem I grew up with. To you they may appear to be a problem. And as it happened, you would have been needlessly concerned. The poor savage but sought the beach, and clung there until my people found him, this morning. Now come, we must attend his execution.'

'His . . .' Kit's hands slowly fell to his side. 'His execution?'

'Of course,' she said. 'There is only one punishment for runaways. He will be burned alive, as soon as you are dressed.'

6

Across the Water

Marguerite had already left the house and was about to mount her horse when Kit caught up with her.

'You cannot mean that,' he said.

A Negro slave held her bridle, and Maurice Peter waited to give her a knee up to her side-saddle. Her six mastiffs trotted from the house to follow her. She settled herself, reins in her left hand, and looked down at him. 'What else can I mean? There is no other punishment for runaways.'

'But . . .' he grasped her stirrup. 'It is barbaric, Marguerite. I . . . I had no idea of what they spoke, when they warned me that I might not find everything here to my liking. But this . . .'

She frowned, very slightly. 'They?'

He waved his hand. 'Everyone. Barnee . . .'

Her forehead cleared. 'What did Barnee have to say about me, Kit?'

He felt his cheeks burning. She was so calm, and so admonitory, as if she were a schoolmarm and he a little boy. 'He said your methods were your own.'

'Ah,' she said. 'Indeed they are, sweet Kit.'

'I could detect no approval in his tone. Rather the reverse.'

She smiled. 'No doubt Barnee's approval is important to you. We will discuss my methods, you and I, my darling. But not in front of the house servants. Will you mount, and ride with me?'

Another horse waited. Kit scrambled into the saddle, and grasped the reins with both hands. She regarded him with a critical look.

'We will have to make you practise, I think. Nothing so earns a man respect as to sit a horse well.'

Now he was angry. 'I assure you, madam, I need to earn respect from no man.'

'I never doubted that for an instant, Kit. I but wished to be sure you always possessed mine.' She walked her horse in front of him, began the descent of the gradual slope towards the slave compound. She pointed, with her whip, at the houses grouped perhaps half a mile to their right. 'I have not had the chance to show you our plantation, my darling. That is the village of the white staff.'

'I had gathered that for myself.'

She half turned her head, then changed her mind and ignored the brusqueness in his tone. 'Have you any idea how many people live there, as you are so knowledgeable?'

'You told me you employed thirty overseers.'

'Only twenty overseers,' she said. 'The other ten are bookkeepers, and men with a knowledge of machinery who are required to keep the grinding house in good repair. For upon that our entire prosperity depends.' Her whip moved, a few inches, to point to the bulk of the boiling house, dominated by its huge square chimney, even larger than that which rose from the kitchen of the Great House. 'But of course,' she said, 'they have their wives and families living with them. I even employ a schoolteacher, a lady from St John's. My intention is to make Green Grove entirely self-supporting. In all, counting you and me, my darling, there are fifty-seven white people on this plantation.'

'A sizeable number.'

'And yet hardly sufficient.' The whip moved again, to point to the rows of barracoons at the bottom of the hill. 'When you consider that there are five hundred blacks. Now tell me, Kit, what do you think keeps them down there, and us up here? For I do assure you, it is a mistake to assume the blacks entirely lack intelligence, or the ability to count. Perhaps you imagine that it is the knowledge of your good right arm, your unerring accuracy with a pistol, your terrible prowess with a sword. But you arrived here only last month, and they have been there for twenty years and more.'

'Now you seek to mock me.'

'I shall never do that, Kit. I give you my word. But I must make you understand that we live in a world which is constructed upon fear, and fear alone. Those blacks fear my overseers, because they know the overseers will punish them savagely for any transgressions, but they fear me more, because they know also that my overseers are but carrying out my will. And now it is our will, Kit. There can be no doubt in anyone's mind that this is so.'

'I understand everything you say, Marguerite. And I appreciate the reasoning behind it. I even appreciate that it may be necessary to execute runaways, although by my faith I find it hard to punish a man so terribly for behaving as I should myself. But if it is to be the case, why not hang him or shoot him or behead him? Is not the mere fact of dying awful enough? To burn a man alive . . . can there be a worse fate?'

'There can indeed,' she remarked. 'But that is reserved for the black who raises his or her hand to a white. As for burning alive, it is barbaric to be sure. But then, you see, we are not concerned with the man who is about to die. He is dead from the moment he makes the fateful decision to break out. We are concerned with the effect we must have upon the brains of those who remain behind upon this earth and more particularly upon this estate. They must hold at the forefront of their minds, for the rest of their lives, the awful spectacle, the awful sound, the awful stench, of a man they know being consumed to ashes, so that whenever the idea of escape enters their minds, they will reject it instinctively. Now come, they are ready.'

They had reached the foot of the hill, and the entrance to the slave compound. Here the majority of the overseers were gathered for in view of the escape there was no field work today, as yet; the white men were mounted, and armed, at once with the fearful cartwhip and with swords and pistols. In front of them, gathered in a vast concourse, dressed uniformly in white calico, drawers for the men and chemises for the women, were the slaves; their children milled about them, but these were permitted to be naked. They looked no different to the previous afternoon, save that today they were silent, and there were no smiles to be seen. They watched the overseers, and they watched their approaching mistress, and they watched too the stake erected outside

THE DEVIL'S OWN

their gate, made of green timber, but surrounded by carefully dried wood and leaves stacked as high as a man's knees.

Passmore waited some distance from his fellows. Now he urged his horse closer to Marguerite's. 'It is ready, Mistress Hilton.' His eyes flickered to Kit, and then back again.

Marguerite turned her head. 'Will you give the order, my darling?'

He gazed at her in utter horror. 'Me? I cannot, Marguerite, I swore an oath, after Panama, that I would never again take a human life, except in defence of my own.'

Her frown was beginning to gather, as Passmore was beginning to smile.

'Surely you were then suffering from the pangs of conscience, my darling,' she said gently. 'Oaths should be sworn only in the clear light of sober day.'

'None the less, it was sworn,' Kit insisted. 'And can you not make an exception, this day of all days? It is the first of your new married life. No one could possibly mistake a gesture of magnanimity as weakness this morning. Why, kings and queens are accustomed to grant an amnesty on the morrow of their coronation.'

Marguerite looked at him for some seconds, then she said, still without taking her eyes from her husband's face, 'You may bring the prisoner out, Passmore.' She waited until the overseer was out of earshot, then she said, still speaking very softly, 'Dear, dear Kit, I do admire your humanity. But please believe me when I say that even if you meant to honour your oath, it would hardly apply to these blacks.'

'Are they not human?' Kit demanded.

A slight shrug of those exquisite shoulders. 'Perhaps, if we stretch the term. But I would not do so. They are certainly an inferior species. Can you doubt that? Oh, you will hold up Agrippa, of course. Then Agrippa is a human amongst the sub-humans. I would willingly hold *you* up, as a demigod. Yet would I not suppose you the Deity Himself. And are we not in His image created? There are classes of things. So there is God, and His angels, and there are men, and there are blacks. Believe me, Kit, as you have studied seamanship and battle, the use of weapons and the leadership of men, I have, perforce, had to study these creatures to whom you would arrogate a humanity equal to your own. If you have a fault at all, it is your own modesty, your own diminution of yourself and your species. I would correct that so slight fault. Now hear me out. You have but to ask of me. No, I would not have it so. Demand of me, Kit, and it shall be yours, of my person and of my wealth. Both are considerable. Would you have a ship, larger than any ever built? I will build it for you. Would you have a sword, made of solid gold, and yet sewn through with steel to make it a serviceable weapon? Be sure that you shall have it. Would you take the whip to my back? Be sure, that in the privacy of our bedchamber, I will bend before you, and smile while the blood flows. In return I ask only two things of you. Nay, I demand only two things of you, in exchange for the immensity I now place within your grasp. Support me in the rule of Green Grove, for upon this rock are all our powers founded. And love me, and me alone. I am sufficiently a woman, who has already been married, to understand that my body may not always satisfy a true man. But *love* only me, Kit, no matter where you may find your comfort. Supposing I should become unable to provide it for you. Now let us, together, supervise this execution.'

For the black man was being brought from the hut in which he had been chained, by four of the Negro foremen, heads held high as they dragged their victim forth, because they were acting for the superior being, the demigoddess, the mistress.

The man himself scarce wasted his time in fighting them or in struggling, and he knew better than to waste his precious breath in begging for mercy. But as he was taken to the stake he stared at Marguerite, and occasionally his lips moved, silently.

'He is cursing you,' Kit said.

'I have been cursed before. But he left his gods behind in Africa. They will not help him here.'

The man was at the stake, and being pressed against it while iron chains were passed around his waist and under his armpits, and secured to keep him upright. Meanwhile his drawers were removed from his thighs, to leave him naked.

'Can you not spare him that, at the least?' Kit asked.

'Material costs money,' Marguerite pointed out. 'Even calico, my darling. One makes a profit from a sugar plantation by saving wherever possible. Not by throwing one's goods away.' She raised her voice. 'You may light the fire, Mr. Passmore.'

Passmore nodded, and dismounted. The torch had already

been kindled, and was held by another of the Negro foremen. Now it was handed to the overseer, and a moment later a puff of smoke rose from the pyre, accompanied by the first tongues of flame. Kit wrapped his hands tight round the reins, and felt the sweat start out on his cheeks and shoulders. But then, the morning was starting to heat as the sun rose above the eastern hilltops, out of that endless ocean from whence this man had come, and upon which he now looked for the last time.

A moan arose from the throats of the slaves, rising and falling like a dirge. Kit glanced at Marguerite, but she gave no indication of having heard it. Certainly she was not affected. Her face was expressionless as she gazed at the man, who still stared at her, through the pain and the anguish which filled his eyes. Her own eyes were soft, almost perhaps filled with tears. The schoolteacher. She regretted what must be done, because there were good muscles being wasted. But done it must be, for the good of all. For the discipline of all.

And now the dying man cried out, time and again, and his own wail joined the chant of the slaves. But it lasted a surprisingly short time. He inhaled smoke and choked, and died, before his body was consumed. Yet must they sit there, and stand there, and watch, as the fire crackled and the smoke pyre reached upwards towards the clear blue of the heavens. Once I was a buccaneer, Kit thought, a common cutpurse, a creature of passion, who fought and robbed and raped while convulsed with passion. But now I am one of the élite. There is none higher than me in all the Caribee Isles. I live like a king, and I command like a king. And I punish like a king, as well, with slow and deliberate enmity. Did I not always dream of possessing such power?

'Be sure the ashes are scattered, Passmore,' Marguerite said. She touched her horse's flanks with her heels. 'You'll stay by my side, Kit,' she said, without looking over her shoulder.

The horse was advancing towards the slave compound. 'You'd go amongst them now?' Kit asked in wonderment.

'Should I not, my darling?' Her voice was low. 'It is my, our, daily duty, Kit. For even plantation owners have duties, alas.'

Kit gazed at the slaves as they approached. Behind him the flames were roaring and the man was silent, and dead. The spectacle was over. The overseers were moving forward as well, barking their orders, and the foremen were taking their whips from their belts. The Negroes were falling into gangs with well disciplined obedience, but Kit saw to his horror that each man, and each woman, was armed with a sharp knife, almost a small sword, although it had no point and no guard to the haft. And now Marguerite was amongst them, and they stood to each side of her horse, touching their foreheads in eager humility, and averting their eyes.

He drew level as they passed the last of the throng and gained the beaten earth of the compound itself. 'They could have torn us to pieces in seconds.'

'I explained that to you, but a minute ago,' she said. 'Because we are we, and they are they, it will never happen. They have brains, but only to feel, and fear, not to reason. Not to aspire to anything more than the food I allow them twice a day, and the mug of rum I allow them once a week.' She reined, and George Frederick stooped to allow her to place her boot in the centre of his back as she dismounted. Kit joined her, pulling the kerchief from his pocket to wipe the sweat from his neck and brow. Another foreman was waiting, an older man, this time, with grizzled hair and bent shoulders, and they were to inspect something Kit had not noticed before, a row of six frames set beyond the houses, placed in the ground like inverted hoops, although with square edges. From the crossbar of each of the frames there hung a naked body, and to his dismay he saw that only four of them were men; the other two were women.

But disgust had not yet come upon him. It grew as he approached, and saw the marks on their backs, great gashes in the black skin, crimson trenches in which the blood had coagulated.

He stared at Marguerite, and his mouth slowly opened in utter horror. Her expression had not changed; not even the faintest wrinkle marked her lip or her forehead. But she slowly pulled the glove from her right hand, and with a bared forefinger actually touched the wounds on the back of the first man. 'Enough,' she said. 'Salt.' She passed on to the next, again touching and this time even stroking the serrated flesh. 'What of him?'

'He does curse, mistress,' the foreman said. 'He does kick and curse you.'

'Another two dozen,' she said. The body quivered, but the man did not speak.

'What crimes have they committed?' Kit asked.

'Insubordination in the fields.' Marguerite was stroking the back of the third man, and commanding him to be cut down.

Kit gazed at the blood on her hands. 'Are you not afraid?'

'Of what?' She had reached the women.

'Of . . . of disease?'

Marguerite smiled. 'It is good blood, Kit. Were they diseased, they would not have been in the fields in the first place. It is also our responsibility to care for that. Take these girls down,' she told the foreman. 'No doubt they will behave in the future.'

'Yes, mistress.' He held out a towel, and a woman waited with a basin of water. Marguerite washed and dried her hands, and then led the entourage, like an inspecting queen, it occurred to Kit, towards another hut, larger than any of the others and set a little apart from them. But then, he realized, she is a queen, here on Green Grove, and I am no more than her consort.

The door was being opened, and they stepped into the gloom. A noisome gloom, for although the interior of the house was carefully washed with lime, and quite recently, and there was clean straw on the floor, yet the smell of human sweat and human excrement could not be excluded.

'Is this, then, your prison house?' Kit muttered.

'We do not have a prison house,' Marguerite said. 'The lash is sufficient for disciplinary purposes.'

Now that his eyes were accustomed to the sudden end of the brilliant sunshine he could see that there were perhaps a score of people in here, men and women, lying on pallets on the straw, most trying to raise themselves on their elbows as their mistress came in, but several unable even to muster that much strength.

One of the men following Marguerite ran forward with a three-cornered stool, and placed it beside the first of the sick men. Marguerite sat down, and leaned forward, over the trembling Negro, a young fellow, whose eyes rolled. 'How is it today, Peter Thomas?' she asked, her voice like a soothing zephyr of breeze.

Peter Thomas's eyes rolled some more. 'Oh, man, mistress, it itch itch too bad.'

'But that is good, Peter Thomas,' she said. 'It shows you are fighting the poison. I will look at it.'

The foreman hastily knelt beside the sick man and pulled the cover away from his leg, which was swollen to twice its size. Peter Thomas screamed as the foreman seized the leg itself, and raised it, for Marguerite to feel and prod the swelling sore which was dominating the misshapen calf.

'What happened to him?' Kit whispered.

'He was stung by some insect in the field. I have no idea what it was. But of course he scratched the puncture, and inflammation set in.' She sighed. 'They are a careless people, of their healths no less than of my profit. But this will heal. It is good, Peter Thomas,' she said. 'You will soon be well. He may have a glass of rum, Henry William.'

'Oh, yes, mistress,' the foreman said. 'He going like that. You hear what the mistress say, Peter Thomas? You ain't happy?'

'I happy, mistress,' Peter Thomas muttered. 'I happy.'

Marguerite stood up, walked on to the next patient, a woman who lay on her back, face drawn with pain.

'Do you remember all of their names?' Kit asked.

'I try to do so. I give them their titles myself. It is of course necessary to have two names for every one or we should soon run out. I keep a roster, of twenty-six names, from Arthur to Zebadiah, and another, from Alice to Zenobia, and merely couple two in strict rotation. This permits me to recall them with some ease, and I have not yet had to use a dead man's name. In fact, I have not yet reached Thomas as a prefix. Peter Thomas is one of my newest arrivals.'

The stool was in place, and as she sat down the coverlet was removed. This time even Kit bent forward; the woman's thigh was enclosed between two boards, drawn tightly one in front and the other behind, and secured by rope bands which ran round the thigh itself and across the pelvis to constrict the body as much as possible.

Marguerite was frowning as she leaned over the girl, and at the shriek of agony which drifted from the clenched lips at her touch.

'It is not knitting,' she said.

'No, mistress,' Henry William agreed. 'I ain't see how it going to do that.'

Marguerite sighed, and stood up. 'A fall,' she explained to Kit. 'It really is very bad. She was a good worker.'

'And can she not be so again?'

'With a deformed thigh? No, I do not see that she can ever be put to useful employment again.' She was standing in the centre of the room now, Henry William attentive at her elbow. 'You'd best see to it, Henry William. This day.'

Kit caught her arm as she would have moved on. 'You cannot mean to murder her?'

Marguerite's head turned. 'I'd be obliged it you'd keep your voice down, my darling. These people are sick, and it would not be good for them to understand our measures. No, I am not going to murder her. I am going to put her to sleep. Believe, she will not feel a thing.'

'And you do not call that murder?'

For God's sake, Kit, how can one murder a slave? You will be speaking next of murdering horses, or cats, or dogs. Would you not shoot your horse were he to break his leg and become a useless encumbrance? And you would shoot it. Hannah Jane will never know what is happening to her.' She turned away, and was already seating herself beside the next patient, when she discovered Kit was no longer at her side. He was in fact pushing the blacks aside as he made for the door.

'Enough,' Marguerite said, standing up again. 'I will see to the rest later.'

The blacks parted, and she reached Kit as he himself gained the open air.

'That must not happen again,' she said. 'You have a duty, to me no less than to the rest of the planting community on Antigua, never to show weakness in front of the blacks. Nor had I supposed you to possess such weakness.'

'No doubt I have similarly misjudged,' he muttered.

She gazed at him, her brows brought together in a frown. 'I doubt that,' she said. 'I doubt that, Kit. Come, we shall leave the sick house and attend to something more congenial.' She seized his hand. For a moment he almost shrank away from her as he recollected that but a few seconds earlier that hand had been covered with blood. But it had been washed, and was cool to the touch. And now she was leading him on, to yet another compound, set at the back of the slave village proper, and reached by a high gate, which was thrown wide as the master and mistress approached. 'Here you will find nothing but happiness, I do assure you, Kit. Here the blacks are kept at stud.'

This time the entourage stopped at the fence, and Marguerite entered by herself, hesitating just long enough to make sure Kit was still at her shoulder. Henry William had rung the bell which waited by the gate, and from the huts there now came a score of young people, equally divided as to sex, naked and apparently delighted to see their mistress. As she seemed delighted to see them, and moved around them, apparently in no way embarrassed by their animated sexuality, speaking with them, laughing and smiling and praising, now and then stopping for a longer chat as if discussing a problem.

Kit remained on the outside of the gathering, watching his wife, watching the naked female flanks and the thrusting male penises, feeling the blood pumping into his own arteries. This was the first morning of his married life. The first morning of an eternity of mornings, which would be spent awakening in those magnificent arms and against that magnificent body, but knowing too that within an hour he would be out here, with the punished and the sick and the productive.

'Are they not splendid?' Marguerite demanded, returning to him. 'They will bear magnificent children.'

'My mind is in a whirl,' he said. 'You control their mating?'

'Of course. Supposing they are of child-bearing age.' She led him back out of the compound. 'For where would be the purpose in investing so much money in these creatures and then allowing them to bed at will, with the inevitable consequences of bearing unhealthy and certainly unwanted children? Ah, our drink.'

George Frederick had returned from the house, bearing a tray on which there waited a jug of sangaree and two glasses. These he now filled, and Marguerite raised her own. 'This will sustain us until it is breakfast time. We will do the animal farm and the nearer canefields this morning, and ride aback proper tomorrow.'

Their horses had also been brought forward, and now George Frederick handed his tray to Henry William so that he could assist his mistress up. Kit mounted in turn, and Marguerite smiled at the assembly. 'I am satisfied,' she said.

They clapped their pleasure and parted to allow the two horses out of the compound. The dogs padded at their heels. Marguerite glanced at Kit. 'But I doubt you are.'

'As I said, madam, I am overwhelmed. I have lived in a world of unbounded passion all my life. Here I find unbounded order, and control. I wonder how you manage events so to your satisfaction.'

'It but takes thought,' she said. 'Certain it is that a woman will conceive on at least one day in every twenty-eight, even if we cannot be sure which day is the true one. So I select ten of my girls, every month, after careful inspection, and send them to that compound, along with ten young men . . .'

'Also carefully selected, no doubt,' Kit said.

She chose to ignore his sarcasm. 'Of course, my darling. The owner of a plantation must be all things, to all things. And then they are commanded to have intercourse on every day of the month. It very seldom fails.'

'Would it not be simpler just to let your slaves couple as they choose? As I am certain they do in any event.'

She drew rein and checked her mount where the path came to a cross. 'They do not,' she said. 'I will cut the stem from any man who takes a child-bearing woman wantonly on Green Grove. I cannot afford more than a strictly limited number of pregnancies. True enough that these girls are uncommonly hardy, and will work until the babe drops between their legs, but I cannot risk that either. I am laying down a stock for the future, Kit. For our children. Slaves are essential, for the operating of the plantation. But they are also uncommonly expensive. And will grow more so. Now, if we can produce our own, generation after generation, why, our children and our grandchildren will depend upon nothing but themselves. But the stock must be strong, and obedient, and healthy. This is our aim.'

'And you will pretend that there is no fornication on this plantation save as instructed by you?'

'Once a woman is past child-bearing, she may couple to her heart's content, and any young man may put her to good use. Girls who may bear children know well that should they do so without my permission they will be punished. And severely, I do warrant that.' But her frown was back as she studied him. 'I wonder if we have not worked enough for the first day of our married life. I think we shall leave the fields and return to the house.'

She urged her horse up to the right-hand path, and Kit rode behind her. Christ, how confused he was. How uncertain.

'And is what you have shown me today common practice on all the plantations in Antigua?'

'By no means. Nor was it common practice here, until four years ago. For the most, my fellow planters allow the blacks, in whom they have invested nearly their entire fortunes, to go their own way, live and die and fornicate and drop their children with as little interference from their masters as possible. Truly are they a thoughtless society. But then, is there a society which is not?'

'And for this they speak of you in whispers.'

Once again she reined her horse. 'For this they feel that I am beyond their understanding. Were I a man, perhaps, with ideas to put into practice, they would be less aghast. That I am a woman, and young, and even beautiful, would you not say, but yet will go amongst my blacks, and feel their wounds, examine a male weapon, deliver, on occasion, a babe myself and cut the cord myself, this they feel is indecent, unbecoming. Would you not say they are fools? I do the same when one of my mares is in foal.'

Kit stared at her.

'Aye,' she said. 'You are, after all, no more than a man, Kit. But you are my man. We'll not forget that, either of us. Now race me to the house.'

Her whip cracked on the rump of her horse, and it started off at a gallop. Dust flew from its heels, and her hair scattered behind her as she charged up the hill. Kit followed more slowly, keeping his hand tight on the reins. He doubted his ability to keep his seat at that speed, and besides, it was an opportunity to think. As if he dared, to think. Marguerite Warner, Marguerite Templeton, Marguerite Hilton. She was everything he had ever wanted. She was everything any man could ever have wanted. She was a walking dream, in her smell, in her confidence, in her very being.

So then, had he supposed he was marrying a doll? A creature without thought or judgement of her own? He had never supposed that. He had wanted her as much for her spirit and her obvious intelligence as for the promise of her thighs. So then, that spirit and that intelligence was now his, had he the spirit and the intelligence to master them. But to master them he must first of all master the world of which she had made herself the mistress.

So she was universally . . . what was the word he sought? He could not be sure. Abhorred by her fellows? Hardly. They had come quickly enough to attend her wedding. Perhaps feared would be a more accurate description of the emotion she inspired, in the planters no less than in her blacks. She was feared for her ruthless certainty. She evaluated her situation, decided what must be done, and then did it, without a glance to left or to right, without hesitation, without a thought as to the possible hardship she might be inflicting.

And he was taking her to task for that? Had she not acted always upon such a principle, and with such determination, he would not now be riding up to the Great House, the master of Green Grove. She had defied family and convention and society in taking a buccaneer as her husband. Because she had chosen to do so. Only a fool would question her for that.

But only a coward would not. Because why had she made that decision? There was a disturbing thought. It could not alone be centred upon his virility, for the decision had been taken long before she had accompanied him to bed.

He was at the house, and George Frederick was hurrying down to take his bridle as he dismounted. Marguerite's horse already waited at the steps. 'The mistress says you must go to her, Captin,' George Frederick looked embarrassed. 'If you please.'

' 'Tis a lecture you'll be receiving, Mr. Hilton,' Dutton remarked. The overseer had come round the corner of the house unobserved. 'For losing your phlegm at the execution.'

Kit stared at him. 'Aye,' he said. 'I have something to learn about the planting business.'

Dutton grinned. 'You'll not find a better teacher than Mrs Templeton. Ah, I must apologize, sir. I had meant Mistress Hilton, had I not?'

Kit went up the steps and handed his hat to the waiting girl. The house was quiet, and cool, and sweet smelling. The house was the Green Grove he loved. The house and its inmate. But to come back here and claim that inmate, he must ride the fields, and the people in them.

'Where is the mistress?' he asked.

'She taking she bath, Captin,' the girl said, and simpered.

Kit nodded, climbed the stairs to the bedchamber used for her tub; it contained nothing else save a gigantic mirror and a low table. From behind the closed door there came the sounds of splashing and the chatter of the girls. But Martha Louise waited outside the door. For him. Because as he approached she knocked, and the sounds within immediately died.

'The master is here,' she said.

Hands clapped, and the door opened. Five girls came running out, their hands still wet, and their dresses also soaked.

They giggled and bowed, and scattered towards the servants' staircase.

'You is to go in, Captin,' Martha Louise said, and drew the back of her hand across her nose; she seemed to have caught a cold.

Kit nodded, hesitated for a last moment, and then stepped through the door, which promptly closed behind him.

'I am the victor,' Marguerite said. She sat in the huge tin tub, which was some four feet in diameter, and round, and filled with bubbling suds. Her hair was bound up on the top of her head to expose that splendid, strong face, but for the rest she was almost lost to sight beneath the bubbles. 'Pour some sangaree, my darling.'

Kit obeyed; the jug and the glasses waited on the low table.

'Now give me a sip.'

He knelt beside the tub, held the glass to her lips. She drank, and smiled at him. 'Did I ever tell you how happy I am, Kit?' she asked. 'Just to look at you, and know you are there. Just to know that this body belongs to you, and will always do so.'

Her eyes held his. She was fighting a battle, with all the intensity of her body, of her mind, with all the power that she could command. But it was a battle for which she had prepared, for at least a month. Whereas he had stumbled into an ambush, unawares.

Nor would she admit less than a total victory. 'And as I won our race,' she said, 'I claim a forfeit. A duty of you, my sweet. I have sent my girls away. I would have you bathe me. Would you not do that, as a forfeit?'

He placed the glass on the floor, empty. As he had drunk he had tasted her perfume, or so it seemed. Now he took off his coat and pushed up his sleeves. Because how much did he want to touch that body? How much had everything he had seen and heard and smelt this morning made him want to renew his possession of that body.

And besides, she was the victor.

'What's this?' Kit stepped out of the front door, flicking his boots with his riding whip; it was remarkable how easily one picked up the habits of the planters and the overseers. 'A carriage?'

'Did you not know that we possessed a carriage?' Marguerite smiled. 'It is housed in that shed yonder.'

'Then you do not mean to go aback today?' But now he looked at her more closely he could see that indeed she did not, for she had abandoned her divided skirt and her boots and her tricorne in favour of a dark blue taffeta gown decorated with cream silk cuffs and matching bows, and wore lace on her head, while her hair was dressed, although loose. And she carried a fan and a cane.

'A surprise,' she said. 'Do you not realize, my sweet, that for six whole months I have not been to St John's? The only occasions on which I have left my plantation have been to visit Goodwood. But now . . . now that I am a bride of a fortnight and more, I thought we might venture forth and show ourselves to the idle populace.'

'St John's?' His heart bounded at the thought. Now why? Had he then been a prisoner? Oh, indeed, in the most splendid prison imaginable. But now he was more master of his surroundings; practice had even taught him to sit a horse at more than a walk. The flogging of a recalcitrant slave no longer had him trembling, as the sight of the blacks' nudity and desires no longer aroused his own manhood. He had realized that he could reconcile his present position with his innermost ambitions. For the slaves on Green Grove were undoubtedly healthy, and cared for, and in so far as a slave could ever be happy, they were happy. Certainly their lot seemed infinitely preferable to those of any other plantation, nor did it seem to interrupt their concept of themselves to be treated as animals. Because at the very least they were treated as valuable animals, and in that sense protected from the worst evils of climate and human frailty. Whereas on most other plantations in Antigua their lot fluctuated between total neglect and a constant apprehension of the worst of human vices, which reached out to encompass all ages and both sexes, and varied from lust to sadistic brutality.

And for looking after her slaves as she cared for her horses and indeed for her cane itself, Marguerite was feared and disliked by her fellows. Well, then, he was proud to stand at her side, now and always.

'As the idea pleases you, my sweet,' she said, 'I suggest you sit beside me. I shall be attending the auction, Dutton, as I am going that way. You will join me with the wagon in an hour.'

'Yes, Mistress Hilton,' the overseer said, and touched his hat. A man to watch, Dutton, with his constant smile, and his determination to take orders from none but his mistress.

As Marguerite had noticed. She settled herself comfortably as the carriage moved off behind George Frederick and the liveried coachman. 'A drive, with my husband, on a cool morning. Is that not a delight?'

'Indeed it is. I wonder that you spare the time.'

'The cane is nearly ripe,' she said. 'There is little harm can come to it, now. Next month, we shall grind. Then, then you shall see us labour. And you shall labour yourself; I would like you to supervise the boiling.'

'Willingly,' he agreed. 'If I could be at all sure how to go about it.'

'I will have Passmore instruct you. But you must be sure that you understand what you are about. Boiling is a time of great effort, and not all are willing to give that effort. You must drive them to it, Kit. I would estimate that you have now completed what we might call your probationary period as master of Green Grove. Now I would have you *be* master. You understand my meaning?'

'As well as I can.'

'I doubt you do,' she said. 'The blacks will not go against you. They dare not, as they know I ride at your side. I would have you be more assertive with the whites. Perhaps they find it hard to consider you as their superior, as when you came here you appeared no more than their equal.'

'I was no more than their equal.'

'You underestimate yourself. Life had perhaps treated you unkindly, but you should never forget that your background is infinitely superior to that of any poor white. Your grandfather was Governor of Tortuga.'

Kit burst out laughing. 'Really, dear one, you must have forgotten that heap of rubble, that colony of cut-throats. And it had improved since my grandfather's day.'

'None the less,' she insisted, with unusual heat. 'Anthony Hilton was a colonial governor, and will remain forever in the history books as a colonial governor. I would have you bear that always in mind, Kit. As for the other, it would be a good thing were you to give one of these fools a proper taste of your character. They know you only by reputation, and your one aggressive act since coming to Antigua earned you a beating from my father's blacks. Believe me, I see no reproach for you in that. You were attacked from behind and by numbers too considerable even for you to manage, but still I would have you remind these louts of what danger they play with when they mock you. I do not think it would be sound policy for me openly to encourage you to brawl in front of them, so I make my request now, and trust that you will act upon it in due course.'

'But Marguerite, darling,' he said. 'Why should I? I assure you that their remarks or sly grins bother me not in the least. And I would really like to turn my back on violence.'

'No man can do that, and be a man, Kit,' she said. 'And if their pinpricks do not bother you, be sure they bother me. Would you have your wife insulted, even at second hand? You are master of Green Grove, Kit. No law can touch you were you to kill a man in the main street of St John's. I give you my word on that. You have but to act the part.'

She turned away from him, almost violently, to signify the conversation was at an end. So now she would have me kill a man, he thought, no doubt just to prove to herself that I am capable of that. Sometimes he almost hated her, a quick eruption of temper, which he knew was mainly the result of her inexpressible arrogance. But did she not only wish that he would show a similar awareness of his own power and superiority? Was that unreasonable in a woman, and such a woman, born to such power and such dominance? And would he not be a fool to risk her disrespect, when her love was all that sustained him?

And besides, how much was he wrapped up in the words, her love. Already, twenty-one unforgettable nights, when only exhausted sleep had separated their mouths, their bodies, their very hearts. He had but to think of her, of her legs and her belly, of her ever-damp love forest, of her swelling breasts, of her always-hard nipples, of her ever-welcoming lips, and his love was renewed, again and again, and again.

He leaned across the seat and picked up her hand. Her head started to turn and then checked.

'Be sure, my darling, darling Marguerite,' he promised. 'No one shall ever again offer you the slightest insult, whether direct, or implied, or through your husband. At least in my hearing or to my knowledge.'

Now her head did turn, and she smiled at him. 'You are the best and truest of men, dear Kit. I knew I had but to mention the matter to have you understand.' She blew him a kiss. 'Now let us purchase ourselves some lusty blacks.'

For they had arrived in St John's, and were already rumbling down the main street, bringing people out of shop doorways and to their windows, for there were not that many carriages in Antigua. And once the couple were identified, the spectators grew. Captain Hilton and his bride. Or would it be more correct to say, Mistress Hilton and her husband, Kit wondered? But then, she had just taught him the way to alter their positions. It was a way he knew well, even if he had not thought to pursue it in these delightful surroundings. But was any aspect of life any different to any other?

George Frederick pulled on the reins, and Henry Bruce came round to release the steps and hold the door for his mistress. They were outside the only building in town which approximated the Ice House in size, and already a crowd was gathered at the steps, gossiping and exchanging views, and prospects for the sale as well, for if the planters came to buy in batches from ten to fifty, there were invariably some slaves who would be cast aside for a minor defect, and these would be sold cheaply; it remained always the ambition of the poor whites to own at least one black, if only to establish a superiority over their fellows.

But they separated into two sides of a lane quickly enough, nodding and touching their hats to Mistress Hilton, and winking and grinning at Kit, whom they had known in less prosperous days. He prayed that there would be no ribald comment, lest Marguerite should feel that she was being insulted, but this day the remarks were confined to congratulations.

The door closed behind them, and they were in a vast warehouse, well enough lit by great skylights in the roof, and large enough to permit the air to circulate from the jalousied shutters over the lower windows, but yet containing to an incredibly distressing degree the scent of humanity, anxious, lustful, and more than anything else, afraid. Already there were more than a dozen planters here, and already the slaves were grouped at the far end, an entire shipload of them, perhaps two hundred and fifty from an original cargo of four hundred, Kit realized with a turning belly. They gazed about themselves in fear and amazement, happy enough at the moment to be off the dread ship, where they would have been confined for several weeks like living corpses already in their coffins, and fortified as well by the swallow of rum which would have been given to each of them before entering the auction hall.

'Marguerite, how good to see you at an auction.' Edward

THE DEVIL'S OWN

Chester, as bustlingly exuberant as ever. 'Can this mean that you are once more going to be seen socially? My word, Kit, old fellow, but should you have accomplished that miracle, you will be the most popular fellow in Antigua.'

'Am I not already?' Kit asked, quietly.

Chester, bending over Marguerite's hand, straightened and frowned. Marguerite also frowned, for just a moment, and then gave a quick and delighted smile.

'Indeed, you shall see me socially, Edward,' she said. 'If only for a short while.' She stepped round him and made her way towards the blacks.

Chester removed his tricorne to scratch the back of his close-cropped head. "Now what the devil did she mean by that?'

'I should ask her, old fellow,' Kit said. 'Whenever she can spare you a moment.'

'The devil,' Chester said. 'A month's bedding that gorgeous creature has changed your stride, by God.'

'By God, it has,' Kit agreed. 'And you'd do well to keep a civil tongue in your head, dear Edward, or be sure I shall twist it out for you.'

He followed his wife. By Christ, had that been Christopher Hilton speaking? By Christ, how Jean would laugh. If he still lived. Naught had been heard of that carefree buccaneer in a year. But Daniel Parke would also laugh, with sheer delight. And Agrippa? Or Lillan Christianssen? He checked, frowning. And then squared his shoulders, and walked on. Was he then to undertake his every action in fear or desire of approbation or criticism? There was only one person in the entire world that Kit Hilton needed to please, and that was no hardship.

'Stand back. Stand back.' The auctioneer was snapping at the men who had quickly gathered about the only lady in the room. 'Give Mrs Templeton space.'

Marguerite all but froze him with a stare. 'Mrs Hilton, Darring. And by God if you forget again you'll have no more of my business.'

'My apologies, Mrs Hilton. My apologies. I am such a thoughtless fellow. And the Captain is here as well. Good morning, Captain Hilton. Good morning to you.'

'And to you, Darring.' Kit leaned on his cane and watched Marguerite step up to the blacks.

'This fellow,' she said, regarding a large young man, who rolled his eyes as he gazed at what must have been the most splendid apparition he had ever seen. And then jerked as Marguerite poked him in the belly with her cane. But his breathing remained even. 'Your mouth, man, open your mouth,' she said, slapping him lightly on the cheek with the cane. His jaw dropped open, and he pulled back his lips to reveal a splendid set of teeth.

'He's a right buck, Mrs Hilton,' Darring said anxiously. 'You'll find no defects in him.'

'No doubt,' Marguerite agreed. But she intended to be sure for herself. The top of the cane lightly touched the man's penis, to jerk away at the first reaction. 'Aye. He seems fit enough. Now what of that woman?' She moved along the line, to repeat the careless yet knowledgeable examination, and Kit felt his belly roll some more. Suddenly the heat and the stench were oppressive. And he was no more than a spectator, here. Marguerite needed none of his assistance in choosing her slaves.

He walked to the back of the room, and thence on to the steps outside.

'Why, Kit,' Philip Warner said. The Deputy Governor had just arrived. 'Can you find nothing suitable?'

'I am afraid as yet I lack the experience to make a decision either way, sir,' Kit said. 'But Marguerite seems to find them much to her requirements.'

'Marguerite, here,' Philip cried. 'By God, that is good news. You'll excuse me.' He hurried through the door.

'Too much for your stomach, eh, Captain Hilton?' Dutton asked, dismounting from his horse and giving the reins to the slave who had ridden in with him. 'Aye, a slave auction is not the prettiest of occasions.'

The crowd outside the auction house had not diminished, and many were grinning. In sympathy or with contempt? But it would not have mattered which. Because how angry Kit was, on a sudden. With Dutton? Hardly. With Marguerite, for being able to treat other human beings, however inferior, as lumps of flesh? Or with himself, for loving her at all? For knowing that his love, allied to his ambition, would keep him at her side, always?

But Dutton was here, and Dutton had a considerable history of sly contempt as regards his new master, and Dutton was the man Marguerite had spoken of, in the carriage.

Kit swept his hand, up from the thigh, and backwards, slashing across the overseer's face, cutting his lip and bringing blood smarting to his chin, sending him reeling across

THE DEVIL'S OWN

the step and to the earth three feet below, with a jar which all but knocked the breath from his body.

His gasp was scarcely louder than that of the assembly. They gazed from the fallen man to Kit, and back again in utter consternation.

'You'd do best to keep a civil tongue in your head, Dutton, when addressing me in the future,' Kit said, and turned away. He walked up the street, in the direction of the harbour, and the ships, and the breeze, and the life for which he had been intended, and heard a sudden shout.

He stopped, and turned. Dutton had scrambled to his feet and pulled from its scabbard the double-barrelled blunderbuss which always rested by his saddle. Now he uttered a bellow of rage, and came down the dusty road, shouldering people apart, and none would make a move to stop him. This was overseer against master, but also planter, of however inferior a species, against buccaneer. And now the shouts and the noise had brought even more people on to the street, and filled the windows, and the doorway of the auction house itself. But for Kit there was only Dutton, slowing now, trying to control his breathing, the firearm thrust forward, the muzzle moving from side to side. There could be no mistaking his intention; his face was deep red, and his eyes stared.

'Roll me in the street, by God,' he said. 'Roll me in the street, you pirating bastard. You bitch's litter. I'll blow you into little bits.'

He was thirty feet away, feet braced as he brought up the blunderbuss. 'Or would you like to start running?' he invited.

It occurred to Kit that he was about to die. That he had no choice. To run from Dutton would mean the end of his life, as Christopher Hilton of Green Grove, just as much as if he stood here and took the charge. But to die, at this moment, when life was opening so entrancingly in front of him...

'Kit.'

He half turned his head. Agrippa stood on the side of the street not twenty feet away, and held a pistol. Now he tossed the weapon through the air in a gentle parabola. Kit leapt to one side, and the blunderbuss exploded. The noise was tremendous, and a stinging pain in his left arm told him that at least one of the pellets had struck home.

'Fight me, would you, scum,' Dutton shouted, turning

and sighting again, with his undischarged barrel looming large and round and deadly.

But Kit had reached the pistol, scooped it up, turned, and sighted all in a single movement, as he and Jean had practised so often in their youths. And as the pistol came into line with Dutton's body, long before the overseer could fire a second time, it had exploded. The bang of the blunderbuss followed half a second later, but Dutton was already dead and his muzzle was pointing aimlessly at the sky.

The sound of the three shots continued to echo over the houses, only slowly fading while an immense hush clamped on the street and the town itself.

Agrippa was first to speak. 'By Christ,' he said. 'You have lost none of your skill.'

'And yet it was a lucky shot,' Kit muttered, and looked at the blood trailing down his sleeve.

The crowd surged forward, to stand around the dead man and stare at him in horror, to gaze at Kit in wonderment.

'Did you see that?' they asked each other. 'A single shot, fired without a proper stance? Man, did you see that?'

Did you see that? Kit gazed over their heads at Lillan, standing on the steps of her father's house, staring at him with a stricken expression. But surely she had been looking from the start, and seen that he had fired in self-defence, that it had been his life or Dutton's, that Dutton had been out of his mind with anger. If she did not know these things, then must she be convinced of their truth.

He stepped towards her, and was checked by the voice behind him.

'Kit. Kit? Oh, my God, you are wounded.' Marguerite touched his arm, allowed the blood to dribble over her glove. 'We must have you back to the plantation.' She pulled the skirt of her gown up and ripped a length from her petticoat, while the onlookers gaped, and tied the linen round the wound. 'Oh, Kit, what a *man* you are.'

He looked down at her. 'I but obeyed your instructions. I had not expected it to go this far.'

Her head came up as she looked at him. 'I saw the shot,' she said. 'I reached the doorway as you fired. I have seen nothing like that in my life. No one on this island can have ever seen that.'

'And suppose I told you that it was no more than luck? I took no proper aim. I but wished to make him miss a second time, so that I could close with him.'

Her face broke into that unforgettable smile. 'You made him miss, Kit,' she said. 'You made him miss. By God, there will not be a man on this island will ever dare look you in the face again, unless invited. By God, Kit, but now I am the proudest woman on earth. Come, we will get you home and tend to that wound.'

The crowd was parting to let the carriage through, and a moment later he was inside and staring at them as they stared at him; Philip Warner stood on the steps of the auction house, Edward Chester at his side. They looked as if they had seen the devil himself. As perhaps they had. Certainly that had been the expression in Lillan's eyes. But when he looked to the Christianssens' house again, it was lost to sight as the carriage thundered out of town.

'Did you secure any of the blacks?' he asked. How desperate he was to return to normal. As if life could ever be normal again.

Marguerite continued to smile. 'I have left a bid on some twelve of them. Obviously I will not be at the auction.' She touched her lip in a gesture of impatience. 'I shall have to arrange Dutton's burial. I had all but forgotten in my concern over your wound. But your wound must be attended first. I will send Passmore to see to Dutton.'

'Will not the other overseers hate me for killing one of them?'

'Oh, indeed they shall,' she agreed. 'But if it is any comfort to you, you may be sure that they hated you before, for being set above them, as they have always hated me, for being their employer. There is not a planter in this island who is not heartily loathed by every white person of inferior station.'

'And now I have joined the minority,' he muttered.

'As you were always intended, by nature and by me, to do,' she said. 'I did not elect to fall in love with you entirely because I hoped and expected that you would fill my womb with eager joy, darling Kit. For near a year I had lived alone on Green Grove, the mistress of all I surveyed, and more, the daughter of the Deputy Governor, but a short ride away from all the succour I could possibly need, and yet I was daily growing more and more aware of my position, a mere woman amongst so many jealous and eager men. I noticed it in their gaze, in the manner with which they would appear at the house, uninvited and unexpected. And they all have wives, you know. But I could read their minds as if their very brains had been exposed to my gaze. Here is a lonely woman, they thought to themselves, young and beautiful and healthy, but none the less lonely and alone; surely she must soon seek to share her bed, and he who is available at the decisive moment may well find himself cock of the walk. And from such hopes and ambitions, Kit, there soon stem plans and plots.'

He stared at her. 'You *wanted* me to kill Dutton.'

'He was the worst of them, certainly. But he was not alone in his insolence. Believe me, Kit, I do not trade in violence. I abhor war, for the damage it can do. But I know enough of life to understand that one example, if properly carried out, may save a world of trouble.' She smiled at his frown. 'You find me too straight a woman, I sometimes think. You would prefer me to blush and dissemble and shrink away from manly talk and manly behaviour. But *would* you wish that, Kit? Could you repose so much confidence in me had you the slightest doubt as to my character?' She kissed her finger, and laid it on his lips. 'I doubt that, somehow.' And a moment later she was staring ahead of the carriage in a frown of irritation. 'Now what in the name of God troubles him? The news cannot have reached Green Grove already.'

For Passmore was whipping his horse towards them.

'Mrs Hilton,' he gasped. 'Thank God you elected to return early, madam . . .' he paused to pant.

'For God's sake,' Marguerite cried. 'We have had crisis enough for one day. What ails you, man?'

'Martha Louise, madam,' he gasped. 'Maurice Peter brought her to my attention, today. He did not know how to approach you, madam.'

'Martha Louise?' Marguerite frowned. 'You had best speak plain. She has been stealing?'

'No, madam. Not Martha Louise. She'd not do that, madam.'

'Then get to the point. God damn you,' Marguerite shouted.

'The marks, madam. She has come out in the stains.'

Marguerite stared at him, her brows slowly knitting, her mouth slowly clamping into a hard line. When she spoke her voice was low. 'Give rein, George Frederick. Give rein.'

'Yes, ma'am,' the black said, and scattered his whip across the horses' backs. The carriage jerked forward and rumbled down the road, throwing Kit and Marguerite back in their seats, while Passmore wheeled his horse and rode behind.

THE DEVIL'S OWN

'What did he mean, the stains?' Kit asked, when he had got his breath back.

'Isn't it strange how troubles never go in ones,' Marguerite mused. 'Stains on the skin. Discolouring of the flesh. It is the first sign of leprosy.'

Kit sat bolt upright. 'Leprosy?'

'Oh, do not be alarmed,' she said, a little irritably. 'It is a common enough occurrence amongst the blacks. I suspect they breed it in their filthy habits. But amongst one of my house servants . . . that has never happened before. And yet, her nose has been dribbling these past few weeks.'

'That is a symptom?'

'It can be. The marks are more positive.'

'What will you do?'

She tapped her chin with her forefinger. 'Have the entire place fumigated, you may be sure of that. And immediately. Believe me, Kit, there is naught for us to be alarmed about. No doubt the disease *can* afflict white people, but be sure that it is first of all necessary for them to exist in conditions which may breed the horror.'

'I meant, what will you do about the girl?'

'Martha Louise,' she said to herself. 'I like the girl. You know that, Kit?'

'I do. Can she not be cared for?'

She glanced at him. 'No. No, there is the terrible thing about leprosy. There is no cure, no treatment. Not even any alleviation of the condition. She must go across the water.'

'Across the water?' Kit asked. 'I do not understand.'

'Have you never wondered to what purpose I put that island of mine?' she asked. 'You should know that it is not in my nature to waste land, or labour.' She smiled. 'It is another manifestation of my peculiar methods which so upset my fellow planters. On any other estate Martha Louise would be taken to sea and thrown overboard with weights tied to her ankles. And then forgotten. I cannot bring myself so to destroy otherwise faithful servants whose only fault is the contraction of an unforeseeable horror. So I send them to the island.'

'Them?'

'I told you, it is a common enough complaint.' She sighed. 'Poor child, she will be upset.'

The carriage was hurtling through the gates, and a moment later it drew up in a cloud of dust before the main steps to the Great House. Marguerite got down without waiting to be assisted, and ran up the stairs, while Kit followed as quickly as he could, quite forgetting the sharp pain in his shoulder and the trickle of blood which had again started to course down his sleeve.

The house slaves were gathered in the dining-room, anxiously awaiting their mistress. They looked terrified.

'Where is she?' Marguerite demanded.

'In the pantry, ma'am,' Maurice Peter said.

Marguerite walked through the doorway without a moment's hesitation. Kit did hesitate, and then followed her. Martha Louise had been sitting on a straight chair, her shoulders bowed, but at the entrance of her mistress she sprang up. Her eyes were filled with tears, and her face about as woebegone as Kit had ever seen.

'Mistress . . .'

'Take off your chemise,' Marguerite commanded.

The girl obeyed, lifting the garment over her head and letting it drop to the floor behind her. Marguerite went closer. Kit remained just inside the doorway, staring at the thin body, aware that the rest of the servants were crowding behind him. Marguerite touched the girl's thigh, ran her gloved finger down the side of her leg. There was undoubtedly a discoloration on the dark flesh there, a slight roughness; and now that Kit looked more closely he could see that there were other, similar marks, one stretching from her right breast almost down to her navel, and another on her right leg.

Marguerite straightened. 'You will launch the boat, Maurice Peter.'

For a moment there was absolute silence, then Martha Louise uttered a most terrible wail. 'Aieeee. Mistress, I ain't sick, mistress. There ain't nothing wrong with me, mistress. I feeling well, mistress. I feeling better than ever, mistress.'

Marguerite stared at the girl for a moment, and then turned and left the room. 'Be sure you wear gloves, Maurice Peter.' She paused at the foot of the stairs to the upper floor, stripped off her own gloves, and dropped them on the floor. 'Burn those.' She commanded. 'And bring me a drink.'

'Sangaree, mistress?'

'Rum,' she said. 'Bring me a glass of rum.' She climbed the stairs.

Kit recollected himself and ran behind her, caught her in the doorway to their bedroom. 'Marguerite, I have just remembered. There is a disease to which the Negroes are subject, called the yaws, which also leads to a roughness of the skin, to a discoloration, but it is not fatal. Can we not wait, to see, if the girl has indeed got leprosy?'

Marguerite shrugged her arm free, and sat on the bed. 'No,' she said. 'I dare not take that risk. By sending her across the water now I may save the disease from spreading. What am I saying? I *will* save the disease from spreading. She may have the yaws, Kit. Then truly she is the least fortunate of humans. But I cannot take the risk.'

'Yet once she is sent to the island, she will certainly contract leprosy from the others there.'

'She will. So let us suppose she already suffers from that disease.'

He stared at her. 'Have you been there yourself?'

'We take them food and drink once a week. Most of them are too far gone to care for themselves. We leave the supplies on the beach. They know better than to approach us, but they stand at a distance and watch us, and ask after their relatives on the plantation.' Her head came up, and he saw that her eyes too were filled with tears. 'Have you ever seen a sufferer from leprosy, Kit?'

'No.'

'It is the most terrible thing you can imagine,' she whispered. 'They rot away. Literally, Kit. Their fingers and toes. Their noses. Their entire skin. And all the time the disease is at work within them, and they know that their vital organs are also just rotting away. Christ, my poor Martha Louise.'

'Yet you will not even have her put aside here for a week, to see if the blotches grow or fade,' he said.

Marguerite stood up. 'No,' she said. 'No, I will not. I said, I cannot take the risk. I cannot take the risk of infecting the rest of my slaves. I cannot take the risk of infecting my overseers and their families. I cannot take the risk of infecting you and me, my darling. But most of all I cannot take the risk of infecting my child.'

'Your . . .' his jaw sagged open.

'I would not have told you now, but for this,' she said. 'We have been married only a month, and I have not bled. So that perhaps is the least conclusive of tests, one month. Yet never have I missed even one month of my entire life before. And besides, I *know*. You have accomplished all that I could have asked of you, this month, Kit, beginning with our first coupling and reaching on to this morning, when you showed the world your mettle. No, no. I will risk none of that, Kit.'

7

The Choice

There was no breeze, and the smoke, belching from the chimney which dominated the Green Grove boiling house, rose into the air like a column, three hundred feet, before spreading itself, in layer after layer, until it obliterated the entire morning sky, hanging over the plantation, and the sea, and the leper colony, like some portent of inescapable doom.

But rather was it a portent of inescapable wealth. It was a sweet-smelling smoke, which titillated the nostrils as it filled the lungs. And beneath it, in the furnace that was Green Grove, the smell of boiling sugar-cane, and then boiling sugar, and then boiling molasses, filled the air, the mind, the body, even the soul. During the grinding season a normal diet was impossible; everything tasted sweet. But then during the grinding season nothing was normal.

Gone was the siesta considered so important to Europeans; even at two in the afternoon, when the sun ruled the heavens, the work went on. Although not even the sun, a Caribbean sun, huge and round and fiery and imperious, could penetrate the smoke blanket which covered the plantation. The sun could do no more than add its heat to the inferno below. Yet it was scarcely noticed.

The plantation looked as if the Spaniards had landed and carried fire and sword from one end of it to the next, saving only the houses in an act of unusual magnanimity. For before grinding the canefields must be burned, to remove the possibility of snakes or noxious insects. Thus over a month earlier had the great smoke clouds rolled across the compounds, and the brilliant white sheets became dotted with black wisps of ash, which dissolved into filthy smudges whenever touched. The house servants had been the first to find their work doubled, as they washed and scrubbed and cleaned.

The fires smouldering, the fields had been assaulted with knife and cutlass. Kit and Passmore had themselves led the van of the charge, while their slaves rolled behind like an army, shouting and cheering, marshalled by the remaining overseers, driven always by the ear-splitting crack of the whip, and followed by the squealing axles of the carts on to which the cut stalks must be placed.

Once this work had been properly commenced, Kit could leave it to Passmore and attend to the factory. For the previous six weeks this had been in preparation, with grease and polish, to take away the rust and the faults which would have accumulated during the growing season. Now it had been put to work. The selected slaves, great strong young fellows, had mounted the treadmill, the signal had been given, the whips had seared their backs, and the huge wheel had started its ponderous turn, rumbling as it did so, setting into motion the rollers and the crushers by a spindle and gearbox, to spread the creaking grind across the morning.

Then it had been time to light the fires. Special fuel had been stored for this purpose over the previous weeks, dried wood and straw. By now the first of Passmore's cartloads were already rumbling down the track from the canefields, heaped with cut stalks, already turning from green to yellow, still showing the scorch marks from the fire; the casualties, despatched from the battlefield, where the dreadful work of execution went on and on and on.

The carts were drawn by mules bred especially for this purpose, up to the raised ground behind the factory, where the giant shutes awaited. Here also there waited another regiment of slaves, controlled and marshalled by Allingham, the second overseer, and armed with spades and pitchforks. These dug into the cane stalks and tumbled them down the shute, smoothed to a treacherous perfection, into the first of the rollers, this one a system of interlocking iron teeth, which seized the cane and crackled it into firewood. This dreadful sound rose even above the whine of the treadmill and the gears, while every so often a stalk escaped, to fall over the side and arrest the process with an almost human scream of tortured metal. To discourage this were four picked hands, for time was not to be lost repairing machinery during grinding. Here was a dangerous job, and Kit could still remember, at his first grinding, the truly human scream which had followed the disappearance of old Charles

Arthur's hand and forearm, his fingers caught by the ceaselessly rolling drums.

That poor fellow had died from loss of blood and shock. But then, would he not have been disposed of as useless, anyway?

And soon forgotten, as the mangled cane was thrown out the far side, on to another shute, being forced through another set of rollers, these no more than drums, touching each other as they rotated, which seized the shattered stalks and compressed them, causing the first drops of the precious white liquid which would eventually be sugar to drip into the gutters beneath.

But still the cane's ordeal was unfinished, for there was yet another shute, and yet a third set of rollers to be negotiated, these so close and fine that their squealing creak against each other dominated all other sounds inside the factory. Here the last of the juice was squeezed free, and the stalks were left no more than wisps of useless wood.

Yet not so useless that they could still not be used. A sugar plantation produced its own fuel, its own energy, wherever possible. Beneath the last of the rollers was an immense pit, into which the stalks fell. But here again was a platoon of slaves with pitchforks and spades, for off the side of the pit there led a single channel, to the fires, and in this gully there were carts and sweating labourers. The stalks were loaded on to the carts, and carried along this surely accurate replica of hell to the great furnaces, and there consumed, for once the fires were started they would feed on anything combustible, even still-damp fibres.

This truly was the end of their journey, until they were belched forth to darken the sky as black smoke. But the juice had only just begun *its* travels. The gutters from beneath the rollers and crushers ran down to the vats, huge iron tubs set exactly over the never cooling furnaces beneath. Here the liquid bubbled and leapt, a witch's brew, constantly being combed through with nets at the end of long sticks held by the factory hands. Beyond were more gutters, more cauldrons, more furnaces, and not until Reed, the factory overseer, was satisfied was the cane juice allowed to flow off into the cooling vats. These were also set over a pit, and these had perforated bottoms. For as the liquid cooled, while the precious crystals would cling to the sides of the vats, the still molten molasses would slip through the sieves and into the fresh vats waiting beneath.

THE DEVIL'S OWN

The manufacture, storage, and bunging of the hogsheads was a separate industry in itself, employing another horde of slaves under the supervision of Webster, the carpenter. And always there were the book-keepers, commanded by their head, Burn, a dapper little fellow who wore spectacles, and was never to be discovered without a note pad in one hand and a pencil in the other, listing, evaluating, checking.

Nor was even the complete hogshead the end of the process, for the molasses in turn were drawn off down yet other gutters to yet other vats, and these were kept simmering, while the additives were carefully measured, for Green Grove, like every sugar plantation, manufactured its own rum. Here waited the chemist, Norton, a happy fellow who had to spend most of his day tasting the slowly fermenting liquid; there was more red in his nose than ever came from the sun.

But perhaps Norton was symptomatic of the whole, because, remarkably, grinding was a happy time. There was not a soul on the plantation, from Kit himself down to the smallest Negro boy or girl able to drag at the bagasse, who did not work harder in this month than throughout the rest of the year taken together. And yet, the change from the unending field labour, the making and mending of roads, the back-breaking weeding, the repairs to houses, was itself pleasant, and during the grinding season there was no daily punishment parade. The whips cracked ceaselessly, and the men and women worked until they dropped, but they knew better than to attempt any insubordination or obvious slackness, for the ships were coming, and would be in St John's on the appointed days to load, and the life of a slave, often valuable enough as part of the estate's assets, became trivial if set against any damage to the crop.

From the smallest, to Kit himself. He stood by the vats, gazing at the bubbling liquid, while the heat from the fires rose around him. Surely, when he went to hell, because planters no less than buccaneers must be destined for hell and he was now astride both professions, he would find it positively cool. And scarcely less demoniac. He would only hope that he found it no less exciting.

He found all of planting exciting. He wondered if, like Morgan, his people had really been farmers before politics and economics had driven them across the sea. The Warners had certainly farmed. So perhaps much of his happiness came from the obvious delight he could see on Marguerite's face, in her entire demeanour, as she watched the crop grow, as she inspected every little ratoon, the name given to the shoots cut from the older plants, which were in turn replanted to provide each successive crop. And then, the climax of grinding.

He watched her coming towards him. Was this the magnificent creature he had first loved on the hill in Tortuga, and in whose slender white arms he renewed his love night after night? She wore only a muslin gown, without a petticoat or a stocking, with no more than a single chemise beneath, and this was more sweat-soaked than the gown itself. They folded themselves together, and wrapped themselves around her legs and her thighs and her shoulders, clung to her breasts, left her all but naked to every gaze. Her hair was invisible, piled on top of her head and lost to sight beneath a bandanna which was itself concealed beneath the wide-brimmed straw hat, Yet sweat dribbled out from the kerchief, and furrowed its way down those smooth cheeks to hang from that pointed, determined chin.

Her fingers were black with dust and grease and dirt. Dirt smudged her face, streaked the skirt of her gown. But she laughed as she approached, and signalled George Frederick forward; if the house servants played no part in the actual grinding, it was their duty to care for their master and mistress. George Frederick carried the inevitable tray of iced sangaree, from which Marguerite now took two glasses, one to hand to her husband. 'The thousand,' she shouted above the grind of the machinery. 'Burn has totalled a thousand hogsheads. By Christ, but we have never reached the thousand before.'

He drank, and felt the chill liquid tracing every vein in his body. 'I promised.'

'And you deliver what you promise.' She stood close to him, put both arms around his naked waist, as filled with sweat as her own, and hugged him. 'Aye. That you do. Did I not love you, Kit. Did I hate the very ground on which you walk, then I would still be happy that I chose you to manage my estate. Every year, without exception, the crop has grown, and grown, and grown. But a thousand . . . if we add every plantation on this island together, I'd wager we shall not find that total. When Papa hears of this, he will go green.' Once again she hugged him. 'Come to the house. We shall celebrate.'

Which they did, often enough. It was part of their life, to find causes for celebration. Often enough, their mutual happiness embraced the entire island. For Marguerite, having spent four years as the wife of a man old enough to be her father, and another year as a widow, considered that she had very nearly been cheated of her true deserts as a woman. Now Green Grove Great House was often enough a blaze of light and laughter and music, and dancing and lovemaking and scandal, over which she presided with the conscious grace of being superior to everything she overlooked. And with an indulgent eye, as well, to every young woman, such as Mary Chester, a perennial flirt, who sidled up to Kit and invited his arms around her waist. There was no waist around which his arm would stay, save hers. She was the victor. She had claimed her prize on the first morning of their married life, and renewed her claim, day after day, week after week, month after month, year after year.

As a woman, she gratified his every whim, no doubt because whatever he desired appealed to her also. She revelled in his strength and his vitality and his enthusiasm; she loved to indulge in all aspects of her personality. Naked she would sit on his shoulders and make him carry her round their bedroom, her strong slender legs clinging to his neck. Daintily she would lie on his chest, her own body but a whisper against his own muscular frame, and squirm him into endless sexual endeavour. Arrogantly would she hold his arm as they descended the great staircase to greet their guests, or as they rode through St John's to a levee at the Ice House, or an auction at the slave warehouse. And primly would she sit at his side as he delivered judgement or offered an opinion. No one, least of all Kit, could doubt that she was Marguerite Hilton, the Lady of Green Grove. But beyond that, no one could doubt that she was, and content to be, Mrs Christopher Hilton.

And devotedly did she accept her pregnancies. And their results. Anthony had all but cost her life, or so it had seemed at the time, although Haines the surgeon had been content even when her cries had filled the house, and Kit, pacing the verandah, had gazed down on the anxious slaves, who without command from their master, had yet assembled at the foot of the hill.

Praying for her survival? Or praying for her death?

But Anthony was a fine, strapping boy, at eight able to fire a pistol and wield a sword to some effect.

'Is that your determination, then?' Marguerite chided. 'To make him into a soldier?' But always her criticism was softened by that unforgettable smile. 'I agree, dearest. A man should be a soldier first, and whatever else he chooses, after.'

And what of a woman, he wondered. But Rebecca was only four, separated from her brother by two miscarriages, each as disturbing as a full birth, each calculated to cause ill temper and disgust, and each, happily, forgotten with the passage of time.

So then, once he had dreamed, and perhaps, without intending or understanding, had even prayed. Once he had thought himself the most miserable and corrupt of men, the most bestial. No doubt, he was still, but if that was the case and he had sold his soul to the devil, then hell was a long time in coming to claim him, and the interval was sweeter than ever a man had known.

Yet retribution was there, always waiting. It had already overtaken those of Morgan's men who had sought to comb the beaches of Port Royal, much as it had overtaken Port Royal itself; he could remember the horror with which they had heard of the earthquake which had sent that city of sin to the bottom of the harbour he had known so well, and carried thousands of men and women with it. Jackman and Relain, and Morgan's corpse? Poor old Harry Morgan, who had died of cirrhosis of the liver almost as soon as he had taken up his post as Deputy Governor of Jamaica. Who could tell. It had not caught Tom Modyford, who had remained in England as a landed gentleman. And it had not yet caught Kit Hilton.

So, what do you think, Kit Hilton, he wondered, as he watched the smoke columns rise into the sky. Of the slaves, miserable fools, who would attempt to run away? Some of them. But then, he could pass on from those unhappy souls to the laughter of the couples in the mating compound, to the inexhaustible fascination of watching the sinuous black bodies coupling and sliding, one against the other. So reality returned in the walks through the sick house, in the occasional ghastly journey across the water. Never had he landed there; it was enough to back oars in the shallows and thrust the unfortunate black over the side. Always were the lepers gathered to wait for the new arrival. Strange people. He suspected that his own resort, on learning that he must literally rot before his own eyes, would be a spasm of madness followed by suicide. Yet these offered no sound, no sign of resentment and no attempts at violence. So perhaps the brain rotted first.

And always there was the escape, back up the hill, horse flogged at a furious gallop, for he rode as well as Marguerite now, to return to her arms, to the ice-cold glasses of sangaree, to the sound of her fingers running softly over the keys of her spinet, the lilt of her voice, for she sang quite beautifully, to the laughter of the children.

And where was the young man who had stormed up to Goodwood to challenge a governor, or who had boasted his ideals to Agrippa and Lillan Christianssen? Why, he had grown older, and there was all that need be said. He played cards with the Deputy Governor now, and they did no more than smile at each other's shortcomings, while again Marguerite played and Celestine Warner smiled at them all, and looked happier than for years. He rode into town with head held high, and should a face peer out at him from the warehouse, then he would raise his hat, were it a woman, and smile courteously enough should it be a man.

What would he do should the man come out of the doorway of the warehouse and greet him? Why, he would rein his horse and pass the time of day, pleasantly enough, congratulate him on his marriage—to which the Hiltons had been invited but which Marguerite had decided they should not attend—and ask after his family. A friend was a friend, no matter the colour of his skin. He had simply realized that the world went on its way, regardless of man's efforts, and that a man must do the best he can while the universe, and the affairs of the universe, went spinning around him. Slavery was a fact of life, and slavery operated on fear. All in all, as he had early discovered, there was less fear on Green Grove than on any other plantation in the island. In the Leewards. And going on Agrippa's own experience, in the entire Caribee Isles. A man who would attempt to tilt against the world, to stop it in its headlong career, or even to alter the course of that career, was a fool, or at the best an immature boy.

So then, was Agrippa a fool? And Lillan Christianssen? For there was the reason they seldom were at the windows to wave at him, and would never dream of speaking with him on the street. They counted him one of the plantocracy, and one could not be a planter and a Quaker at the same time. Not in this world.

But were they, in their goodness and the purity of their

ambitions, doing any more for the slaves than he was? He could take much of the credit for Green Grove's peace on his own shoulders. His overseers feared him as much as they feared their mistress, and for that reason were they less inclined to give rein to their own desires and their own rages. And the blacks could at least expect fairness; savage fairness should they transgress the laws laid down by their mistress and supported by the right arm of her husband, but none the less, the law applied to all. The transportation of Martha Louise across the water had proved that to them.

And how long ago was that? Nine years? Surely she was dead, by now. But none knew, who lived and who died across the water. And none dare ask.

Oh, indeed, the Hiltons had much to celebrate. But the best of all celebrations were those they enjoyed by themselves, with Anthony marshalling his tin soldiers in the centre of the drawing-room floor, with Henry Morgan always to the fore, but not yet the tallest and best set up of the models; that place was reserved for Captain Hilton, marching at his commander's elbow, while the rest followed behind, eternally and interminably assaulting the hassock which was Panama City. Amongst these others was Jean DuCasse. His was not an unfamiliar name, in the Leewards, as England and France had found a more fruitful war was to be fought between themselves. Now he commanded a buccaneer fleet himself, which only last year had ravaged the north coast of Jamaica. A successful raid, carried out with a fleet of five ships. Perhaps in time he would equal the fame of Morgan himself.

Kit wondered if Jean, careering around the Caribbean at the head of his veteran freebooters, ever spared a thought for the successful Antiguan planter, Kit Hilton, the man who had been with him at Panama?

On the far side of the room Rebecca played with her dolls, a strange collection, some home-made, bits of wool on the ends of sticks which represented arms and legs and bodies, others imported from Holland via the enormous warehouses of St Eustatius. She seldom joined her brother in his games; they fought whenever they intended to do anything together. But they were both happy and healthy children.

He wanted no more. He had his son and heir, to carry on the Hilton name, to inherit this magnificent house and these magnificent fields, and he had his daughter, to take after her mother, he hoped and prayed, and to be married, well—no doubt, an occasion to look forward to in the distant future. But another child, even another pregnancy, would rob him yet again of the comfort of that superb body which had so strangely come into his possession. For on these private celebratory occasions the group was completed by Marguerite and himself. They shared the settee, and watched their children. She wore her undressing-robe and lay back in his arms, while their glasses of sangaree stood waiting at their elbows.

Her head rested on his shoulder, and every time he breathed he inhaled her perfume. She would employ no wet nurse, and had brought both her children to their first birthdays without saving herself. Yet did her breasts remain swollen to his touch, and delicious to feel. Nor was there more than the slightest stretch marks on her belly, the slightest thickening of her thighs. And she was past thirty. He had had the very best of her. But surely there was so much more to come.

He squeezed, gently, and she nuzzled him with the back of her head. 'And are you, now, content, dearest?' she asked.

'Should a man ever be content?'

'No. Except on the day of his death, and few reach that climax with contentment in their hearts. But few men have accomplished so much as you, in these short years you have lived.'

'Flatterer.'

'My business is with facts. How else do I operate my plantation without being robbed by my own book-keepers? Shall I itemize your prowess? For let us not suppose that you began your career with even the normal drawbacks to which your name and fortune might have reduced you. In addition, you were left an orphan with no more than the clothes on your back and the brains in your head and the courage in your heart. Yet did you survive and prosper, command a squad of musketeers before Panama, and when that venture turned out badly, yet did you once again pick yourself up from the floor.'

'Not so simply,' he smiled. 'I was dragged from the floor, by our friend Daniel.'

'No friend, Kit,' she said, twisting her body to slide right down the settee beside him, so that her head lay on his lap and she could face him. 'Not that demon, believe me. He may be regarded as an instrument of fate, as an evil instrument, surely, but here accomplishing only good. And so you sought me once again. When I had almost despaired of waiting. And thus you came, and saw, and conquered. But even then were you not content. Now you have raised the efficiency and the accomplishments of my plantation. Now you bestride the narrow world of planting like the colossus you are. You have no more fields to conquer, where sugar-cane is concerned. Nor have you anything left to accomplish as regards my bed. You have made me the happiest woman in the world, and the most content. You have brought from my belly two splendidly healthy children. You thrill me with desire and with love and with admiration whenever I look upon you.'

'But yet you are not satisfied,' he suggested.

She frowned at him. 'What makes you say that?'

'Your tone, sweetheart. The suggestions that you are leaving something unsaid.'

She sat up, violently, her hair flying and her undressing-robe trembling. She seized his hands. 'Yes. Yes, my darling. Now I would have you take your talents and your courage to a wider field.'

'You are seeking another plantation?'

'Sometimes I wonder if you are deliberately dense, or if you merely seek to mock me. Listen to me, Kit. You are master of the richest plantation in this island. Nay, in the entire Leewards. Yet you have no say in the management of the island which protects you and from which you take your wealth. There is a dangerous imbalance. Listen to me,' she insisted as he would have kissed her. ' 'Tis not of you I speak. 'Tis of Green Grove itself. It is twenty years since the master of Green Grove took his seat in the Assembly. Poor Harry had no interest in politics, and besides, twenty years ago things were different. Harry, and my father, and his brother, made their way here despite politics, not because of them. They used to smile, in the old days, at the King's Commissioners, and agree with what they said, and then ignore them. Then when the King's head was cut off, and Ayscue's Commonwealth fleet ranged these waters, there was no choice but to smile once again, and rely on the fact that three thousand miles is a deal of salt water. Then, with the restoration, when the new King also sought to impose his iniquitous taxes on us, to lease us yet again to his court favourites, we were accomplished in the arts of dissembling.'

THE DEVIL'S OWN

'I had heard that the new lessor, Willoughby, came himself to manage his new estates.'

Marguerite smiled. 'He did, and found us rather more than he had bargained for. He settled in Barbados, and soon took to buccaneering, and disappeared at sea. No doubt he was drowned, although it suits certain parties to pretend that he may yet languish in a Spanish prison. Certain it is that he accomplished nothing for either good or evil in these parts. But then, then, Kit, politics began to hit home. The four and a half per cent tax, why, 'tis nothing while we prosper. Yet it is an iniquitous example of blatant despotism. The quarrel between King James and his people. That were bad enough. But now this infernal Dutchman has got us involved in a seemingly endless war with the French . . .'

'When I first came here, your uncle told me that our only friends in these islands were the Dutch.'

'Oh, indeed, the Dutch of Eustatius. Believe me, Kit, they abhor our forcible involvement in European politics no less than we. Our business is to make what profit we may. God knows in accomplishing that we receive no assistance from Europe. But they are quick enough to get their fingers into our money. And if their squabbling should mean that our plantations are burned and our profit lost, be sure that they will still want their taxes.' She paused for breath, her face flushed.

Now at last he could manage his kiss. 'It seems to me that it is *you* they require in the House.'

'Aye,' she said. 'I'd sing them a song. But, being men, they have turned the Assembly into a men's club, to which no woman can be admitted. There you have the saga of Green Grove. Harry would take no part in politics during the last ten years of his life, and I was barred by my sex. While these last ten years you have been concentrating, rightly, my love, believe me when I say that, on the plantation and on me. I would have you neglect neither of us. But it behoves me to spread your protecting, your encouraging, your advancing wings over a larger canvas.'

'The Assembly?' he wondered.

'The seat is yours, by right, Kit. Every owner of a plantation has a seat, by right.'

'I know that, sweetheart. My imagination was but failing at the thought of Kit Hilton, buccaneer and *matelot*, robber and rapist, pretending to Parliament.'

'Oh, what rubbish you do talk,' she cried, and slipped a

stage further, to her knees beside the couch, while Anthony and Rebecca abandoned their games to stare at their parents with wide eyes. 'Today you are only Kit Hilton, planter and gentleman. The past is the past. Only the present and the future is of importance. Say you will go, Kit. The House always sits as soon as the ships are loaded with the crop, and we all have more time to ourselves. Say you will go, my darling.'

Kit poured them each a glass of sangaree. 'Why,' he said, 'perhaps it is a secret ambition of mine, to strut a wider stage. Let us drink to the political career of Captain Christopher Hilton.'

* * *

The Negro majordomo, resplendent in dark blue coat over white breeches and white stockings, banged the floor four times with his staff, and the room fell silent. 'Captain Christopher Hilton.'

Kit stepped through the doorway, and stopped, and took a long breath. It had been Marguerite's idea that he should arrive late. 'For I know you too well,' she had said. 'Left to yourself you will sneak into the Assembly like a thief in the night. You must arrive as the master of Green Grove.'

He was simply enough dressed, in a plain blue broadcloth coat over buckskin trousers, and he wore no wig. He carried his black tricorne under his left arm, and was unarmed, apparently. But the right-hand pocket of his coat sagged beneath the weight of a loaded pistol. He was well enough aware that he had enemies, merely by being what he was, and he doubted that the next time someone elected to murder him Agrippa would be standing by.

And he had accomplished her desire. The ripple of whispering ran across the benches in front of him, uncomfortable looking things, but it was no part of the Assembly's plans to have its members falling asleep on a hot afternoon. Now the heads turned and the muttering commenced, while the speaker, John Trumbull of Plantation Paradise, peered at the newcomer. Nor was the disturbance confined to the chamber; in the gallery which looked down on it, and where the ladies were seated, together with such of the town merchants who conceived themselves interested in what was likely to happen to their island, there was a ripple of comment. There Marguerite had just taken her seat, and was smiling at him.

'Welcome, Captain Hilton,' Mr Trumbull said. 'It is too long since we have had the pleasure of the company of the master of Green Grove. Pray take a seat.'

'Here, Kit, here,' Edward Chester said, and Kit sat on the bench beside him.

'You may continue, Mr Harding,' Trumbull said.

The planter who had been speaking bowed towards the chair, and turned to face his fellows, and more particularly Kit. 'May I also,' he said, grasping the lapels of his coat, 'welcome the master of Green Grove to our midst. And indeed, sir, he could not have come at a more appropriate time. For be sure that Green Grove's future welfare is as much at stake as are any of ours, in this crisis. I repeat gentlemen, this war is no affair of ours. This . . . this Dutchman came to the throne by virtue of his being the husband of Queen Mary, God bless her soul. Thus the sanctity of the English crown, of the succession, of the divine right that governs the succession, was preserved. No doubt we feared then, and rightly, the consequences of this over-close identification of England with Europe. Traditionally have we stood apart from the endless quarrels which have destroyed all that is of value to that tortured continent. None of the devastation of the Thirty Years' War ever afflicted England's green and pleasant land. And no doubt the accession of Dutch William was necessary, to prevent the equal horrors of a religious conflict at home, which might in course of time have spread its destruction to these beautiful islands. But the Queen has now been dead these several years. That man has no legal or historical justification for remaining on the throne, for involving us further in his schemes.'

'Was he not elected?' someone asked.

'Bah,' Harding said. 'Kings are not elected, sir. We are not members of some savage tribe of antiquity. And even they preserved a proper sequence of events. How may a man be king, if the blood of kings does not run through his veins? If he has not been bred to it?'

'Yet is William surely a ruling prince in his own right,' Kit suggested. 'And indeed, is he not a member of the English royal house in his own right?'

Harding frowned at him. 'I was not aware, sir, that a knowledge of English domestic history was included in your many and dazzling accomplishments.'

'Yet is my friend entirely correct,' Chester said. 'His Majesty's mother was the Princess Mary, daughter of King

Charles the First. The Queen, God bless her memory, was his own first cousin.'

'That may be so,' Harding declared. 'But I have not heard it expressed as a principle of succession that the crown should pass to cousins. No, no. King James had proved himself an unlucky monarch, and England must have a monarch, so Dutch William was installed, as the consort of Queen Mary...'

'Not so, sir,' interrupted another voice. 'They were jointly installed, as equal authority on the throne.'

'Expedience, sir,' Harding shouted. 'Expedience. Then it was necessary, for the good of the realm. Now it is no longer necessary. But now we are fatally embroiled in a war with France.'

'Fatally, sir?' Chester inquired.

'Name me a Dutch victory, sir, in the last five years,' Harding demanded. 'This William prides himself upon extricating his armies, summer after summer, from the worst consequences of defeat. Yet are the defeats continual. But that, sir, is not the question we debate here today. England, Europe, are three thousand miles away. We are here, surrounded by perils enough, God knows. There is at this moment a French fleet rampaging through the Caribbean Sea. And it is not even a fleet of war. It is a fleet of buccaneers, commanded by the dreadful DuCasse. It will visit upon us the frightful calamities which Morgan was wont to inflict upon the Spaniards. We have all heard what happened in Jamaica. The graves were torn open and the very bodies of the dead violated. Common decency forbids me relating what happened to the living. Jamaica is not so very far from us here, and be sure, that when a French fleet appears off our shores, there will be no succour to be expected from St Kitts, divided as it is between the two nations. Why, I have heard that they already face each other along a line of entrenchments, but awaiting the first shot.'

'They have done that often enough,' a voice said.

'Aye, to their ruination,' Harding declared. 'But, sirs, the point I put to you now is this. We are, so we are told, part of England. We must pay taxes for the support of this abominable war, this abominable foreign government. We must transport our goods in English bottoms and none other. But, gentlemen, what do we receive in return?'

'Admiral Benbow,' said a voice.

'Benbow?' Harding demanded contemptuously. 'There is

indeed the measure of King William's regard for us. We appeal for a fleet and an admiral, and he sends us a few worm-eaten second-raters commanded by a man who has risen from the lower deck. A common seaman, by God, intended to protect cane-planters. Why, tell me this? Where was Benbow when DuCasse landed in Jamaica?'

'Out looking for the French,' someone said.

'Aye,' Harding said. 'Port Royal is the home of the English fleet, yet when the French land, they are away, looking for the French. There is an example of Benbow's genius. Think not of him as your protection, gentlemen.'

'There is the revenue frigate in St Kitts,' a voice said, and brought general laughter.

'Aye, the revenue frigate,' Harding said. 'Did not a respected member of our own assembly show that tub the strength in his teeth, the speed of his heels, when occasion demanded?'

There was a storm of applause, and Chester slapped Kit on the back. He frowned, and stared at the Speaker in confusion. He had not expected to be congratulated on his illegal activities in this body.

'Indeed that is so,' Mr Trumbull said. 'And it occurs to me, gentlemen, that this would be a good opportunity for Captain Hilton to give us the benefit of his experience. I have heard it said that you know DuCasse, Captain. There you are a measure more knowledgeable than us all.'

Kit stood up. 'Indeed, gentlemen,' he said. 'I have known Jean DuCasse since boyhood. We were *matelots*, in Hispaniola. We sailed with Morgan. Our paths only separated after the disbandment of that fleet. Jean elected to stay with the sea, I elected to take the path of planting and peace.'

'Well said, indeed, Captain,' Chester said. 'But what of this man you know so well? Is he the brilliant admiral, the devil incarnate, we are led to believe?'

'We were *matelots*,' Kit repeated. 'Without Jean DuCasse at my side, gentlemen, I would not have survived to be here today. He is a man of many parts, sirs. Give him a pistol and he will have your eye at twenty paces. Give him a cutlass and he will fight until you drop from weariness. Give him a ship, and yes, sirs, he will navigate her to safety. And give him a task, as he has now been given by his country, and gentlemen, he will carry it to a successful conclusion or die in the attempt. He is a born leader of men. That I can assure you without hesitation. But a devil incarnate? By no means. He is more of a gentleman than I would claim to be.'

'Yet are the atrocities in Jamaica attested by eye witnesses,' Harding insisted.

'No doubt the French were there assisted by their allies, the Caribs,' someone said.

'Perhaps Captain Hilton can tell us of these also,' Mr Trumbull remarked.

'To my knowledge, sir,' Kit said. 'I have never yet set eyes on a Carib.'

'Yet you have a Carib relative, at least by marriage,' a voice muttered.

Instantly there was uproar, with Trumbull banging on the desk with his gavel, and gentlemen shouting at each other from opposite sides of the room, and being assisted in their cacophony by their wives from the gallery.

'Order,' bellowed Mr Trumbull. 'Order. And gentlemen, I must ask you to be so good as to leave our Deputy Governor and his family from these debates. A man is not responsible for the excesses of his parents, unless he chooses to continue such excesses. Colonel Warner has shown us where his heart and his strength lies, time and again. It is here, in Antigua. He loathes and abhors the name of Indian Warner as much as any man present. I'd lay my life on that. Now I thank Captain Hilton for his exposition upon the talents and restraints of Monsieur DuCasse. I would but remind the gallant captain that a man can be considered only as good as the company he keeps, and in that regard we must anticipate in Monsieur DuCasse not only an enemy, but an enemy of a peculiarly vicious and bloodthirsty stamp. It behoves us, as responsible for the well-being and prosperity of our colony, to keep that thought ever-present in our minds, and to seek our best solution to the problem it presents. But emotions are running too high today for a continuance of this debate. The House is adjourned until tomorrow week.'

The planters rose as he left the chair and joined them on the floor, and now the doors were thrown open, and the laides were permitted to descend.

'That was a splendid opening to your career in the Assembly, Kit,' Chester declared. 'Was he not splendid, Mary?'

Mary Chester put up her cheek for Kit to kiss. 'Indeed you were, Kit. You looked so handsome, standing there. Why, I was more than ever jealous of Marguerite.'

Marguerite smiled at her, benevolently. 'Sometimes I am

even jealous of myself, my sweet child.' She held Kit's arm. 'But you were the most handsome and the most authoritative man there, Kit. While they have spent their lives in talk, you have spent your life in action. You are a natural leader, just as you claimed that French boy to be. And I take odds with you on that point. I met them both together, you know, Edward. And even then Kit was the leader. Monsieur DuCasse but trailed behind to pick up the pieces. I will not pretend that at the time I appreciated my husband at his true worth, but I was only a girl.' She laughed, and squeezed his arm. Yet her eyes were uncommonly serious. 'Would you not say that he is a natural leader, Edward?'

Chester frowned at her, and then glanced at Kit, and smiled. 'Why, you may well be right, my sweet. For depend upon it, when we need a leader, we shall truly need a leader.'

'My own thoughts entirely,' Marguerite agreed. 'Now we must hurry off to Goodwood for lunch. Papa will be anxious to hear how Kit got on.' She led him from the chamber and down the steps, to where George Frederick waited with the carriage, on the edge of a crowd of onlookers. 'Why so serious, after such a triumph, my darling?'

Kit sat beside her. 'I had forgot the history which surrounds your family.'

'And does the presence of a skeleton in my closet now disturb you?'

'Not in the least. I but wish to know where I must stand, if I am to be at your shoulder.'

Marguerite's eyes glinted. 'Just hate the very name of Indian Warner, Kit.'

'Have you ever met him?'

'I saw him once, as a child. And I knew him then for an evil thing. He was my grandfather's bastard, Kit. There is an apt description. And after old Sir Thomas died, Papa tried to make the boy into a human being, and failed. With his Indian mother he fled back to the forest of Dominica, where they belonged. Yet were they not allowed to disappear into eternity. The French sought them out, and ever anxious to make capital of dissensions amongst the English, appointed him Governor of Dominica, as if Dominica was theirs to govern. There you have the sorry tale. Be sure that should he ever re-enter our lives Papa will hang him higher than Haman, and with much less ado.'

'Who knows,' Kit mused. 'Perhaps he is already dead, and your fears are groundless.'

'He is not dead,' she said. 'We would have heard of *that* good fortune. Nor do I have fears. Have I not you at my side?' She seized his hand. 'I am so proud of you, my darling. Your first day in the House, and you left them in no doubts as to the part you would play.'

'I fail to understand your enthusiasm. I did no more than make a point of accuracy, during Harding's diatribe. And then I answered a question put to me by the Speaker.'

'Ah, but it is the way you did both those things, your confidence and assurance, your very appearance, both as you entered the room and as you stood there, that impressed us all, my darling. They knew a man had come amongst them. They will not forget that. And yet, I think you were a trifle inhibited, by my presence, no doubt. I shall not attend the House again. I shall leave it to others to bring me news of your prowess. I will say only this to you, Kit; there are great things afoot, and men, once embarked upon large and perilous ventures, need talented and courageous captains. You are such a man, and today they recognized that. I would but ask you to keep that fact in mind.'

George Frederick had cracked his whip, and the carriage was moving forward. Kit looked through the window, beyond the crowd, at the warehouse. At the top of the steps Lillan Christianssen stood beside Agrippa and his wife. Many in the crowd waved and cheered at the master and mistress of Green Grove. But not that trio.

'A victory.' Harding waved the piece of paper. 'So it is described. Dutch William has recaptured the fortress of Namur. This is his crowning achievement, gentlemen, after near ten years of war.'

The house broke into a storm of cheering and shouting, stamping on the floor.

'Aye,' Harding said, striding up and down. 'You may well celebrate, this night. But I would ask you this, my friends. What are we celebrating? Had not the war all but ground to a halt? Was there not talk of peace between England and France? Are not negotiations always liable to be lengthy, where such a conflict must be ended? Not so, says Dutch William. The French are tardy, so I will once again take the field. And by God, I will win a victory. Because they are not looking. They are thinking only of peace. So think well, as you raise your glasses. This is the victor of Glencoe you are toasting. This is the man who would bring ruin upon all our heads. For mark my words, gentlemen, Louis will now be tearing up his projected offers and proffers. He will not suffer Namur to be wrenched from his hands, treacherously. I see no end to this war. I see only disaster staring us in the face.'

'Surely you are speaking treason,' Chester said quietly.

Harding rounded on him. 'Do you accuse me of that, sir?'

'By no means,' Chester said. 'I merely point out how your words might be construed, should they reach English ears.'

'Aye,' Harding said. 'And so they would. But I speak for Antiguan ears. You have all been so dumbfounded by this remarkable news, this unexpected blessing, this resounding victory so splendidly gained by our noble monarch, that you have omitted to look further. I did, gentlemen. I spoke with the captain of the *Southern Queen*. Because he had a tale to tell. Of five ships he sighted but three days ago when becalmed off Barbuda. Ships steering south of St Kitts, reconnoitring these waters, he estimated. Five ships, gentlemen. There is a number to conjure with. Do we possess five ships? Perhaps there are five, recently loaded with sugar, but leaving St John's on the day they were laden. Does Sir William Stapleton command five ships? We all know of his motheaten frigate. Could it be Benbow? Oh, happy day. But would Benbow sail the Leewards without visiting St John's, without making his presence known? But yet the number is familiar. I seem to remember that when Monsieur DuCasse made his raid on Jamaica, it was with five ships.'

He paused, gazed at the consternation in their faces.

'Five ships,' he said again, after a moment. 'In the Leewards, and at this time. Because, as Captain Hilton has told us, this is no ignorant seaman we deal with. This is a man of intelligence, an intelligence, I would swear, far surpassing that of Morgan. Morgan sought only gold, gentlemen, and counted himself a patriot because he took it from the Dons. DuCasse is also a patriot, and seeks to harm England, not enrich himself. Suppose he had landed here two months ago, gentlemen, and burned our canefields? Would we have wept? Or would we have laughed at his ignorance, at his kindness, in saving us the labour of doing it ourselves? For then the cane was ripe. But now, gentlemen, now. Supposing Monsieur DuCasse lands here next week, or even next month, and supposing we defeat him, so that he is enabled only to set fire to our cane? Our young shoots, gentlemen, from around which our slaves gather the weeds every day of the week, just to preserve those infinitely valuable lives. Where is our prosperity then? Where is the future of this island, then? Where is the inheritance we choose to leave our sons and daughters, then? And this is supposing that we defeat the French. But now, let us consider with what shall we defeat them? With the garrison in St John's? A hundred men on the muster roll, of whom at least thirty are ever sick? Our overseers? A pack of mutinous dogs. Our slaves? Who wait only to get their black fingers at our own throats? Think on that, gentlemen.'

Once again he paused, to enjoy their expressions.

'But what remedy have we?' asked a voice. 'If the captain of the *Southern Queen* saw DuCasse's fleet already in these waters, may we not expect an assault any day?'

'Aye,' said another. 'We must place ourselves in the best condition of defence we may. Perhaps Captain Hilton would advise us on this matter also.'

'Willingly,' Kit said. 'It would seem to me that the obvious way to discourage these pirates, because however patriotic, they are no more than pirates, would be to prevent their landing at all.'

'And how do you do that, pray?' demanded Harding. 'There are fifty odd miles of coastline to be defended. Would you create earthworks along the entire beach? It would take you years, and the threat is present now.'

'I agree with you entirely, sir,' Kit said. 'So let us take a lesson from history. Was not King Alfred confronted with the same problem, seven hundred years ago? He had no fleet, but was assailed by one. His solution was a band of mounted warriors, always at the ready, able to gather in haste wherever the Vikings were seen making for the shore. Now, gentlemen, he had all southern England to defend. We have but Antigua. And we certainly have the horses, and the men.'

'By God, sir,' said Mr Trumbull. 'That is a brilliant suggestion.'

'Brilliant?' Harding shouted. 'It is the suggestion, indeed, of a man who knows nothing but warfare and fighting. And believe me, gentlemen, I am grateful to have so distinguished a warrior in our midst, should we ever need him. But my contention is that we do not need him in this present crisis. Because it is not *our* crisis. It is none of our making, and indeed, we hate the thought of it. It can reflect no profit on us, either in money or in fame. On the contrary, it can bring only disaster. We are being dragooned, gentlemen, into a quarrel in which we can only lose, as we have been so often dragooned in the past. I say that we should have none of it.'

'And like an ostrich, bury our heads in the sand while Du-Casse does his worst to our backsides?' Chester inquired.

'I'll take no offence today, Edward,' Harding said. 'The matter is too grave for levity. It is to preserve your miserable backside, aye, and that of your pretty little wife, that I am speaking. Gentlemen, listen to me, I beg of you. We receive no good of England, neither succour, nor credit, nor compliments. The sole result of our being English is to suffer for it. But are we, then, English? Are we not prouder to describe ourselves as Antiguans? Hear me out,' he bellowed, as the hubbub rose. 'What are you afraid of? The truth? Our future lies in this island and this island alone. Be sure the Dutch in St Eustatius will never let us down. They need us, and they hate their own government in Amsterdam, as much as we need them and hate those stuffed-up prigs in Whitehall. The future can bring us only disaster if we remain tied to Dutch William's apron-strings, and even if he is succeeded by the Princess Anne, as is the present intention, then think back on this, gentlemen, did the rule of the Stuarts bring us any prosperity? Or is it not a fact that most of our fathers and grandfathers came to these islands to escape those very fickle Scots?'

'By God, but you are changeable,' Kit said. 'A week ago you were defending their divine right.'

'No inconsistency in that, sir,' Harding insisted. 'I believe they do have a divine right, to the throne of England. We are under no divine command to remain in England to be ruled by them. That is why we are here, sir. I say have done with it. Now, while we may.'

The planters stared at him, and at each other, and at the Speaker. But already there was a hum of whispering, and it had spread to the gallery. By this evening, Kit realized, it would be all over the island.

'And pray, sir,' Chester said, 'supposing we all followed your suggestion, which I assume is to declare ourselves the free and sovereign state of Antigua, how then would we save ourselves from the French? Would we not be even more vulnerable? Would they even know of our decision?'

'They'd do that quick enough,' Harding said. 'We would immediately inform Sir William Stapleton that we no longer recognize him as our governor, and be sure the news would spread to French ground soon enough.'

'And then, by God, we could raise that mounted force of which Captain Hilton spoke,' someone said. ' 'Tis a fact that the buccaneers, if actuated by a desire for profit, will bite on no hard nut, and if forced on by patriotism, would far rather pass us by should we declare ourselves free of England.'

'By God,' Kit said. 'By God.' He got to his feet. 'That I should sit here in an English Assembly, in a gathering of men of repute, and hear such unmitigated treason. By God, sir, had I that troop of horse of which we spoke earlier at my back, my very first act would be to place you under arrest.'

'Treason?' Harding shouted. 'Why, sir, you seek a quarrel.'

'Oh, aye,' Kit said. 'I seek a quarrel, John Harding. You may be sure of that. I'll quarrel with any man who preaches treason.'

'Yet are we not already guilty of treason, Kit,' Chester murmured, 'in acknowledging Dutch William at all? 'Tis a specious point to be sure. Is a man required to give his unflinching loyalty to his country, or to the man who happens to sit on the throne at the moment? The latter were an easy sop to the conscience.'

'You, Edward?' Kit demanded. 'Of all people, you? We accepted William and Mary, when they came to the throne . . .'

'Were we asked to accept them, sir?' Harding demanded. 'No, no, we were informed of the event, in the course of time.'

'Yet has it been sanctified by time,' Kit insisted. 'You'll withdraw your suggestion, sir, or be sure I'll call you to account.'

A hush fell on the chamber. Harding stared at Kit, his gaze flickering down to the right arm which hovered by the weighted pocket.

'By God, sir,' he said at last. 'Fight you? A professional murderer? When I duel, sir, it is with a gentleman.'

'By God,' Kit shouted. 'You'll . . .'

The sound of the gavel battered on his words. 'Gentlemen, gentlemen,' called Mr Trumbull. 'This business has gone far enough. The house is adjourned. We'll let these tempers cool a while, and resume the debate in a more rational atmosphere.'

Kit turned his stare from Harding to the Speaker, then

crammed his hat on his head and marched from the chamber.

To encounter Marguerite on the stairs. 'Why, sweetheart,' he said. 'I had no idea that you would be here today. You said . . .'

'That I would no longer attend,' she said, speaking quietly, but he frowned as he saw the anger in her eyes. It was an expression he had not witnessed in a very long time. 'I did not wish to inhibit you, Kit. But it seems I made a mistake.'

'You . . . did you not hear what that man was proposing? What do you think your father, as Deputy Governor, would have said?'

'Oh, you fool, Kit. You fool. You see life going on its way all around you, and you have not the wit to understand it. Papa hates England more than John Harding. But he is not important this day. It is you. You had them at your feet, but a week ago. They would have followed your lead, willingly, given a few more hours of such straight talking, such authority. Did you know that Trumbull retires from his post within the year? Did you not realize that this was the reason I was so anxious for you to take your seat? Speaker of the Antigua House of Assembly. There is no more important post in the entire Caribee Isles. Perhaps in the world.'

He frowned at her. 'You planned that, for me?'

'Of course I did. Does not every wife wish for her husband to aspire to the very summit? But now . . . yet it can be done, still. A reappraisal of the situation . . .'

'Madam, you disgust me,' Kit said. 'Reappraisal? You have scant knowledge of your husband if you suppose I would change my tune for a position. You have scant knowledge of my ambitions if you think I would seek to lead a pack of traitors. And you have scant knowledge of the world if you think this little rock is of the slightest importance to anyone who does not live on it.'

Her turn to stare. No doubt it was the first time in her life she had been so addressed, at least since that fateful day on the hill-top in Tortuga. Pin-points of rage gathered in the centres of the green eyes. Yet was she still perfectly controlled, aware that the usual crowd had gathered in, the planters at the top of the steps, the hangers-on at the foot. Here was a ripe source of scandal, for many a long day.

Marguerite smiled. 'You are angry, my darling,' she said softly, 'and upset. Come on back to Green Grove, and we shall discuss the matter further over a jug of sangaree. I had forgot the speed and vehemence of your temper, darling Kit.' She had raised her arm while she spoke, and already the crowd was parting to allow George Frederick to bring the carriage to the foot of the steps.

'I'll come to Green Grove,' Kit said, 'when my belly feels the urge.'

He turned away and went down the steps. People stepped aside, and he walked down the street. Where? He neither knew nor cared. He felt the whole world was swirling about his head. On what a senseless, silly issue. Did he care whether Antigua was independent or a part of England? What hold had England on him? Was not every word that John Harding had spoken absolutely true?

And did he not, through Marguerite, have a greater stake in this island than any other man there today?

Through Marguerite.

And what a stake. He found himself standing on the dock, gazing at the almost empty harbour. Two weeks ago all had been hustle and bustle here, as the last of the sugar ships had been loaded. Now the port was again sleepy. God, to be at sea. What had Marguerite promised him, once? The biggest, the finest ship that could be built. He should have taken that. But would she have come with him? Perhaps not. Perhaps it would have been better had she not. At sea men were free. All men, regardless of the colour of their skins.

So then, he was a good deal of a hypocrite. But he had known this for a very long time. He hated slavery. He hated it from the first and he hated it still. He pretended that he led his blacks as a general might command his army, but yet was the lash in constant use, and worse. He would take part in this life, because of the wealth and the power and the admiration and the love it brought him, but he would not put his seal on the decision that it was better than any other life, better than the freedom so hardly gained in England, better than the world, that Antigua was the world. To do that would be to condemn himself to being one of them.

And was he not already, one of them?

'They say,' Agrippa remarked, 'that no man can ever fight his true nature for all of his life. But that hot tongue of yours will get you into trouble, one day, Kit. Unless it has already done so.'

Kit half turned his head. 'Were you there?'

'I am a typical St John's layabout,' Agrippa pointed out.

'I always attend the Assembly. It is like being present on Olympus at a gathering of the gods.'

'It is a relief to discover that at least one person on this island can regard our proceedings as a joke.'

'I hope to be laughing the day I die, too. You are invited to dinner.'

Now Kit did turn. 'By you?'

'By Dag Christianssen. If you are not above accepting the hospitality of a Quaker.'

Kit frowned at him. 'And he is not below inviting a planter to his table?'

Agrippa grinned. 'We both figure you put on a suit of clothes, Kit. Clothes are easy. You can always take them off.'

'For which, Lord, we humbly thank thee.' Dag raised his head, smiled at his guest. 'You'll finish the bottle, Kit.'

'Why, I . . .' Kit looked the length of the table, to where Astrid Christianssen also smiled at him. 'It is strange, to be drinking alone.'

'Why so?' Astrid asked. 'If you like the taste, and the quality.'

'The taste and the quality are delicious. The meal was delicious.' His gaze drifted across to Lillan, sitting opposite; her hair was loose and she wore a simple grey gown, as shapeless as ever. He had not spoken to her in nine years. Then she had been seventeen. Now she would be twenty-six, a tall, handsome, grave young woman. 'I really do not know how to thank you all.'

You all. Agrippa sat next to Lillan, and Abigail sat next to himself. She was a plump, pretty girl, very dark-skinned, and looking more so in her white dress. She was a true Negress, as opposed to the many northern tribes included in the generic term by the planters. There was memory from the past. Sitting down to dinner with a Negro and his wife. Sitting down to dinner with a friend.

'You may pay for your dinner, Kit,' Dag said. 'By telling us whether you feel we are really in imminent danger of a French invasion.'

'I'm afraid I believe we are,' Kit said.

'Oh, no,' Astrid cried. 'But what must we do?'

'I'm afraid we will have to fight them,' Kit said. 'They are, as we are constantly reminded, no more than buccaneers, not soldiers. Any Great House, properly defended, will be discouraging to them. If you will remember their raid on

Jamaica, the only plantations which fell were those which were surrendered or abandoned. As for St John's, I do not think they would even consider an assault.'

'Right,' Dag said, half to himself. And sighed. 'No doubt you are right.'

'But you would not contradict your beliefs, old friend. Nor should you. On the unlikely mischance that a Frenchman should break in here, you may safely leave your life in the care of Agrippa, surely.'

'I pray it will not come to that,' the Negro said.

Dag smiled at Kit's astonishment. 'Agrippa thinks as we do, now. And Abigail.'

'By God.' Kit scratched his head. 'You'll forgive me. I had not supposed Christianity was of interest to you.'

'Nor was it,' Agrippa acknowledged. 'Until Dag got to talking.'

Kit picked up Abigail's left hand; she wore a thin gold band. 'And you also?'

She smiled at him. 'You got for . . . I'm sorry, Agrippa spends so much time making me speak good English. You have to thank Dag for that too.'

'I wish you would tell me how it came about.'

'He purchased my freedom, Captin. You could say he bought me. I belong to him, double.'

'And you've children?'

'No, Kit,' Agrippa said. 'I'd not wish a child on this world unless his skin could be as white as snow.'

Astrid gave a nervous smile. 'Or perhaps until the world changes for the better, he means, Kit. It must.'

'Aye,' Kit said. 'But I'd have thought yours was not a Christian concept, Agrippa.'

'I am new to the religion, Kit. Would you describe planting in Antigua as a Christian profession?'

'You'll not quarrel at my table,' Dag said.

'I'll not quarrel with Agrippa under any circumstances, Dag. But our conversation leads me to wonder why you have not tried your persuasive tongue on more of the Negroes.'

'Would that I could, Kit. But I have been expelled from too many plantations in my efforts to do so.'

'I fail to see why, You can hardly be accused of preaching sedition.'

'Oh, but I am. You cannot enslave the body of a man, efficiently, unless you also enslave his soul. It is impossible to be a Christian, and not believe in the eternal freedom of your soul. Therefore it is impossible to be a slave and Christian at the same time. Logic.'

'Yes,' Kit said. 'You are all too deep for me. I can only say that you have not attempted to preach on Green Grove.'

Dag smiled, sadly. 'And what do you suppose would be the reaction of your wife to that, Kit?'

Kit gazed at him for several seconds.

'I must see if I can find you a horse,' Agrippa said.

'At this late hour?' Dag demanded. 'You'll spend the night here, Kit.'

'Of course you will, Kit,' Astrid insisted. 'We shall be pleased. Unless you feel your wife will be worried.'

'To say truth,' Kit admitted, 'Marguerite is not at the moment very pleased with me. She sympathizes more with the point of view of Mr Harding than I supposed.'

Dag smiled at him. 'Then perhaps it would be as well not to return until tomorrow. Time is the great healer in family differences. They are infinitely preferable to quarrels and harsh words, or harsher deeds, which may be regretted.'

'Yet must we not interfere between husband and wife, Astrid said. 'Believe me, Kit, we should be more than happy to offer you a bed. But only if you feel it would be best.'

Kit scratched his head again, and found himself staring at Lillan. He had drunk the entire bottle of wine himself, and he had drunk it while still in a state of some agitation. The room was swaying unevenly, and he had an erection. He was angry with Marguerite and with himself. He had wanted to fight Harding. Instead he had all but quarrelled with his oldest friends. His only friends. Now he wanted . . . what?

And Lillan had taken no part in the discussion, either for her religion or against the planters. And now, having met his eyes for only an instant, she lowered her head to stare at the plate.

'No doubt Dag is right,' he heard himself saying, 'Marguerite's rages seldom last very long.'

'Then it is settled,' Dag said. 'And the hour is late. I am sure we shall all be better for a good night's sleep. Lillan, you'll make up a bed on the floor of the office, and sleep there. Kit, you can have Lillan's bed.'

'I could not possibly evict Lillan,' Kit protested.

'You may have our bed, Kit,' Agrippa said. 'If it does not concern you.'

'Now why should it do that?' Kit demanded.

'Gentlemen,' Dag said. 'This happens to be my house, and you will surely allow me to make the arrangements within it. I am sure Lillan has no objection to sleeping in the office, Kit.'

'I should be delighted to offer Kit the use of my bed,' Lillan said.

'Then you will show him up,' Astrid said. 'Dag, you and Kit are much of a size. No doubt you can discover a nightshirt to fit him.'

'That I shall.' Dag left the table, bustled towards the back of the house. Kit stood up, found Agrippa looking at him.

'Sleep well, Kit,' the Negro said. 'And sound.'

'I usually do.'

Lillan had already gone up the steps, and waited for him there.

'I'll say good night, Astrid.'

'It is our great pleasure to have you under our roof once again, Kit,' Astrid said. 'I hope, in the future, that you will not only seek to visit us in times of crisis.'

'Be sure that I shall not.' He climbed the stairs, watching the gown moving in front of him, obscured in the gloom, for she carried the candle. 'Your parents are uncommonly kind.'

'I think they look on you as the son they never had.' She opened the door on the landing. ' 'Tis a small room, and uncommonly untidy.'

He stood in the doorway beside her, and his arm brushed hers. Here was no magnificently scented rush of air as with Marguerite, but a subtle quality of freshness, such as he had not known in a very long time. But he had known it once. In Panama City.

'I wish you would allow me to sleep downstairs,' he said. 'It is not right.'

'You are our guest.' She moved forward, lifted the pillow on the pallet bed, and took out a wisp of white. Then she placed the candle in the holder. 'It is also a somewhat hard bed.'

'I am tired enough to sleep on anything.' He stood beside her again. I want you, his mind said. I wanted you years ago, and then my wanting was overwhelmed by my desire for Marguerite. Now . . . was it just the anger talking? The anger and the wine? The desire to spite Marguerite? But was that not the reason he was here at all? Come down to it, was that not the reason he had been invited? Antigua was cleaving down the centre, and Kit Hilton was a catch, for the common party. Could they but hold him. If that were so, then why should he spare them a thought of gratitude, of concern? This night he wanted a soft, fresh, unexpected home for his weapon. His body demanded it. And here it was, in front of him.

God curse the invention of wine.

'I will wish you good night,' she said, and made to step round him. His left arm moved, and she stopped, his hand just brushing her thigh. 'Why, Papa,' she said, 'you have found a clean nightshirt after all.'

'It is old, and mere linen,' Dag confessed. 'Yet will it cover your nakedness, Kit.'

He took the garment. 'And I am again grateful. If I can ever repay this kindness, you have but to ask.'

'Debts, repayments, are for enemies, Kit,' Dag said. 'A friend is just happy to help a friend. Now we shall bid you good night.'

He changed his clothes, put on the borrowed nightshirt, blew out the candle, and lay on the bed. What torture. It also smelt of her, and wherever he moved, whenever he turned from side to side, his body touched sheets which only twelve hours before had brushed against her. Yet surely would he soon be asleep, and awake, sober and controlled, once again.

He settled on his back, staring at the darkened ceiling, listening to the creaking of the stairs outside as the Christianssens mounted to their bedroom. What did Quakers do, in bed, together? Was there an abandonment of humanity, a realization of the joys of being animals, such as existed between Marguerite and himself? Such as had existed. And would again. Today she was angry. She was ambitious. And because she was a woman, she could never realize her ambitions in herself, and so desired them for her husband. What cruelty, what a waste of talent, was caused by the historical conception that women were inferior. What a magnificent Speaker of the House would Marguerite make. And had she not already proved herself without an equal at that most masculine of tasks, plantation management?

But was she not also the possessor of that most feminine of attributes, an imperious, unforgiving rage? Which was now no doubt in full flow.

So then, was he afraid of her? He sat up. By God, why

should he be? He was her husband. She belonged to him. To his bed, whenever he chose to summon her. To his will, whenever he chose to make it known. To his hand, if he chose to inflict it upon her. By God, and he had run away from her this morning. As she had herself pointed out, time and again, he was unable to recognize his true stature, his true place in the world. But she knew it. Then she could expect nothing less than to feel the weight of his anger. And soon.

He stood up, found himself swaying, and steadied himself against the wall. He had no tinder, and could not relight the candle; he found his clothes by feeling towards the chair where he had left them. Yet was he making too much noise. He scooped them under his arm, opened the door, and blinked. Out here was much lighter; there was a full moon, shining through the skylight at the top of the stairs. And reaching all the way down to the foot. This was safer. His last sway had all but set him tumbling downwards.

He descended the stairs, cautiously, hugging his clothes to his chest, grasping the rail with his left hand, and saw Lillan, standing below him.

'Kit?' she whispered.

'Oh, Christ,' he muttered. 'Oh, Christ.'

'I heard you move,' she said. 'The office is beneath my room. Is something the matter?'

He reached the floor, and could pause for breath. But surely this was a mistake. A sway of less than a foot to his left would carry him against her. 'I want to go home,' he said.

'Now?'

'I must...'

'You did not feel that way earlier, Kit.'

'Then the wine spoke for me.'

'As it is doing now,' she said severely. 'But in a different voice. I doubt you could sit a horse the distance.' And then her face broke into a smile, so relieving when set against her normal solemnity. 'And you have none, unless you will take Papa's mule. Then will you ride until this hour tomorrow.'

He leaned against the wall, gazing at her. The moon shone full on her nightdress. Not through it, certainly. Her body was a dark shadow. Yet it was there.

'I must go,' he said. 'And so must you. Back to bed. You do not know me, Lillan. You do not know of my crimes.'

'I know you well enough,' she said. 'I know the goodness in you, Kit, which you are constantly trying to bury beneath some assumed characteristic of villainy. I think I know the true Kit Hilton. Now come, I will assist you back to your bed.'

Her hands closed on his arms, and he sat down on the steps. Perhaps his weight was too much for her. But not enough. His clothes slipped to the floor, and he found his fingers on her thighs.

'Kit,' she whispered. 'Let me help you, Kit.'

He pulled her down, on to his knee, and his right hand searched the front of her nightdress.

'Kit,' she whispered, suddenly alarmed. 'No, Kit, you cannot.'

Here was softness. Softness he must know better. There were ties at the neck of her nightdress, neatly bowed. He wrapped his fingers in them and pulled them apart, carrying the material with it, laying her bare to the waist. She gasped, and pushed against him, found she could not get free herself, and swung at his face instead with her closed fist. He ducked beneath it, and found his face against her breasts. He nuzzled them and kissed them, sucked the nipples into his mouth. The arm swung round his head and came to rest on it, for a moment hugging him yet closer.

'Kit,' she whispered. 'Kit, in the name of God . . .' she bit the words back. Because God was not present here. Kit was already slipping from the step, turning as he did so, completing the ruin of her nightdress as his mouth moved from her breasts to sink lower. Her legs closed, but too late; they only enveloped his neck, and now her body sank forward, over his head, and he felt her fingers on his back.

Nothing had changed. Green Grove was basked as ever in the warm morning sun, flooding out of the eastern coast of the island to bathe the western, brilliantly illuminating the bright green of the young cane shoots.

He rode into the compound, slowly, because the mule would go no faster, and the dogs raced forward, growling and barking, to greet him. The mule stopped, and scraped at the dust with its hooves. But George Frederick was also running forward, to take the bridle, and Kit was dropping from the saddle, to stroke and slap the eager mastiffs.

'The mistress does be aback, Captin,' George Frederick said. 'But she going come home soon.'

Kit nodded, walked up the steps, stopped to look along the verandah to where Miss Johnson was leading Anthony in his Latin grammar while Rebecca played by herself at their feet. But Anthony had also seen his father come in, and now jumped up and down in his seat. 'Papa, Papa, you're home.'

'Hush, child,' Miss Johnson insisted. No doubt she was not as old as she looked and pretended, but she was older than either Kit or Marguerite, and was severely conscientious in her duties as governess; her father was the manager of the Ice House, and so she occupied a privileged position, by no means a planter's daughter, but by no means a poor white either; she approximated Lillan on the social scale, he supposed, although she would never have admitted to equality with a Quaker.

'Aye,' he said. 'You'd best obey Miss Johnson, or she'll have her stick to you, I've no doubt. I'm back, Tony. I'm back.'

He took off his hat, and went inside. Lillan, Lillan, Lillan. Then what was he doing here? There was an unanswerable question. Save that here was the fount of his strength, and if he was to put this behind him, then must he be sure what he was doing.

If he must put this behind him. There was the opportunist speaking.

Ellen Jane waited at the foot of the stairs. 'Is good to see you home, Captin,' she said. 'You going aback?'

'No. I'll have a bath, I think. And a jug of sangaree.' He went upstairs, into the great bedroom. The bed was made, and the room might never have been touched by human hand. But Marguerite's perfume filled the air. Was he afraid of her? Of her reactions? Of her denunciations? Or was he more afraid of what he had done to Lillan? Of what he had caused Lillan to do to herself.

He took off his coat, threw it across the bed, and sat beside it, staring through the window at the canefields. Now he was sober, and sufficiently tired to be dispirited. Thus true evaluation of the situation should wait until he had had a rest, and a chance to think. And before these, a hot bath. There was the solution.

He stripped off his shirt, turned to face the still open door, and gazed at Marguerite, hatless, her coat open.

'Welcome home,' she said.

He licked his lips. Christ, how nervous he was, on a second. 'Am I then, welcome.'

'Silly darling,' she said, coming into the room and closing the door behind her. 'I apologize for yesterday, without reservation. It was the one thing I was determined we should never do, air our differences in public. Be sure that on our next appearance in St John's I shall be the most contrite of wives.'

'I disappointed you,' he said. 'You were entitled to anger.'

'No wife is entitled to do anything but support her husband,' she insisted. 'I had forgot that.' She picked up his shirt, held it close for a moment, and then put it down again. 'Was your dinner satisfactory?' Her head half turned. 'I had George Frederick return to oversee the situation. I should also ask, was her bed soft?'

Kit inhaled. There was never any possibility of subterfuge or dissembling, with Marguerite. In that she was superior to any of her sex.

'I returned to speak with you of that.'

'Indeed?' She sat on the bed, her hands on her lap. 'Your bath is ready. I will assist you, and you can say what you want, then.'

'Will you want to listen? It must be mainly goodbye.'

A slight frown, but gone in a moment. 'Is she then, so much softer than I? So much more willing than I? So much more passionate, than I?'

He cursed the flush on his cheeks. 'None of those things, Meg.'

'Is she, then, insistent that you declare your love, and make an honest woman of her to the world?'

'Of course not.'

'Are you, then, bent on becoming a Quaker yourself?'

'Good lord, no. But . . .'

'But you fear my displeasure, my jealousy, will remain ever between us, like a bolster across our bed.'

'I . . .' he chewed his lip. 'No doubt you have said it.'

'Then tell me this, my darling. Do you love your Danish mate?'

He sighed. 'I wish I knew. God, I wish I knew. I have liked her, admired her, perhaps even have I wanted her, since the day we met, and this is a long while ago. I have felt guilty in my friendship with her, because I am not of her people, her faith, even her persuasion about life.'

'And you have loved me since the day *we* met, which was

well before you knew that creature existed. Or can a man's love only burn for a limited number of years?'

'I told you,' he shouted. 'I do not *know*. I do not know anything, for certain, at this moment. Last night I was drunk. I got drunk because of our quarrel. And then there was Lillan...'

'And you are still the buccaneer,' she said. 'When drunk. Oh, do not suppose I am carping. That is why I love you. But when you are sober you are the man who would set the world to rights, and you imagine this particular world can be set right by leaving me to live with that girl.'

'Can you suggest an alternative?'

'To such folly? That would be hard. I told you, when first we lay together in this bed, Kit, when the time comes, you may lie on whom you please. Only do not love her as you love me. I do not believe that you do love this girl as you love me. If you must have her body, then do so. Build her a house, and set her up as your mistress. If I may offer a word of advice, do it down in Falmouth, where she will be removed from the immediate criticism of the Quakers or those who thoroughly dislike them. Visit her as you please. But be sure you come back to Green Grove when you are done. And be sure that I will be waiting for you.'

'You would accept such a situation?'

Marguerite smiled at him. 'You are my husband, my darling. Those children down there on the verandah are yours as much as mine. This plantation is held in our joint names, our joint strengths, for our joint purpose. I have had the best ten years of your life, and you have had the best ten years of mine. We shall come together again, God willing. I shall not throw you over for the first hole that attracts you, when drunk. And I shall expect you to possess, or to cultivate, a similar sense of perspective.' She got up, put her hands on his shoulders, and kissed him on the cheek. 'Now come, and I will assist you in your bath.'

So, then, there were two qualities of fear. Or apprehension. Or concern. This was a much more gentle emotion.

It was a glorious morning, with the sun reaching out of the ocean to dominate a cloudless sky. His horse nibbled grass by the road, and to his left he could just make out the steeple of the St John's church. But on the beach to the south of the town and the harbour was he sufficiently alone. And here he waited. He had left the message with Agrippa,

THE DEVIL'S OWN

and Agrippa had looked at him for some seconds, his eyes sadly aware of the truth. And yet, what more could he do? He would have to be a man of steel to turn his back on this.

And yet he could not doubt the evil he was setting in motion at this moment.

For she was here, walking her horse along the side of the road, right knee high on the saddle, left toes firmly thrust into her stirrup. She wore her grey gown and her grey hat; seen from a distance she was no more than a woman. Only as she turned off the road to walk her mount down the beach did he recognize the glint of golden hair at her shoulder, the solemn face relaxing into a smile as she saw him.

He stood beside the horse, held up his hands, and she slipped from the saddle. He caught her under the armpits, and as he set her on the sand, brought her close. How tall she was. He had not noticed before. To kiss her on the mouth he had to do no more than bend his head, whereas to kiss Marguerite on the mouth involved the movement of his own body.

'I was not sure you'd come,' he said.

He could feel her breath on his face. And now memory come flooding back like a wave from the sea. So it had been four days, and he had been drunk, when it had begun. He had spent the four days thinking of her, and he had been sober when it had finished. He remembered the silence, so unlike the murmurs and gasps of Marguerite, somewhat salutary in itself, but then he remembered too the strength in her arms as he would have released her, the power in her legs, as they wrapped themselves around him.

'Could I do otherwise?' she whispered.

And he remembered too, the blood on the sheet. For the second time in his life, he had taken a virgin, brutally and savagely. But this one had not sought to end to her own life.

He kissed her on the mouth, and her arms went round his waist.

'What of your parents?'

'I explained that you had chosen to return to Green Grove early, and had taken the mule. They asked no questions.'

'And could they not see?'

Gently she freed herself from his embrace, and walked across the sand, to stand by the rippling wavelets on the beach. 'That I was exhilarated, excited, delighted, delirious with joy, Kit? Oh, they could see that. And accurately guessed its source. But again, no more. They know that I have loved you for ten years, since that day in St Eustatius. Who else on this island of demons and blacks might a woman love, Kit? You are like this breeze which blows in from the Atlantic, fresh and clean where all is sweat and filth. But they trust my good sense, my good judgement. Even as they trust yours. I was happy to have you in the house, no more.'

'Then am I doubly damned,' he said, walking beside her. 'Marguerite?'

He gave a short laugh. 'She bears you no grudge, Lillan. Oh, I did not tell her. She greeted me with a simple statement of fact. She judges all others in the light of herself, and who knows that she is not entirely correct.'

'And she was not angry?'

'Not in the least. I think she almost knew it must happen, one day.'

Lillan stopped, and turned to face him. 'But she will not let you go.'

'She produced convincing arguments to prove not only how impossible it was, but how unnecessary.'

Lillan gazed at him for some seconds. 'I never doubted she was a woman of character. And now she demands of us a similar character. Am I right?'

'Lillan . . .'

'I understand my situation, Kit, believe me. I also understand yours, and hers. She is your wife. She has the first call upon your protection and your honour and your love. I am in a position of a second mortgagee. And yet, what am I to do without you? I shall never marry. I shall never know another man. I had resigned myself to never knowing one at all, before last week. How can I resign myself to that again, having known you?'

'Lillan . . .' he seized her hands. 'I must be several kinds of a cur.'

She smiled at him. 'You are a man, Kit. I think and believe that you are an honourable man, so it is your misfortune to attract women. And latecomers must be trespassers. What would you have me do?'

He sucked air into his lungs. 'I could build you a house, Lillan. In Falmouth, or in the English Harbour. A house of your own, where . . .'

'Where I could be alone, except when you chose to visit me, and where I would hoist a banner, here lies Christopher Hilton's mistress.'

'Lillan...' but he bit his lip. She was speaking nothing less than the truth.

'And yet the alternative, of not seeing you again, is no less unthinkable. And I cannot see you again in my parents' house, or even secretly like this, more than once or twice. Antigua is too small.'

'Would you brave your father's displeasure? He certainly cannot take a stick to you.'

'He has that right,' she argued. 'As long as I acknowledge him as my father. But I am not afraid of sticks. I am afraid of his understanding that I, and you, Kit, are after all merely bits of flesh. He counts us both higher than that, as he counts my mother also, and Agrippa. He is a man who sees people as very very white or very very black; I am talking of their characters, you understand.'

Behind her, in St John's, a bell began to toll, steadily, incessantly.

'But if I left Marguerite, turned my back on all my responsibilities, on my children and my plantation, on my entire past and a good deal of my future, you would still be, only my mistress, Lillan.'

'Oh, of course,' she said. 'I should curse the day you sailed into St Eustatius harbour, Kit. I wish I could.' She looked along the beach towards the town. 'It is not Sunday.'

For still the bell tolled, unceasingly, urgently. And now they heard the sound of hooves, and watched Agrippa spurring his horse along the track, leaving the road to kick great clouds of sand into the air as he located them.

'Kit,' he bellowed. 'Kit. The French have landed.'

Kit released Lillan's hand, ran forward. 'The French? Du-Casse, you mean?'

'Who knows, Kit? A fleet, they say, of five French ships, down at Falmouth. But that is not the worst of it. You will remember that Mr Harding claimed they have been in these waters for some time. No doubt he was right. They were waiting for assistance. There are Carib war canoes with them.'

'Caribs?' For a moment his imagination could not grasp the fact. There had been no Carib raid on Antigua for forty years. 'Christ Almighty. I must...' he checked, and turned, and felt her hand on his arm.

'You must go to Green Grove, Kit. And quickly. You yourself said St John's would be safe enough. It is the plantations they will attack.'

Still he hesitated.

'She is right, Kit.' Agrippa said. 'You must defend your wife and family. I will see Lillan safely home, and protect her afterwards, and come to your aid as soon as it may be done.'

Marguerite, in the hands of naked red men. He had heard all the tales from the past. Anthony and Rebecca, their brains carelessly dashed away. He hesitated for the last time, kissed Lillan on the mouth, and then ran for his horse.

8

The Avengers

Wisps of smoke, clinging to the clear morning air. Goodwood? Goodwood was surely farther inland. And even if it was Goodwood, Kit could spare no aid in that direction. In front of him the sky remained clear. For how long?

He reined at the top of the rise, drew the back of his hand across his forehead. Now the smoke clung to his right. And now too he looked down on Green Grove. And on a scene he had not expected to witness in his life. He watched the slaves streaming out of the fields, running carelessly across the ratoons, across the paths, shouting and screaming as they made for the village. But what would they find there? Even the leper colony would be safer.

And then the house. The shutters were being closed, and muskets were emerging at the loopholes. He watched two of the overseers driving the horses from the stables; they bore the Green Grove brand and could be easily rounded up again after the invaders had gone. But time was already short. There were people moving to the right, on the very borders of the plantation. People or ants? Their numbers seemed to grow as he watched; a horde of little specks. Red ants.

Kit kicked his horse and sent it down the road, bending low over the animal's neck. This day he was unarmed. He had not left the plantation to fight anyone this morning.

He thundered through the opened gate and up the drive,

THE DEVIL'S OWN

scattering the fleeing slaves, while the men on the verandah of the Great House stopped work to stare at him.

'Kit.' Marguerite ran out of the front door. 'Oh, thank God you are here. I did not know . . .' She checked, aware that her overseers were staring at her, at the unaccustomed sight of their mistress afraid. She wore her planting clothes but yet looked more untidy than usual; Rebecca clung to her skirt. She knew where he had gone this morning, and why. She had not known which he would choose at a moment like this. An invasion was beyond the experience of even Marguerite Hilton.

'I came as soon as I heard the news.' He hurried up the steps. 'There are Indians not a mile away.'

'Oh, Christ,' she said. 'Oh, Christ. Kit, what are we to do?'

He turned, gazed at the plantation, at the slaves flooding through the gate. They seemed to lose their purpose as they entered the compound itself, and milled around, shouting and weeping.

'Give me that,' Kit snapped, and whipped a musket from Burns' trembling hands, pointed it in the air, and fired. The hubbub stopped, and the crowd faced the verandah. 'Go to the village,' Kit shouted. 'Go to your huts and stay there. These people have no quarrel with you. Their fight is with us. Stay inside until the Indians have been beaten off.'

The Negroes stared at him, but already the foremen were marshalling them and pushing them down the hill.

'Their huts will not save them,' Marguerite said.

'From what? Slavery by the Indians? Their lot will hardly be worsened,' Kit said. 'And it is our best hope of retaining any of them afterwards.'

'If we are alive to do so. Look there.' She pointed up the hill behind the house, at the smoke rising from the fields, and at the row of figures which stood on the skyline, constantly growing in numbers, naked men, carrying hatchets and bows and arrows, their copper-brown bodies glinting in the sun.

'Quickly,' Kit snapped. 'Women and children into the cellar. Mr Burn, you will stand by the trap and make ready to close it. And be sure, Burn, when I give the order to bolt the trap, do so and open it for no one save your mistress or myself, and even then when you are sure the savages have withdrawn. Mr Passmore, get those windows shuttered, and quickly. Muskets, lads, muskets. Three to every man, and loaded. A man to each window. They may well assault all four walls at once.' Christ, to remember, what Susan would have done. What Susan had done, once. Without success. But surely, as he had boasted, this house resolutely defended, would prove too strong for naked savages.

'You are splendid,' Marguerite whispered. 'Splendid. I never knew how splendid until this moment, Kit.'

'Tell me that after I have won. Now get downstairs with the children. And take your domestic girls, too.'

'I have already sent them,' Marguerite said. 'But I will stay here. I have no wish to be incarcerated in that cellar. And I can handle a musket as well as any man here, saving yourself.'

He stared into her face, his emotion sucking at her sparkling green eyes, her flared nostrils, her parted lips. Here was beauty, and more than beauty, because of the strength which supported it. Which supported him. Christ, that a man should ever have to choose between such demoniac magnificence and such perfect femininity.

He kissed her on the forehead. 'Then stay close to me.'

The shriek alerted him, and he looked at the charging Caribs, flooding down the hillside, waving their weapons, howling like a pack of dogs.

Dogs. 'Loose the dogs,' he shouted at Webster the carpenter. 'Loose the dogs. Poor beasts,' he muttered. 'Yet will they slow them up.'

The mastiffs issued from the kennels below the front steps, setting up a howl to match that of the Caribs, bounding across the compound as the first of the redmen came swarming through the gate. And even the dread cannibals were given pause by the dozen monsters hurling themselves forward.

'Mr Allingham,' Kit bellowed. 'Twenty men. Here, with muskets and spares on the front verandah. Here will be the main attack.'

The overseers and book-keepers came clattering on to the verandah, crouched there, muskets primed. At the gate the Caribs checked to receive the onslaught of the dogs, coming straight as bullets themselves, hurling themselves at the copper-brown throats before them. Several of the Caribs fell, then the others rallied, encouraged by the waving sword held by a tall man who now hurried to the front.

'There,' Marguerite said, pointing. 'Bring him down, Kit, and the battle is won. Bring him down.'

Kit strained his eyes; the tall man was too far away to see his face clearly. 'He is beyond range.'

THE DEVIL'S OWN

'Then when he comes within range. He will lead them, Kit. He has all the courage of my family. I will say that for him. He will be in the front. So bring him down.' The words came from her lips like drops of vitriol. Kit stared at her, and then turned back to look at the big man.

Indian Warner, he thought. The legend, come to life. To raid his own niece's plantation? Did his hatred run as deep, have a core as vicious, as hers?

'They're coming,' Passmore's voice shook.

The dogs were dead, scattered mounds of red flesh. And half a dozen of the Caribs also lay on the trampled earth of the compound, the earth where, he suddenly remembered, the Negroes had danced and cheered on his wedding night, ten years ago.

'Sight your pieces,' he said. 'Easy now, lads. Sight your pieces. Make each shot tell.'

But their hands shook, and their faces were ashen. They were overseers. They rode confidently enough behind a cart-whip, with pistols in their belts, when those opposed to them had nothing. But these swarming red men were armed, and as vicious as themselves. So their hands shook, and the sweat stood out on their foreheads.

All except one. Marguerite was at the end of the line, her hands tiny wisps of white on the stock and barrel of her musket. She sweated, but her hands were steady. By Christ, he thought, to have no more than a dozen of Morgan's men beside me here. To have but one. To have Agrippa.

The Caribs ran across the yard, whooping and waving their weapons.

'Give fire,' Kit roared. 'Give fire.'

The verandah shook, and the black smoke eddied about them, setting them coughing and spitting.

'Replace your weapons,' Kit shouted. 'Replace your weapons.'

The overseers scrabbled at the floor, found the fresh muskets. The smoke began to clear, and they looked at near a score of men, lying wounded and dead in their blood, some thirty feet from the steps. 'Aieee,' Kit shrieked, as he had not shrieked since the day he had charged the Spaniards at Panama. 'Well done, lads. Well done. Sight your pieces. Sight your pieces.'

But there were so many red men. And if they were temporarily halted, they were once again being rallied by the tall man, and now those with the bows were drawing their strings, and the deadly wooden shafts clouded across the morning. Allingham gave a moan and fell forward, an arrow thrusting from his chest. Another man also screamed, although he had only been hit in the leg. There was a clatter, and Passmore had dropped his musket.

Kit realized he would not hold his people here. 'Aye,' he said. 'Withdraw, lads, into the house. We'll fire from shelter. In you go, Marguerite, for God's sake.'

She still stared at the Caribs, as if she would destroy them by the very venom of her hate. But now she moved for the door, and at the sight Indian Warner pointed his sword at the house, and yelled an order.

The Caribs surged forward in a long peal of angry inhumanity. The overseers, getting to their feet to withdraw into the doorway, stared at their foes for a fraction of a second, and then uttered a howl of their own. But this one was of fear, and their muskets hit the floor in unison as they crowded through the doorway, wailing their terror. Desperately Kit ran behind them, thrusting men aside as he reached the door itself, finding it blocked by a body. But this was immediately dragged aside. Kit looked up, stared at George Frederick.

'You should be in the cellar,' he said.

'You give me a sword, Captin,' George Frederick said. 'I's fighting with you.'

The door boomed shut as the first Carib reached the verandah, and bolts thudded into place. But still the morning was hideous with the whoops of the red men outside, with the terrified screams of the white men within. For they had continued on their way, to the pantry, and there had wrenched open the trap to the cellar, and were pouring down the stone steps with all the haste they could manage.

'By Christ,' Kit drew his sword, and ran across the dining-room. 'You'll return,' he shouted. He straddled the stairway, elbowing Burn out of the way. 'I'll run through the last man up.'

A mustket butt slammed his skull, and he fell forward, on to his hands and knees. He crouched there, shaking his head, and was kicked in the ribs, to go rolling across the floor. Dimly he heard Marguerite's voice, shouting desperate commands, then she was behind him, raising his head.

'Kit,' she gasped. 'Kit?'

'Go with them,' he muttered. 'For Christ's sake, go with them.'

THE DEVIL'S OWN

'And you,' she said. 'Come on, Kit. Up, for God's sake.'

He struggled to his knees, and listened to the clang of the trap. He flung himself across the floor, battered on the inches-thick wood. 'Open up,' he yelled. 'Open up. Your mistress is out here.'

She knelt beside him, panting, tearing at the wood with her fingers, striking it with her closed fists. 'The curs,' she moaned. 'The filthy curs.'

Glass shattered behind them, and the whooping filled the entire house. Kit grasped his sword, turned round, and faced Indian Warner.

Easy enough to recognize, certainly, for all his nakedness. Tall; far taller than his half-brother, and thin, with ribs showing against the smooth pale brown of his flesh, but heavily muscled too, at thigh and bicep and shoulder. But it was the face which was unmistakable, the features softly rounded, so unlike the sharpness of the more typical red men about him. But the roundness was tempered with the Warner steel, and the eyes, a pair of blue stars in the surrounding darkness, stared at Marguerite as though she were a scorpion. And directed the right hand, extended to full length, and ending in a pistol.

'You'll drop your sword,' he said. 'Or shall I shoot her in the belly?'

'She is your niece,' Kit said. 'Do you not know that?'

Indian Warner smiled. His lips seemed to ripple away from the sharpened teeth. 'Oh, indeed, my niece,' he said. 'I know that, white man. I know that.'

'Kill him,' Marguerite whispered. 'Kill him now. Let us die together. Kill him, Kit, as you love me.'

But the moment's hesitation had been a moment too long. Already hands were scrabbling at Kit's shoulders, other red bodies clouding between himself and the chieftain. And there were red hands on Marguerite's body as well. The sword fell to the floor.

'She is right, white man,' Indian Warner said. 'You could have killed me then. And you would have suffered no more than you suffer now. But she must watch.' He gave an order in his own language, and Kit was half thrust, half carried across the dining-room and to the foot of the stairs. Here the banisters were almost as high as a man, and against these he was placed. Rawhide cords were produced, and his arms carried behind his back and the wrists secured. Another cord went round his neck, and was made fast to the banisters, and another round his waist, so that he was held upright, and was yet unable to move. He gasped for breath, and attempted to face his tormentors without flinching. But he knew now what they intended. He could remember Susan's stories clearly enough.

The knives were already out, and he closed his eyes. But the time was not yet. They were merely stripping the clothes from his body, the very boots from his feet, all with exquisite care, to leave not a scratch on his flesh. For that privilege must lie with the cacique. Slowly he inhaled, and allowed the air to hiss through his nostrils, and wanted to weep. For suddenly he looked at Marguerite, held in front of him.

'Oh, God,' she whispered. 'Oh, God.'

Indian Warner stood at her shoulder, his fingers thrust into her hair, so that as he chose he could bend her head back to make her eyes stare into his. And now he chose. 'You love him, this man of yours?'

'Oh, God,' she said. 'Your fight is with me. With mine. He is no part of it.'

'Has he not shared your body, shared your love, shared your hate? Will you not partake of his body now?'

Her mouth sagged open as she stared up at him, her head pulled so far back Kit could see the convulsions of her throat.

'Then hate *me*,' he said. 'Let her go. Do the Warners make war upon women?'

The blue eyes seemed to impale him, and the woman's hair was slowly released. 'Love,' Indian Warner said. 'A loving couple. There is a rare sight. You would die for each other. Then you shall, die for each other.' He smiled at Kit. 'For how may a white man die, how may a gentleman die, how may a *planter* die, white man, more cruelly than in watching his wife violated before his own eyes? Answer me that, white man.'

'You'd rape your own niece?' Kit demanded.

'Niece.' The hands were back at her hair, twisting her face this way and that. 'I'd not touch her body, save with a burning brand. That I shall do. But that you shall not see. Your vision, your last vision, white man, will be that of your woman enjoying the embraces of another. For you will enjoy it, sweet Marguerite.' Again the tug, and the flop of her

THE DEVIL'S OWN

mouth as she gasped for breath. Tom Warner smiled down at her. 'Fetch me that black fellow we found by the door.'

Three of the Indians brought a struggling George Frederick across the room. 'I ain't done nothing, suh,' he said. 'I ain't done nothing. You know I ain't no planter, suh.'

'I know that, black man,' Tom Warner said. 'I know that you are a slave. I was a slave once, black man. I have known the lash.' Again the savage tug. 'Her father gave me the lash, with his own hands. So now you will take your revenge.' The orders were given in Indian, and the fingers released Marguerite's hair.

Those fingers, but there were too many others. For just an instant her head came forward, and she stared at Kit, and then she was on the floor at his feet, as Susan had once been, on the floor of her own house. But how kind, how gentle, how humane, were the Spaniards by comparison with these naked warriors? And in only seconds she was as naked as they, spread-eagled on the floor, a red man kneeling on each wrist and each ankle, her breasts inflating as she gasped for breath, her belly fluttering in its pelvic cage, the muscles of her thighs twisting as she stared at her uncle. Yet she had spoken not a word, uttered not a cry. Her eyes spoke for her.

'Take her,' Indian Warner commanded. 'Take her, black man, until your loins can do no more.'

'She?' George Frederick's voice went up an octave. 'Oh, no, suh, no, suh. Not the mistress, suh. I ain't going to harm the mistress, suh. Oh, no, suh, I can't do that.'

'Take her,' Tom Warner commanded. 'And you shall live. I give you my word on that. You shall return with us to Dominica, not as a slave, but as a member of my people. You shall have honours heaped upon your head. Refuse me this, and you shall die, but slowly, and your blood will yet drip upon that body you fear to touch. Choose.'

George Frederick stared at the chieftain, and his eyes slowly dropped to the trembling body at his feet. For the moment he was ruled by fear, of the future no less than of the past, and was thus less than a man. But as Marguerite continued to fight her captors, and got one leg free, to kick in the air, and half roll on her side, to dominate even the horror of the morning with white buttock and brown hair, fear diminished beneath an irresistible lust.

'You got for see, mistress,' he said. 'I can't just die so, mistress.'

Marguerite's gaze had turned from her uncle to her slave, and George Frederick closed his eyes. Kit wished also to close his eyes, and yet he too was impaled upon the hate emanating from the slight white glory which was his dearest possession. And so he stared, while the Caribs whooped their amusement, and Tom Warner smiled. Kit stared, not at the black upon white, not at the eyes, not at the rigidly clamped mouth, but instead at the right hand, held immobile by the red foot on her wrist, but still clenched and clenched, and clenched, so that before George Frederick lay still there was a trickle of blood rolling across the hand to drip on to the floor, and her fingers were thrust so deeply into her palm that it was difficult to see how they could ever be released.

Tom Warner smiled. 'Now, white man,' he said. 'Now, you are dead, in your mind. Or would you like to follow your slave, for the last time, before I take your manhood, and then your life?'

'Truly must you have suffered, friend, to have so far forgotten your true stature,' Kit said.

Tom Warner frowned at him. 'You are a man of some courage, white man. No doubt it takes courage, to bed with that she-viper. Your name?'

'Christopher Hilton.'

The frown deepened. 'Hilton?' A look of almost pain crossed his features. 'You are called Kit?'

'By my friends.'

The chieftain gazed at him for several seconds, and then spoke in Indian, without taking his eyes from Kit's face. One of the braves ran from the room. The others sliced through the rawhide ropes holding their prisoner.

'Susan's grandson?'

Kit rubbed his wrists. 'By Christ,' he said. 'You remember her?'

'In my life,' Tom Warner said. 'But three white people showed me kindness. My brother Edward, his wife Aline, and Susan Hilton. Now all are dead. I do not ask your forgiveness, Kit.' He looked at the couple on the floor, for George Frederick still lay there, perhaps afraid to release her, now that his passion was spent and he understood the enormity of his crime. 'But I would have you understand. She is my niece. Aye. Her father is my brother. Yet did he send my mother and me to the slave compound, and have us in the fields, my mother, who had cared for him *like* a mother when Rebecca died. And when we faltered, he himself used the whip. Only a Warner may flog a Warner, were his words.'

'You escaped,' Kit said.

'Aye,' Tom Warner said. 'And waited. For twenty years I waited. To deal with him, and his brood. He has escaped me this time. But she . . .' he turned as feet clumped on the verandah. 'I have found your friend, Jean.'

Jean DuCasse hurried in, panting, sweat soaking his shirt. His head was bound in a bandanna, and he carried a cutlass. He had put on weight, and had allowed his moustache to grow and droop beside his mouth. 'Kit.' He frowned at his naked friend. 'Mon Dieu.'

'I discovered in time,' Tom Warner said.

'In time.' Kit seized George Frederick's shoulder, threw him away from Marguerite, dropped to his knees. She said not a word, and her fists were still clenched.

'Kit,' Jean said. 'Ill met, after too long. I knew you were a planter, but not the name of your estate. I should have guessed.'

'Aye.' Kit smoothed the hair from her forehead; it was matted with sweat, and there was sweat on her face as well. But no tears in her eyes.

A tablecloth fell on her shoulders. Hastily Kit wrapped it round her, and gazed across her at his friend.

'You'll take my hand, Kit. I would not have had it so.'

Kit hesitated, and then thrust out his hand. Jean squeezed it. 'And you, madam? Do you remember me?'

Marguerite's head turned. 'I remember you, Monsieur Du-Casse. I shall, remember you.'

'I would not have had it so,' Jean said again. 'It is war, and a savage war. No doubt my time will come. But they shall not burn your house. This I swear. Nor will they take your blacks.'

'Leave me only that one.' Marguerite's voice was hardly more than a whisper, but George Frederick, crouching six feet away from her, jerked his head, and stared at them with wide eyes.

'You cannot, suh,' he screamed. 'You cannot leave me, suh.'

'Leave him,' Marguerite said. 'Or take my curse.'

Jean sighed. 'Then must I accept both, madam. You will murder him for a crime he was forced to? Then are both Kit and I deserving of a far worse fate.'

'Leave him,' Marguerite said.

'No,' Tom Warner said. 'I leave you your life. I had not intended that. Be grateful, bitch.'

Kit stood up. 'Can there not be an end to hating, Mr Warner? You have done my wife a mortal injury. I understand, that her father . . .' he hesitated, glancing at her. 'Her father did you and your mother nothing less. Can there not be satisfaction?'

Tom Warner pointed at the slight figure on the floor. 'She lives,' he said, 'because she is your wife. I pity you, Kit Hilton. You know not where you rest your head of a night. As she is Philip's blood, so does she reek with his venom. Had my braves sliced the skin from your bones, you could scarce have suffered more than you will suffer, tied to that reptilian creature. I shall not see you again, Kit. Will you take my hand?'

Kit looked down at the proffered fingers. Christ, to end emotion, to do what mattered. If one could tell, what mattered. 'Perhaps,' he said. 'When we meet again. If that should happen.'

Indian Warner looked into his eyes, then nodded, and gave his orders. And left the room, his braves at his heels.

Jean hesitated in the doorway. ' 'Tis your government you must blame for this, Kit,' he said. 'Benbow needs more ships in these waters. Then must DuCasse meet his end. Until then, why, DuCasse must injure the English wherever he can. But not Kit Hilton. Nor his wife.' He bowed to Marguerite. 'I am truly sorry, madam. Had I the power to accomplish one miracle, I would command time to turn back, for but a scant half hour. I would beg you to believe that.' He gazed at George Frederick. 'You'd best run behind me, fellow.'

Marguerite crawled across the floor to the door, the tablecloth forgotten. 'Bring him back,' she whispered. 'Bring him back, Kit. Take who you need, what you need. Bring that bastard back.'

'We are all bastards,' Kit said.

Her head started to turn, and then checked. The house echoed to shouted questions from the cellar.

'Our heroes,' she said. 'The Indians would have fired the house, Kit. Why do you not, and leave them to perish of suffocation?'

'Your own children are down there.'

She got to her feet. Slowly she inflated her lungs until her

THE DEVIL'S OWN

belly swelled amd her breasts stood away from her chest, then she released it again, and her body sagged. 'Then no doubt you should release them,' she said, and climbed the stairs.

Kit knelt by the trap. 'Open up. It is done,' he said. They stared at him in amazement; he had forgotten he was naked. 'They have gone,' he said, and followed Marguerite up the stairs, closed the bedroom door behind him.

She lay on her belly across the bed. Perhaps now she wept. But he knew better than to expect that. 'I am in a unique position,' she said. How steady was her voice. 'For me. My situation is beyond my experience, or my comprehension. What does one do, Kit, with a woman, after she has been raped, by a slave?'

'One loves her the more. For her courage.'

'And could you bear to touch me?'

He crawled on to the bed beside her, kissed the nape of her neck, parting the matted hair with his tongue. 'Should you wish it, I would enter you now.'

She rolled away from him, sat up at the foot of the bed, legs dangling, back held to him. 'No. No, no, no, no, no, no.'

'The stigma is in your mind.'

'Of course.' She got up, walked to the window, gazed at the smouldering fields, inhaled the crisp smell of the burned cane.

'It will rise again. Everything will rise again. Had they burned this house, it too would rise again,' Kit said. 'Had they slaughtered your slaves, they would have been replaced. Had they murdered your children, I would have given you others.'

'And had they torn the flesh from your bones, before my eyes?'

'Then would you have secured for yourself another, more able, more virile husband.'

At last she turned. How beautiful she was, through all the marks on her body, through all the agony on her face. Or did the agony itself, and the knowledge of how it was gained, add to her beauty? To her desirability? For how perverse is the mind of man.

'No, not more virile,' she whispered. 'Do you not fear that this may also have happened to Lillan?'

'It has not,' he said. 'They had no means of storming St John's. But had it happened, Meg, I would pray she would have borne it with as much fortitude.'

Marguerite crossed the room, looked out of the other window, at the slaves milling about in the village. 'Poor creatures,' she said. 'Had they but an ounce of vigour in their gut they would have used their temporary freedom to murder us all. And I have had one of their black tools inside my body. Christ, had I a knife.'

He held her shoulders, brought her back against him. 'You'll not give way now, Meg.'

She turned, in his arms. 'Then say you'll avenge me, Kit. Bring me back that slave. I want no more.' She smiled, and it was a terrible sight. 'No. I set my sights too low. Bring me back Tom Warner as well, Kit. Bring them back alive. With *men* at your back, that were not difficult, for Kit Hilton.'

He stared down into her eyes, hardened facets of gleaming green. 'To perpetuate this hatred, which may well rise up again and overwhelm my own children? That makes little sense to me. Your uncle claims to have been savagely mistreated by your father. No doubt this raid satisfies his sense of revenge. Yet he is not a savage, Meg. He would not take my life, or yours.'

'My life?' she whispered. 'What is my life, when I have lain beneath a black man? How do I look at myself in the mirror, Kit Hilton? How do I touch myself, as I must, if I live? How do I accept your lust, if indeed you can ever feel such for me again? Tell me, Kit. Tell me.'

'Would you be easier in your mind with George Frederick at your mercy?'

'I would be easier in my mind,' she said. 'I would be easier, knowing that he will no longer dream, of that moment of glory, that he will no longer remember, how his belly pressed against mine, how his semen mingled with my own juice. By Christ, I would be easier.'

'Aye,' Kit said. 'I have no answer, to such a memory. Save to overlay it with others. With sweeter thoughts. Have no fear of my love, my darling Meg. Command it, and it belongs to you alone. Be my wife. That is all I ask. Say the word, and I will never go near Lillan Christianssen again.'

'And I almost believe you,' she said. 'Oh, God, to be alone with you, now and always, shipwrecked upon some lonely isle where we should have none but each other, and our love. I have sought only yours. I will ever seek, only yours. So perhaps you are right. Perhaps with your sweet aid I may overcome that memory. Then let it commence now. Quickly, I beg of you, Kit.'

Her eyes were shut. He swept her from the floor and laid her on the bed, and knelt above her, and looked up as the door opened.

'Papa,' Tony cried. 'We were so afraid, Papa, when you did not come.'

He led his sister by the hand, and she still cried.

'But we are here now,' Kit said. 'Safe and well. Eh, sweetheart?'

Marguerite also sat up, and smiled at her children. 'Come here,' she said.

They crossed the room, slowly and timidly. They were unused to their mother, naked and dishevelled. They found her a stranger, and Tony, at the least, was old enough to link her appearance with the whispered gossip which already seeped through the house.

Marguerite took a child in each arm, hugging them against her. 'We are all here now,' she said. 'Safe and well, as your father says.'

'And did you beat them, Papa?' Tony cried.

'No,' Kit said.

'There were too many,' Marguerite said. 'Too many even for your father. But he fought as no other man could have fought, for there is no other man of his stature. And when they finally overcame him, Tony, and would have killed him, they learned his name, and their anger turned to respect. Thus we live, and our plantation lives, and we will prosper.' They buried their heads in her shoulders, and she looked over them at her husband. Now at last, after so long, the tears came, rolling silently down her cheeks. The gates of hell had opened wide, and she had stumbled in, and then been dragged back to the light and air outside. So perhaps she would need to lie and cheat a little to remain above the ground, but she would do that. And surely, he thought, as he leaned forward to kiss her eyes, if I can but keep her this high for a short time, the gaping chasm which yawns before her mind will fill, and disappear.

Marguerite Hilton.

The crowd roared its anger. It stamped its feet, and dust eddied into the air. It whistled, and the noise pierced the very heavens. St John's was an ant-heap of outraged manhood. Their anger swelled up towards the dais on which their Governor, and his deputy, stood, and the redcoats grasped their firepieces tighter as they formed line before the steps, and stared at the people who were their brothers-in-law and fathers-in-law and drinking companions, in saner moments, and prayed that the explosion of hate would lead to no more than words.

Sir William Stapleton regarded them without the slightest emotion other than a frosty smile. He had confronted hostile crowds before. Now he waved the paper again.

'Peace,' he shouted. 'We must all be grateful for that, my friends. Certainly while the French are so superior in strength in these waters.' Once again he paused, and smiled at Philip Warner, standing beside him, mopping his red neck against the heat of the sun.

The noise subsided. 'Grateful,' he bellowed, 'because it permits us to devote our attention to the real enemy. To the Caribs, my friends. What say you to that?'

There was a moment of surprised silence, and then a roar of rapturous approval set the glasses tinkling in the windows bordering the street.

'Aye,' Stapleton said, holding up his hands, confident that this time they would obey him. 'Did you think I had forgotten them? Did you think that your Governor would allow such an outrage to pass unavenged? No, no, my friends, my people, for every life they took, nay, for every stalk of sugar-cane they burned, we shall exact a full retribution.'

The crowd cheered.

'But I would have you know,' Stapleton shouted, 'that the path will not be easy. No sooner did I learn of the attack upon our fair island, than I wrote letters to our countrymen in Jamaica and in Barbados, requesting their assistance in settling this matter once and for all. The Governor of Jamaica has replied to say that his heart, and those of his people, march with us, but that owing to the devastation caused by the dreadful earthquake at Port Royal only a few years ago, he can assist us with no military force. We are grateful for their good wishes. But the Governor of Barbados has replied to say that we must fight our own war.' He paused to allow the boos and hisses to run their course. 'Further, he says that the more the Leeward Islands are reduced, the happier will the Barbadians be.'

This time, the howl of execration sent the gulls scattering from the harbour.

'I cannot believe,' Stapleton shouted, 'that such a sentiment expresses the true feelings of the Barbadian people. But it is the point of view taken by their governor. So we must act

THE DEVIL'S OWN

on our own. Yet we are not so bereft, dear friends. Have we not many good men and true in these islands who will bear arms to avenge our recent catastrophe?'

The crowd roared.

'And have we not, living in our midst, nay, standing beside me, a man of vast experience in dealing with the Caribs? Gentlemen, I give you Colonel Philip Warner. His father and brother faced no less a challenge, and carried it to a successful conclusion. Shall we be lesser men than those heroes of the past? Colonel Warner.'

The men and women stamped their feet and cheered and clapped their hands, and dust and sweat and passion filled the morning air. The horses shuffled restlessly, and Kit had to rein hard to keep still. The trap waited at the back of the crowd, and Marguerite's fingers were tight on his arm.

'They will not lack for volunteers,' he said.

'Nor should they.' She smiled, a tight-lipped smile. 'Although Papa here exists on reputation. He did not accompany my grandfather and my uncle on that famous expedition.' She glanced at him. 'But he will have you at his side.'

Kit said nothing. He watched the Deputy Governor calling for silence.

'Aye,' Philip Warner shouted. 'I know these brooding devils. I know them well. They are led by my own brother.'

The crowd fell silent. They had not expected such frankness.

'But does not the Bible itself command me,' Philip said. 'Should your right eye offend thee, cast it out? My brother will pay for this outrage, and I shall see that he does. I need men. Men of courage. Men of purpose. But more than that, I need men of anger. Are you such men?'

The loudest of all the shouts came crashing through the still air.

'So then,' Philip shouted. 'If you are such men, enter your names on the tables set out by the Ice House. Enter them, and assemble this time tomorrow, to be given arms, and to be told what we intend.'

The crowd cheered, and the two governors turned and left the platform to enter the Ice House itself. Kit urged the horses forward, and the people parted before him.

' 'Tis Captain Hilton,' someone said.

'You'll lead us, Captain,' shouted another man.

'Aye, we'll march with you, Captain,' someone else bellowed.

"Or are you afraid to meet Monsieur DuCasse again?' a voice said.

For everyone present knew that Green Grove had been spared the worst of the assault.

Kit turned his head, and his eyes searched the crowd, but found no man looking sufficiently defiant. And now they were abreast of the warehouse, and he could see Agrippa and Abigail, and the Christianssens. And Lillan. He had sent a message into town, the moment the roads were safe, both to inform her of his own survival, and to learn of hers. But now . . . the rumours were already spreading of what had happened to Marguerite. Lillan would not expect him to return.

As the crowd knew.

'You'll lead us, Captain,' said the man who had first spoken, grasping the bridle. 'You've a cause, same as us.'

Marguerite stared at them as the carriage stopped, and she stepped down. 'Aye,' she said, not speaking loudly, but with an edge to her voice which cut across even that huge assembly. 'He has a cause. The Captain will lead you.'

The crowd cheered, and hands reached up, both to assist Marguerite to the ground and to slap Kit on the back as he followed her up the steps. He sighed with relief when the doors closed behind them. But here was a new kind of ordeal. For every planter on the island was present, coming forward to greet the new arrivals.

'Marguerite,' Philip said. 'Thank God you are safe. We had heard such rumours.'

'All of them true,' she said, and faced the men, and their women.

'Oh, *sweetheart*,' screamed Mary Chester, throwing herself at her friend. 'Could you not reach St John's?'

Marguerite embraced her. 'I chose to fight for my plantation,' she said, looking over the young woman's head at the rest of them. 'And we were defeated, thanks to the cowardice of our overseers. And so I was thrown on the ground and raped, by one of my own blacks. Is that not what you wished to hear, gentlemen? But I am still alive, and my husband still stands by my side, as he fought at my side, and lost at my side.'

'Kit,' Philip Warner squeezed his hand. 'It seems a miracle.'

'No miracle,' Kit said. 'Your brother spared my life when he discovered my relationship to Susan. And then DuCasse

THE DEVIL'S OWN

arrived, and called a truce. You'll recall that we sailed together as lads.'

'A fortunate circumstance,' Edward Chester remarked.

'But you will march with me, Kit,' Philip said hastily, before Kit could take offence. 'I have need of men with experience of the jungle.'

'I would know your purpose,' Kit said.

'Our purpose?' Stapleton demanded. 'Why, Captain Hilton, it is to avenge this catastrophe.'

'Scarce a Christian thought, Your Excellency.'

'Christian? You speak to me of Christianity, in regard to these heathen monsters? You, who have seen your own wife . . .'

'And you are indelicate, sir,' Kit said. 'If my wife chooses to mention her own misfortune, that is her decision, but the next man to speak of it, uninvited, before her or before me, will face my pistol, be he governor or book-keeper.'

'By God, sir,' said one of the St Kitts planters who had accompanied Stapleton. 'You cannot speak to the King's representative in that tone.'

'Be quiet,' Stapleton said. His face was red, and yet he smiled. 'I had expected no less a reaction from Captain Hilton, and I honour him for it. Yet, sir, if you will turn such anger on me for reminding you of the guilt of these savages, can you not spare some for the Indians themselves?'

'I doubt whether anger would accomplish anything of value, Your Excellency,' Kit said. 'You ask me to accompany the expedition because I have been on such an expedition before. Well, sir, if you wish my experience, then kindly do me the honour of accepting it. I marched with Morgan. He took a year and more to prepare his expedition against Panama, reconnoitred the ground over which we had to travel, handpicked his followers, understood truly what he was about.'

'He fought the Dons,' Harding said. 'We plan to fight naked savages.'

'I would have thought we oppose the more deadly foe, sir,' Kit said.

'Yet must it be done,' Stapleton pointed out. 'Although certainly it will be necessary to proceed with caution.'

'And there are ships, sir,' Kit said. 'Where will we find the vessels to transport our men at short notice?'

'Now there we are fortunate,' Philip Warner said. 'As the news of the peace with France was brought to us by a flotilla of three vessels, all anxious to lend their support in our expedition to Dominica.'

'The three anchored in the bay?' Kit demanded, with a sinking heart.

'None others,' said a man who had hitherto been lurking in the shadows at the corner of the room. 'And happy to make your acquaintance after all these years, Kit.'

Kit frowned. 'Bale? Can that be you?'

'Captain Bale, lad. Captain Bale.'

Certainly the buccaneer had prospered. His coat was of broadcloth, and his shirt cambric, if somewhat dirty. But his cutlass was bright enough and there were two pistols at his belt.

'I had thought you long dead.'

'I'm not that easy to kill, lad. As I told you gentlemen, I was a good friend of this lad's grandfather. We sailed together, when I was but a boy, Tony Hilton and I.' He gestured his companions forward. 'Captain William Hamblyn, and Captain Edward England, at your service, gentlemen.'

'Pirates,' Kit muttered.

'Privateers, Kit, privateers,' Bale insisted. 'Temporarily out of employment, with the news of this peace, and eager to play our part in your campaign.'

'With good crews, Captain Hilton,' Stapleton said.

'If allowed to plunder, sir,' Kit said.

'And yet,' Stapleton mused, 'on the last occasion that it was necessary to mount an expedition against the Caribs, did not old Sir Thomas and Edward Warner, good men and true, happily avail themselves of the aid of two famous buccaneers to gain their victory? One of these men, as I recall, was named John Painton. And the other . . . now strange, his name escapes me.'

'It was Tony Hilton, sir,' Kit said. 'Like Colonel Warner here, Your Excellency, I make no apology for my family. Or indeed, for my own past. But you have raised the most important point of all, sir, in my opinion. The objective of the expedition.'

'Why, to kill as many of the devils as possible,' Chester said.

'And to regain as many of our kidnapped slaves as possible,' Philip Warner said.

'And the women, gentlemen,' Stapleton observed, drily. 'Were not a dozen white women also carried off?'

Feet shuffled. 'Aye,' someone said. 'The women.'

THE DEVIL'S OWN

'The slaves and the women must be regained,' Kit said. 'But I wonder if we achieve anything by mounting an expedition of pure vengeance.

'Sir?' A dozen voices shouted the query.

'Hear me out,' Kit bawled. 'I but seek to know whether we approach this affair as angry men, or as statesmen. There is all the difference in the world between the two. Sir William has just reminded us that there was a previous expedition, which cost many lives, which was intended to avenge many lives. Yet it did not end the Carib menace. Nor will this one, if we seek to do nothing more than kill. Do you imagine we can destroy the Carib nation in Dominica? Has any one of you the slightest concept of the shape of that island? Of the forest there? Of the precipitous mountains up which we must march? Can we do more than raid, as they raided us? And by doing that, will we not be exposing our own sons and daughters, and ourselves, in our old ages, to another violent and bloody conflict? Were we not discussing our own futures but a few weeks gone, and planning even treason with but one objective in mind, the security of our plantations and of our families?'

'The only secure Carib is a dead Carib,' Chester said.

'Yet it would seem that Captain Hilton has an alternative scheme, and I have no doubt at all that it is worth hearing,' Stapleton said.

'Well, gentlemen,' Kit said. 'I was neither born nor brought to manhood in these islands. But my grandmother knew them well, and remembered them sufficiently to impart some of their history to me. And no doubt Colonel Warner can confirm much of it, and point out where I err. Is it not a fact, Colonel, that your illustrious father, and my illustrious grandfather, were welcomed to St Kitts by the chieftain of that island, the cacique Tegramond, and given land to plant their tobacco, and treated as friends? And more. Did Tegramond raise any objections when his own daughter Yarico became your father's mistress? I speak no slander; it is a well enough attested fact. It is that fact that we are discussing now. The men quarrelled, or there was a suspicion of treachery. No one will ever know the truth. Suffice that the white men, outnumbered and insecure, felt themselves menaced by the Carib peril, and forestalled it by a surprise attack, which led to the massacre of Tegramond and his people, and which began this deadly feud. Which was fanned by the adherence of Yarico to her English lover.

And is it not true, Colonel, that you and your half-brother, the fruit of that liaison, quarrelled, and that he and his mother fled to Dominica to perpetuate a hatred which might otherwise have died a natural death?'

'I early saw the villain in him, if that is what you mean,' Philip Warner said. But his face glowed with angry embarrassment.

'And is it not true that the French, seeking to make capital between Englishman and Indian, elected Tom Warner to the Governorship of Dominica, meaning thus to enlist him for all time on their side? Yet is he half-Warner, and half-English. And so he proved at Green Grove, that he has not finally turned his back on that glorious heritage.'

'Yet would he revenge himself upon my body, and as he hoped, upon my mind,' Marguerite said.

Kit turned to her. 'Indeed, my sweet. But there is the nub of the matter. The quarrel is entirely between Warner and Warner. Sad it is that it should involve so many innocent people.'

'And would you leave it to my father to fight it out with my uncle?' she demanded angrily. 'And stand to one side, and congratulate the victor?'

'That were no less a pre-Christian solution,' Kit said. 'But gentlemen, suppose Tom Warner and Philip Warner were to shake their hands together, and attest their names to a treaty of peace between Indian and Englishman, between Dominica and the Leewards? Suppose that could be done, gentlemen. What then of the future? For be sure that we will have fighting enough, against the French and the Dons, to satisfy the most bloodthirsty belly, without raising the redskins against us into the bargain.'

'Balderdash,' Harding shouted. 'What treaty could a savage understand?'

'I speak of no savage,' Kit insisted. 'But of a man who can bend the savages to his will.'

'Yet it is still specious talk,' Philip Warner said. 'There is much hatred between Tom and myself. Too much to be reconciled at the snap of a finger. I know not how I should go about it. Nor do I know how I could force my nature to speak friendship with a devil from hell.'

'Then allow me, Colonel Warner,' Kit said. 'For as you once pointed out, I too am a devil from hell.'

The assembly fell silent, afraid to agree with him, unable to argue that point.

THE DEVIL'S OWN

'And why should he listen to you, Captain Hilton?' Stapleton inquired.

'Because, sir, as he told me but a few days gone, my grandmother, and her lover, Edward Warner, were the only white people ever to show him kindness.'

'And you'd put your trust in that, buccaneer?' someone asked.

'They'd have you stripped and tied to a stake before you could draw your sword,' Bale remarked.

'The risk is mine, gentlemen. I will take it. I have a son and a daughter. I have no wish to see them on the ground at the feet of a red man. And be sure that that fate is one which may overtake the family of every man here if this feud is allowed to fester.'

They stared at him. Stapleton was first to speak. 'If you have sufficient faith, in yourself and in this savage, to attempt such a solution to our problem, why then, we were men of little sense, and certainly of little Christianity, did we not consider the attempt worth our while. What say you, Colonel Warner?'

Philip Warner hesitated, and then snorted, 'Let the captain pursue his aims, Sir William. But he'll go alone, by God. Bring my brother, and his fellow chieftains, down to the beach, Kit, unarmed and in a mood for talk, and by God, we shall meet them, unarmed, and in a mood for talk. But until they appear beside you, why, by God, my armament and my ships and I will stand in a posture of defence, and if need be, we shall avenge you together with all our other dead.'

'Aye,' Edward Chester said. 'Spoken like a sensible man, Philip.'

'Then it seems we have arrived at an equitable solution,' Stapleton said. 'We shall recruit our army, and send it across the sea, and pray that it shall not need its strength. Aye, there were a Christian intent.'

'And do I have no say in this matter?' Marguerite demanded. 'As it is my body you partly seek to avenge, and my husband you are so carelessly sending to his death?'

'At his request, Mrs Hilton,' Stapleton protested.

'It is the best way, Marguerite,' Kit said. 'You know of what we spoke. I cannot give you back those terrible moments on the floor. I can but erase their memory with moments as beautiful as those were horrible, time and again. I can only give you happiness where you have known misery. But we are both young. We have a great time to live, God willing, and be happy. Can we really swear to do so with the Carib menace hanging above us like a cloud for the rest of our lives, and knowing too that it will similarly overhang the lives of our children?'

Marguerite gazed at him, her lips parted as if she would have spoken again. Then her eyes flickered, across his right shoulder, and he knew she looked at her father. Still she hesitated, for several seconds. Then she muttered, 'So be it,' and turned, and left the chamber.

The sun filled the sky with all the splendid power of a Caribbean noon. But the island remained dark. A green so intense it seemed almost black, clustering over rock and valley, headland and bay, appearing to grow out of the black sand beach itself, which did no more than form a narrow bridge between the forest mass and the deep blue of the sea. Susan had never seen Dominica, but she had spoken of it, often enough, and it must have appeared no different, Kit realized, to Tony Hilton and Edward Warner when they had come here more than half a century ago.

'No peace in *their* hearts,' Philip said at his elbow, and he turned in surprise. The Deputy Governor had avoided him during the overnight sail from Antigua, even as he had studiously avoided being alone with him during the week of frenzied preparation just past. Now he smiled, grimly. 'Aye, I can read your thoughts, Kit. They can be little different to mine.'

'You were not on that expedition.'

'No. My father wanted one of his sons, at the least, to survive. But they accomplished their objective, which was to destroy the Carib power for a generation. And to regain Edward's wife, Aline. What the devil is that leadsman doing?'

For indeed the dark mountains seemed to overhang the three ships.

'Yet have I heard that deep water extends practically up to the beaches,' Kit said.

'In places. I would not like us to go aground, just in case the savages do not respond to your peaceful notions, Kit.' Philip went to the rail. 'You'll wear ship and prepare to anchor, sir.'

Bale looked up. 'We have not that much chain, Colonel Warner.'

THE DEVIL'S OWN

'The weather is settled, man. So long as the anchor but nudges the bottom to hold us from drifting, there will be no danger. We are not planning to abandon our vessels here. And break out the longboat.' He came back to the stern. 'You'll not change your mind, Kit?'

'That would scarce be either honourable or wise, sir,' Kit said. 'And in any event, it would certainly be unnecessary. I perceived in your brother a heritage he could not throw off no matter how hard he tried. And a wisdom which was all I had expected, of a Warner. An appeal to both of those things must have results.'

'Then here is my hand.' Their fingers clasped. 'But mark me well. Stand once again on the beach by noon tomorrow, or I shall mount an assault in which quarter will be an unknown word.'

'I shall be there. And you will guarantee the safety of whomsoever I bring with me? There are some right cut-throats in this fleet.'

'Their safety will be my responsibility, Kit,' Philip said.

'Then I am content. 'Til noon tomorrow.'

He climbed down the ladder, sat in the stern of the boat as it pulled for the shore. Now they were in the shelter of the mountains the breeze had dropped, and the day was steaming hot. The sun seemed to hang over the stern of the longboat, and the men sweated as they pulled. But then, Kit realized, he also sweated. With fear? He did not think so. But memory kept crowding him, of that day off Hispaniola, when they had lain in the swell, and watched the Spanish coaster drifting. The commencement of a lifetime of violence, from which he only vainly attempted to escape. There was a specious statement. Could any man, or woman, own a plantation and turn his back on violence?

The keel grated, and the sailors backed their oars. Two men jumped over the bows to hold the boat steady, and Kit made his way forward. Now there was cause for fear; the crowding trees were certainly within bowshot, and waiting beneath them were six of the great war canoes, upturned on the black volcanic sand. Yet not a leaf moved, and there was no sound above the gentle splash of the little surf.

He jumped on to the beach, and the men immediately pushed the boat back into the swell before scrambling on board. 'God go with you, Captain Hilton,' the coxswain called.

'I thank you, friend.' Kit gazed at the ships, nodding to

their anchors a hundred yards away. The ports were opened and the guns run out, and they presented a splendid sight. His last, of European humanity? But now was scarce the time for backsliding. He turned, to face the trees, and instinctively dropped his left hand to rest on the hilt of his sword, only to have it fall uselessly at his side. For he had left his sword, as he had left his pistols, on board. Kit Hilton, alone and unarmed. And how alone he felt.

Slowly he walked up the beach towards the trees, seeking some sort of path. And there it was, a distinct thinning in the forest, immediately behind the war canoes, a roadway of earth and leaves beaten flat by the tramplings of innumerable feet. But still the canoes lay there, untended. But not unwatched. He was sure of that, and turned again, sharply, hoping to catch the forest unawares.

The green wall stared at him.

He took off his hat, and the bandanna he wore underneath, and dried the sweat from his face and neck. Then he replaced both, and stepped beneath the trees, following the uneven path up a shallow hillside. After a few minutes he paused, and looked back, and saw nothing but trees and bushes. The forest had closed around him like a living creature. Perhaps the beach was not there, nor the sea, nor the ships. Certainly that was easy to believe.

But in here it was no longer silent. He was surrounded by the rustle of flowing water, to suggest a stream nearby. And the air was cooler too, as the glare was diminished. Not even the Caribbean sun could fully penetrate these leafy rooftops.

He climbed, and lost track of time as rapidly as he had lost track of his whereabouts. Often the path became too steep for walking, and he had to use his hands as well as his toes to pull himself upwards, while the sweat drained from his hair and shoulders and soaked his clothes. It was while climbing thus that he suddenly faced naked feet, and reared back so violently he all but fell. His head jerked, and he stared at a savage standing above him, bow already bent and arrow fitted, scarce seeming to breathe, perhaps a statue, but for the venom in his eyes.

Kit balanced himself as best he could, and raised both his arms high into the air. 'Don't shoot,' he shouted. 'I am unarmed. I come in peace. I seek your cacique. I seek the Governor.'

'Why, Captain Hilton?' asked Indian Warner, and Kit

dropped his hands to grasp the rock as he turned his head. Tom Warner stood behind and below him, with a dozen of his braves. And now he realized there were others on either side of him. They had been there, no doubt, since he had started his climb.

'Why?' Tom Warner asked again. 'You come as the representative of a fleet of white men. Do you know what happened last when the white men landed in Dominica, Captain Hilton? They fought a battle, and won, by their superior arms, and then they burned and pillaged. They seized the wounded braves, and any women they could find, and they hanged them, Captain Hilton. Why should I not have my men strip the flesh from your bones, now?'

Kit got his breathing under control. 'Because I hope to convince you that it would be to your interest to listen to me, and even to agree with me. If my people have wronged you, Mr Warner, be sure that you have wronged me. Thus we can meet on equal ground, at least this once.'

Tom Warner hesitated. And then smiled. 'You speak the truth, Captain Hilton. By your lights, at the least. Come, we will talk with my people. And with my mother.'

'Your mother still lives?' Kit asked in amazement.

'Should she not, Captain Hilton? And she will be glad to talk with Tony Hilton's grandson. Now come.'

He climbed up to Kit and past him, and Kit hastily scrambled behind him. The Indian with the bow loosened his string and put away his arrow, and the other Caribs followed. Some of them. More melted away into the forest, to watch the white man's fleet. They suspected treachery. That must be his principal concern, Kit realized, to overcome the suspicion which afflicted both, but which had been started by the massacre of the Indian tribe in St Kitts by this very man's father.

They climbed for more than two hours, and then they must have been high above the sea, Kit thought, perhaps a thousand feet and more. Yet the trees never thinned, and it was not possible to see the ocean, and the peaks covered in trees went on soaring on either side. Then they at last descended, and soon enough his nostrils were afflicted by the ghastly taint of sulphur. But Susan had warned him of this also, and he was prepared for the sudden cessation of the forest, which ended with an abruptness as if some deity had drawn a line, as perhaps He had, to allow below them only a valley of empty rock, dotted with pools and crossed by a stream, all of which seethed and bubbled and emitted clouds of noxious vapour. The Valley of Desolation.

Here Tom Warner stopped for a moment, and glanced at his companion. 'This was the site of the battle, between Edward Warner and Tony Hilton, and the Carib Wapisiane,' he said. 'A good place for men to die, would you not say,' Captain Hilton? We must cross it. But beware. Do not allow your feet to slip into any of that water, or you will be stripped to the bone with a speed far greater than my men could accomplish. Follow me, closely.'

He scrambled down the side of the hill, and Kit followed. The Caribs fell into single file behind him, and they made their way across the valley. Here the heat really was intense; not even the boiling house at the height of grinding quite equalled it, and instead of the sickly smell of evaporating sugar juice there was the lung-blocking stench of sulphur, which rose around them and blotted out the sun; the clouds themselves were a sickly yellow.

And now there came a roar from somewhere to his left, and the earth shook. He checked, and Tom Warner turned with a smile. 'That is the volcano. My people call it the Boiling Lake, because it bubbles without ceasing. But it has not actually exploded within the memory of any man of my tribe; I think it is because the excess of steam is carried off by these pools and this stream. We shall soon be across.'

And indeed already the air was clearing, and the ground beginning to rise, and there were other sounds to be heard above the hissing of the steam. Soon Kit saw green leaves again, and a puff of wind dispelled the worst of the vapour, and now he saw the palm-thatched roofs of the Carib benabs. A few moments later he was surrounded by women and children, all entirely naked, leaping and shouting, reaching out to touch his clothes, to squeeze his arms and belly, to fumble at his thighs.

'They suppose you are for the stake,' Tom Warner said.

'I hope you will be able to persuade them otherwise,' Kit remarked.

Once again Tom Warner smiled, and stopped and clapped his hands. The Indians fell silent, to listen to their Governor. His voice echoed across the clearing, while Kit seized the opportunity to look around him. The breeze still blew, but he was not at all sure that the scents which now afflicted his nostrils were preferable to that of the sulphur. Apart from the expected odours of a savage village, there was another, more intense tang in the air, the stench of putrefying flesh, and now he saw, to his horror, three stakes erected in the centre of the rough circle formed by the houses. To each of the stakes there clung a skeleton, suspended by throat and waist as he had been strapped to his own banisters, tatters of rotting flesh dripping from shoulder and thigh, faces the more horrible because the heads had been untouched, and were mouldering on the bones as they grinned at him, expressions still caricatures of ghastly fear and pain.

Tom Warner ceased speaking, and the crowd melted away, casting glances over their shoulders at the white man they would not possess. 'They will not harm you,' Tom said.

'As they did those poor devils?' Kit demanded. 'Tell me, Governor, did you partake in that feast?'

'I thought you came here to talk peace, Kit,' Tom remarked. 'Indeed, I have eaten human flesh. Those were brave men, before they were tied to the stakes. They died screaming, yet there was sufficient courage left in them to impart some to those who tasted their flesh. Come.'

He walked across the clearing, and Kit followed, acutely aware that he was being watched by every man, woman and child in the tribe, and there seemed to be a great number of them, more than he had expected, crouching in shaded doorways and standing in clusters beneath the overhanging branches of trees. And suddenly his courage and the confidence of his demeanour was assailed by a new threat.

'Captain Hilton,' a woman screamed. 'Captain Hilton.'

He checked, and saw a white body, naked and stained with dirt and filth, tumbling from a doorway to his right, to be seized by the ankle and dragged back into the shade.

'Captain Hilton.' The sound wailed on the wind.

'By Christ,' Kit said, once again feeling for his absent sword hilt.

'She is one of our captives,' Tom Warner said. 'There are eleven of them, and some slaves. Fear not, Kit. We do not eat either blacks or women. As for their misuse, I have been told that you sailed with Morgan, and were at Panama. Women, like gold, are the spoils of war, are they not?'

'Yet must they form part of any negotiation between us,' Kit said.

Tom nodded. 'If your people would have it so.' He stooped, to enter a house somewhat different to the others, in that the palm fronds which composed the roof had been thickened and allowed to droop closer to the ground, to provide more shade and more privacy to those within. Kit had to bend almost double to gain the interior, but here he could straighten without difficulty, and blink into the gloom. Tom stood beside a gently swaying hammock, perhaps six feet away from him. 'I would have you meet my mother,' he said. 'Yarico.'

For the first time in too many years Kit was embarrassed, unable to move, uncertain what words to use, or even if to use any. But the woman in the hammock knew no such restrictions. 'Kit Hilton,' she said, in amazingly good English. 'Come closer, Kit.'

He crossed the beaten earth floor, frowning into the shade, and stood beside the hammock. His impression was first of all of white hair, descending to the shoulders, and this truck him as odd, because in the the village there had not been a single white-haired Indian, of either sex. Then there was brown flesh, surprisingly firm. She did not bother with the apron of the other married women, nor was her body, which could hardly be younger than seventy years old, he realized, less attractive than those outside, and her grasp, which now fastened on his hand, was as strong as a man's.

But it was her face he searched. And without disappointment here either. Like all Carib faces it was long, and the features were prominent, high cheekbones, straight, thrusting nose, firm chin, wide mouth. And glowing black eyes. It seemed the most natural thing in all the world, to drop to his knees next to the hammock, to feel her fingers rippling up his arm and across his shoulder and into his hair.

'Susan's grandson,' she said, softly. 'Did she tell you of me?'

'Endlessly, princess,' Kit said. 'Of how you loved and laughed together, and how you fought together, too.'

'A long time,' Yarico said. 'A long time. Now all are dead, from those days.' Her voice changed. 'Save Philip.'

'He waits with his fleet.'

'I know that, Kit. My son has told me. Philip was my son, too. Not of my belly. He was Rebecca's child. But when she died, I felt guilty. Because his father had neglected her, for me. I was beautiful then, Kit. There was no man could look upon me and not wish to share my hammock.'

'You are beautiful now,' Kit whispered.

Yarico smiled. Her teeth were the whitest he had ever

THE DEVIL'S OWN

seen. 'Now,' she said. 'Now I am a goddess. I am unique, Kit. My people do not grow old. It is the custom amongst the Caribs for any man or woman feeling the onset of infirmity to take themselves alone into the forest, there to die of starvation. But my people would not let such a fate overtake me. Because I have known the great white man, Sir Thomas Warner, and his even greater son, Edward.' Once again the change of tone. 'Would that the white people had felt it also.'

'It is my purpose,' Kit said. 'To bring an end to that strife.'

Her eyes searched his face, in the gloom. 'Aye. You have the breadth of spirit of your grandfather. I would speak of him again. And of you. But now my son's chieftains await you.'

Kit realized that Tom Warner had left his side, and that almost the entire Carib nation, it seemed, had gathered beyond the hut to wait for the white man. He stooped, and returned to the sunlight, gazed at the assembled warriors. Here were men. He wondered if Philip Warner understood the force by which he might be opposed, should these talks come to nothing. But then, did he understand what would be *his* fate, should these talks come to nothing.

'Speak to them, Kit,' Tom Warner said. 'I will relate your words, as faithfully as I can.'

Kit hesitated, once again staring at the stern red-brown faces, the muscular arms, each one holding a spear or a bow, the heaving chests, the powerful limbs. But was he not just such a man, to them? To all men? As white men were ranked, he was more of a warrior than any man present, even Indian Warner himself. He inhaled. 'Tell them that I know of the past, Mr Warner. That I know how Tegramond and his people welcomed the Warners and their people to St Kitts, and how the English and the French repaid that kindness and that trust with blood. Tell them that I know how the Caribs were expelled from all the Leewards by Edward Warner. Tell them that I know how the Caribs under Wapisiane sought to avenge themselves, and how they kidnapped Edward Warner's wife after destroying his colony in Antigua. Tell them that I know how the Warners, aided by the Hiltons and their people, came to Dominica and won a great victory, and killed and murdered and raped and plundered, also in the name of revenge. And say also, that I understand why the Caribs came to Antigua last month, once again in revenge, and why they murdered and plundered and raped. Tell them that my own wife suffered, and that I know why she did. Because her name was Warner.'

Tom Warner gazed at him for a moment, and then slowly translated. The language was guttural, and brief. No flowery phrases for the Caribs.

'You may continue,' he said.

'Then tell them that, knowing all this, I have accompanied the fleet of Colonel Philip Warner to these shores. They know it is there. Then let them know this also, that there are two hundred and fifty men on board those ships, more men, every one of them armed and determined to fight, than all the people in this tribe, from the newest babe to your mother. I come here in no consciousness of weakness, from no fear of the Caribs. But knowing too that the fight, when it comes, will be long and terrible, and that many brave men on both sides will die. No Carib fears to die. Every Carib may wish to do so in battle. But there is more. The white man is coming, in ever-increasing numbers, finding his way across the sea to live in these magnificent islands, to make himself rich from the sale of his sugar-cane. Every Carib warrior who dies is gone for ever. Every white man who dies will be replaced a hundred-, a thousandfold. This struggle is one the Carib nation cannot hope to win. And why did it begin? Because of an act of the Warners. Why does it continue? Because of the hatred of Warner for Warner. Now there are so many wrongs on both sides, there is no hope of surrender. There is only hope of a mutual forgiveness. It is to see if this can be done that I have come to your village. Here is your noble and valiant chieftain, your Governor, Thomas Warner, and down there on the ship is our noble and valiant leader and Governor, Philip Warner. They are brothers. Now is the time for them to shake hands, as is the white man's way, to look together at the great Sun, as is the Carib way, and to break their swords together.'

He paused, and Tom Warner frowned. 'My brother will do this?'

'He has promised. There will be some argument, I am sure. But he wishes to talk with you, and your chiefs. No harm can come out of that. You have my word, and his, that your lives will be safeguarded.'

Tom Warner nodded. 'I will tell my people. Then we will feast.'

The Carib women were already preparing the slaughtered

THE DEVIL'S OWN

birds and the fried fish, and pouring the cups of piwarri, the fermented juice of the cassava plant. Now they waited to serve their men as the braves sat in a vast circle, and ate, and drank, with much solemnity, and muttered at each other, and watched the white man sitting next to their cacique, while the heat left the sun as it dipped towards the mountains. And Kit stared back at them, and beyond, at the ghastly things that had been men hanging from their stakes, and listened, to the whimperings of the white women confined to the huts behind him. As the afternoon wore on, and the piwarri mounted its attack on his senses, he ceased to believe that he was here at all, eating and drinking with the fiercest people on earth. And by the time the feast ended the day had become a long dream. He found himself in a hammock, and there was a soft body next to his. Carib custom, or Tom Warner's way of making some atonement for the crime he had committed on Marguerite? Or perhaps it was Yarico herself, moving her ancient limbs silently against his, bringing him to enticing orgasm time and again. Or was that also a dream, for certainly the ground no longer existed, but he floated on air, and the night no longer existed, as bright lights hovered around his brain, and the darkness dissolved into eternity, which ended with the rising of the sun, with a nudge in the thigh, and with a sudden return to reality.

He was in a hammock, and alone, and the day was already hot.

'My chieftains say they will come, to hear what my brother has to say,' Tom Warner said.

Kit sat up, and scratched his head. 'When will we leave?'

'Immediately. But my mother wishes to speak with you again, before you go.'

Kit followed him across the still mist-steaming clearing, into the sheltered hut. Here Yarico swung in her hammock. Yarico? It could not be.

She smiled at him. 'My son tells me you have brought a proposal of peace, between your people and mine.'

'It is my hope. And if they will come and talk, then it is a possibility.'

'Aye,' she said. 'It will allow me to die happy. And you also. For these are your people no less than mine. Do you look often in a glass, Kit?'

He frowned. 'No more than any other man.'

She nodded. 'But you have been taught enough about

your family's history, I have no doubt. Susan has told you much about her past.'

'She valued her experiences.'

'And so she should,' Yarico said. 'We were in the forest of St Kitts together, Susan and I. And Edward Warner. We shared everything, the three of us, and Aline. But Susan was ever his favourite. Do not doubt that, Kit. Aline's son was murdered by Wapisiane. Her daughter hated the islands, hated the memory of what my people did to her family, of the anger of her own father, and so she returned to England. She lives and prospers in that far off land. My son still lives and propers, outside. And Susan's son also lived and prospered, and died. And yet lives on, in his son. But they are all Warners.'

Kit's frown deepened. 'I do not understand you, Yarico. Is there yet another Warner, tucked away amongst these islands?'

She smiled. He would never forget the flash of her teeth. 'Aye,' she said. 'Yet another. Perhaps the best of them all. Now kiss me before you go, Kit. I doubt we shall meet again.'

He lowered his head to hers, and she seized his face between her hands and brought his lips to hers. 'Now go,' she whispered. 'Go, and prosper.'

She held his hand for a moment longer, and then released him. He stepped outside, found Tom Warner waiting for him, with seven other chieftains, wearing bright feathers in their hair. Behind them were the women captives, roped together, and guarded by a dozen braves, and then a good score of Negroes. He could not resist inspecting them, before asking Tom Warner, 'What has happened to George Frederick?'

'You would demand him as well?'

'I would know where he is.'

'He sailed with DuCasse, for which I thank our mutual good fortune, Kit.'

'Aye,' Kit agreed. He stepped past the Indians, smiled at the women. 'Have no fear, ladies. You shall soon be returned to your husbands and families.'

They gaped at him. Several of them he had met, although none was a planter's wife; they were the families of overseers and book-keepers, and one or two came from Falmouth. All were clearly still suffering from the shock of their ordeal. And no doubt they also had spent a busy night, as every night

THE DEVIL'S OWN

since they had been captured would have been similarly busy.

Tom touched him on the shoulder. 'If we are to reach the beach by noon, it would be best to hurry.'

They descended from the village into the Valley of Desolation, made their way across, and then climbed into the mountains before beginning their descent to the beach. They made a vast array, the chieftains leading the way, Kit in their midst, the captives following, and behind them the warriors of the tribe, fully armed and ready for war. But having come this far, it would not reach the ultimate. Of that Kit was sure, now. Even Philip Warner must respond to this willingness on the part of the Caribs.

'You are doing right,' he said to Tom Warner.

The half-caste thought for a while before replying. 'I am doing the best for my people, Kit, because I too am well aware of the growing strength of the white men. As to what is right, no man can tell that, because no man knows what is right. There is a risk that with the determination to live at peace with our invaders, my braves might degenerate into a nation of women, like the Arawaks.'

'That is not necessarily so,' Kit said. 'Do not the white men desire to live at peace with their neighbours? And are they not still capable of waging war?'

Tom looked at him, and burst out laughing. 'Do you honestly believe what you are saying? There is no more warlike creature on the face of this earth than the white man. He merely endeavours to disguise it under a variety of specious pleas for peace. We are at least honest about our pleasures. But come, we have arrived.'

The beach opened in front of them, and the ships waited, patiently at anchor, guns still run out. The Indians halted at the fringe of the trees, and Kit went on alone down the beach, past the war canoes, and waved his arms.

A cheer broke out from the ships, and a moment later the longboat pulled away from the side of the flagship. 'Welcome back, Captain Hilton,' said the coxswain. 'We were all but giving you up for lost.'

'Not so, friend,' Kit said. 'I have brought the chieftains with me.' He turned to the forest, and Tom and his seven caciques came down the sand.

'Your men are armed,' Tom observed. 'I had expected to meet my brother on the beach.'

'Will you not take his word? He gave it to me personally,' Kit said.

Tom hesitated, glanced at his companions, and then climbed into the boat. The other Indians followed his example. The white sailors looked towards the trees, and the women they could see there.

'They will come, when the talking is finished,' Kit said.

The boat pulled across the calm sea, into the looming side of the ship. How enormous she looked from down here, and how powerful, with the ugly muzzles of the cannon protruding from the row of ports. But there at the gangway were Bale and Philip Warner, waiting to receive their guests.

Kit was first up the ladder, to grasp hands with his father-in-law.

'Well done, lad,' Philip said. 'Well done. Welcome aboard, Tom.'

The brothers gazed at each other. Then Tom took the proffered hand. 'My chieftains,' he said.

Slowly the seven Indians came up the ladder, looked around them at the sailors and the great cannon, and up at the towering masts and the furled sails.

Tom made a remark in the Carib tongue, and then smiled at Kit and his brother. 'They are amazed, at the size and strength of the white man's ship. They do not understand why you should seek for peace when possessed of such strength.'

'We seek for peace because we, too, respect the Carib strength,' Kit said.

'Aye,' Philip Warner agreed, glancing at the people on the beach. 'You'll bring your people below, brother.'

Tom hesitated yet again, and he also looked from the armed seamen to the distant shore. Then he nodded, and ducked his head to follow Kit into the great cabin.

'You'll stay on my right hand, Kit,' Philip Warner said. 'And you, Bale, on my left.'

The captain grinned, and nodded. He appeared to be in a high good humour this morning. Kit found himself on the opposite side of the table to the Indians.

'I feel that we outnumber you unfairly, Philip,' Tom said with a smile. 'Eight to three.'

Philip also smiled. 'But you are on my ship, brother, and therefore in my power,' he said. 'And perhaps it were best to put an end to this farce immediately.' He clapped his hands, and the door opened once again, to admit six seamen, four carrying pistols and the other two carrying lengths of chain.

Tom frowned. 'What's this?'

'As you have seen fit to surrender yourselves,' Philip said. 'I intend to clap you in irons before taking you back to St John's, where you will be hanged.'

Kit's jaw dropped in consternation. Tom's reaction was more violent. With a roar of rage he leapt across the table, his fingers searching for his brother's throat. But Philip was already shouting, 'Now,' and at the same time throwing both arms around Kit's shoulders and stretching him full length on the deck.

The doors to the cabins behind the white men swung open, and the entire morning exploded into a crash of musketry.

9

The Traitor

The deafening crash of the explosions, the cloud of nostril-clogging black smoke, the cries of the assailed men, the entire suddenness of the event, for a moment removed Kit's senses. He was aware of sprawling on the deck of the cabin, Philip Warner on top of him, and then of feet stamping on him as men swarmed over him, their passage being marked by the rasp of their swords. The confined space was filled with curses and groans, and the shrieks of the dying. But now he was understanding what was happening, and with an effort forced himself to gaze up at the companion-way to the main deck, and watch a Carib chieftain running up, to pause at the top, and then come tumbling back down the narrow steps, a pike protruding from his breast.

The thump as he cannoned into the door was the end of the brief conflict. Now there were only the gasps of exertion issuing from the lungs of the victors. Perhaps the entire task had taken them ten seconds, and yet they panted as if they had been fighting for several hours. This was the measure of the guilty effort they had put forth.

Slowly Kit climbed to his feet. Someone threw open the

stern windows, and the smoke began to clear. Men stared at the bloody swords in their hands, and began to pick up their discarded muskets, and from the hatchways and skylights other men peered in, gaping at the scene of destruction below them.

Someone laughed. ' 'Twas easy, after all, Colonel Warner.'

Kit stood at the end of the table, looking down at the dead bodies, looking down at Indian Tom Warner. Perhaps he had fallen in the first volley; there were two gaping bullet wounds in his chest, but no cut marks. His eyes were open, and he stared, at Kit and beyond. The expression in his eyes was the most terrible Kit had ever seen.

Revulsion filled his belly, bubbled to his chest, took control of his brain and the muscles of his body. He uttered a yell which outdid that of any of the Caribs, and as Tom Warner had done, threw himself clear across the table to wrap his fingers around the Deputy Governor's throat.

'Stop him,' Philip bawled, as he fell back on to a chair. Kit's knees ground into his belly, and he landed, and swung his fists. But already men were clawing at him, throwing him to one side, stamping on his arms and legs, regaining their own weapons as they sought to put an end to his anger.

'Do not harm him,' Philip commanded. He sat up, straightened his cravat. 'He has cause for distress. It was his word we pledged.'

They dragged Kit to his feet. 'My word,' he said. 'You cur. You crawling thing. You . . .'

Philip Warner slashed the back of his hand across Kit's mouth. 'My decision,' he said. 'As commander of this expedition, as Deputy Governor of Antigua. You'll convince no one that I was wrong, Kit. And if you'd keep my friendship, you'll maintain a civil tongue in your head.'

'Your friendship?' Kit demanded. 'I'd as soon take the hand of a snake. That creature at the least pretends to nothing more than its own belly-crawling treachery.'

Philip's brows drew angrily together, but he was interrupted by a cry from Bale, who had gone on deck.

'Colonel Warner, sir. They must suspect something is afoot. They are launching their canoes.'

'By Christ.' Philip ran for the steps. 'Raise your anchor, Mr Bale. Make sail, man. Make sail. And signal the fleet to do likewise.'

The rest of the men ran behind him, and Kit was left alone, with the dead. But he too had reason to be on deck.

THE DEVIL'S OWN

He climbed the ladder, emerged into the afternoon heat, gazed at the six great canoes being dragged down the sand and launched into the water, at the spears being waved, the arrows being fitted to the bows.

'Would you compound crime upon crime?' he yelled. 'The women are still there. Our women.'

Philip Warner looked down on him from the poop deck. 'Not our women Kit. They belong to the Indians, now.'

'You'd desert them?' He could not believe his own words.

'Would any white man want them back?' Bale demanded. 'After they'd shared a cannibal's hammock?'

Kit continued to stare at Philip, who had the grace to flush. 'Aye, my brother took *his* wife back,' he said. 'But Edward was always an unusual fellow. Like you, Kit. You'd do well to ponder that.'

Kit turned away to look at the beach, at the green mountains which towered upwards towards the sky, at the myriad figures running up and down the sand, at the men already digging their paddles into the water as they urged their canoes towards the ships. Too much had happened, too quickly and too relentlessly, this past fortnight. Too much for his mind to assimilate. His brain rejected utterly the conception placed there, firstly by Yarico and now by Philip himself. He was the victim of a gigantic conspiracy. For if this deed had been planned before the fleet left St John's, then the decision to abandon the women had also been taken, before the fleet left St John's. And every word that had been agreed there had been a lie.

But the women. Almost he thought he could see them, waving their arms and calling, nay begging, for deliverance from the impossible fate to which they had been deserted.

Impossible was the word. He left the stern of the ship and ran forward. Men were heaving on the capstan to raise the anchor; others were already aloft unfurling the sails, and still others were gathered by the forehatch from which the boatswain was passing up cutlasses and muskets, for the canoes were fast approaching.

'Listen to me,' he shouted. 'There are white women back there. Eleven white women. Women from Antigua. We cannot just sail away and leave them to the mercy of the Indians. Would you abandon your wife or your daughter? You cannot do that.'

They turned to look at him, at a man demented.

'You have arms in your hands, and the cannon will cover us,' he shouted. 'God knows I wanted no bloodshed, but as it is come upon us, at least let us get ashore and rescue them. Will no man follow me?' He seized a sword and ran to the side of the longboat. 'I, Kit Hilton, call for volunteers. I will lead you, my bravos. I marched with Morgan on Panama. You'll find no better leader in these islands. Who'll follow me?'

They stared at him. Perhaps, had he been Morgan, they might have come. Perhaps, had he been Jean DuCasse, they might have come. But then, perhaps not. He offered them no gold and no glory. He could not even offer them beautiful women. He could offer them only death, for the sake of eleven women they already counted as dead.

Bale stood before him, a pistol in his hand. ''Tis mutiny you're after, Captain Hilton,' he said. 'To suborn men from their duty in the face of the enemy is downright treason. I've orders to place you under arrest in your cabin.'

Kit looked down at the weapon he held. How he wanted to thrust it forward, to kill Bale, as could easily be done, and to confront the lot of them. And then make his way aft and settle with Philip Warner. His father-in-law? His own uncle? But was that not part of the hate and anger he felt? That he should be a part of this unhappy family?

But would it avail anyone for him to die now, when there was so much for him to do, by living?

He dropped his sword to the deck. 'I've a long memory, Bale.'

The pirate flushed, and jerked his head towards the after companion-way.

'Be sure he is secured, Mr Bale,' Philip Warner called down from the poop. 'We can stand no more eruptions of this nature. 'Tis certain we shall have to fire into these men.'

'Aye, aye, Colonel Warner.' Bale pushed Kit inside the cabin, hesitated. 'Remain in here, I beg of you, Kit. And remember if you will that this was not my doing.'

'Not your doing?' Kit turned on him. 'By God, you prating coward.'

'Hear me,' Bale begged. 'I knew naught of this plan until I was given my instructions, after you had left the ship, yesterday afternoon. This I swear. And who was I, Kit, to gainsay the Deputy Governor? I am no planter, protected by wealth and precedent. You yourself were quick enough to accuse me of piracy. He'd have had me under arrest and on

THE DEVIL'S OWN

my way to Execution Dock before I'd have known what was happening.'

'On your own ship, and surrounded by your own men?' Kit asked, bitterly.

Bale flushed. 'There are sufficient of his volunteers on board as well. There is the truth of the matter, Kit. You'll believe it or not as you choose. My conscience is clear.'

Kit seized his shoulder as the captain turned for the door. 'Then you'll so testify, Bale, when the time comes. Or be sure that you will indeed find yourself on that ship for London.'

Bale hesitated, and then nodded. 'When the time comes, Kit. But it'll not come at all if I do not con this ship to open water.'

Kit let him go. He could hear the cries of the savages as they came alongside, and now the cannon began to speak, causing the vessel to shudder and roll. Kit sat on the narrow bunk, and listened. He had never been below deck in a fight before, found it difficult to decide exactly what was happening. But soon enough the ship began to heel to the wind, and he could hear the sluicing of water past the hull as she gathered speed. Now the cannon were silent, and the shouts of the Caribs faded.

Soon he heard the tramp of feet in the great cabin beyond the door, followed by the splashes from astern as the dead bodies were thrown to the sharks. After that there was nothing to do but wait, as the little fleet beat north. To wait and to think, to remember and to vow vengeance. His door opened but once, to admit two sailors, one with his breakfast.

'We'll be home soon enough, Captain Hilton,' one of them said with a grin. 'Antigua is rising fair on the port bow.'

Mocking him? Or revealing their sympathy. As if he cared for their sympathy. As if he cared for anything beyond his own sense of outrage, his own determination to have justice done to Tom Warner.

Now the cannon was firing again, but this time expelling empty air from their blank charges, and even as he heard the anchor rattling through the hawse-pipe, he could also hear the distant cheering from the Antigua waterfront. They were celebrating a victory.

The door opened. Philip Warner stood there, backed by six of the Antiguan volunteers, all armed. 'Good morning to you, Kit,' he said. 'I have some hope that by now you will have come to your senses. Sir William approaches in his barge, and I have no doubt that he will wish to congratulate you as much as me. We were sent to destroy the possibility of the Caribs ever mounting such a raid again, and we have accomplished our purpose, without the loss of a single man. They will not grow eight such caciques again in a hundred years. Leaderless, they will fall to squabbling amongst themselves, and perhaps into a pattern of mutual destruction, and our islands, our plantations, and our families, will be safe. I'd have you stand at my side to receive the plaudits due to the victors.'

Kit did not reply. He picked up his hat and went outside, to blink in the sunlight, to look at the trim rooftops and the sharp church steeples, now all echoing joyous sound as the other ships in the fleet also brought up to anchor.

The Governor's barge was already alongside, and Stapleton clambered up the ladder. 'Philip,' he cried. 'By God, sir, but it is right glad I am to see you. Kit. By God, sir, and you fly the pennants of victory. But it was so rapidly accomplished. Tell us straight, man, you suffered heavily?'

'We lost not a man, Sir William,' Philip Warner said. 'And we seized the eight most prominent Carib chieftains.'

'By God.' Stapleton looked around him as if expecting to see the Indians on deck. 'They're confined?'

'No, sir. They resisted arrest, and we were forced to execute them.'

Stapleton's smile slowly faded, and he frowned at the Deputy Governor. 'Executed, you say? Your own brother?'

'My father's bastard son, Sir William,' Philip said, speaking very evenly. 'I knew him only as the man who had my daughter raped by her own slave.'

'By God,' Stapleton said. He turned to Kit. 'Your plans came to naught, then?'

'My plans were successful, Sir William.' Kit also spoke with great deliberation. 'I visited the Carib village, alone and unarmed, and I spoke with their caciques, and I persuaded them to attend a conference on board Colonel Warner's ship. in order to discuss a just treaty of peace between the Caribs and the English. They came, willingly and unarmed. And no sooner were they seated in that cabin than they were set upon and most foully murdered.'

'Murdered?' Stapleton gazed from one to the other in horror.

'By God, Kit,' Philip Warner said. 'But you make it hard.'

'Murdered?' Stapleton repeated. 'Now come, the pair of

you, confess to having had another of your interminable quarrels.'

'You'd best ask the crew,' Kit said.

'For God's sake,' Philip shouted. 'Were *they* not murderers? Were they not the inhuman creatures who have been butchering defenceless people for too long? By God, sir, the question of how they were done to death does not enter into it. One does not ask the hunter, how did you kill that pack of wolves, the fisherman how he managed to destroy the shark that was taking from his line. You merely say, thank God the deed is done.'

'By God, sir,' Stapleton said. 'You do not deny the crime?'

'I deny any crime. The deed I will admit. You charged me with avenging our losses here, and with ensuring that no such raid could ever take place again. Well, sir, I have accomplished both of these objectives, in the shortest possible space of time, and with the least possible loss to ourselves. You should be doubling your congratulations rather than wasting your time in listening to this . . . this pirate become Quaker.'

'By God, sir,' Stapleton said. 'And you the Deputy Governor of this island, the representative of the King, God bless him. Where would English justice be, sir, were it always carried out in so arbitrary a spirit? The men were on board your ship, sir. And you arrested them. As they had been granted safe conduct, why, that would have been treachery enough for the most hardened blackguard. But to slay them in that cabin there, why sir, my brain still finds it difficult to grasp the enormity of such a deed.'

'They endeavoured to resist,' Philip said again.

'And so they were killed. Eight unarmed men before the entire crew of this ship. By God. You'll consider yourself under arrest, sir, until this charge is proved or disproved.'

'Bah,' Philip said. 'You'll not find a jury in this island, in all the Leewards, to convict me on any charge arising out of this affair. Those men were Caribs. There you have my defence.'

'Aye,' Stapleton said. 'No doubt you make a fair point. But there are other courts of law, Colonel Warner. As of this moment you are relieved of the duties and responsibilities, and prerogatives, of the Deputy Governor of this island, and you will be placed upon the next ship bound for England, to stand your trial there, and may God have mercy on your soul.'

' 'Tis done.' Kit laid down the quill, and slowly straightened his fingers. He had never written so much in his life.

The clerk scattered fine sand across the ink, raised the papers, one after the other, blew them clean. Stapleton was already reading the first sheet, standing by the window where the best light was to be found, every few seconds jerking his head at the steady cacophony outside.

'This will serve admirably,' he said. 'You'll dictate your statement as well, Mr Bale. My clerk will pen it.'

'And then I'll be free to leave?' Bale was sweating with fear.

'Aye. You'll be free to leave. Now make haste, man.' The Governor put down Kit's statement. 'You hear those people, Captain Hilton? You'll need a file of soldiers to see you from town.'

Kit set his hat on his head. 'Do you mean to leave me a file of soldiers for the rest of my life?'

Stapleton frowned. 'Why, that would be impossible.'

'My own opinion entirely. I've never needed protection in the past, Sir William. I'll not require it now, I promise you.'

Stapleton walked with him to the courthouse door. 'I do not rightly understand my feelings for you, Kit,' he said. 'I know you for what you were: a buccaneer. No doubt you will claim provocation, but 'tis little enough excuse for the mayhem caused in these fair islands by Morgan and DuCasse. I know you for what you are now, a planter, as stiff-necked a profession as I have ever had the misfortune to encounter. Neither of those are reasons for me to like you. And now you see fit to oppose public opinion and who knows, even public welfare, in the cause of an abstract concept of justice. I see you as a man who will cause trouble wherever he goes, because you will not bend with the times, with opinion. You will merely stand rigid until you break. But I would be doing you less than justice did I not also say that, as a man would rather look upon the towering oak, knowing full well that its rigidity must in time bring its downfall when the winds grow too strong for it, than upon the blade of grass which but lies flat and then recovers its stance when the gale is over, so I wish there were a few more like you. In all the world, to be sure. But here in the West Indies most of all. My hand, sir. Be sure you will ever have my support should you seek justice.'

Kit grasped his hand. 'I thank you, sir.'

'And now you go home to Green Grove?'

THE DEVIL'S OWN

No idle question, that. It was twenty-four hours since the fleet's return, twenty-four hours since Philip Warner's arrest. The news had spread throughout the island, as the angry mob outside testified. But Marguerite had not come into town. She, who was usually in the forefront of any public occasion. But perhaps that was a happy sign.

'Yes, Sir William. I shall return to Green Grove.'

Stapleton nodded. 'Then I will wish you God speed. But Kit, be careful, I do beg of you. Watch your back. Tempers are running high, and we have seen how careless these people can be of honour.'

Kit nodded. 'At least they will know the risk they run.' He pressed his tricorne a little more firmly on his head, opened the door and stepped through. The crowd were baying and shouting, and for the moment did not notice him; their attention was taken by the tall figure of Agrippa, who stood with the two horses at the foot of the steps.

'Nigger,' they chanted. 'Pirate. Nigger pirate.'

'He should be hanged,' someone yelled. ' 'Tis the pirates should be suffering justice, not our Governor.'

'Aye, to the gallows with him,' someone else yelled.

Agrippa stared at them, and they made no move to close him. But their temper was rising.

Kit walked down the steps. His own anger simmered only just below the surface. And he had recognized Chester in the throng.

'Edward,' he called. 'Dear chap, you'd best send your friends home, lest someone gets hurt.'

There was a sudden silence, as they turned to look at him. He continued to walk down the steps, and now reached the foot. Agrippa held his stirrup for him, and he swung himself into the saddle.

'Indian lover,' someone yelled.

'What did you do?' asked someone else. 'Hold your own wife on the floor for the red devils to make at her?'

Kit swung his horse smartly aside, knocking two men from their feet, reached the last speaker, bent from the saddle to seize the man by his coat and whip him from the ground. He held the wriggling body close, while the fellow's feet kicked feebly and the crowd gaped a such a display of strength and determination.

'The next time you address me, sir,' Kit said, 'have a weapon in your hand, or take a whipping.' He threw the man away from him; the flying body cannoned into three more men and all fell. The crowd surged back, and then surged forward again, to check and once more retreat as Kit's hands dropped to the pistols at his belt. And Agrippa was also armed.

'Ow, ow me God,' screamed the man he had thrown down. 'My leg is broken.'

'Now there is a pity,' Kit said. 'I had intended it to be your head. Will you gentlemen stand aside, or must I clear a way with my sword?'

'By God, Kit Hilton,' Chester shouted. 'Would you declare war on us all?'

'If need be, Edward. Will you be the first? These people can make a space for us. I have here pistols and a sword. Or would you prefer daggers and bare hands? Name it, man. Name it. Let us be at it.'

Chester stared at him, the colour slowly draining from his face. The crowd stared also, from one to the other of the planters. But others were separating from in front of the two horses. Kit urged his mount forward, and Agrippa clattered immediately behind him. A few moments later they were through the crowd and trotting along the road leading south.

'I thought we would have to fight our way out,' Agrippa remarked.

Kit shook his head. 'They have too high a regard for their own skins. They have to be whipped to it, or shown the way, and the planters lack the belly to draw on me.'

'Yet can they still harm you, Kit.' Agrippa urged his mount level. 'For how may a man exist, without human companionship?'

'And am I that bereft? I have you, old friend. And any others?'

'They support you entirely, Kit. They are distressed you would not immediately call upon them.'

'I'll have no man be forced to declare his support for me, Agrippa, especially one who lives in the centre of that rabble and yet refuses the use of weapons. Nor could I expose Lillan to such contumely.'

'Yet is she already exposed,' Agrippa said.

'How can that be?'

'God alone knows, Kit. But it is common knowledge in St John's that she is your mistress.'

Kit frowned at him. 'Dag has heard this?'

'He has said nothing to me. But if he is not stone deaf, he has heard it.'

'By God,' Kit said. 'But no one in the island knew of it,

THE DEVIL'S OWN

save you, and me, and Marguerite . . . by God.' He kicked his horse in the ribs, set it to a gallop. A man, rushing to disaster, with anger in his heart. For did not his strength truly depend upon Marguerite, and the wealth of Green Grove? And he could expect nothing but anger there, at what he had done. That indeed was why he was hurrying home now, to placate her. And how could he do that, with anger colouring his own emotions?

Yet he would not slacken his pace. He felt like a ship caught in the full force of a hurricane wind, blown hither and thither and unable to do more than keep afloat, by doing the correct things, trimming the sails, manning the pumps, shifting the ballast, from hour to hour, intent only upon survival, but without any knowledge of where in the ocean the storm would eventually leave him floating, or if, indeed, he would be left floating at all, and not stranded upon some rocky shore.

He galloped down the last of the road and into the drive. The Negroes stopped work to stare at him. They were busy clearing the burned-out fields, saving which of the plants could be used as ratoons for a fresh crop. Others laboured on the Great House, plugging bullet holes, removing the shattered doors where the Caribs had broken in, standing by with pots of paint to remove the last traces of the conflict, as were still others working down in the overseers' village. But all stopped to stare at their master, flogging his horse into the compound, throwing the reins to Maurice Peter and stamping up the stairs on to the verandah, while Agrippa also reined in beneath him, but remained mounted.

'Father,' Tony came tumbling through the withdrawing-room, starkly empty as most of the furniture had been removed, to be repaired or consigned to the flames. Only the spinet remained, strangely overlooked by the marauding Indians, or untouched because they did not recognize its meaning.

'Boy.' Kit swept him from the floor, hugged him close.

'Did you win, Father? The news from town is that all the Caribs are dead.'

'Not all.' Kit set him back on the floor, stooped to kiss Rebecca on the cheek. 'Where is Miss Johnson?'

'She has not come out today, Father. There is so much tumult and excitement she feared to ride alone.'

'And your mother?'

'Mama is upstairs, in bed.'

Kit frowned at the boy. 'Marguerite, in bed, at this hour?'

'She has been in bed for two days, Captin,' Maurice Peter said. 'Since the fleet sailed, almost.'

'By God,' Kit said, bounding up the stairs. But how his heart overflowed with relief. Because there was surely the reason she had not come to town.

He pulled the door open. She sat up in bed wearing a shawl over her shoulders, but nothing else so far as he could see. Her hair was loose on the pillows propped behind her head. She looked as well, and as beautiful, as ever he had known her, and there was a jug of iced sangaree on the table beside her.

'Meg. They told me you were ill.'

'A slight fever,' she said. 'Nothing more.'

He crossed the room, and noticed the thin lines running away from her eyes, the bunches of muscle at the corners of her mouth. She had been under some strain, and she was nervous. 'Sweetheart.' He held her arms, and kissed her on the mouth.

'I expected you yesterday,' she said. 'Did not the fleet return, yesterday?'

'Indeed we did. There was much to be done.'

Their eyes seemed to lock. 'Indeed,' she said. 'A victory to be celebrated, as I have heard.'

'We were ever straight with each other in the past, sweet Meg.'

'So be straight with me now, Kit. I have heard so much, and all of it garbled and contradictory. I would not injure your projects by appearing in town. I also would believe nothing of what those foul-mouthed gossips brought to me. I would hear it all, from no other lips than yours.'

He got up, and her fingers left his, reluctantly. He paced the room, paused to pour himself a drink. 'You knew my purpose?'

'I doubted it would succeed.'

'It would have. Unfortunately, your . . . father did not respect it. I gave Tom Warner my word, Meg. I gave his people my word. And they were shot and stabbed and carved in cold blood. You have mirrors scattered throughout this house, in which we have enjoyed preening ourselves and thinking, and saying to each other, what a splendid pair we make. Had I not accused your father of the crime he committed I should have had to break them all.'

'Then the rumours are true.' She spoke very quietly.

THE DEVIL'S OWN

'Philip Warner has been removed from the position of Deputy Governor, and is under arrest. He leaves St John's tomorrow, for London, and his trial.'

Marguerite gazed at him for some seconds, then she threw back the covers and got out of bed. She left the shawl behind her, went to the door, and threw it wide. 'Ellen Jane,' she called, her voice clear and high as a bell.

'Yes, mistress?'

'You'll prepare my bath. And my town clothes. Quickly, girl.'

'You'll go to town?' Kit asked.

Marguerite draped her undressing-robe around her shoulders. 'Should I led my father go to his trial without saying goodbye?'

'No,' Kit agreed. 'I had not expected that. Shall I ride with you?'

'No.' She extended her left hand, looked at the ring which glinted there. 'No. I prefer to go alone. But it would be best for you to return there, before I return *here*.'

'To be with my mistress, you mean, as you have so carefully put about?'

Her head came up, and her gaze scorched his face. 'You can be with whomsoever you please, Kit. But I do not wish to see you again.'

How quietly she spoke. And how ridiculous her words.

'*You*, do you wish to see *me*?'

'You have forced me to understand my own stupidity. You watched me lie on the floor beneath a black man, and then sought to forgive the man who caused it. I do not understand the mind of a man who could do that. I endeavoured to understand. I endeavoured to tell myself that perhaps you have a stature, a breadth of vision, that exceeds mine. I placed you above other men, ten years ago, when I elected to marry you. Father endeavoured to dissuade me, and I would not listen to him. But it would seem he was right. Or I overestimated my own powers. I knew you then for what you are, Kit. At least, I knew your strengths and your weaknesses, your past crimes and your possibilities. I did not understand, alas, that streak of deep wayward revolution that runs through your soul. I should have. Not only did my father warn me of it, but it was there in your own past, in the history of your family. Tony Hilton was ever a rebel. Edward Warner was ever a rebel. Susan Hilton was the daughter of an outlaw and the wife of another. Perhaps it is simply that too much of the wild Irish runs in your veins. I knew all of these things, ten years ago. But I thought I could change you.'

Almost she smiled.

'How many women make that mistake? I thought I could take that strength and that vigour and that demoniac energy and harness it, for the use of Green Grove, for the use of the Warners, for the use of Antigua. And you have proved me wrong, time and again. So leave this place, Kit. I took you from the dust. I'll not return you there. Sign what bills you wish, find what happiness you wish, with your Danish whore. I'll not gainsay you. God knows . . .' she hesitated. 'I love you. I have never loved any man but you. I shall never love any man but you. But to have you in my bed now would sicken me no less than the memory of George Frederick.'

The sun dropped into the Caribbean Sea with its invariable suddenness, and darkness swept across Antigua. The two horsemen walked their mounts slowly through the main street of St John's.

They had waited till dusk, deliberately, to avoid the mobs, the risk of giving offence. Out of fear? That at least was not true. Out of a desire to cause no more harm, to bring about no more of a catastrophe than had already happened.

What was it Jean had said, only a short fortnight ago? He had wanted to turn back the clock a brief half hour. But how far should the clock be turned back now? To the minute before he had accepted Philip Warner's offer of the command of the *Bonaventure*? Yet would he still have met Marguerite, soon enough. Well, then, to the moment before he had thrown his cutlass to Daniel Parke? He had done then what he had always done since, what he had believed to be right, at the moment, without any thought of the consequences. He had always been proud of that.

And he had left Green Grove this afternoon, in that spirit. It had been the most difficult decision of his life, especially knowing the shortness, as he also knew the vehemence, of her anger. But the plantation was hers, and she was entitled to be bitter, about what had happened to her, about her father, and about Lillan. Nor could he expect her to do anything but hate the Indians. So he had ridden away into the darkness, away from wife and children and wealth and prosperity, as she had commanded, with only his sword

THE DEVIL'S OWN

and his pistols and his faithful friend at his shoulder. As he had done before.

And yet his instincts had not always led him down the path of right. Else why was he here, seeking once again a girl he had cruelly wronged, and could now wrong only some more.

He dismounted, and knocked on the door. St John's was quiet, save for the occasional burst of laughter from the tavern, where, no doubt, they were consigning Kit Hilton to hell for all eternity.

Astrid Christianssen opened the door. 'Kit?' Almost he could read the dismay in her tone, although her face was indistinct. 'Agrippa? We had feared for you.'

'We are sound enough, in wind and limb,' Kit said. 'May we come in?'

'Come in? Oh . . .'

'You may come in, Kit.' Dag came out of the parlour.

'I thank you.' Kit took off his hat and stepped into the hall, Agrippa at his shoulder.

'What has happened?' Dag asked.

'I have left Green Grove.'

Astrid frowned at him. 'You have left your wife? And your children?'

'It was a mutual decision, between Marguerite and myself. She feels that I have betrayed her father. Everyone feels that I have betrayed Philip Warner, by not permitting him to get away with fratricide. I am probably the most unpopular man in Antigua at this moment. Do you share that view?'

Dag shook his head. 'No, no we honour what you did, in that respect. And we grieve for the sorrow it has brought upon you. I grieve even more than we cannot offer you a bed for the night.'

'As you see best, Dag. I would like to speak with Lillan.'

'She has retired.'

'And it is scarce an hour since dusk? You are playing the father.'

'And should I not, as she is my daughter?' He sighed. 'Whom you have outraged.'

'And have you, then, taken your stick to her?' Kit asked softly. 'For be sure that I will see her, Dag, and should she be harmed, then will I harm you.'

The Quaker hesitated, glancing at Agrippa. 'Truly, you

revert easily enough to the buccaneer, Kit. You'd see mayhem where we have given you a home, Agrippa?'

'I'll not draw against Kit, Dag,' the Negro said. 'I'd beg you not to force that issue.'

'Good evening, Kit,' Lillan said from the foot of the stairs. Her undressing-robe was pulled close across her nightdress.

'I told you . . .' Dag began.

'And I wish differently.'

'You are a common slut,' he shouted. 'Your name is bandied about in this town like a piece of filth. You fill me with disgust every time I look upon you.'

'Then look upon her no more,' Kit said. 'I have come to take her with me.'

'To . . . why, sir . . .'

'I am appealing to your common sense, Dag. As you say, her name is being used too freely. That was not my doing. It is Marguerite's. But as it has been done, why, nothing we can do will unsay it, except openly to declare ourselves. I have in mind a house down in Falmouth, somewhat removed from the tumults of St John's, where Lillan may live in peace, with me as her protector.'

'Protector?'

'You are still married to Marguerite Warner,' Astrid said. 'How can you gainsay that?'

'I cannot gainsay that. I know what I am asking of Lillan. I would not have done so, had the event not been made public.'

'Aye,' Dag said. 'No doubt you can, as always, explain your motives to your own satisfaction. Well, that is not our way. You were no doubt sent by the Lord to try our patience and our spirit, Kit. I hold nothing against you for that. But now you would compound another moral crime on top of your first, just as you have spent your life compounding crime against crime, always in the hope of expiating the original sin. Crimes are not expiated by other crimes, Kit Hilton, but by prayer and resolution, by patience and by good works. You have dragged our daughter's name through the gutter. It will be her punishment, and ours, to live in the gutter for a while. But in time we shall re-emerge from that filthy place, cleaner and better than before. Sure it is that Lillan will not need to crawl from one gutter to the next.'

Kit stared at him, his brows slowly drawing together. 'I respect your morality, Dag, even if I think you set too much store by it. But then, I have no such advantage of faith, in either people or the hereafter. Morality in my world consists of honour and courage; there has never been room for patient resignation. I ask Lillan to let me honour her, as publicly as I may, and I ask her also to show the courage I know she possesses, the courage to take life and circumstances by the throat and say, I will live, and be happy, no matter what the odds against it. These things I ask of her, not you, Dag. And by God, I'll not leave this house until I hear the answer from her own lips.'

Dag turned to look at his daughter. 'You'll be a whore, now and for ever.'

'Oh, Lillan,' Astrid cried. 'You cannot. You . . .'

'Will you stop me by force, Father?' Lillan asked, very quietly.

He opened his mouth, glanced at Kit, and closed it again. 'You'll do as you see fit, daughter. But once pass through that door in this man's company, do not seek ever to re-enter.'

'Well, then,' she said. 'It seems I must bid you farewell.'

They rode, four mounted figures under a darkening midnight sky, south for Falmouth. Their clothes were tied to the backs of their horses, and the two men possessed their weapons. They said little. They had hardly exchanged a word since leaving the town. There was too much to be thought about. And perhaps even some things to be anticipated. They were four against the world. The thought made Kit's blood tingle.

Lillan yawned, and swayed in the saddle. 'Should we not rest by the roadside, Kit? It wants another six hours to dawn.'

'But only two to Falmouth,' he said. 'There is a tavern, where we shall find ourselves shelter and comfort. Unless you are truly too tired to continue.'

'No. I will ride. I am but ill-prepared.' She smiled at him. 'I have slept little this last week. There has been too much to keep awake for.'

He reached across to squeeze her hand. 'But from henceforth you will sleep sound every night, Lillan. I give you my word for that.'

'Kit Hilton's woman,' she whispered. 'I want no more than that, Kit. I have wanted no more than that, since the day I met you, in the harbour at St Eustatius.'

'And fool that I was, I looked elsewhere, and became involved in events which were too big for me.'

'Too big for you, Kit? That I deny. There is no man will not honour your courage in denouncing Philip Warner's crime, when they give themselves time to consider the event.'

'Pray God you are right.' Not a man. But what of a woman? And then, what terrible thoughts were those, to have while riding in the company of yet another woman, who, like the first, was giving everything she possessed into his care. But Christ, Marguerite, all the memory of her, that glorious animal sexuality which shrouded so much beauty, that confident laughter, that arrogant awareness of herself as a person and as a power, that aura in which she moved. And she was the mother of his children.

Almost he wanted to weep. And then he whipped their horses into a faster trot. Marguerite could only be lost in the softness of Lillan's arms.

And these were not for the taking, that night. She was asleep in the saddle when they rode into Falmouth, and banged on the door of the inn, to get an irate innkeeper out of bed, to watch his anger change to fear as he discovered the identity of his visitor. Beds and rooms were hastily made available, and in one of these Kit placed his mistress. She wore a grey gown, and her hat was tied firmly under her chin. He removed the hat, and took off her boots, to marvel at the straight slender toes, so white, so perfectly shaped. Now she smiled in her sleep, and sighed. She was his. He could undress her completely. Indeed, he should do that, for she did not possess so many clothes that she could afford to sleep in her gown. But he did not dare touch her. To touch her, while she slept, to strip her while she slept, to love her while she slept, was to conjure up too many visions from the past. And here was one vision he did not dare risk losing.

He bade Agrippa and Abigail good night, and slept in the chair, removing only his own boots and weapons and hat. He snuffed the candle, and leaned his head, and stared into the darkness. He felt the emptiness which comes after battle. For ten days he had charged forward at the head of his mental troops, first of all in rising above the catastrophe of the French and Indian invasion, then in recruiting and preparing the expedition, then on his march into the interior of Dominica, and since then in his attack upon Philip Warner. Culminating in his assault upon the Christianssens themselves.

THE DEVIL'S OWN

Why, Daniel Parke would be proud of him, for that was how that wild-eyed Virginian lived every moment of every day of every year. And where was he now, Kit wondered. By God, what would he give to have Daniel Parke standing beside him, laughing at opposition, careless of life or fame in the pursuit of his own ambitions.

There was a dream. And now he must awake into reality. He had done the right things, by Lillan. He was sure of this, as he must be sure of this. But in doing that, he had burned his last bridge. Marguerite had tossed the girl in his face, as a man might toss a glove. And he had picked it up. She would not forgive. And he would not have her forgive, ever, for that would be to betray Lillan, in turn.

And now, too, his last friends in St John's were his most bitter enemies. When Kit Hilton fell, as fall he must, eventually, with a bullet in his gut or a sword thrust through his heart, there would be only three mourners.

He slept, uneasily, and awoke with a start, at the touch of a hand on his arm. She stood beside his chair, looking down on him. He gazed at a vision, for now she was rested, and she had washed her face to remove the dust of the journey and the tears of her quarrel with her family. And she had undressed, and waited. How tall she was, and how slender. Her height seemed increased by the long, straight golden hair which drifted past her shoulders almost to her thighs, a fine-spun web of purest delight.

It occurred to him with a thrill of surprise that he had never actually looked at her body before. They had shared but one brief hour together, and then it had been in the dark. He had felt, and he had inhaled, her loveliness, but he had not been able to see it, at his leisure. Now she waited, on his leisure; long, long legs, lightly muscled and therefore thin; narrow hips, almost a youth's hips, surely never meant for childbearing; a flat, scantily forested belly stretching up to a clearly marked rib-cage and narrow shoulders, from which came the small, up-tilted breasts of an utter virgin, in thought and in deed, for twenty-six years.

And then the face, which matched the body, in its natural solemnity, yet in the suggestion of calm pleasure which lay behind the mask. The face he knew. The face he had always wanted to possess. And the face displayed all the promise of the body.

'I do believe,' she said softly, 'that you have forgotten how we came to be here.'

He shook his head. 'I am but marvelling that a man of my character and my past should be so fortunate.'

'Fortune generally comes to those who deserve it,' she said. 'I would not have had you sleep in a chair.'

'And I would not have had you disturbed.' His arms went round her waist and he drew her down to his lap. His fingers explored the firm texture of her skin, dry where Marguerite's had ever been damp; cool where Marguerite's had ever been warm. And yet she knew passion. He remembered that she had known passion before, and now she knew it again, anxiously and eagerly. Her lips sought his, and her mouth was wide open. Here were none of the extravagant gestures and movements of Marguerite, and yet because of this the intimacies she sought, the intimacies she permitted, the way she inhaled whenever he would cup her breasts, to grow into his hand, the way she would spread her legs, slowly and yet insistently whenever his fingers slid lower than her ribs, the soft sighs with which she reached orgasm, so contrasted to the tumultuous groans of Marguerite, all filled him with an immense satisfaction, where in Marguerite's arms all had been temporary, a mere passage on the road to the next set to, where morning had been no more than the prelude to lunch, and afternoon no more than the overture to the night, and the night itself no more than the hallway which led to the awakening in the dawn. Marguerite had consumed. Lillan gave only peace. And where even the quiescent moments, with Marguerite, had had their fingers always busy, here there was time to talk, and think.

'You have not asked me how we shall live.' He lay on his belly, across the bed, chin on his hands, gazing through the window at the brilliant sunlight, hearing the distant rumble of the surf.

She brushed her hair, standing before the spotted mirror. She used long, slow strokes, turning her head and drooping her shoulder to allow the passage of her hand and her arm. 'I do not care how we shall live.'

'Yet must it be my care. My credit remains, although I would not impose upon it more than I must.'

'I do not care how we shall live,' she said again.

'I will write to Sir William Stapleton, and ask him for a position. It was an idea I had, many years ago, before other events overtook my common sense. I have never been a planter. The sea is my home, as it is in my blood. I will sail with the revenue frigate.'

THE DEVIL'S OWN

The brush slowly travelled to the end of the last strand of hair, and remained there, at the end of her fingers. 'You will go to sea?'

'Oh, fear not, sweetheart. Only on overnight passages, and Agrippa will remain here always, to guard you and protect you.'

She turned. 'You spoke of a house.'

He laughed, and swung his legs from the bed. 'That first. Come, dress yourself, and we shall breakfast, and go forth to inspect our new kingdom.'

It was no more than a cottage, set somewhat apart from the village itself, and therefore overlooked by the Caribs, nestling amidst the trees and looking down at the beach and the sea beyond. From the bedroom window they could see St Kitts, with the pointed finger of Mount Misery aiming at the sky.

'But there is only one bedroom,' Lillan wondered.

'We will build another at the back,' Agrippa said. But he was more interested in the amount of flat land surrounding the building. 'Space for a garden. Flowers, man,' he said to Kit. 'Have you never seen flowers?'

'There are flowers on Green Grove,' Kit said.

'We shall outmatch them here.'

'You, a gardener?'

'I like to watch things grow.' Agrippa said. 'I like to feel them come to life under my hands.' He slapped Kit on the shoulder. 'Man, for the first time since I was a little boy, I am happy. You can't be happy as a slave. And you shouldn't be happy as a buccaneer. And it is hard to be happy when the only man in all the world you love has got himself into something outside his nature. I can say that now, Kit. That woman was an obsession. She turned you inside out, made you something you were not. Kit Hilton, a planter? Kit Hilton, armed with a whip instead of a sword? That was unnatural. Maybe you didn't treat the Christianssens quite right. But I figure a man is a man and a woman is a woman, and when they want each other, they should take each other, religion or no religion. Be sure now, that you have done the right thing at last, Kit. And going back to sea is the right thing, too. And so I am happy.'

'To stay here? I cannot leave her alone.'

'To stay here, Kit. I will guard your woman, and I will tend my garden, and I will be happy.'

'Then it is decided. I'll see the attorney this day.'

Not that Mr Walker was happy with the situation. He perused the bill for several seconds. ' 'Tis a confused world we live in, Captain.'

'You'd question my credit?'

Mr Walker gazed at the big man in front of him, at the cutlass and the bulges in the pockets of the coat which denoted the presence of the pistols. Then he removed his periwig and scratched his bald head. 'I'd not dream of doing so, Captain. I have no doubt at all that if I present this paper at the Ice House, at Christianssen's Warehouse, or at Green Grove itself, it will be exchanged.'

He was asking a question. 'It will,' Kit promised.

'Aye,' Mr Walker said. 'And it will be done this day, I do promise you, Captain. As I have said, we live in too confused and uncertain a world for credit.'

'Meaning that some rogue may seek to strike me down, before I leave town?'

'I doubt there is a man on this island possesses the courage to risk such an attempt, Captain. No, no, I merely suggest that the island is in such a state of flux, with family divided against family, with our Deputy Governor by now, no doubt, incarcerated in the Tower of London, with the owners of the richest plantation on the island at loggerheads, with the House of Assembly prorogued, why, no man may tell what tomorrow will bring.' He took the conveyance from his clerk; the ink was still wet. 'There is your deed, sir. The house is yours. You at least should be content.'

'You make me feel a villain,' Kit muttered. 'Who has extracted this document from you by force of arms.'

Mr Walker permitted himself a dry smile. 'Indeed, sir, were this bill *not* to be honoured, then you would have done nothing less. But we are entering the realms of speculation. That is ever an unsound practice for lawyers, would you not agree? Should I need to contact you about any small matter, no doubt I will know where to find you.'

'You will.' Kit went outside into the street. Passersby averted their eyes and hurried on their way. There was no one in St John's would challenge him now. Philip Warner had been gone a fortnight, and memories were short. There was work to be done, and rum to be drunk, and lives to be led. Dominica was a long way away, and England even farther, and the war was done. No doubt there would be a stir, when the outcome of the trial was learned, but even that would cause little of a ripple at this distance, saving in the Warner family.

His family. He mounted, and rode for Green Grove, following the roads he knew so well. Already the fields were restored, the houses repaired and repainted. Save that the crop had been set back perhaps two months the raid might never have been.

And the sun was just beginning to dominate the sky. She would have returned from aback, and be in her bath.

Maurice Peter took the bridle. 'Welcome home, Captin.'

' 'Tis only a visit, Maurice Peter. Where are the children?'

'Here I am, Papa.' Tony stood on the verandah, staring at him with solemn eyes. 'Where have you been, Papa?'

'Away. Here, I've a present for you.'

It was a short sword, hardly more than a dirk. Tony took it even more solemnly, turned it over.

'It is very beautiful, Papa. Have you something for Rebecca?'

'Aye.' He kissed the girl, gave her the doll. 'All for you.'

'Oh, Papa,' she squeaked. 'It has eyes, Papa. It has eyes.'

None of Rebecca's dolls had eyes, after the first twenty-four hours.

'All the better to see us.' He entered the drawing-room, and Miss Johnson hastily stood up.

'We had not expected you, Captain Hilton.'

'Or you'd have dressed them in their best? Am I that much of a stranger?'

'Indeed you are,' Marguerite said from the top of the stairs. 'But none the less welcome.'

She wore her crimson undressing-robe, and her skin glowed; she must just have left the tub. And how beautiful, how arrogant, how confident she was. Because he had come home? But if ever he might have thought of staying, here was reason to leave again.

'Ellen Jane,' she called. 'Sangaree, for the master and myself. Will you come up, Kit?'

He slowly climbed the stairs. She did not wait for him, but turned and entered the bedroom. Yet was there still a memory; she did not take off her robe.

'Do you wish me to apologize?' she asked.

'Why should you do that?'

She sat on the bed. 'I lost my temper. I lose my temper too easily.'

'You had every reason, on that occasion.' He watched the

maid bring in the tray, and fill the two glasses. He took his, and raised it. 'I wish good fortune to your father.'

She smiled. 'Oh, he will have that, never fear. You sailed with Morgan. You no doubt recall the terrible fate which overtook him, and you must also remember that his crime was far greater, in political eyes, at any rate, than Father's.'

'Indeed it was. Then you imagine that he will be returned here, in triumph.'

She poured some more sangaree. 'I anticipate that, Kit, certainly. But I do not suppose that you have come here to speak of my father. You have had a honeymoon with your Danish charmer, and you are purchasing her a house down in Falmouth. Capital. It is exactly what I suggested.'

'I signed the bill for that, and for some other necessaries, this morning,' Kit said.

'Very good,' she said. 'I am sure you were not robbed. Now, when are you returning here?'

''Tis that I come to see you about. I shall not be returning here.'

She set down her glass. 'Do not be a fool, Kit.'

'I think I have always been a fool, when it comes to expediency,' Kit said. 'Lillan has given up a great deal, for me. I will not have her nothing more than a kept woman.'

'I do not see how you can change her status,' Marguerite pointed out. 'There can be no question of a divorce between us. I have committed no crime against you.'

'That I know, and appreciate. I but wished to make my position clear.'

'Your position,' she said contemptuously. 'You are a man who carries deep grudges, and for a long time. Very well, then, Kit. Go to your blonde bitch. You will soon weary of her. You will soon remember where your rightful place lies. And then you will be back.' She smiled at him, but her mouth was twisted. 'And I shall have the coverlet turned down, for that day.'

'I shall not trouble you for money, after this bill is settled.'

'You will seek employment, in St John's?' she inquired. 'I know. You can be foreman of the stevedores. Oh, Kit, Kit, were you not so serious, so determined, so *upright*, you would be amusing. Your expenses are Green Grove's expenses, for you are master of Green Grove. What, would you suddenly decide not to be a man any more, but instead a dog, because you fancy a dog's life is more acceptable? Are you a magician, that you can throw off your humanity? You are

THE DEVIL'S OWN

master of Green Grove. I made you that, Kit. And the day you die, regardless of where it may be, in what stinking hole it may be, what stinking disease may be the cause of it, you will still be master of Green Grove.'

'I wish I could understand you,' Kit said. 'If it is a matter of pride . . .'

'Pride,' she shouted, coming upright on the bed, her eyes molten pits of green hell. 'Pride? Fear? Avarice? Greed? Courage? Anger? Love? What have I to do with words? Do you think I rule the slaves because I am prouder than they? Because I am braver? Because I fear less? Because I love more? Should I ever stop to consider what emotion must govern my power I am lost. As you are continually lost by making just that inquiry. I am here, and they are there, because I accept no limitations, no puerile humanities.'

'By God,' he said. 'You *do* see yourself as a demigoddess.'

'And am I not, to them? To everyone on this island? To everyone in the world who knows of my existence? And I placed you beside me, Kit Hilton. After due consideration. So even I can make a mistake. But there you have it. I cannot make a mistake. Go to your Danish whore. Love her and love her and love her, until she makes you sick, and then come back here and take your place. I will not reproach you. For who should dare to criticize a god? Not even another god. Go. Hurry. The sooner you leave here, the sooner will you be tired of her.'

Be tired of Lillan. As if such an eventuality could ever be imagined, much less be considered possible. Lillan was not a tiring person. Where Marguerite had always exhausted, she sought only to soothe. Their love play was cool, almost restrained, in its beginning, and yet always with the promise of more, of the sudden overflow of passion which convulsed her as much as him. And yet even the passion contained a different quality. Lillan sought to please him, and in doing that found pleasure herself. She demanded nothing more, nor could he persuade her to accept anything more. But in pleasing him she was anxious to accept his every whim, his every mood, his every desire, and could any man *ask* for anything more?

But loving and possessing Lillan's body was no more than a part of it. On Green Grove, he was coming to realize, he had loved Marguerite, physically, or managed the estate, physically. When she had played the spinet it had been to consume the tireless energy of her own fingers; just as when he had opened a book it had inevitably been an account book. There was no stress, no goal in sight, with Lillan. She liked to walk, and they strolled for miles along the foreshore, holding hands. Marguerite had never walked anywhere except up a flight of steps in her life; it would never have occurred to her to do so.

And when she walked, Lillan talked, about Denmark, about the frost-bitten winters, about the balmy summers, fluctuations of climate which Kit had never known and found it difficult to appreciate. But she could talk of other places too, for her father had wandered for much of his life before coming to rest in Antigua. She spoke of Holland and of France and of England. And she grew excited when he told her of Morgan and Panama. She was a young girl in her mind, avid for tales of adventure and faraway places, unaware that she had more of a tale to tell than he, that she was in herself a more interesting person.

And she worked in the garden. This was a continually amazing sight, to watch her kneeling beside Abigail, tending some new plant with the care she might have bestowed upon a dying man, those slender white fingers stained with dirt, that golden glory starting to drop in disorganized wisps about her ears and over her forehead.

She revealed happiness, in herself, and in her being. To awake in the morning, and to inhale, was happiness, for Lillan Christianssen. Whatever followed would also be happiness, she had no doubt, but she was content to have it follow in its proper course, at its proper time, and then to enjoy it as fully as she enjoyed merely stretching, and knowing her health, and her immediate comfort. She never spoke of her parents or her religion, beyond a tendency always to place his weapons out of sight when he took them off. When she prayed it was by herself, in a corner of the bedroom, on her knees, her face turned to the wall. He was not invited to join her. So, for what did she pray? For her forgiveness, or for his conversion? And indeed he was tempted, time and again, to kneel beside her. But in no religious spirit. Only to share the one part of her being which was barred to him.

And she did not speak of the future. The future was perhaps too uncertain even for her. She revealed this in her tears at Abigail's pregnancy. Agrippa was beside himself with joy, and Kit felt vastly complimented. His friends would not bring a child into the world they had known in St John's,

THE DEVIL'S OWN

but this world, the world he had created for them, was acceptable. But not for Lillan, yet. There was no permanence, in Falmouth, for a fugitive from family and convention. And for all the delights of a continual honeymoon, with nothing to do but eat, sleep, love and laugh, tend the garden and help Agrippa spread the nets for the fish which formed the main part of their diet, they both knew that he could not continue to stagnate for the rest of his life.

Yet he needed a crisis to stir him from his lethargy. The death of the King reminded him that time waited for no man. Still would he not leave Lillan's side. 'You will have to go, Agrippa, old friend,' he said. 'I will give you letters, and you will take the sloop from English Harbour, and go to Sandy Point, and request an audience of Sir William. He will grant it readily enough when he learns it comes from me. I wish a post, with the Government. The Government of the Leeward Islands, not the Government of Antigua, and preferably at sea, although I will command on land if need be. He promised me no less, and now I would ask it of him.'

'Aye,' Agrippa said, with satisfaction. For he too had feared that the sharpness of the blade which was his friend would be blunted by inactivity.

'Necessary?' Lillan asked, as they watched the sloop bobbing across the passage to the sister island. 'Why must men always *do*?'

'Because they are men. But I shall not be doing so very much, lover, or be so very far away from you.'

'I would like you, always, right here at my side, Kit.'

'Because when I am gone you begin to doubt.'

She glanced at him, frowning, surprised that he should be capable of that much understanding. 'I am not as strong as you would wish, perhaps.'

He laughed, and held her hand for the walk back along the beach to their little house. 'Allow me to have the strength, and you rest content with the goodness which bubbles out of you like steam from a volcano.'

Yet was she invested with more passion than ever in the past, at the thought of losing him, if only for a few days a week, and they resumed their honeymoon with more intensity than ever before, to awake one morning to the sight of Agrippa hurrying up the beach from English Harbour, accompanied by an officer of the St Kitts garrsion.

Kit pulled on his breeches and ran down the stairs. 'Holloa,' he shouted. 'Am I then to be arrested for being happy?'

The officer panted, and removed his hat as he reached the cottage. 'Ensign Frankland at your service, sir. And right glad am I to meet you, Captain Hilton.'

'I am sure the pleasure will be mutual,' Kit said. 'Come in, man, come in. You'll take a glass of rum?'

'Indeed, sir, that would be most pleasant.' Frankland sat down without being invited, and mopped his face. Abigail hurried forward with a glass.

Kit glanced at Agrippa. 'There has been some mishap?'

'Well, that is hard to say.'

'We hope not, sir. We hope not.' Frankland drank deeply, and seemed to feel more in command of himself. 'First of all, sir, I am charged to say that you shall have whatever employment you wish, when the other matter is settled.'

'The other matter?'

'Your first duty must be to act as a witness for the Crown in the affair of Philip Warner.'

Kit frowned at him. 'Witness? I wrote out and signed my deposition before the Governor himself. What, would they have me travel to England?'

'No, sir, and there is the point. The English Government, having due regard to their distance from the alleged crime, and the distinguished services which are laid to the credit of Colonel Warner, have concluded that it would be invidious of them to try him for his life. He is being returned.'

'To St Johns?' Kit could not believe his ears.

'No, sir. Even Her Majesty's councillors recognize that there would be little prospect of acquiring an unbiased jury here in the Leewards. His trial is to be held in Barbados. Before a jury of Barbadian planters. Yet, sir, is Sir William Stapleton determined to mount as firm as assault as he may upon this vicious murderer. He is despatching a ship from Sandy Point, which will call at St John's to take on board all the witnesses to the deed that can be found. And at the top of the list, sir, must necessarily rest your name.'

10

The Trial

'The devil,' Kit said. 'Barbados.' He gazed at Agrippa. 'They bear Philip no great love.'

'He is a planter, as are they,' Agrippa said.

'You'd not contemplate refusing the Governor's subpoena?' Frankland demanded. 'By God, sir, coming from that quarter it is a command.'

'Aye,' Kit said. 'Nor did it cross my mind to refuse it.'

'You'll go to Barbados?' Lillan asked softly.

'I must, sweetheart. Agrippa will remain with you, and see to your every requirement. Will you not, old friend?'

'Of course, Kit.'

'And you'll pledge my credit, where necessary,' Kit said.

'It is not that that concerns me,' Lillan protested. 'It is the time. A trial of this nature can take weeks, perhaps months, and then there is the journeying to and from that distant land, and the dangers attendant upon it...'

'Sweetheart,' Kit cried, taking her shoulders to hold her against him. 'I have spent my life surviving the worst that these Caribbean waters can attempt. And can you not see, this must be done? I was informed, by no less a person than Marguerite, that Philip had powerful friends working for him in England. She was under the impression that he would, indeed, be subjected to nothing more than an inquiry, like Henry Morgan, and perhaps a month or two in the Tower, to make him aware of the King's displeasure, before being released and returned here, no doubt with a knighthood. But we also seem to have friends at court; if they will not try Philip there, at least they have not acquitted him. He is our responsibiltiy now, and who knows, this may be a most important principle they concede. Yet must we carry the case to a proper conclusion. For should he be returned here, and the case against him go badly for lack of evidence, why, I had better have kept silent from the beginning.'

She gazed at him from those clear blue eyes. 'And suppose, despite all, he is acquitted?'

'That is not possible, madam, with the evidence Captain Hilton shall give,' Frankland said. 'He was there. He saw the deed. And it was his word pledged to the Caribs.'

'Yet will it still be my word against Philip's,' Kit said, frowning. 'We meed Bale, at the least.'

Frankland nodded. 'The Governor is aware of that sir, and the search is on. But that confounded pirate has disappeared.'

'He must be found, Mr Frankland. Make no mistake about that.'

'And he shall, sir. Believe me, have no fear on that score. Certain it is that he was last heard of in Jamaica, and our agents are looking for him there. But come, sir, the frigate will already be entering St John's Harbour, as she left Sandy Point at the same time as your friend here and I took the sloop for Falmouth.'

'I will pack, and do you breakfast, Mr Frankland.' He ran upstairs, hastily threw his clothes into a satchel, put on his coat and hat. Lillan stood in the doorway and watched him.

'They will hate you for this, Kit. For evermore.'

'Would you have me remain, on that score?'

She hesitated, and then sighed. 'Yes. Yes, I would have you remain, on that score, Kit. I would have you do nothing more with your life than hold me in your arms, and love me, and keep the world at the length of your strong right arm. But I know that to do that, you must first of all love yourself. And men have strange ways of professing *that* love. So go to your duty. But come back soon, Kit. And come back safe. I possess nothing in this world, nor do I wish to possess anything, in this world, save your love.'

He kissed her on the mouth. 'Then be sure of it, now and always, sweetheart.' He went downstairs, where the horses waited, procured by Agrippa from the Falmouth stable, clasped his friend's hand. 'Will I like Barbados?'

'It is an island much like this one.'

'And the people?'

Agrippa shrugged. 'Perhaps you will enjoy them also, Kit, as your skin is white.'

'Aye. You'll watch over Lillan, old friend.'

'With my life, Kit.'

'I did not doubt that.' He mounted and urged his horse out

THE DEVIL'S OWN

of the little yard, Frankland at his side. At the top of the rise which took them away from the beach he reined in, to look back, at the house, and the garden, and the beach, and the sea beyond, leading to St Kitts. Certainly he felt reluctant to leave such peaceful surroundings, such willing and undemanding love. But he would have had to do so in the near future, in any event. His sadness, his uncertainty, was compounded by what lay ahead. So in that, like all men, he was something of a coward. He had no wish to face Philip Warner again, again attempt to send him to his doom, and this time with his voice rather than merely the written word. Six months ago it had all been white hot anger, and he would have throttled the man with his bare hands. But now he was to accuse him in cold blood and after sober reflection.

Yet it must be done, or the very foundations of these islands would crumble away in contempt. And when it was over, perhaps he could again return to Dominica. How he wanted to do that, once again to see Yarico, and hear that ageless voice, to kneel beside her hammock, and tell her how her son had been avenged. And then, perhaps, to ask her more of himself. To seek an explanation to the thoughts and fears which had risen up to torture him night after night since his return to Antigua.

But that, too, could not be answered, could not even be investigated, until this business was completed, else would his resolution seep away from his boots like the sand from the beach after a hurricane.

They rode in silence, and at a good pace. Frankland could see well enough that Kit wished to think, and he did not encroach, until they were close to St John's itself.

'Supposing the ship is already at anchor, Captain Hilton,' he said. 'The town will be filled with rumour. No doubt it is, already, as the news of Her Majesty's decision will have been carried on every vessel making for these waters. There may well be some hostility in the town.'

'Believe me, sir, I am well enough used to hostility, in the layabouts of Antigua,' Kit said.

'Still, I beg of you, Captain, let us make our way to the harbour without a riot, if that is possible.'

They entered the main street. By now it was early afternoon, as they had ridden since breakfast, and the shops and businesses were beginning to close. The townspeople stood on the sidewalks and stared at the two riders.

'Captain Hilton,' someone said, and it was taken up as a shout. 'Captain Hilton, Captain Hilton, Captain Hilton.'

' 'Tis hard to tell whether they hate you or love you,' Frankland said.

'I would not count on their love.' Kit kept his head straight, and looked at the street in front of him.

'Traitor,' someone yelled.

'Indian lover,' another voice took up the chant.

'Negro lover,' added another section.

Then the first missile flew. Kit did not move his head, and the stone hurtled through the air, to strike someone on the far side and bring a howl of pain and anger.

'By God,' Frankland said. 'We had best hurry.'

'We'll run from no mob, Mr Frankland,' Kit said. 'Now, if you've a mind to run our horses *at* them, I am your man.'

'Not that, sir, I beg of you. Sir William said no violence. Thank God, there is the harbour.'

Now the air was full of flying debris, much of it, fortunately, either eggs or tomatoes or soft mud. Something struck Kit on the shoulder with a squelch, and an egg burst on the head of his horse, causing the animal to jerk and sidestep. He turned his head to find his tormentors, looked at the Christianssens, standing on their porch. They were not part of the mob, but their lips were tight and their faces hard.

'God bless you, Captain Hilton, and good luck.'

A lone voice in the multitude. Kit turned his head the other way, and Barnee waved. A bold action, not only for the jostles which he immediately received, but because his prosperity depended on the goodwill of the planters, and his sentiments would very rapidly be spread across the island.

But at last they were at the waterfront, and the seamen were gathered on the wharf, facing the mob. Kit and Frankland dismounted, and the ship's lieutenant touched his hat.

'Good day, Captain Hilton, and well met. I think we had best leave this instant, as all is ready.'

Kit got into the longboat. Frankland raised his hat. The sailors cast off, and the boat rowed for the waiting frigate while the crowd flowed along the jetties, shouting their execrations.

'Indeed, sir, I wonder at your courage in coming through that mob,' the ship's lieutenant said.

Kit did not reply. He wondered at his courage in coming out here in the frigate's boat. Ten years ago he had fired into this ship. And surely by now rumour would have spread the

THE DEVIL'S OWN

name of the perpetrator of that deed? Yet the lieutenant seemed no more than anxious to be the perfect host.

'You will, sir, at any rate be pleased to know that we arranged things better for your wife,' he said.

Kit turned his head to frown at him, but the longboat was already pulling under the side of the frigate, and the pipes were sounding as he scrambled up the ladder and into the waist of the warship, where Captain Holgate awaited him.

'Welcome on board *Euryalus,* Captain Hilton. I have given you my own cabin.'

'Why, sir, that is far too good of you,' Kit protested.

'Orders from Sir William,' Holgate assured him. 'And in any event, sir, we wish you and your lady to enjoy the voyage. It is a difficult business, beating down to Barbados, and may well take us upwards of a fortnight.'

'My wife?' Kit demanded. 'This is the second time her presence has been intimated. I was not aware that she was accompanying me. Indeed, I am sure there must be some mistake.'

Captain Holgate looked embarrassed. 'I do not see how there can have been a mistake, Captain Hilton. Should she not, as this whole affair touches her so closely?'

'Let me understand this,' Kit said. 'Marguerite is on board this vessel?'

'And awaiting you in my cabin, sir,' the Captain said. 'Now, I think I had best get under way, as the wind is for the moment fair, and the tide as well.'

* * *

Kit ran down the companion ladder, made his way across the great cabin, and reached for the door of the Captain's quarters. Here he checked, for a moment, getting his anger under control, and then threw the door open.

Marguerite wore her riding habit, her coat open, her hat resting on the table beside her. Oh, the cunning hussy. For she had never in her life, to his knowledge, allowed herself to be seen off her plantation except dressed as the great lady. But she remembered full well that she had been dressed like this when first he had seen her, and had first renewed his love for her.

And that would be easy to do all over again. For had she aged at all? Oh, indeed she had. There were crowsfeet tracing away from the corners of each splendid green eye; a combination of strain and the constant squinting necessary to withstand the glare of the West Indian sun. But these gave that marvellous girl's face a maturity it had previously lacked. And now the breasts were heavy, and sagged against the thin cambric of the shirt. But how they demanded to be caressed, and how his own chest demanded to feel them against it. And beneath the belt her belly would be pouted, but none the less soft and sweet to the touch.

She smiled; there was sweat on her upper lip. 'You may leave us, Patience Jane,' she said, and the maid hastily sidled round Kit and out of the cabin. 'Kit. Do you know, I heard the tumult in town even from here? I was so worried for you. I wanted the Captain to run out his guns, and the swine would not.'

'It would have been a remarkable misjudgement of the situation,' Kit said. 'To fire into a crowd of people doing no more than express their feelings, on account of one man.'

'Oh, what rubbish,' she said, and got up. 'There are men, and there are people. One man is worth a thousand, perhaps a million people.' She came towards him. 'Listen. They are raising the anchor. Isn't it exciting. I have never been on a sea voyage, with you. I have never been on a sea voyage at all, since that visit to England, my God, seventeen years ago.'

He held her shoulders. Christ, had it only been a few hours ago that he had similarly held Lillan? But this action was to keep her at arm's length. 'What are you doing on board this ship?'

Her eyes were wide. 'I am going to Barbados with you.'

'Why?'

'My husband is giving evidence against my father, Kit; is it not a matter of concern for me?'

'I would have thought you'd try to stop me from going at all.'

'What, me prevent Captain Christopher Hilton from doing what he thinks best? Then would I be putting my head in danger.'

'Now you seek to mock me.'

'I do not. Nor would I seek to humiliate you by requiring you to submit to my wishes in this matter. But I wish to be at your side, for the next few weeks may well be the most important in your life, Kit. And in mine.' Her laughter rippled across the cabin. 'And, of course, in Father's.'

Still he held her as she would have come forward. 'Be sure that the evidence I shall give will send him to the gallows.'

THE DEVIL'S OWN

'I have no doubt it shall,' she agreed. 'But do we have to discuss it now? We have a voyage of at least a fortnight in front of us, so Captain Holgate assures me. Let us keep our serious talk for when we are far away from land, and able thus to see life more clearly, perhaps.'

'If you do not discuss it now, Marguerite,' he said. 'I doubt we shall discuss it at all. I have no intention of sharing this cabin with you. I am about to ask the Captain for separate accommodation.'

She frowned at him. 'Kit, I have just said that I would not dream of humiliating you by demanding that you not testify against my father. May I ask of you a small favour in return? That you not consider humiliating me by refusing my bed?'

'I should have thought the humiliation would lie in accepting your bed, Marguerite. There can be no member of this crew does not know of our relationship.'

'Of *your* relationship, with Lillan Christianssen. Thus I stand already sufficiently humiliated, would you not say? What ails you, Kit? Would you be utterly faithful to your Danish lady? Can you swear that you will always be? I should have thought you of all men would know better than that. What shall I do, Kit? You know that no human finger has touched this body, saving my maids in my bath, since you left. And saving my own, of course. For be sure that I have torn at my own body, out of lonely desperation. Be sure that I have awakened in the middle of the night, and cried out for you, and sweated for want of you, and been called upon myself to atone for your absence, as Onan might have overlooked me and felt pity for me, in my needy turmoil. Must I humiliate myself further? Must I crawl on the deck at your feet? Must I weep, and beg? See, I do both of those things. You once said I consider myself a demigoddess. Well, so I do. So here stands before you a demigoddess, weeping and begging, willing to humble herself, before her demigod. Demand of me what you will. Be sure that I will grant your most ambitious, or your most debased wish. I ask only your love, Kit. I ask it even at second hand. As I have given you mine, at cost of fame, and family, and fortune, I ask only your kiss in return.'

Could there ever be a woman so demanding, so insistent? If he could but believe that she acted out of passion, and not carefully calculated determination to achieve. But on that score he knew her a shade too well.

Desperately he thrust her away. 'You are a temptress, madam. You seek to suborn me from my duty, and from my responsibility as a man. Had you been in the cabin of *that* ship with me perhaps you would have known better. I will not declare they were innocent men. Perhaps there are no such things on the face of this earth. But they were men, such as I, or your father, or any other that you may have known, and to those men I had pledged my word. To them, no less than to their people. And even had I not, they came to your father's ship in good faith and believing in his good faith. I had made them believe that there was a new era of peace and perhaps prosperity opening for both our peoples. And your father took that possibility, nay, that probability, and tore it into shreds with his hands, before my eyes. Should he not pay for it, our children will have to do so. I will have *him* do the paying, madam. Believe me, I do not seek to insult you or to hurt you. You remain, before God, the most beautiful and the most desirable female I have ever known, or can possibly hope to know. But while you support that evil, you *are* evil, and I will have no part of you. Come to me again when the trial is finished, and your father condemned, and we will speak again.'

He freed her hands, and stepped for the door, and hesitated, expecting her to speak. But she said nothing, nor could he make himself turn to face her again.

'Gentlemen.' Captain Holgate struggled to his feet, and swayed with the ship. He swayed thus at most meals, and it made little difference the state of the weather. So no doubt in a gale he was a very good fellow to have in command, as the trembling of the hull itself would have little effect upon his already trembling body. Now he watched the wine in his glass flowing to and fro, although the wind was light and the frigate did no more than roll in the swell. 'I give you the Queen, God bless her, Anne.'

The men rose, Kit in the midst of the officers, and the toast was drunk. As usual, he found himself staring at Marguerite. As he sat on the Captain's left, and she on the Captain's right, at table were they in closest proximity. At least no questions had been asked by the courteous officers concerning his request for a separate cabin, although equally certainly this strange pair must be a fruitful source of gossip for the entire crew.

Now, as ever, she smiled at him, her face a delightful

THE DEVIL'S OWN

mask concealing whatever anger seethed behind those brittle green eyes. But then, for her part, she seldom came on deck, and spent most of her time in her cabin.

'The land rising on our port bow is Barbados,' Holgate declared. 'And by dusk we shall be anchored in Carlisle Bay. Now tell me truly, Mrs Hilton; has the voyage been so violent, so unpleasant?'

Marguerite shook her head. 'I am sure that as sea voyages go, this has been as peaceful a venture as one could wish, Captain. But will we truly be on land by this evening?'

'Indeed, Mrs Hilton. Unless the wind should entirely drop, and that is not its custom in these parts.'

'Then I hope you will excuse me now, as I should prepare myself.' Her chair scraped as she stood up, and the assembled officers hastily got to their feet. 'Pray be seated, gentlemen. I would not interfere with your port.' Her gaze swept them all, and came to rest upon Kit. 'I would be obliged if you would attend me, for a moment, dear one. It is a matter of some importance.'

It was the first time on the voyage she had made such a request in front of the assembled afterguard.

'Gentlemen.' Kit went round the table and opened the door for her. She swept past him in a cloud of scent, and snapped her fingers at Patience Jane. 'You may return later to complete the packing, girl.'

'Yes'm.' Patience Jane gave Kit a hasty, anxious glance, and hurried out of the cabin. Kit closed the door, but remained standing by it.

Marguerite sank on to the seat beneath the great stern window. 'Cannot you now have done with humiliating me? Can any woman have suffered the outrageous gossip of these last few days? I cannot even command my husband to my bed? Oh, perhaps I went about it in error. I assumed, as I am a woman, a woman you once loved, that I had but to approach you in that guise to regain your love. I had forgot the inconsistency of man.'

'Did you summon me to hear a tirade, madam?' he asked. 'You yourself commanded me from your bed, if I would not cease opposing your father. Any further relationship between us can only come under the guise of corruption, at least until this affair is concluded.'

'Then sit down,' she said. 'I beg of you, dear Kit. Be sure that I shall keep my distance, on this side of the cabin. I but wish to have this conversation with you, as it is a matter which so greatly affects us all, and be sure that this will be the last occasion on which we shall discuss it, if you will not admit me to your love.'

Kit sat down, on the far side of the cabin. He gazed at his wife, so strangely uncertain of herself, as her fingers plucked at the cushion beside her, so unutterably beautiful.

'I ask you now,' she said, 'Without coquetry or subterfuge, but as your wife and as Philip Warner's daughter, to abandon this peculiar vendetta against my father. Hear me out, Kit, please. in your eyes he has committed an abominable crime, and you have taken all possible action against him. He has been removed from his position as Deputy Governor of Antigua, a misfortune which affects him keenly. I have read his letters to Aunt Celestine. Nor is he likely to be reinstated, whatever the outcome of this trial. In addition, his fame has been dragged in the dust, as this event has been discussed wherever civilized men get together. He has been pilloried before the English public, and now is returned to Barbados, a place where he has never attained much popularity, to be tried like a common malefactor. This is the man whose father founded these colonies, who bears a proud name, a name which will surely ring as long as these islands remain above water. Be sure that Philip Warner's will ever remain associated with the death of that Carib monster. So, I ask you, what more can he suffer? Yet would you hound him to his death. But he is already past his middle age. I doubt he has more than ten years left before him, at the best of things. Is that, then, too long for you to wait?'

Kit sighed. 'I understand your plea, Marguerite, and I respect it. No man could wish for more devotion from his daughter. Yet must I follow this path, because there is too much at stake. I do not speak of my good name, my reputation. God knows, that was sufficiently compromised long before I ever set foot in Antigua. But these colonies which are your, and my, pride and joy, do we not hope and expect to see them grow, and become even wealthier, and of more importance in the world? Do we not hope and trust that they will spread, to take in St Lucia and St Vincent and indeed all the Windwards, perhaps even Dominica itself? Must we be subjected always to the taint that there go a band of cold-blooded murderers? Why, the acceptance of your father's deed brands us as worse than the Dons, and they at least were always actuated by mindless religious fervour. Where was your father's fervour? Only a certainty that he had already wronged his brother and the Princess Yarico so grievously that his stomach rebelled against accepting them in friendship.'

'The Princess Yarico,' she said contemptuously. 'Aye, I have heard tales enough of that whore. So you visited her hammock. Was her body sweeter than mine?'

'I had supposed we intended to conduct this conversation in a civilized fashion,' Kit said.

Marguerite's turn to sigh. 'I apologize. I will retain my temper, I do promise you.'

'Well, then, let it be certain that a great deal depends upon justice being done in this sad event, and even more, a great deal rests upon justice being *seen* to be done. Or who, be he Carib or Frenchman, Dutchman or Don, will ever attend a conference with us again?'

Her shoulders rose and fell. 'You persist in seeing life in these large canvasses. I can see only the figure of my father, on trial for his life. Tell me this, Kit. Do you despise me for attempting to defend him?'

'Rather do I honour you for that, Meg.'

'Well, then, would you not do the same for your own father, regardless of the crime he had committed?'

'No doubt I should.'

'And suppose I could convince you that this is a family affair, for you as well.'

He stared at her, Yarico's words bubbling in his brain.

'Aye,' she said. 'You have thought on that score, Kit. I can see it in your face. But does it not occur to you every time you use a mirror?'

'Then would we have sinned beyond measure,' he said.

'What nonsense. If indeed Edward Warner coupled too successfully with Susan Hilton, as is generally accepted, then your father was my first cousin. But *you* cannot be more than my second cousin.'

'Still too close. I shudder for our children.'

'I still say, nonsense,' Marguerite insisted. 'Do not kings and queens marry within such constrained limits? I would declare before any court in the world, that knowing this as I did, when first I elected to pick you from that ditch in which you lay, I yet had not the slightest doubt that it was you I should take to my heart and my bed. What, marry anyone other than a Warner? There was the crime, so to weaken the blood.'

Kit's shoulders were hunched. 'So there is more drawing

us together than either love or lust. I never doubted that, Meg. Yet are we now burst further apart than you can have imagined possible. So Philip is my great-uncle, as he is your father. Yet must I send him to the gallows if I can. For do you not realize, that if indeed he is my uncle, then so was Indian Tom?'

'That ... that bastard?'

'Are you not a bastard? And am I not descended from one, certainly?'

Her eyes shrouded him, and he remembered the sparkling angry determination with which she had looked at Philip himself on the day she had announced her intention of marrying. Oh, God, he thought, to turn back the clock that far and exorcize all of this bitterness, all of this hate.

Knuckles drummed on the door, and still she stared at him. He was glad to turn away, and open it. A midshipman waited there. 'Begging your pardon, Captain Hilton, but Captain Holgate presents his compliments, and says the Careenage is now in full sight.'

'I will be there in a moment,' Kit said. And frowned. 'There is more?'

'The Captain begs me to inform you, sir, and the lady, that there appears to have been some misfortune. The signals flying from the fort indicate that we are again at war with France.'

'By God,' Kit said. 'That was a brief interlude.'

'War,' Marguerite said softly.

He turned to her. 'You think this will make a difference?'

She smiled at him, and held a handkerchief to her nose. She seemed to have caught a slight cold. 'Wars make men more aware of reality, and less of abstract notions. Will you stand there the day, boy?'

'I beg your pardon, madam.' The midshipman hastily withdrew. Kit closed the door.

'Then is your father perhaps fortunate,' he said.

'Yet your duty remains clear.'

'More than ever.'

'And nothing I can say or do or beg or promise will alter your resolution?'

'Nothing,' Kit said. 'For me to turn aside now, for fear of punishment or in hopes of reward, for love or for hate, would be to make myself a party to that crime. I will not do that, Marguerite. I am sorry. More sorry than you know, perhaps.'

THE DEVIL'S OWN

She stood up. 'Then be sorry, Kit Hilton,' she said. 'And suffer. For be sure you will find in me an enemy you shall fear.'

'I trust these lodgings will prove satisfactory, Captain Hilton.' Mr. Sergeant Pratt could not speak without apparently considering himself in a court of law. Now he held the lapels of his coat, one in each hand, and peered around the bedchamber with a censorious frown.

'They will do very nicely, sir, thank you.' Kit went to the window, looked out at the palm-trees and the beach. Barbados was indeed remarkably like Antigua, lacking mountains or volcanic springs and being entirely devoted to cane-growing. Even the little town of Bridgetown was reminiscent of St John's. But there was no true harbour here, and no protecting ring of islands. Barbados was exposed, lonely in the Atlantic swell.

'I will have one of my own blacks attend you, of course,' the lawyer said. 'And you shall be the guest of my wife and myself once the trial is concluded. I but wish we could similarly express ourselves to your good lady, but I understand that is not possible.'

'We maintain separate positions in this affair,' Kit said.

'And yet you came to Bridgetown in the same vessel.'

'In separate cabins, Mr Pratt. Nor do I see that our domestic differences are any concern of yours, or the court's.'

'Indeed, sir, I wish to agree with you, were this whole affair not a domestic one. Brother against brother. Niece against uncle and husband. Husband against wife and father-in-law. Oh, Her Majesty's Commissioners did this island no great favour when they commanded the trial to be held here. But justice will be done, Captain Hilton. You may rest assured of that.'

'I have no doubt of that, Mr Pratt. What of the man Bale?'

'Ah.' Pratt took a turn up and down the room, his hands clasped beneath the tails of his coat. 'We have had no fortune there, I am sorry to say. We have hunted for him in Jamaica, and in the Caymans, and even as far afield as the Virgins. Most know of him in those parts, but none have seen him in these past four weeks. It seems. There is the problem with relying upon a pirate as a witness. Yet we shall be permitted to read his deposition, I do assure you of that, Captain. And we have Hamblyn.'

'Now, there is good news,' Kit cried. 'He was present at the conference in St John's when our plans were agreed. There was also a Captain England.'

'Aye. Pirates all. But England has himself vanished. 'Tis said that he seeks a fortune in the Indian Ocean, sailing out of Madagascar, and endeavouring to follow in the footsteps of that rogue Avery. We shall not have him back from there, and must do our best with this Hamblyn. However, these are but corroboratory witnesses, Captain. We may liken them to the icing upon the cake which is your case. The substance, sir, the substance stands before me. You have no doubts?'

'Should I have?'

'I assume that pressure has been brought to bear upon you, in Antigua, from your family no less than your friends, to withdraw.'

'I cannot very well do that, Mr Pratt, having been served with a subpoena.'

'Indeed. Indeed. But there will be other pressures to withstand, even here. There are some gentlemen now waiting to see you.'

Kit frowned. 'Why did you not say so sooner?'

'I wished to have this talk with you myself, first. It is a matter of some importance, you know, Captain Hilton. As the eyes of the West Indies will be upon our courtroom here in Bridgetown, be sure that the eyes of the world will be upon this small island of ours. I would have us receive nothing but praise for the way we handle this unfortunate affair. Now, do you wish to receive these gentlemen?'

'Should I not, as I must live in their midst these coming weeks?'

'Oh, indeed, sir. Indeed. Then, if you will permit me, I will take my leave now, and make my way out by the back door. It would not be good for us to be found together at this juncture. I will see you in court, Captain Hilton. Until then, may I wish you Godspeed.'

'I thank you Mr Pratt.' The Attorney General was frightened, he thought. But surely the affair could not so concern the Barbadians? They had but to supply judge and jury. He went downstairs, and was greeted with a nervous smile by the young woman who managed the hotel for her father.

'I hope your chambers are satisfactory, Captain.'

'Indeed they are,' Kit agreed. 'I was informed that there are some gentlemen waiting to see me.'

'Oh, yes, sir,' Miss Blaine said. 'They are in the parlour.'

Her face was pale, and her lips trembled. Kit smiled at her. 'Then show me the way.'

'Yes, sir. Through here, sir.' She hurried in front of him, opened the door. 'Captain Hilton, gentlemen.'

The three men turned to face him. They were obviously planters from their dress, and straight from the fields, although he noticed that they wore swords for this visit to Bridgetown.

'Good morning, gentlemen,' Kit said. 'It is good of you to call. I am Christopher Hilton, of Antigua.'

'The pleasure is ours, sir,' said the first of the men, the smallest of the three, with swarthy features and a large belly. 'Rodney Alleyne, at your service.'

'Percival Browne, Captain Hilton.' This man was taller than Alleyne, fair, and with blunt, friendly features, now severely composed.

'Arthur Harrison, Captain Hilton.' The tallest of the three, with lank black hair and an ugly pout to his lips.

'Gentlemen,' Kit said. 'I imagine we can procure some punch. I will summon Miss Blaine.'

'If you would be so kind, sir, as to speak with us first,' Alleyne said. 'Then, no doubt, we can all take a glass together to celebrate our mutual understanding.'

'Certainly, if that is what you wish. Sit down, gentlemen, sit down.' Kit sat himself by the door. 'Well?'

The three Barbadians exchanged glances. 'You'll understand that the coming trial is the sole subject of conversation in Barbados, sir,' Alleyne said. 'Why, even the renewal of the war pales into insignificance beside it.'

Kit waited. He did not suppose a comment was required at this stage.

Alleyne cleared his throat, glanced once again at his companions.

'Sir,' Browne said. 'We are convinced that this is no good thing.'

'Indeed, I agree with you,' Kit said.

'Thus we feel that there must be some considerable misunderstanding at work to have brought things to this pass,' Harrison said.

'After all, Captain Hilton, you are a planter, as is Colonel Warner, as are all of us. Upon our prosperity, sir, depends the prosperity of these islands. And upon our unity depends the prosperity which is so important.'

'Believe us, Captain, when we say that it was no decision

of ours that your late expedition to Dominica was assisted by no Barbadian contingent. We were more than willing to participate, and it was the will of our Governor, a scurvy rascal if ever there was one, which prevented us. And now sir, we cannot help but feel that this whole affair has been magnified out of reasonable proportion by the governments of these islands, oh, and of Whitehall too, you may be sure of that.

'Therefore, sir,' Alleyne resumed, 'we feel it incumbent upon the planters of all these islands to forget the narrow bounds of self-interest which have separated us in the past, and present a united front against this overseas' and governmental encroachment upon our rights and privileges. Do you, as a planter, not agree with us?'

'I am entirely for a united plantocracy, gentlemen,' Kit said. 'I agree that it is most necessary, for our protection and our prosperity.'

'Well, then . . .'

'But I cannot concede that the mere fact of being a planter places me, or you, or any one of us, above the laws of God and of morality.'

'Expedience, sir. Expedience. Unity demands expedience,' Harrison declared.

'You had best speak plain, Mr Harrison,' Kit said.

'Why, sir, our purpose is simply this, since you will have it so. We would have you abandon this trial, and leave it to us here in Barbados to settle the matter to our own satisfaction.'

'And my subpoena, sir?'

'A minor matter, I do assure you, Captain Hilton,' Alleyne insisted. 'What will they do, impose on you a fine? They can do no more. We guarantee that every penny will be paid by public subscription.'

'And my own honour?'

'Is due first of all to the plantocracy, Captain, rather than any red-skinned savage.'

'Then would I consider myself a blackguard, sirs. Believe me, I have been subjected to considerable pressure, from quarters where I place more importance than any represented by you three gentlemen. I understand your motives, and you may believe that I respect them. So I am entitled to request you to extend to me a smiliar courtesy. I came here to see justice done, and by God, I will see justice done.'

'You refuse to co-operate with your fellow planters, sir?' Browne demanded.

THE DEVIL'S OWN 287

'I refuse to co-operate with anyone who seeks to pervert the course of justice.'

'Then, sir, believe me, but we shall put a stop to your nefarious game,' Harrison cried, getting up.

'Indeed?' Kit asked. But he was as angry as they, and also stood up. 'How do you propose to do that?'

'By calling you, firstly, a coward and a blackguard, sir,' Harrison said. 'And secondly, by drawing my hand across your face.' He was as good as his word; the buffet was so forceful Kit stepped back.

And smiled. 'Ah. You seek to murder me, I think, Mr Harrison.'

'I have my own concept of justice, Captain Hilton, and you lie beyond it.'

'Very well,' Kit said. 'Allow me to repay your challenge.'

His big fist was closed, and now he hurled it at Harrison's chin. The planter saw the blow coming and hastily attempted to get out of the way, he stumbled over a chair, lost his balance, and sat down. His companions retreated against the wall.

'Why, you . . . you brawler, sir,' Harrison shouted, getting to his feet and whipping his sword from its scabbard.

'Gentlemen, gentlemen,' shouted Miss Blaine, coming in from the back. 'You cannot fight in my parlour. I'll have the constables on you.'

'There is a beach, at the bottom of the garden,' Kit pointed out.

'Aye. Let us adjourn there promptly,' Harrison said. 'You'll second me, Mr Alleyne?'

'Indeed I will. Mr Browne, perhaps you would be good enough to act for Captain Hilton?'

'Willingly.'

'Gentlemen,' Miss Blaine pleaded. 'Can this matter not be settled without bloodshed? I do implore you. It will make no good appearance in the press, and with the trial due to start in twenty-four hours, and King William barely cold in his grave.'

'The remedy lies with Captain Hilton,' Harrison declared.

'On the contrary, sir,' Kit insisted. 'It lies entirely with you, gentlemen, to withdraw. I know my duty and I shall do it. And if you force me to kill you, sir, well then, be sure that I will do that too.'

Harrison stared at him, seemed for the first time to take in his heavy shoulders and the strength of the fingers in his right hand, to notice that it was no display rapier hanging by his side but a most serviceable sword, and perhaps also to recall something of his reputation.

'Aye,' he said at last. 'I have no doubt you would, sir. Your background of violence is well known.'

'Nor do I seek to deny it, sir,' Kit said. 'Come, do we make for the beach, or not?'

Harrison glanced at his fellows. 'I'll not be butchered by a professional swordsman,' he said. 'Be sure, sir, that your sins will find you out.' He crammed his hat on his head and left the room, followed by his friends.

The clerk opened the door. 'They are ready for you now, Captain Hilton.'

Kit got up. He had grown sufficiently tired of the bare-walled little room in which he had been confined all the morning, not even allowed out for lunch, but forced to eat his meal from a tray, for all the world as if he were the prisoner and himself awaiting trial.

But Mr Sergeant Pratt and the other law officers had considered it necessary, first of all that he be confined away from the other witnesses until his turn came, and that he should be as far as possible protected from public insult which might have him once again reaching for his sword. The news of the abortive duel with Harrison had made the round of the Bridgetown clubs, and caused as much sensation as the whole trial. For apparently Mr Harrison was a man of some repute as a duellist. Not, of course, that anyone blamed him publicly, or indeed would have dared to do so, for refusing to draw his sword upon an ex-buccaneer, one of Morgan's men. How would that episode in his past dog him to the end of his days, Kit thought.

He followed the clerk along the corridor, entered the courtroom, paused for a few seconds to allow his eyes to become accustomed to the brilliant light and the still more brilliant colours, for the windows were huge sheets of glass which admitted the full force of the sun, and it seemed all Barbados was here, from the Governor himself, acting as Chief Justice, and wearing a scarlet robe, to the ladies in the gallery in their sparkling dresses and hats and fans. And not only all Barbados; in their midst Marguerite sat, wearing her favourite crimson, her handkerchief held to her nose and lips.

'If you will, Captain Hilton.' The clerk waited.

THE DEVIL'S OWN

Kit climbed the spiral stairs to the witness box. Here he was on a level with the dais where sat the judge. The dock was below him and to his left. He cast a hasty glance in that direction. Philip Warner was soberly dressed in dark brown, and might have been an agent rather than a wealthy planter. He returned Kit's stare without hostility. Indeed, his face was remarkably relaxed.

'You'll take the oath, Captain.'

The Bible was in front of him, and the printed card waited by it. 'I swear to tell the truth, the whole truth, and nothing but the truth, so help me God. He faced Mr Pratt.

'Will you state your full name, and your occupation, and your address, sir.'

'Christopher Hilton, planter, late of Plantation Green Grove in the colony of Antigua.'

Pratt frowned at him. 'Did you say *late* of Plantation Green Grove, Captain Hilton?'

'I am no longer living on the . . .' he cast a defiant look at the gallery. 'On my plantation.'

'Why is that?'

'I am estranged from my wife.'

'Ah.' Pratt appeared to consult his notes. 'Would you tell the court your relationship with the accused?'

'He is my father-in-law.'

'Ah,' Pratt said. 'Now, sir, will you tell the court in your own words the circumstances surrounding the recent assault made by the people of Antigua on the Carib tribes in Dominica?'

'The Caribs, in company with the French, had made a raid upon Antigua,' Kit said. 'Some loss of life, and much more of property, was sustained. It was the wish of the people of Antigua to be avenged.'

'But you opposed this?'

'No, sir. Not in the last resort. It was my wish to bring about an end to the fighting between the two peoples which had been carried on for over fifty years.'

'And you thought you could achieve this?'

'I thought, sir, as we of Antigua were led by Colonel Philip Warner, and the Caribs in Dominica were led by Mr Thomas Warner, and these two gentlemen were brothers, that it should be possible to make a treaty of peace with the Indians.'

'You would not describe this as an ambitious scheme, Captain Hilton?'

'No, sir. I knew both gentlemen. I felt it was worth trying, in order both to end the present strife, and to prevent future strife, with its attendant loss of life and property. Besides, sir, peace had been agreed between England and France, shortly after the raid on Antigua. In the circumstances it seemed to be the proper thing to agree peace with the French allies, the Indians. Nor, sir, was I risking anything more than my own life, I thought. There was a fleet of three ships out of St John's, with nearly three hundred armed men on board. Had I failed in my mission, they could have carried on the assault as they had planned.'

'But you did not fail, Captain Hilton.'

'I persuaded the Caribs to talk peace, sir. I visited their village, I spoke with Thomas Warner and his caciques, and I persuaded them to come down to the shore to speak with Colonel Warner.'

'Now, Captain Hilton, tell the court whether Colonel Warner was privy to your plans.'

'He was, sir. The plan had been decided at a meeting in St John's at which all the principal residents of Antigua were present, as well as the ships' captains, as well as Sir William Stapleton.'

'And what arrangements had you made to safeguard the Indian chieftains when they came to the conference?'

'I had received Colonel Warner's personal assurance of their safety.'

Mr Pratt paused, and looked around the court, which was tensely silent. 'And what happened when the eight caciques arrived at the beach, Captain Hilton?'

'They were taken out to Captain Bale's ship, where Colonel Warner waited, and they were shown into the great cabin, and informed that they were under arrest. When they would have made their escape, the doors to the sleeping cabins behind us were opened and Colonel Warner's men opened fire with muskets and pistols.'

'And what were you and Colonel Warner doing this while?'

'Colonel Warner threw me to the deck and lay on top of me,' Kit said. 'I was too surprised at what had happened immediately to attempt to get up. By the time I did get up, the massacre was over. The crew used their cutlasses to complete the work of their firearms.'

'And what was your reaction to this crime, Captain Hilton?'

'I assaulted Colonel Warner.'

'And what happened then?'

THE DEVIL'S OWN

'I was placed under arrest until the ship regained St John's.'

'And then?'

'I accused Colonel Warner of the crime, before Sir William Stapleton.'

'Following which the accused was sent home for trial, before being returned here. Yes, indeed, Captain Hilton. That will do admirably. Your witness, Mr Harley.'

The Defence Advocate slowly stood up. It seemed to take him a very long time, because he was a very tall man. Like so many tall men he was also untidy; his wig was askew. Which did not mean Kit realized, that he was a poor advocate; perhaps the reverse.

'Captain Hilton,' he said, slowly and thoughtfully. 'An honorary title? Or is there some great event in your past of which this court is unaware?'

Kit flushed. 'Mainly honorary, sir. I once commanded a trading sloop out of St John's.'

'In the employ of whom?'

'Several planters of Antigua.'

'Of whom the principal was Colonel Warner?'

'Yes.'

A murmur went round the court.

'But of course,' Harley said, 'you and Colonel Warner are old acquaintances. Indeed, your two families have been closely connected since the first Englishmen settled these islands. Is that not so?'

'It is,' Kit agreed.

'Your grandfather was one of Sir Thomas Warner's associates?'

'He was.'

'And your grandmother was one of Sir Thomas Warner's servants, I understand.'

Kit felt his cheeks burning. But he kept his voice even. 'She was.'

'And on one occasion she was flogged for absconding?'

'Yes,' Kit said.

'A sad case,' Mr Harley said, regretfully. 'One can understand . . . but no matter. At a later date she was a close, an, ah, intimate friend of Mr Edward Warner, I believe.'

'I was not alive then,' Kit said.

'Nevertheless you will have heard this story.'

'I have been told many stories about my family, sir,' Kit

said. 'I doubt they have any bearing on our reasons for being here today.'

'On the contrary, sir, they have every bearing on our presence here today. But I will touch on that matter in a moment. Now, sir, your grandfather left St Kitts and settled in Tortuga. And achieved high office.'

'He was first Governor of Tortuga.'

'Where you grew to manhood. Tell the court if Colonel Warner ever visited your home.'

'He did. On one occasion.'

'When was this?'

'Oh, a considerable time ago. Nearly twenty years.'

'And was he made welcome?'

'As I remember, sir.'

'There was no quarrel between your grandmother and Colonel Warner?'

'No, sir.'

'I would remind you that you are under oath, Captain Hilton. Is it not a fact that Colonel Warner left Tortuga in haste, with a jury rig still holing up the foremast of his ship, after a quarrel with your grandmother?'

'Colonel Warner did not quarrel with my grandmother, sir,' Kit said. 'The quarrel was with me. I . . .' he glanced at the gallery. 'I was rude to Miss Warner. My future wife.'

Again the murmur. But Harley, naturally enough, did not choose to pursue that line. 'Then tragedy struck. Tortuga was overrun by the Spaniards. May I ask what happened to your family?'

'My grandmother was murdered by the Dons,' Kit said. 'I took refuge on the mainland of Hispaniola.'

'You escaped the holocaust. By yourself?'

'No, sir. I had a companion.'

'Would you tell the court the name of this companion?'

Kit looked at the gallery. What a mine of information she had proved, to be sure. 'His name was Jean DuCasse.'

'DuCasse,' Harley said thoughtfully. 'Do you know, Captain Hilton, that name is vaguely familiar to me. Yet I cannot place it. Perhaps you would be good enough to tell me why it should be familiar?'

'Admiral DuCasse now commands a French fleet in these waters.'

'Indeed he does. How silly of me to have forgotten. And Admiral DuCasse was in command of the French fleet when it invaded Antigua last year.'

THE DEVIL'S OWN

'That is correct,' Kit said.

'Which is no doubt why Plantation Green Grove was spared the worst effects of the outrage. Because he is an old acquaintance of yours. Or do I do you both an injustice. Is acquaintance the word you would choose, Captain Hilton?'

'Monsieur DuCasse is my oldest friend,' Kit said. 'We survived together more than two years in the jungles of Hispaniola, and afterwards . . .' he hesitated.

'You were *matelots*. But please continue, Captain Hilton.'

'Afterwards we marched together through the jungle of Central America, on Panama.'

'Under the command of the late Sir Henry Morgan. So another facet of your remarkable career comes to light. You were a buccaneer.'

'I have never denied that, sir.'

'Indeed you have not. And then, the buccaneer fleet having been disbanded, at least by Morgan, you took yourself to Antigua and a new career. But in the first instance you commanded a sloop owned by Colonel Warner.'

'And others.'

'Indeed. But the employment was granted by Colonel Warner. It would seem that he had decided to let bygones be bygones, in his desire to help the orphaned son of his old servant.'

'He needed a sea captain,' Kit said evenly. 'I was a sea captain.'

'You had been a buccaneer, yes. But you will agree that it was magnanimous of Colonel Warner.'

'He needed a seaman,' Kit said again.

Harley stared at him for some seconds, and then shrugged. 'However, the animosity which you bear him, which lies constantly just beneath the surface, would not remain for long dormant.'

'Your Lordship,' Mr Pratt said, getting up. 'I must object. My learned friend has not proved there was any animosity between this witness and the accused, nor has this witness suggested it.'

The Governor nodded. 'I must agree with that point, Mr Harley.'

'As you wish, Your Lordship,' Harley said. 'You remained in Colonel Warner's employment for a month, Captain Hilton, and then you resigned your command. I will not enter into your reasons for wishing to leave Colonel Warner's employ, but is it not a fact that when you resigned your position there was a violent quarrel?'

'There was,' Kit said. 'But...'

'In the course of which you were set upon by Colonel Warner's servants, beaten, and thrown off the plantation?'

'That is what happened,' Kit agreed.

'But of course you bore the Colonel no ill will for this.'

'I...'

'And soon afterwards you married Mrs Marguerite Templeton, Colonel Warner's daughter.' Mr Harley held up his hand. 'I have no wish, it would be improper, for me to inquire into the methods used by a man in his courting, or to inquire into the wiles and fascinations a man may exercise over members of the female sex. Yet I would like your opinion on whether or not Colonel Warner approved of this marriage?'

'He did not approve of the marriage,' Kit said. 'But he became reconciled to it as time went by.'

'Ah, indeed. The power which time possesses, Captain Hilton, of enabling us poor mortals to become reconciled to our lot is in many ways the only thing which makes life tolerable. Would you not agree?'

'I would say that is a remarkably passive point of view.'

'You do not agree. I thought you might not. Would you deny that, if Colonel Warner became reconciled to your new position in the bosom of his family, you never became reconciled to the many injuries you conceived he had done to you, and to *your* family?'

'If you mean by that, sir,' Kit said, 'that I have never actually liked Colonel Warner, then I would have to say that you are right.'

'I thank you, sir,' Harley said.

Pratt sat back and looked at the ceiling. He seemed to have indigestion.

'I'm afraid,' Kit said, 'that I did not prove a very successful witness.'

Mr Pratt snapped his fingers, and the boy brought two more glasses of rum punch; the tavern was close by the court-house, and indeed was entirely filled with spectators from the trial; but the Advocate General had secured a corner table in some privacy.

'You were transparently honest, Captain, which is what I anticipated you would be, as you are a transparently honest

THE DEVIL'S OWN

man. There are pitfalls in such honesty, and there are great advantages. Nor do I think you came off worst in your encounter with Harley. I have known him for many years, as you may imagine. He did not look particularly satisfied with the results he achieved. And in any event, I expected nothing less than an endeavour to discredit you. For how else may he possibly hope to gain the day for his client? You will note that he made no attempt to deny the truth of your allegations, only to impugn your motives for bringing them at all.'

'And supposing he has failed to discredit me in the minds of the jury?' Kit asked. 'What then? Will he place Philip on the stand?'

'I do not see how he can possibly do anything else. The facts of the case are indisputable. No one, least of all Colonel Warner, has attempted to deny that Indian Warner and seven other caciques were killed in the cabin of that ship.'

'And cannot Mr Harley see all this?'

'Indeed he can,' Pratt agreed. 'And in any event he knows me as well as I know him. I see nothing for him but an appeal to mercy. And do not underestimate the power of that. But at the very least Colonel Warner will stand condemned, fined, perhaps imprisoned, and the infamy of the deed, and the quality of British justice, will be seen to be untarnished, and your name will be cleared before the world, and will indeed be honoured by men everywhere.'

Kit smiled, somewhat wryly. 'I had not supposed it was my name needed clearing. Anyway, I have no wish to hound Colonel Warner to his grave. That he is condemned will be sufficient.'

'An honourable sentiment,' Pratt agreed, and got up. 'I must go back to court. Will you attend this afternoon?'

'How could I stay away?' Kit asked. 'I have but to finish my drink.'

'Well, then, soon I fancy we shall see the end of this nefarious business, and then, sir, we shall show you the quality of Barbadian hospitality. My wife is longing to meet you. Until this afternoon.'

He hurried across the room, and heads turned to watch him go, and then turned back to stare at Kit. He smiled at them, and sipped his drink. Let them take which side they chose. As Pratt had said, this afternoon would see an end to the matter.

But he frowned as a man left the far end of the room and came towards him. He did not recognize the man's face, nor was it a face he would have chosen to remember; the fellow was slight, and his thinning hair was not concealed by a wig. He wore horn-rimmed spectacles, from which he peered at the room with a slight air of alarm, and his clothes were threadbare.

'Captain Hilton?' he whispered.

'I am he,' Kit agreed.

'May I have a word, sir?'

'By all means. A pot of punch?'

'I would rather not, sir, if you'd not take offence. I find the wine of this country a shade too vehement for my brain.'

'Now why should I take offence at that?' Kit demanded. 'But you have the advantage of me, sir.'

'My name is Ligon, Captain. Richard Ligon.' He paused.

'The pleasure is mine, Mr Ligon. Have we met before?'

'No, sir. I have not had that privilege before this minute. But we have mutual friends.' Ligon rested his elbows on the table. 'I am on a voyage of discovery, sir. The most fabulous adventure ever undertaken by man. At least, by a man such as I when compared with a man such as you, to be sure.'

Kit sipped his drink; he wondered if Mr Ligon's discovery that rum was too strong for him had not been very recently made.

'I am, sir, a writer. A mere scribbler, I do assure you. No Dryden I, much less a Donne. Hobbes is as the sun, scorching down upon some rutted pit beneath, and even Defoe must rank as the moon, shedding a fitful light upon those darknesses he would illuminate. But in my own way, sir, I do what I can.'

'Indeed,' Kit observed. 'I must confess I have not heard of you.'

'Nor is that to be wondered at, sir, as I have never yet been published. I am in the course of preparation, sir, a work of great value. In my youth, sir, what were my imaginings constantly seeking? Why, tales of the Indies, of the Americas, of Raleigh and Gilbert, of Tom Warner, and if I dare say it, of Anthony Hilton, and more recently, of Henry Morgan and Jean L'Olonnais, and even of yourself.'

'You are a flatterer, sir.'

'I seek the truth, sir. I would record the fact and the fancy of this beautiful sea. But while it is a great privilege to meet one of my central characters in person, sir, it is not for that purpose that I have inflicted my company upon you. No, sir, I was in court yesterday, and this morning, and I heard your

THE DEVIL'S OWN

spirited words in the witness box, and I gathered, even at my distance, some of the anguish which pursues you now, and which must so much have pursued you in the black-sanded forest of Dominica.'

'You had best speak plain,' Kit suggested.

'Then, sir, so encouraged, I shall. I have recently come from that island.'

Kit frowned at him. 'You have been to Dominica? And retain the flesh on your bones?'

'Indeed, sir, as you know the Caribs better than I, where would be the benefit to any warrior in eating one such as I? His eyes could only grow weak, and his muscles flabby, and his heart and will to victory, why, they would dwindle right away. No, sir, Captain. I was in no danger in that dismal place. I was permitted to penetrate even the dread valley, and speak with the Empress herself.'

Kit put down his glass. 'The Empress? You mean the Princess?'

'What is in a title, sir? She spoke of you.'

'Aye,' Kit said. 'And you hastened to Barbados to bring me that dread message, no doubt.'

'On the contrary, sir. She exalts and admires you, and looks back upon her meeting with you as one of the events of her life. Even if it cost her the life of her son.'

'Could I but believe that . . .'

'Then do so sir, I beg of you. As I was able to relay to her the news of your enmity for Colonel Warner, to inform her of this trial and all that would devolve from it, so did she bid me seek you out, and assure you of her love, and more, her admiration, for your determination to avenge Indian Warner's death.'

'Then, Mr Ligon,' Kit said, 'I shall shake your hand, and invite you to accompany me back to the courtroom, that we may oversee the end of this affair.'

'The pleasure will be all mine, sir. I have but one request to make of you. That I may be permitted to say in my book that I have sat at table with Captain Christopher Hilton.'

Kit laughed, and slapped him on the shoulder. 'Why, Mr Ligon, will you not in any event? Let us go to court.'

'Well, Mr Harley?' inquired the Governor.

Harley tucked his thumbs into his armpits. 'I have no witnesses, Your Lordship.'

The Governor frowned at him. 'No witnesses? What?

What? Does your client then change his plea to guilty?' He bent his glare on Philip Warner to suggest that in this event the sentence would be a severe one.

'By no means, sir. But this case is an unusual one. More, it could be described as unique. The facts are not in dispute here, merely the interpretation to be placed upon the facts. I waive the right to call any witnesses, on the clear understanding that I thereby obtain the right to address the gentlemen of the jury last.'

'Well,' said the Governor, and pulled his nose. 'Well. What say you to that, Mr Pratt?'

Pratt cast a somewhat angry glance at his colleague. 'If that is how my learned friend chooses to discharge his obligation, sir, why should I object.'

'Ha. Ha. Well then, Mr Pratt, as we have the entire afternoon in front of us, I suggest you make your address to the jury now.' He turned his frown on the Attorney General. 'You have your speech prepared?'

'Oh, indeed, Your Lordship,' Pratt agreed. Yet it was obvious even to Kit, seated at the back of the room with Ligon beside him, that the prosecutor was thrown off his stride. He kept shooting bitter glances at Mr Harley. 'However, my address can be nothing more than a restatement of the case I have just presented. It appears that Mr Harley chooses to deny nothing about this case. He mentions that a different interpretation may be placed upon it. Well, gentlemen, that is a reasonable enough point of view in any crime. Were I to charge the bench at this moment and thrust my sword through the breast of His Lordship the Governor seated there, I would wager you my life to a penny that he and I would place different interpretations upon my reasons and indeed upon the deed itself.' He paused to enjoy the laughter, and give an apologetic smile to the Governor.

'But yet, gentlemen,' he said, when the noise had subsided, 'would I still be guilty of murder. The only possible justification for my deed could be that His Excellency and myself were already in armed conflict, that we were, in fact, at war. My learned friend may care to suggest that point. But I would make a point now that he cannot, he dare not dispute. It is that there was no state of war between the Caribs and the Antiguans. There had been. This I grant you. As the French claim dominion over Dominica, so they installed Mr Thomas Warner with the trappings of governorship, and recognized him as their representative there. Thus, upon the outbreak of the last war, when Monsieur DuCasse was loosed upon the Leewards, and upon Jamaica, he was entitled to call upon the French subjects everywhere to follow him into battle. Thus he called upon the savages of Dominica. Now, gentlemen, this is a course of action we may well deplore, yet it was certainly justified by the fact that our country was in a state of war with France. But almost immediately following that infamous raid peace was signed. We have Sir William Stapleton's own testimony, and I quote . . .' Mr Pratt ruffled his papers, 'that, "as peace had lately been signed with the French, we decided to do what we could about the Caribs." '

Mr Pratt raised his head sorrowfully. 'His Excellency, alas, was in error, as I have indicated. If peace was signed with Louis, then no less was peace signed with all of Louis's subjects, whatever the colour of their skins. Thus peace was signed with Tom Warner and his Caribs just as much as with Monsieur DuCasse and his buccaneers. Yet is Sir William exonerated by virtue of his own humanity. He wishes to see what he can do about the Caribs, but the moment the proposal is put to him, as it was put to him, by Captain Hilton, that it might be possible to sign a separate and lasting treaty of peace with the savages, he gives that idea his support. More, he called upon all the gentlemen present, including the Deputy Governor of Antigua, who was to command the expedition, to give the idea their support. And this was agreed. However falsely, it was agreed. Now gentlemen, therefore, put aside these specious arguments. There was no war between the Caribs and the people of Antigua. There had been war. No doubt there will be a war in the future; in the circumstances I do not see how this can be avoided. But when that expedition sailed, and when it landed in Dominica, there was no war. And more, the expedition was aware of this and instructed to proceed accordingly. Its purpose was to meet the Indian caciques around a table, and discuss a mutual treaty and restoration of the captives. That was the purpose of the expedition. But Colonel Warner's purpose was far different. He meant to put an end to the Caribs' capacity for making war, for at least a generation. And he also meant to put an end to this family feud which has distorted the Caribbean scene for so very long. Do not be misled by this story of resisted arrest. Colonel Warner has lived in the Leewards all his life. He has known the Caribs all his life. He of all people can have had not the slightest doubt what would be the reaction of a Carib to being arrested, especially following a promise of safe conduct.

'His problem was, how to get the Indians into his power. But for this he possessed a willing tool. My learned friend has attempted to suggest that there was bad blood between Colonel Warner and Captain Hilton. No doubt the two men had quarrelled in the past. Have any of you never quarrelled with a man later to become your friend? Captain Hilton has even admitted that perhaps he has never liked his father-in-law. Can any of you gentlemen honestly admit to liking your wife's father? That is not a part of human nature. And Captain Hilton has here been as honest as he has been everywhere else. If it were possible to look around this courtroom and say, with my hand on my heart, there is an honest man, I would point to Captain Hilton. And no matter what the relationship between Captain Hilton and Colonel Warner, no one can deny that Captain Hilton *trusted* his father-in-law. Why should he not? He had been present in Antigua when the plan of campaign, the determination to invite Tom Warner and his caciques to a conference, to give them safe conduct while the conference continued, was put forward and accepted, by Sir William Stapleton, and by Colonel Warner. This assurance was later repeated by Colonel Warner to Captain Hilton. So Captain Hilton says. There are no witnesses to the event. But are witnesses necessary, when the principle was already agreed? Nor, may I say, has there been any denial that this second assurance was given. Philip Warner has elected not to take the stand. That is his prerogative. But this cannot alter the facts: that there was an agreement between the Governor of the Leeward Islands and his Deputy in Antigua and the officers of the expedition; that safe conduct should be given to the Caribs; that Christopher Hilton, at great personal risk, visited the Carib village with this offer, and had it accepted by Tom Warner; that the eight Indians accompanied Captain Hilton back to the ship where Philip Warner waited; and that the moment they were safely secured in the great cabin, they were done to death, on the orders of Philip Warner. Gentlemen of the jury, no one has denied any of these facts. No one *can* deny any of these facts, because this is what happened. Therefore no argument put forward by my learned friend can alter the *facts,* that Philip Warner stands before you guilty of a most foul and unnatural murder, which resounds to the discredit of Englishmen everywhere, but of Englishmen in the West Indies more than any other. He deserves to be punished, and it is our duty, and our necessity, to see that he is punished. I call for a verdict of guilty against this man who has so betrayed his position, his trust, and his family.'

Mr Pratt sat down, and mopped his brow.

'It is difficult to see even Colonel Warner surviving that onslaught,' Ligon whispered.

Kit did not reply. He watched the gallery, where Marguerite stared down into the court with burning eyes.

And from Marguerite he looked at the planters in the jury. They whispered amongst themselves, and even smiled.

'Mr Harley?' invited the Governor.

Harley stood up, his thumbs tucked into his armpits. 'My friends,' he said. 'Gentlemen of the jury. My learned associate has taken me to task, implicitly, at the least, for not putting my client into the witness box; for not, apparently, offering a case. Gentlemen, I can only repeat what I said at the beginning of this hearing, that there is no case for my client to answer. Now, gentlemen, we in Barbados are a fortunate people. We lie outside the mainstream of the Caribee Islands, and more important, we lie to windward of them. Even a sailing ship, with a clean bottom and fully manned, must prepare herself for a hard week's work to make the Careenage from St Vincent or St Lucia, much less from Dominica. Thus we have never seen a pirate bring his guns to bear, and indeed, we have never been visited by a Spanish warship. The only contest we have witnessed in these waters was when Sir George Ayscue brought his Commonwealth fleet to overawe us, and we were his first landfall.

'So then, gentlemen, it has proved doubly impossible for any Indians, depending only upon their own muscles for propulsion, to force themselves into the broad bosom of the Atlantic, to contest with the wind for so long and so unequal a struggle, which must necessarily take them out of sight of the islands they know so well, and leave them with scant prospect of getting back. I repeat, gentlemen, we are the most fortunate of people. We have never seen a Carib on the warpath.

'Yet there are men amongst us who have. Barbadian men, forced by contrary weather or in the normal course of business, to make their way amongst those dangerous and treacherous islands. *They* know the Caribs, and you know *them*. How much more do the peoples of the Leewards, of Antigua and St Kitts and Nevis and Montserrat, know the

Caribs? I doubt that Captain Christopher Hilton knows them half as well as any of us, any of them, his new compatriots. For he was born and bred in Tortuga, as he has told us, far to the north of the Carib countries, and he spent his young manhood with Morgan, in Jamaica or on the Main, again, far removed from the spread of Carib power.

'But for those of us who know these savages, there can be no doubt about their humanity, their right to be treated as creatures of God. For they are not. Be sure of that. They are creatures of the devil. They acknowledge no god, save their primitive deities. They acknowledge no rules of morality such as govern us in our daily tasks. They acknowledge no treaties of peace amongst themselves. Their rule is the law of the strongest, the most brutal, the most terrible. And when they have won, they tie their victim to a stake, while still living, and they tear the flesh from his bones, while he still lives. Are these men? I doubt that, gentlemen. I doubt that very strongly. If these are men, then am I ashamed of my own humanity.'

He ruffled his papers; no other sound was to be heard in the crowded courtroom. 'I have heard a report, of an event on the plantation of Mr Alleyne, but a year gone. A mad dog was found to be on Mr Alleyne's estate. There was a great deal of concern. This was a huge, a terrible beast, and it had belonged to Mr Porter.' He stared at one of the members of the jury. 'I am sure all you gentlemen remember it well. Everyone who could bear arms was called out and the dog was hunted down. Yet did it eventually take refuge in a barn, where it could not be reached by the hunters. It was necessary to bring the dog out, or to burn a barn with the consequent risk of life and property. According to my report, gentlemen, Mr Porter himself advanced with great courage, and held out a piece of raw meat, the scent of which brought the dangerous, the starving animal from its lair, whence it was immediately shot dead. Gentlemen, the report I have in my hand praises Mr Alleyne and his friends for their prompt and vigorous and decisive action, when any hesitation might have allowed the animal to escape and begin a reign of terror in this island, and it also praises Mr Porter, for the gallant subterfuge with which he brought the beast from its lair.

'Gentlemen, I ask you, which would you rather face, in your garden? A mad dog, or a Carib? Much less a horde of Caribs. Does anyone here imagine that Colonel Warner was

THE DEVIL'S OWN

happy in what he had to do? Does anyone here imagine that Mr Porter was happy to see his dog, his favourite dog, lying dead at his feet? Yet it had to be done, and it was done. And Mr Porter was praised for it.

'My learned friend has made a great deal of the fact that a safe conduct was discussed and agreed. By whom was it agreed? By Sir William Stapleton and Captain Christopher Hilton. Captain Hilton's knowledge of the Indians we have already discussed. So now, what of Sir William? Has he ever taken the field against the Caribs? Indeed he has not. In that respect, his has been a fortunate term of office. Until last year, to be precise. Perhaps it is a measure of his ability as a governor that his reaction was to attempt to talk peace, with a tribe of mad dogs.

'There will be comment on the fact, again as suggested by my learned friend, that the Caribs, in their raid on Antigua, were acting as no more than allies of the French, indeed, that they were French citizens. I dismiss this last suggestion as absurd, if indeed it is not plain treason. The English Government recognizes no French jurisdiction over Dominica, nor do we. As for the Caribs being called into action by Monsieur DuCasse, were they so called when last they raided the Leewards, looting, burning, raping, kidnapping, eating at the stake? Is it not the truth that, as the Leeward Islanders had built up their defences, the Caribs found themselves unable to assault these bastions of English civilization unless *they* could secure allies. And these were eventually forthcoming in the presence of the French buccaneer fleet. But even if Monsieur DuCasse were to appear in this court today, the claim that he had brought the Caribs to Antigua at his personal invitation, I would put him no more than in the position of Mr Porter, whose dog was mad, and who saw what had to be done, and did it. Monsieur DuCasse thought differently, and acted differently. But do we not condemn Monsieur DuCasse upon a score of grounds? Is he not a most guilty man? Gentlemen, we praised Mr Porter's action. We could not also praise a determination by him, or any other, to turn mad dogs loose to do their damndest.

'And then, gentlemen, there is the point that Tom Warner was Colonel Philip Warner's brother. Gentlemen, how much do we owe this splendid family which has made it possible for us all to be here, and prosper. Is there a man amongst us who does not have a mistress, whose father did not have a mistress, who does not, perhaps, have a bastard half-brother? We all would hope that our bastard half-brother, or our bastard sons, will inherit sufficient of our family characteristics to play their full, their valuable part in the onward march of the human race. But, let us be frank, gentlemen, when, convulsed by passion for a pretty face, an alluring body, we seek a woman's bed, we are not then concerned with the probable result of our immorality. We take it on trust. We are all sinners before the Lord, and yet we have the effrontery to believe that should a child result from our sin, he or she will contain only the virtues we are conscious of, and none of the vices we may fear in the mother.

'Gentlemen, Sir Thomas Warner, far from the country whence he was born, far from friends and from religion, concerned only with building an empire, working from dawn until dusk, fell in love with a beautiful woman. But she was an Indian. From that liaison terrible consequences were to flow. The enmity of Carib for white man. But this was perhaps inevitable, as they were rivals for these islands. But the union also produced this man, Tom Warner. See the note of love, the confident expectation, with which Sir Thomas received this bastard son; he gave the child his own name. But alas, like so many of us, he was wrong. The child inherited none of the splendid virtues of the father. He inherited only the crazed blood-lust of the mother. Gentlemen, when your bastard disappoints you, you show him the door, allow him perhaps a shilling or two to keep him from starving, and think no more on the matter. For what can the lad do, save disappear? But Indian Warner was no mere bastard. He was the son of a princess, herself the daughter of a great cacique. When his crimes caused the new head of the family, Philip Warner, to expel him from Antigua, he did not disappear into the world. He disappeared into the forests of Dominica, to seek his people, carrying his demoniac mother with him. And there, gentlemen, was he sought out by the no less demoniac French, and made governor over this savage place, and told to support them in their dreams of conquest.

'Gentlemen, from birth, Tom Warner was a mad dog. He should have been strangled at his mother's breast. He was not. He was a Warner. Philip Warner, and his stepmother, attempted to make the boy into a civilized human being. They failed. Gentlemen, we may well say *there* was the crime, if ever a crime was committed, which should be laid at the door of Philip Warner. He did not hang this foul spawn of his father's lust on the instant; he still counted on the mere fact that there was Warner blood in the monster's veins, and he let him go, on condition that he left the Leewards for ever. Gentlemen, there was weakness. But the test of a man is whether weakness is an act of policy, or an act of character. It was Philip Warner's decision to let his brother go, perhaps out of love for his father's memory, perhaps, who knows, out of love for the boy himself. They had shared their youths together.

'That decision was a terrible mistake. But at least Philip Warner was prepared to rectify it. There is no weakness of character here. When this terrible figure reappeared, blood dripping from his ghastly mouth, Philip Warner knew what had to be done, and he knew too, that he must do it. There was a mad dog at large, and it had to be destroyed. But it had retired to its lair. It had to be enticed out. He could not do that himself. The hatred he bore for his brother was well known. So he employed his son-in-law.

'Gentlemen, let us not be hard on Captain Hilton. Here is a man who, in spite of his irregular youth, his piratical background, would indeed appear to be a sincere and honest fellow, as suggested by my learned friend, if perhaps he also appears to be weak. Some of his recent actions, indeed, may be called irrational. His own wife was dreadfully assaulted by the Caribs. Yet he wished to make peace with them. He wished to deal with them as honourable men. Perhaps because he has been forced to act dishonourably so often in his past, he has cultivated an unnatural regard for honour, regardless of the fact that honour must be respected and therefore shared, it cannot be imposed upon those who do not understand the meaning of the word. Philip Warner, a born leader of men, knew this fact well enough. To have told Christopher Hilton what he intended would have been to negate his every plan. So Captain Hilton was made a dupe. Yet was the cause itself worthy. Colonel Warner sought an end to warfare and bloodshed, to rape and mayhem, and like a born leader of men, he sought this end with the least possible risk to his own people. Gentlemen, I ask you to imagine the agony this decision must have cost Colonel Warner, the heartsearching and the despair. But I ask you also to be glad that in our midst there are yet men of such decision, and such courage. And I ask you more, whether any man of you, faced with a similar problem, would have acted differently. And gentlemen, when you have asked yourselves these questions, I ask you to acquit my client, and indeed, to praise him, as a man who did what was necessary, at whatever cost to himself.'

Mr Harley sat down, and the court remained absolutely silent. His Excellency once again was pulling at his nose.

'Gentlemen of the jury,' he said. 'This is one of the saddest cases I have ever had to hear. You have listened to the evidence carefully put together by Mr Pratt, so honestly attested by Captain Hilton, and so literately stated by those who cannot be with us. This evidence is incontestable, nor has it been contested. Mr Pratt is right when he states that the issue as to whether or not Colonel Warner repeated his assurance of safe conduct for the Indians to Captain Hilton, when the fleet anchored off Dominica, is irrelevant. He is right when he suggests that this was already established in St John's. There can be no other point at issue. And let me make this plain. A criminal case is tried upon facts before the law. Colonel Warner, as an executive of English justice, and as he acted on board an English ship, is subjected to English law. It is not your place to decide the moral issues at stake here. It is your question to decide the fact of Colonel Warner's guilt before the law, and the facts are these, that a safe conduct was agreed, that in view of this safe conduct the Carib chieftains attended Colonel Warner's ship, and that there, on Colonel Warner's orders, they were done to death. These are the facts of the case. I can add nothing to them, and you have no right to take anything away from them. I will now ask you to retire to consider your verdict.'

The foreman of the jury stood up. 'We have no wish to retire, Your Lordship.'

The Governor frowned. 'What? What?'

'Our verdict is already decided, Your Lordship.'

'Bless my soul,' said the Governor. 'Bless my soul. May I ask what the verdict is?'

'We find the accused, Colonel Philip Warner, not guilty of either murder or treachery, Your Lordship.'

'Bless my soul,' the Governor said again. 'Is that the verdict of you all?'

'It is a unanimous verdict, Your Lordship.'

But the end of his statement was lost in a roar of approval which seemed to emanate from every corner of the room.

11

The Outcast

'Sail ho,' shouted the main top, and Captain Holgate hurried to the taffrail, Kit at his side.

'The Warners, you think?' Kit asked.

Victors and vanquished had left Barbados within hours of each other, in different ships, two days previously, and had remained in sight until the previous night.

'Only if she has passed under our stern.' Holgate levelled his telescope. 'This is a sloop. Out of St Kitts, I would say.'

Both the islands could be seen on the northern horizon, with Nevis and Montserrat clinging to port, and Guadeloupe still high astern.

'Aye,' Kit said. 'They'll have made St John's by now. I suspected they'd show you their heels when the wind dropped.'

Holgate closed his telescope with a snap. 'Ah, well, maybe it's to the good, Captain Hilton. There'll be a crowd to welcome him, you can be sure of that. You'll not be the most popular man there.'

' 'Tis not my own popularity I worry about,' Kit muttered. 'How much longer, do you think?'

'By nightfall,' Holgate said. 'We shall have to beat up.'

'Then do so,' Kit suggested. 'I do beseech you, sir.'

Holgate nodded. His passenger had kept mainly to his cabin on the return voyage; only the sight of Antigua on the bow had brought him on deck now. Well, he could hardly be blamed for that. Holgate could not help but wonder what would be Sir William Stapleton's reaction to the court judgement. What indeed, would happen in Antigua. If it were possible to pass a vote of no confidence in a governor, then the Barbadian jury had done just that. But were they not merely reflecting prevailing opinion in all the islands?

But nothing is this unhappy situation could compare with the position in which Captain Hilton must now find himself.

'She approaches, the deck,' shouted the main top.

Holgate frowned and turned back to the rail. Once again he levelled his glass. 'The government sloop, by God. And flying a signal. You'll heave to, Mr Hartopp.'

'For God's sake,' Kit shouted. 'I am in haste, Captain. Can you not appreciate that?'

'I appreciate that, well enough, Captain Hilton,' Holgate said. 'But you must appreciate that we are once again at war, with France. In obeying His Excellency's instructions and remaining in Carlisle Bay these past weeks in order to bring you back to Antigua, I have sadly neglected my true responsibilities. If now the St Kitts sloop wishes to communicate with me, sir, I have no alternative but to await its news, whether good or bad.'

Kit sighed, and nodded. 'Aye, you are right, of course, sir. You have my apology.'

He moved away, gazed at the calm sea behind them. And of course his agitation was founded on no reasonable apprehension. So perhaps Philip Warner and Marguerite would land in St John's a few hours before he would reach Falmouth. What, would they immediately seek to avenge themselves? And why should they attempt to avenge themselves in any event, on Lillan? Their enemy was Kit Hilton, and they would wait for him.

He hoped and prayed.

But in any event, there would be celebrations, which would certainly consume the rest of this night. With the wind fair there was no question but that the *Euryalus* would make English Harbour by dawn, no matter how long the delay.

The sloop had by now also hove to, and was lowering a boat. Kit watched the oars dipping, coming out of the water sparkling wet, little rainbows scintillating through the scattered drops of water. How appreciative had he suddenly become of the true beauty in life. Because he was so tired, of antagonism. But now was no time to be tired. Now would the antagonisms be more determined than ever.

The boat came under the lee of the frigate, and the captain of the sloop scrambled up the ladder. 'Captain Holgate, sir.' He saluted the bridge while the bosun's pipes shrilled.

'Come up, Mr Lewis. Come up.' Holgate met the lieutenant at the top of the companion-way. 'What news, man, what news?'

Lewis's face was grim. 'The very worst, sir. There has been a battle off the Main, and Benbow has been worsted.'

THE DEVIL'S OWN

'Benbow, defeated?' Holgate cried.

'DuCasse?' Kit asked.

'The same,' Lewis said. 'Mind you, gentlemen, there was little glory in it for the Frenchman. It would appear that there was cowardice amongst the English. Indeed Monsieur DuCasse recognized as much, and has written to Port Royal suggesting they be hanged.'

'Aye,' Holgate said thoughtfully. 'And I'll wager I can name at least two of their number. Wade for a start, and Hampton . . . no doubt they influenced the rest. They would never accept the authority of a man from the lower deck. And Benbow?'

'Grievous wounded, Captain Holgate. 'Tis said he will lose a leg, if indeed his life can be saved.'

'And DuCasse runs free once again. You'll see we had reason to halt, Captain Hilton.'

'I've already begged your forgiveness, friend. You'll but set me on the beach before taking your station.'

Holgate nodded, but Lewis was frowning.

'I did not halt you, gentlemen, to impart that news, grave as it is. My message concerns Captain Hilton.'

'What?' Kit cried. 'What, man? Out with it.'

'Sir William begs me to inform you, sir, that he has been relieved of his post, and is already on his way back to England.'

'Stapleton gone?' Holgate said. 'But . . .'

'He lays the deed at the door of the planters, sir,' Lewis said. 'To condemn their most prominent member is to make an enemy of the entire breed, and so it was felt by Her Majesty's ministers that government would become impossible. But by the same token, he begged me to inform Captain Hilton that life in Antigua for Philip Warner's enemy will become impossible. He suggests, sir, that you remove yourself to St Kitts, or even farther afield.'

'By God,' Kit said. 'Does His Excellency suppose that I am afraid to face any one of that scum with a sword in my hand?'

'By no means, sir,' Lewis agreed. 'But it is not your face he is concerned with. Tempers have run high these last years, and angry men may stoop to no reasonable act.'

Holgate glanced at Kit. 'I can easily alter course for St Kitts. You have but to say the words.'

'And you know that I must return to Antigua, at least for a while. There are people there whose safety requires it.'

'Well, sir,' Lewis said, looking very distressed.

'And of course much will depend on the character of the new governor,' Holgate said. 'Any word of him?'

'None, sir, at the moment. The islands are to be ruled separately by the Speakers of their Houses, pending the appointment.'

'Trumbull, by God,' Kit said. 'There is at least an honest man.'

'Honesty is not always a buffer against angry majorities,' Holgate reminded him. 'None the less, we shall make for English Harbour with all speed. My thanks, Mr Lewis.'

Lewis was not looking definitely embarrassed. He glanced from Captain Holgate to Kit, and then back again, and his face was red. 'Aye,' he said at last. 'You'll be there by nightfall. 'Tis what must happen, I've no doubt. I'll take my leave, sir. And wish you Godspeed, Captain Hilton.'

Kit frowned after him. 'Now what the devil did he mean by those words?'

'Less his words,' Holgate agreed. 'Than his manner. You do not suppose...'

'There has already been some disturbance? By God, sir, make sail, I beg of you, and land me at Falmouth.'

The frigate could not approach the shore too closely, and dropped its anchor in the centre of the bay. Kit was already waiting in the gangway as the boat was swung out.

'You'll understand that I must make haste for Sandy Point, Kit,' Holgate explained.

'I understand that, Captain. There are sufficient boats here to bring me across if I should feel it necessary. If I have to I'll seize one, by God. With Agrippa as crew we'll have no trouble.' He shook hands, and climbed down the ladder. 'Give way, lads, give way.'

So yet again he approached a hostile shore, he thought. But there yet surely was only his imagination loosing itself without cause. English Harbour? Where he and Lillan had walked on the sand often enough, hand in hand, acknowledging the greetings of the fishermen who were all that lived here? Certainly this place had not changed. The cottages still clung to the edge of the beach, the boats needing repair were dragged up, for the main part of the fishing fleet was out, the fluttering skirts still denoted where the fishermen's wives were gathered for an afternoon gossip. But now they were

THE DEVIL'S OWN

straying closer to the shore to watch the frigate and the approaching boat.

The keel grated, and the oars were backed. Kit made his way forward and jumped to the sand. The coxswain saluted and the oars were thrust down again. Kit adjusted his sword belt, felt the comforting weight of the pistols in his pockets, turned to face the houses and the clustering trees. The women stared at him. He knew most of them by sight if not by name. He walked up the beach, the sand crunching under his boots, and raised his hat. 'Good day to you, ladies. 'Tis good to be home.'

Still they stared at him, in horror it seemed to his eyes. But they could not yet have learned the result of the trial. And now other faces appeared at windows and at doors. But for their complexion he might almost have supposed himself back in the Carib village beyond the Valley of Desolation. Certainly these people seemed to regard him as a creature from another world.

He shrugged, and walked on, taking the path by the shore for Falmouth, a mile distant, and the cottage. On his left the longboat had already regained the frigate and was being taken up, even as the anchor was hoisted and the sails were loosed. So, Jean had once again triumphed, even if, as he had been quick to recognize, the honour of the victory was not his alone. But what would happen now? Would he return amongst the islands, burning and plundering? Or would he not consider it worth his while, after his earlier visits. Certainly, with the destruction of Benbow's fleet the Caribbean was his.

The trees on his right thinned, and he saw the cottage. How peaceful it looked, surrounded by its flower garden, waiting apart from the main body of houses farther down the road. And how deserted it appeared. But for the open windows on the upper floor he would have supposed it empty. No doubt they were enjoying their afternoon meal, like everyone else unaware of the disaster which had overtaken their lives. He had not properly assimilated the event himself; his sole concern since the end of the trial had been to get home.

He pushed the gate open, paused in surprise. The path, which Agrippa had ever kept neat and tidy, and smoothed, was scuffed and pitted, and already weeds were attempting to thrust their way through the disordered earth. And the flowerbeds to either side were also scattered, although farther back they seemed in good enough order, if they all needed weeding.

He reached the front door, an uneasy feeling causing his belly to roll. The door was locked. He banged on it with his first, and shouted. 'Holloa. Holloa there. Is nobody home? Agrippa?'

There were startled sounds from above him, and he stepped back to look up, gazed at Astrid Christianssen in amazement.

'Astrid? What brings you here?'

She regarded him with equal astonishment, but hers was tinged with a strange mixture of distress and relief. 'Kit? Oh, my God, Kit.'

'There is something the matter? By God. Lillan is ill? Open up, Astrid. Open up.'

Her head disappeared, and he waited, looking over his shoulder, and espying some of the children from English Harbour, lurking in the bushes on the far side of the path. They must have followed him the entire way. The rascals, and with dusk coming on too. Their parents would have sticks in their hands.

But why had they followed him the whole way?

The front door swung inwards, and Astrid stood there. Her face was lined and tired, her shoulders seemed to sag.

'Astrid?' He stepped inside, closed the door behind him, looked around the parlour. Nothing seemed to have changed. 'Where is Agrippa?'

He heard the rasp of air in her nostrils as she breathed. 'Dead.'

'Dead?' For a moment the word did not register. Then he seized her shoulders. 'Dead? Agrippa? But . . .' he thrust her aside and ran for the stairs.

'Kit,' she shrieked, grasping at his arm. 'Do not go up. I beg of you, Kit. Do not go up.'

He checked and turned, slowly. 'Lillan . . .'

'Is alive, and will be well. Perhaps. But do not go up, Kit. I beg of you. Do not go up.'

'Not go to Lillan? Then what has happened to her?'

Astrid licked her lips, and her knees seemed to give way. She sat on the chair by the door, a collapsed woman. 'She will be well,' she muttered.

There was a sound, and Kit peered up the stairs. Abigail stood there. Her belly had not yet started to swell, and she seemed no different to the girl he had left behind. But she

THE DEVIL'S OWN

no longer smiled. It was difficult to imagine that face ever smiling.

'Captin,' she said. 'You'll get them. Captin. You'll get those who killed my man.'

Kit instinctively took another step. Then halted.

He had known Lillan, always poised and dignified. And overwhelmingly healthy. Besides, he distrusted his own emotions at this moment. He could identify none of them, save a raging fury.

He went to the sideboard, poured a glass of rum, returned to stand by the white woman. 'Drink this.'

She raised her head, and frowned at him. But she took the glass in both hands, and drank.

'Now tell me what happened, and when, and how, and who was responsible.'

'Four days ago,' Astrid whispered. 'That close, Kit. That close.'

'You were here?'

She shook her head. 'I could only gather, from Abigail. From ... people.'

'And Lillan is unharmed?'

'Unharmed,' Astrid muttered. 'Aye, Kit, the surgeon says she is unharmed.'

'Then what happened?' he asked again.

'Four days ago,' Abigail came down the steps. 'But it was night. A band of horsemen appeared at the gate, Captin. They were masked, with hoods over their faces, and only slits for their eyes.'

'White men?'

'Oh, yes, they were white men, Captin. Lillan even thought she recognized one or two of their voices. But she could not be sure.'

'And what happened?'

'Three of them dismounted, and came to the door. It was late, you understand, Captin, and we had retired. But the noise of the banging awoke us and Agrippa went down, unbolted the door and opened it to see what the matter was, and Captin, without saying a word, they ran him through with their swords, again and again and again. I was at the head of the stairs, there, looking down. He died right where you is standing, Captin. If you look close you will yet see the bloodstains.'

Kit's fingers curled into fists.

'We supposed we was also to be murdered, Captin. Me, I

hid under the bed. But it was Lillan they wanted. She says she was unable to move for a few seconds, but when they started towards her she ran for the bedroom and bolted the door. But Captin, they knocked it down in a single charge. She had no weapon save a single pistol, and this was struck from her hand before she could aim it. Then she was dragged down here, and taken out of the house, and set on a horse.'

'Did she not cry out for help?'

'She screamed until her voice cracked, Kit,' Astrid said. 'But Falmouth remained shuttered and dark. 'Tis certain the villagers had been warned not to interfere.'

'They raped her?'

Astrid's head moved to and fro. 'No. No, she was not violated, Kit. Far worse.'

'Worse? Worse than death or assault? By Christ, Astrid, you had best speak plain.'

'They took her away, she says, into the canefields. They rode for a good time, and she cannot be sure of the direction. But when they reached their selected place they halted their mounts and set her down. And the place had been prepared. There was a fire, and barrels, she said.'

Kit stared at the woman, his mouth dry. Abigail at last started to sob.

'They held her down and cut off her hair, Kit. They cut off every strand, and then they lathered her with soap and shaved the rest. But not yet were they satisfied, Kit. They took away her nightdress, and applied tar to her body. They coated her with hot tar, Kit, from her neck to her toes, and accompanied the deed with every act of lewdity that you can imagine, save the ultimate. Then she was rolled in the dust and covered all over with leaves and filth, and placed in a cart.'

'And taken where?'

'To St John's, Kit. By now it was close to dawn. The masked men rode her into town, and stopped in the middle of the main street, and took her out of the cart and tied her wrists and her ankles all together in the small of her back, and left her there. In the middle of the street, Kit. Then they thrust a gag into her mouth so that she could not cry out, and rode away.'

'Who found her?'

'The entire town found her, Kit. As her kidnappers intended. It was a fisherman first. And he roused the Pinneys at the store, and they roused Barnee. They knew not who it was, you see, and supposed in fact that she was some Negress. It was not until they took the gag from her mouth and she spoke that they understood.'

Slowly Kit straightened. Lillan, tarred and naked, in the midst of the St John's mob. With her head shaved. He looked down at his right hand; his nails had eaten into his palm, as Marguerite's had done on that terrible day at Green Grove.

'Dag would not have her in the house, Kit,' Astrid whispered. 'He said she had sinned most terribly, and this was but a punishment on her for that sin. I called upon Mr Barnee for help, and he gave it willingly enough. We got his own wagon, and placed her in that, and brought her back here, Kit. It was then for the first time I understood what had happened to Agrippa. Lillan would not speak, then.'

Marguerite. And Green Grove.

'We got Dr Haines to come out,' Astrid said. 'And he examined her, and bathed her, and tried to get the worst of the tar off. And he gave her a salve for the burns . . . tar burns, Kit. It leaves scorch-marks on the skin.'

Because who else could possibly have done it? She had virtually threatened him, the last day on the boat before they had reached Barbados. Her decision must have been taken then, and the message despatched by the mail sloop almost immediately. She had intended to avenge herself on him, without even knowing which way the trial would go. At a time, indeed, when all had prophesied Philip Warner's condemnation.

'And then we put her to bed, Kit. And there she has remained. Mr Barnee looked after the burial of Agrippa, Kit. He has been very good.'

Her voice was a distant mumble; her face was indistinct. So this, then, was what Lewis would have said, and thought better of it.

'But Dag, Kit. He won't come near her. He says she is accursed. He even condemns me for being here. But she is my daughter, Kit. How could I leave her alone, at a time like this? Why, she would have starved to death. But now you are back, Kit . . . Kit?'

Her fingers closed on his, and he started.

'You'll stay a while longer, Astrid. I beg of you.'

'Of course I will, if you wish. But . . .'

He had already turned away, and was climbing the stairs.

'Kit, no,' Astrid screamed. 'You must not. She begged me that you would not see her. Please, Kit. Give her time, Kit. Every day she improves. Every day we get more of the tar off. Every day her complexion recovers. Every day her hair sprouts a little more, Kit. Do not go in to her now.'

Every day. He hesitated, his hand tight on the banister. 'You'll stay with her?'

'I will stay as long as you wish me to, Kit. But what will you do?'

'Do, Astrid? My first concern will be to seize the vermin who carried out this deed, and have them on their bellies before Kit.'

'But Kit . . .' she chewed her lip. 'It will mean violence, and anger, and perhaps even bloodshed.'

'And do you, Astrid, not feel anger, and a desire for violence, and perhaps even a demand for bloodshed?'

'It is not part of our philosophy,' she said. 'Life is there to be made the best of.'

'Aye,' he said. 'But it is not achieved by bowing your back to every lash that fate or hideous humanity would inflict upon it. You'll not stop me, Astrid.'

She hesitated, and then shook her head. 'I'll not stop you, Kit. I'll wish you good fortune, and success. And may God have mercy on my soul.'

'You bring them men, Captin,' Abigail muttered. 'You bring them men. God going smile on that.'

But once again, no God was involved here. This was an affair of the devil. And it would be rewarded with devil's work. The sun was already dropping behind the protection of St Kitts as he strode into Falmouth, to demand a horse from the inn-keeper. The animal was immediately available. People gathered on street corners to look at Christopher Hilton, but to avert their eyes whenever his gaze swung in their direction. They knew well enough he was on the path to hell, this night, and that anyone who should cross him would surely accompany him on that dread journey.

He rode out of the village, his sword slapping on his thigh, his pistols heavy in his pockets. What did he intend. Murder? Only if forced to it. But confession and atonement. An atonement so abject that it would make it possible for Lillan once again to venture forth into public, with not an obscene smile or an obscene gesture to be noticed. He could settle for nothing less. The alternative was death.

THE DEVIL'S OWN

It rained, a steady patter which suggested the onset of the storm season. A suitable night for such a venture. The rain was not heavy enough to penetrate his coat and dampen his powder, and the distant lightning suited his mood. He expected nothing more; Antigua was seldom troubled with hurricanes, and in any event it was too early in the season.

He was aware of being hungry. He had deliberately eaten a light lunch, looking forward to his dinner with Lilian, after their separation. But his belly would not stomach food now, in any event.

At the crossroads he hesitated, for the first time uncertain. The ship carrying the Warners might have been ahead of the frigate, but it would have docked only hours before. And he had already estimated the scope of the celebrations which would be enjoyed in St John's. There was no possibility of Marguerite already having returned to Green Grove.

On the other hand, she *would* return there, soon enough. And on Green Grove he had no doubt he would find the actual perpetrators of the assault and the murder.

He turned his horse to the right, through the lanes and between the fields he knew so well, topped the hill and looked down on the glimmering lights of the village, the glowing windows of the Great House. It was close to midnight.

He walked the horse down the hill, travelling with deliberate slowness, determined to alert no one on the plantation, enjoying the seething anger which bubbled in his belly. He entered the compound as quietly as he had come the whole way, for the gate was open, and guided his horse towards the Great House. To his left the slave compound lay in silence; above it the white village was also dark, and beyond even that the huge bulk of the boiling house loomed through the night. But a lantern hung above the main steps to the Great House verandah, and now the mastiffs barked, and a moment later they came bounding from the kennels beneath the steps, for they were always unchained at night, perpetual watchdogs to restrain marauders, be they white burglars or vengeful slaves.

And these were fresh dogs. They did not know the master of Green Grove. They charged down the slope with high-pitched venom baying from their throats, and the hired horse whinnied nervously.

Hastily Kit dismounted. He let the bridle go and walked in front of the animal, up to the house. The dogs roared at him, and checked to bark, and to ascertain his nature before loosing themselves at his throat. They panted and dripped saliva, and inhaled some more, and smelt only the anger standing out on his face and shoulders. Their growls turned to whines and they formed a circle around him, ever parting as he strode towards the steps.

'But what is that?' Maurice Peter demanded from the night. He stood on the steps, a blunderbuss in his hands, and peered at the dark figure in front of him. 'And the dogs done bite you, man? Ow, me God, is a jumbie.'

'No ghost, Maurice Peter,' Kit said. 'Not yet, at any rate.'

'Ow, me God,' Maurice Peter said again. 'The Captin? But we ain't expecting you this night, Captin.'

Kit went up the steps. 'Is the mistress home?'

'No, suh, Captin. Not yet. But she arrive back in St John's this afternoon, and she send word that she coming this night. So I waiting for she.' Maurice Peter peered more closely at the white man. 'You did hear that the Colonel done been set free, Captin?'

'I was there,' Kit said.

'Ow, me God,' Maurice Peter said. 'But you there. Yes, you there.'

'And now I wish to have a word with my wife, so I'll do the waiting up, Maurice Peter. Fetch me a jug of sangaree. I have ridden long and hard. And then you may retire.'

Maurice Peter hesitated, then thought better of arguing. 'Yes, Captin.'

'Where are the children?'

"Oh they in bed, Captin. Mistress Johnson done been sleeping in since the mistress gone to Barbados, and she does put them to bed too early.'

Kit nodded. 'Sangaree, Maurice Peter.'

He tiptoed up the stairs, pausing only when a board creaked beneath his weight. But the whole upper part of the house was silent; the only sound the faint patter of the drizzling rain on the skylights.

He reached the gallery, opened Tony's room, stood above the bed to look down on the boy. Tony slept deeply, and quietly, half turned on his side. What did he think of it all, Kit wondered? Because surely he was old enough to understand that his mother and father were enemies. But after this night his father would be gone for ever.

He closed the door, softly, and went to Rebecca's room. She slept violently, tossing and turning, although fast asleep.

THE DEVIL'S OWN

But she was too young to understand what was happening, yet she was aware enough to know that something was happening, and was disturbed by it.

He resisted the temptation to kiss the child, for fear she would awake, and closed her door in turn. No doubt they would grow up looking on Miss Johnson as a parent more than either their mother or their father. But then, no doubt, that was how Marguerite intended it.

He went back down the stairs, stopped at the foot to listen to the drumming hooves, ran on to the verandah. The lantern still hung above his head, its light attracting swarms of insects. But the blunderbuss was gone. In its place a jug of iced sangaree and a glass waited by the door. Maurice Peter was on his way to warn his mistress.

Kit sat down with a sigh. How tired he was. He seemed to have been tired for a very long time. He wanted to rest, with Lilian, in some quiet place. He wanted to recapture the delight of Falmouth as they had first known it. But they could never find pleasure or contentment in Falmouth again. In all of Antigua again. Perhaps in all of the Leewards, or all of the West Indies. Unless he guarded her honour and her reputation with his sword and his pistols. Well, he would be prepared to do that. Once he had had a rest.

His head jerked, and he discovered himself awake. After how long? The rain still drizzled downwards, and the night was still dark, but now increasingly chill. It could not want so many hours to dawn. And the carriage was rumbling through the gate below him and starting to mount the slope. It was driven by two slaves, and Maurice Peter rode alongside, carrying his blunderbuss.

Kit got up. The carriage came to a halt and one of the drivers got down to fix the step. Patience Jane came out, casting her master a fearful glance. She held the door for her mistress.

Marguerite wore a light brown cloak over her gown, with a hood to protect her hair from the rain. She came up the steps, slowly, smiling at him. But it was an arranged smile. Her face was tired, with dark shadows beneath her eyes. At least the cold seemed to have cleared up; she no longer held a kerchief to her nose.

'Kit,' she said. 'What a pleasant surprise. But the frigate did not make St John's. Or we would have invited you to the celebration.'

'Captain Holgate set me ashore at English Harbour,' Kit

said. 'He was in haste to make Sandy Point. You'll have heard that Benbow has been defeated?'

'There is a rumour to that effect, certainly. Fetch me a glass, Patience Jane. I will have some sangaree. By God, but I am weary.' She sat down. 'So your friend Monsieur Du-Casse is once again triumphant. What a pity you did not drown *him* in your water butt, all those years ago. You may put the carriage away, Henry Kenneth.'

The vehicle rumbled towards the stable. Maurice Peter dismounted and led his horse behind it.

Patience Jane returned with the glass, and Marguerite drank, with great satisfaction.

'You may retire also, Patience Jane,' Kit said.

The girl hesitated, looking at her mistress.

'Do as the master says, child.' Marguerite watched her go into the house. 'What brings you to Green Grove in the middle of the night, Kit, sweetheart? There is surely no more harm you can wish to do to my family?'

Kit leaned against the upright of the verandah. 'I came to learn the names of the men who assaulted Lillan Christianssen, and who murdered Agrippa.'

She gazed at him, once again sipping her drink. 'Agrippa, murdered? Then indeed there must have been an army. Lillan, assaulted? She wasn't harmed, I hope?'

'That depends on your interpretation of the word. We'll have no dissembling here, Marguerite. I came for those names, as I came for you. The men I will arrest for murder. You are going to make a public apology in the centre of St John's tomorrow morning at noon.'

She frowned at him. 'You have lost your senses, Kit. The disappointment of the court case, the exertions of travelling . . . who knows. It may even be some deep-seated ailment which afflicts you. Why not come to bed, my darling, and tomorrow you will look on the world in a different light.'

Kit reached across the verandah. She saw him coming and tried to rise, and he caught her arm as she would have stepped round the chair. She struck at him with her other hand, which still held the glass. He leaned away from her fist and the glass flew against the wall, to smash. She panted, and spat at him. Here was the girl crawling out of the water butt in Tortuga all over again.

But this time her beauty could no longer affect him. The force of her attempted blow had carried her against him, and he seized her shoulder and twisted her round so that her

THE DEVIL'S OWN

back was to him, then he pulled the hood from her head and buried his fingers deep in that luxuriant brown hair, closing his fist to put all the pressure he could on the roots. It was, he remembered with a start of surprise, how Indian Tom Warner had held her. And as before, she gapsed for breath, and her mouth sagged open.

'You . . .' she inhaled, slowly. 'You are hurting me.'

'I shall hurt you more,' he promised. 'You know full well what was done to Lillan, Meg. Count yourself fortunate that I do not tie you up and inflict the same humiliation upon you. But I will have a public acknowledgment of your guilt, and a public apology.'

She tried to turn, and to kick him in the same instant. But her cloak was wet and tied itself round her legs, and she fell to her knees, her face twisted with anger and pain as he retained his grip on her hair. Her hands snaked out to catch his thighs, and he threw her away from him, releasing his hold. She fell across the verandah and through the doorway into the hall at the foot of the great staircase, lay there for a moment, then scrambled to her hands and knees, and checked as he placed his foot on her gown.

'You will have to kill me,' she said.

'I doubt that, sweetheart. I suspect, having always inflicted pain and disgrace upon others, you will be unused to enduring any yourself.'

'You . . .' she dragged on her skirt with both hands, and the material split. But when she reached her feet he had again seized her hair. 'Aye,' she panted. 'You'll do well at beating a defenceless woman. 'Tis the first lesson on becoming a buccaneer, is it not?'

He shook her; as usual she wore her strand of pearls, and he could hear them clicking beneath her gown. Her eyes rolled, and her teeth clattered together.

'Bastard,' she shouted. 'Help,' she screamed. 'Help me. For God's sake, help me.'

'Hush,' he said, and shook her some more. 'You'll awaken the children. You have but to do as I ask you, my darling. Give me the names of the men. I believe there were perhaps half a dozen of them. And then signify your own agreement to my request, and you may retire to bed, and tomorrow we shall ride into town and put an end to this business.'

'You . . .' vainly her fists swung, but she was held too far away from him. 'Bitch's litter,' she yelled. 'Hellspawn.'

'Why, Mama, whatever are you doing?' Tony asked from the top of the stairs.

'Mama, Mama, Mama,' Rebecca shouted, jumping up and down. 'And Papa. You've come home.'

'Children, children.' Miss Johnson bustled along the verandah in her undressing-robe, her hair in plaits. 'Why, Mrs Hilton. And Captain Hilton?'

'Help me,' Marguerite screamed. 'He's gone mad. He's lost his wits. He means to kill me. Help me.'

'Papa?' Tony asked.

'Go back to bed,' Kit said. 'Your mother and I are having a discussion on a matter that need not concern you.'

'But Papa . . .'

'You'll take the children back to bed, Miss Johnson,' Kit said.

'Yes, sir, Captain Hilton. Come along, children.' She put an arm round each of their shoulders. 'You're sure there is nothing I can do?' She did not specify whom she was addressing.

'Get help,' Marguerite shouted, once again attempting to kick her tormentor and once again falling over, to sit down heavily. Kit had to go with her to avoid tearing her hair out by the roots. 'Fetch help.'

He knelt beside her. Her perfume rose from her hair and out of the bodice of her gown to shroud him in that magical scent; her teeth gleamed only inches from his face, and her pink tongue darted at no greater distance. Her breasts heaved against his thigh. Oh, God, he thought, that nothing should ever have come between this tremendous creature and me.

But yet he loved her too dearly to harm her. Having come this far, and stretched her on the floor, he had to do no more than slap his hand to and fro to bring blood gushing from her cheeks and mouth; with his powerful fingers he could squeeze agony from her belly and her breasts; he had to do nothing more than increase the pressure in his fist to have her head seething with agony. But he could do none of those things. She was now, as she had always been, the victor in their relationship. Because she never doubted her own superiority.

She frowned at him. She could see the sudden fading of decision, perhaps even of anger, in his eyes. And she could not believe it. This time she had counted herself lost.

But how there were feet on the verandah outside, hurrying, summoned by her shouts.

THE DEVIL'S OWN

'Seize him,' Marguerite shouted. 'Seize him and bind him. He is not fit to be loose.'

Kit released her and jumped away from her, drawing his sword as he did so. There were half a dozen overseers on the verandah, most of them men he did not know; Marguerite had dismissed her old staff following their failure to defend the Great House against the Caribs. But these men were the sweepings of St John's. Those of them he did recognize were sufficient evidence of that.

Marguerite was on her knees, straightening her gown, smoothing her hair. 'Well?' she demanded, her voice harsh. 'What, a half dozen afraid of one man? He is only one man, and his sword has grown rusty with lack of use. As has his mind. He is naught but half a man, now. Advance on him, and he will be yours.'

Kit smiled at them. He had no doubt that these scoundrels who had so eagerly responded to their mistress's screams were the same men who had, with equal eagerness, carried out her instructions regarding Lillan. 'Well, gentlemen?' he inquired.

Still they hesitated, their swords in their hands, unable to make up their minds who would be the first to step forward.

'Cowards,' Marguerite shouted. 'Lily-livered eunuchs. Afraid of him are you? Give me a sword and I will show you the way.'

She forced herself into their midst, and checked at the sound of hooves. And turned, to face her husband. 'Ah,' she said. 'Here are men. You see, dear Kit, when Maurice Peter warned me that you were waiting, I thought it best to send back to St John's for a file of soldiers, just in case they were needed. As indeed they are.'

'Then I must make haste.' Kit leapt forward before they understood his meaning, swung his sword round his head to send them tumbling back, and had plucked Marguerite out of their midst before a hand could be raised against him. 'We will continue this discussion, gentlemen, I do promise you that,' he said to the discomforted overseers, and ran for the steps.

'Then have at you,' one of the white men yelled, regaining his courage when he was presented with Kit's back.

Kit turned on the instant, Marguerite still held under his left arm; she was just regaining her breath and commencing to wriggle and scratch at his face, but his attention was held by the sword-point snaking towards him. His own weapon came up, and the blades clanged, for just an instant, before his own swept along his opponent's, with a screech of tortured steel, and his point thrust deeply into the overseer's chest.

The man stared down at the blood which suddenly welled from the front of his white shirt, while his sword-point drooped and struck the floor, and a moment later he followed it, his knees striking first before his entire body slumped.

'Murderer,' Marguerite shrieked, digging her nails into his groin.

Kit faced the remaining men. 'One down,' he said. 'You'll not let him go alone, gentlemen?'

But now the hooves were close, and the horsemen were bringing their mounts to a stop. 'Hold there,' shouted the officer.

Kit glanced at them, still backing towards the steps. But there were six of them, as well as the officer, and they carried muskets. And now they all dismounted, and presented their firepieces.

'Hold there,' the officer called again. 'You'll put down your swords, sirs, I beg of you.'

The overseers were obviously willing enough for that. Their blades clattered to the floor.

'Yet one is dead,' Marguerite shouted, at last freeing herself and landing on her hands and knees. 'Run through by this . . . this brigand.'

'Captain Hilton?' inquired the officer.

'You'll see he held a sword in his hand when he died,' Kit pointed out.

'Yet was it murder,' Marguerite insisted. 'He made no play with it. But sought to bar Captain Hilton's departure, as he was bent on kidnapping me against my will.'

'You'll stand aside,' Kit said. 'How may a man kidnap his own wife? I would speak with Mrs Hilton, and as this place is crowded, I intend to remove her to a more private situation.'

'Stop him,' Marguerite shouted, 'Stop him. Shoot him down if you have to. Only endeavour not to kill him. Yet.'

Kit faced them, his sword at the ready. The officer looked truly distressed.

'I do beg of you, sir, not to commit violence upon my men. Be sure that they will defend themselves, and you are grievously outnumbered.'

'Then why try to stop me?' Kit asked. 'I have committed no crime.'

'Indeed he has,' Marguerite shouted. 'He has murdered that man. So shall I swear. So shall everyone present swear.'

'And did you not promise me, my sweet,' Kit said, 'that as master of Green Grove I am above the law in such matters?'

'When you were master of Green Grove,' she said, her voice at last regaining its more usual timbre, but as filled with venom as ever he had heard before. 'But you are no longer master of Green Grove, Kit. I disown you, as my husband, as my lover, as the father of my children, as the manager of my plantation. Get out of here with these men, and hope and pray that your bald-headed Dane will be able to bring you some solace.'

'My bald-headed Dane,' he whispered. 'Now you have condemned yourself out of your own mouth, Meg. I did not tell you what happened to Lillan. But you knew, as you yourself commanded it.'

'Take him,' she shouted, her voice again shrill. 'Take him.'

The soldiers were close. He had no wish to kill any innocent man. Kit reversed his sword, held it out to the officer.

'You'll inform me of the charge,' he said.

'It is murder,' Marguerite said. 'Before witnesses. We shall so attest.'

The cell was to all intents and purposes his alone. The five other inmates crowded down at the far end, and eyed him fearfully. They were drunks and brawlers, shut up for the night. And into their midst had been thrust a tiger, or so they had supposed. Even without his weapons, there was no man would oppose Christopher Hilton.

Only a woman would dare do that.

He sat on the pallet-bed, close by the bars, and stared into the office, where the gaoler sat at a table and ate his breakfast. He had sat here the night, and stared, and waited. They could not leave him here for ever. And if they did, word would still spread, to his friends, if he had any. And if he lacked that commodity in Antigua, then word would in time spread to Sandy Point. Sir William Stapleton might have departed, but Holgate would be there, and in due course he would come to St John's to demand Kit's release.

He could but hope that much. Yet it had been a long and lonely night.

But now it was ending. There were booted-feet outside,

and voices, and the door to the office was opening. Kit stood up, as did the gaoler, and the other inmates hastily left the far wall to join him at the bars.

Five men came in. Kit frowned as he recognized the red hair of Edward Chester, and then the short, stout figure of Philip Warner. A word with the gaoler and they came towards him.

'Well, Edward,' Philip said. 'Would you not say he is at last where he belongs, behind bars?'

'Oh, indeed, Philip', Chester agreed. 'The whole island seems a safer place.'

But Kit was determined to keep his temper this day. 'Good morning to you, Philip,' he said. 'I never had an opportunity to congratulate you on your fortunate verdict.'

'By God, sir,' Philip declared. 'But you are a cool rogue. Nevertheless, we shall see how long your humour survives this gaol.'

'I have no doubt it will survive my release,' Kit said. 'I have already despatched a message to Mr Walker, requesting him to take out a writ of habeas corpus.'

'Indeed you have,' Philip agreed. 'He showed me it not an hour gone.'

'Showed it to you?' Kit asked, frowning as a sudden alarm gripped at his belly.

'And should he not?' Philip inquired. 'Alas, I doubt it will be possible for him immediately to act on your behalf, Kit. Mr Walker, being the only attorney on the island, is most uncommonly busy. Oh, yes, indeed, he has not a moment to call his own. Of course he has no intention of abandoning so valuable a client as yourself. He has placed your name on his list, and hopes to be able to attend to you just as soon as he is able; certainly within a twelvemonth.'

'Within a twelvemonth?' Kit asked, slowly.

'But then, you see, Kit,' Philip explained. 'It will be at least a twelvemonth before the case against you is prepared and ready. There are witnesses to be interrogated, and briefs to be prepared, and I do not see how it is possible for a mere magistrate to hear a charge of murder against so illustrious a personage as yourself. But alas, you see, Kit, we lack a governor at this moment. For which sad state of affairs, you have no one but yourself to hold responsible. Worse, it seems we even lack a governor in St Kitts. So you will have to wait. But let me give you a word of advice, from the depths of my experience, lad. Do not despair. Eat sparingly, take regular exercise, and all will be well. Why, man, I spent all but a year in prison, awaiting trial. And near two months of that time was upon the sea, coming and going. I doubt there can be a worse fate than that, sir. And look at me. I have survived, and am as hale and hearty as ever before in my life, and believe me, sir, to my regret, I lack the sustenance of your youth.'

'By God,' Kit said. 'You but seek to avenge yourself upon me for your own misfortunes.'

'Indeed not, sir. You did kill a man.'

'In self-defence.'

'Your story, Kit. And if I may say so, it is no more than natural that you should insist upon it. But there are witnesses, including your own wife, against you. Now she may not testify, but the overseers were there, full half a dozen of them. And their tale is sadly different.'

'By God, sir,' Kit said. 'You have it all decided to your satisfaction, no doubt. Yet there is still justice in this world. The Queen's Majesty is still represented here in Antigua, and I will seek my freedom at that door. I will set my case before Mr Trumbull in his capacity as Speaker of the House.'

Philip Warner continued to smile. 'You are indeed entitled to set your case before the Speaker, Kit, as he is charged with preserving the Queen's authority in this island pending the arrival of a new governor. But you would waste your time to approach Mr Trumbull. Had you attended the Chamber more often you would be aware that he has long desired to lay down his burden, and has in fact now done so, a suitable replacement having been discovered.'

'A suitable replacement? Kit demanded. But now the weights in his belly were more than he could bear.

'Indeed, sir,' Chester put in, 'by unanimous vote of the Assembly, we have elected Colonel Warner to the vacant speakership, there surely being no gentlemen more deserving of the honour, both on account of his past services to the community, and the past suffering he has undergone on behalf of the community.'

'So, now, Kit.' Philip said. 'You may put your case before me. Or have you, indeed, just done so?'

12

The Challenge

'A visitor to see you,' said Jacks the gaoler.

Kit scrambled to his feet, and the drunk retreated to the far end of the cell.

Jacks grinned at him, safe on the outside of the bars. 'Oh, you've not been forgotten, Captain Hilton. Not a man like you.'

Desperately Kit straightened his clothes; they would have stood up by themselves, he had no doubt, so soaked were they with sweat and dirt. And with equal desperation he thrust his fingers through his hair, and even scraped at the fortnight old beard. Because it surely had to be . . . Barnee?

'Captain Hilton,' the tailor said. 'By Christ, what have they done to you?'

'Why, they have done nothing to me,' Kit said. 'Save confine me in this filthy hole. I am allowed into the yard for half an hour every morning. And I am fed twice a day. I suppose you would call it food. And for the rest, I am ignored. But I have constantly changing company, so I am never bored.'

Barnee glanced at the drunk. 'Nobody could blame you for being bitter, Captain. I'd have come sooner, had I supposed it wise. But now, why, the tumult has all but died away.'

'Then they will bring me to trial?'

Barnee sighed. 'Somehow, sir, I doubt that is their purpose.' He frowned at Kit's clothes. 'Such a tragedy. Why, do you know I spent three weeks on those breeches?'

Kit grasped the bars. 'What do you mean, Barnee? Have no papers been prepared against me?'

Barnee shook his head. 'Not to my knowledge, sir.'

'By God,' Kit said. 'But my wife, has she not been after the matter?'

'Mrs Hilton has not been seen in St John's, sir, since the night she and the Colonel returned in triumph.'

'Not seen? The devil. Two weeks?'

'Indeed, sir. Nor has there been any entertainment in Green Grove in that time. There are rumours, certainly. To the effect that she regrets her quarrel with you, and is ashamed of the outcome, or even that she regrets what happened to Miss Christianssen. And then her overseers say she is unwell, and spends much time in her room, visits the canefields but occasionally, and then heavily veiled as if she had been weeping.'

'I doubt that, somehow,' Kit said. 'But Lillan, Barnee. You spoke of Lillan. What news of her?'

'Now that is why I came, Captain.'

'And you have dawdled these last ten minutes? Speak up, man.'

'She is well, sir. At least, she is much better.'

'Her mother is still with her?'

'Better than that, sir. She is with her mother and father.' 'Here in town?'

'Indeed, sir. It was my fortune to play the part of mediator between them, and now she is in good hands, and indeed, asks of you continuously.'

'But . . . what of her condition? The shame of it?'

'Oh, well, sir, we brought her into St. John's privily, and she remains indoors of a day, only occasionally venturing out after dark to enjoy the breeze. Her hair is not yet grown, you understand, nor is her complexion clear. Indeed, I fear it may be some time before she will again be the girl you remember, Captain. But it will be.'

'You have seen her?'

'In a manner of speaking, sir. She wears a hooded cloak, and a veil, when in company.'

'But what of her manner? Her spirits?'

'Ah, well, sir, there is more of a problem for those who love her. You will know that she was always a solemn girl, sir, given to quiet thought. That side of her character now entirely dominates. She does not smile, and she speaks seldom. Indeed, she gives the impression of a woman wrestling with some deep, and possibly irremediable, problem.'

'And would you not be similarly downcast, had you suffered but a tithe of what she suffered?' Kit demanded. 'That I should be here, behind bars, while she is in such despair . . . I sometimes feel like taking that gaoler by the neck and choking the life from his body. It were an easy thing.'

'And then would you truly be hanged, Captain,' Barnee pointed out. 'No, no, sir. Patience is the key to your problem. I have said, I do not believe they mean to bring matters to a trial. For one thing it could set a dangerous precedent, should a planter be tried for the death of an employee; God knows that is not such an uncommon occurrence. And for another, I believe the answer rests with your wife, and I cannot believe, despite all that has passed between you, that she hates you to that extent. It is she who is paying for your keep here.'

'And for that I must be grateful?' Kit asked. 'She will know better than ever to let me come near her again. For, by God, I will finish what I began.'

'No doubt, sir,' Barnee said soothingly. 'But I would again beg of you, be patient. The gossips have it that a new governor has been appointed for the Leewards, and he could already be on his way here. There is an end to your problem, surely, as he will bring the approbation of Her Majesty, and 'tis well known that she is displeased with the attitude of the planters in favour of Colonel Warner.'

'Aye,' Kit agreed. 'Yet much will depend on the character of the man himself. It will take no little resolution to oppose so unitedly stiff-necked a body. Have you no word of his name?'

'None, sir,' Barnee said. 'Yet am I convinced that his arrival cannot but mean a speedy end to your imprisonment. Now I must be away.'

'You'll take a message for Lillan,' Kit said. 'Tell her that I love her, now and always. Tell her that she shall be avenged, this I swear. Convince her, Barnee, that this is but a brief episode in our lives. She must be sure of that.'

'She is, Captain. Of that I am certain. Yet will I give her your words, of course.'

'And you'll come again, Barnee? This place is almighty tedious.'

'I will come again, Captain. And until then, take care.'

Take care. Of what, he wondered. Of his safety? That was well looked after. The other inmates, all transients, feared him and shunned him as if he suffered from the plague. Of his appearance? There was an impossible task. He possessed no mirror, and could only judge on feel, and smell. Thus his hair and his beard both grew, untidily and dirtily, and the dirt accumulated beneath his fingernails as the sweat accumulated throughout his body to give him an extra skin, he thought. As for his clothing, that surely was beyond recall, as he slept in his suit, lived in it, took his scanty exercise in it. Of his health, then? Oh, he would take care of his health, in so far

THE DEVIL'S OWN

as it was possible. The first meal after Barnee's departure he had almost rejected. Marguerite's money? But then it had occurred to him that if she meant to keep him alive it would be foolish of him to reject that. She fought in her way, and he must fight in his, counting upon the ultimate victory.

Of his mind? Here was the true nub of the matter. To sit in a noisome, over-heated cell, minute after minute, hour after hour, day after day, week after week, and even month after month was surely more than man had been intended to suffer. Certainly a man like Kit Hilton, to whom the sea and the sky and the breeze on his face were a large part of what was worth possessing. Not to know what was happening, what Marguerite was doing and planning, tucked away behind the protection of her cane-filled acres and her scent-filled house, what Philip Warner was saying and doing, in the House of Assembly, and what Lilian was suffering and feeling. To know that she was just down the street, in fact, and yet as distant as if she had been on another planet, was the bitterest thought of all.

Perhaps, then, his sanity depended on Barnee. For the tailor came every week with what news he could glean, of John Benbow's death, but strangely of no new depredations by DuCasse, of the execution of two of Benbow's captains for cowardice in the battle of Santa Marta, of the successes of the Anglo-Dutch army in Europe, where the Duke of Marlborough was making his reputation, of the soaring price of sugar, and of more domestic matters, too.

Philip Warner had resigned the Speakership. He had, in fact, but taken the post in acknowledgment of the planters' wish, and to complete his triumph. But age and infirmity were making it less easy for him to get about, and impossible for him to sustain the burden of hours of debate in the Chamber.

'Now there is good news, at the least,' Kit said. 'Surely his successor can hardly be so opposed to my interest.'

'You think so, Captain?' Barnee asked sorrowfully.

'It cannot be John Harding?'

'No, indeed, Captain. From your point of view it is worse. The new Speaker is Colonel Warner's nominee, as you may suppose; Edward Chester.'

Chester, by God. Dear Edward. Possibly the one man in Antigua who hated Kit more than the Colonel himself.

But the change in the speakership had no effect upon his imprisonment. Because he was here on the orders of the mistress of Green Grove, and he would stay here, no matter what the men say or wish or do, until the mistress of Green Grove chose to hang him or release him. What had she boasted when first they had met and loved? That she was at once the wealthiest, the most beautiful, and the most powerful woman in the Leewards. Easy words to say. And yet how true.

But Barnee was also able to reassure him about Lillan. Her health improved every day, and her hair was grown. She looked as she had always done, apparently. But what of *her* mind? There was a cause for concern. She seldom spoke and never laughed. She sent her love by every message, but would not venture into the street. How deep must be the degradation of what had happened bitten into that delicate, reserved mind.

It was time to draw on the past. For what indeed, was the value of the past, if not to bolster the future. Time then to remember the endless horror of Hispaniola. He had never doubted then that he would survive. Untrue. He had doubted. After Bart Le Grand's *matelot* had been stuck like a pig, and had died squealing like a pig, then he had despaired. And been rescued, by Jean and by Bart himself.

Well, then, what of the march across Panama, spurred on always by that heroic villain Morgan? But always then an early end had been in sight. This was more akin to that long year on the beach at Port Royal, when he had been sustained only by the energy of Agrippa. Another who had suffered on his behalf, and died, on his behalf.

Agrippa. So much had happened since that dreadful night of his return from Barbados, the fact of his friend's death had scarcely penetrated his understanding. And he could offer nothing more than revenge, if that were ever possible. But he had never been very effective at vengeance. He had always looked to the future rather than the past. Even in Jamaica, he had never doubted that he would eventually be lifted frrom his despair.

As he had been, by Daniel Parke. A blessing, or a curse? Oh, surely, no matter what had happened since, a blessing, which had brought him Marguerite, and more of life than he had ever dreamed to be possible, for ten splendid years before their world had fallen apart, and which had eventually brought him Lillan, still there, could she but be reached.

Daniel Parke. He listened to the salute of guns from the fort, billowing forth noise to welcome the new governor, and to the name which suddenly seemed to spread on the wind. He clung to the bars, and gazed at the corridor and the distant office, unable to see the door to the street, unable to hear distinctly, aware only that his heart was pounding fit to burst. It was incredible, but it was true. Because there he was, wearing a gold satin coat over a silver waistcoat, face heavy with good living, and yet lacking none of its old arrogance and contempt, lips pouted a trifle petulantly, but eyes brilliantly embracing as ever, speech and manner unchangingly peremptory. He stood in the office and gazed at the prisoner, and his colour seemed to darken.

'By God,' he said. 'By God, sir. I could not credit my ears. By God, sirs, but there will be atonement for this.'

So then, what can be the greatest pleasure known to man? To sit in a hot bath, after so very long, having been shaved and knowing that the best in food and drink awaits only a decision to leave the embracing warmth. And to be in the company of a friend. And what a friend.

'My head swings,' he said. 'I doubt not that I am dreaming.'

Parke sat in a chair, and sipped a glass of wine. He had removed his coat and his wig, and yet looked hot. He had indeed put on a great deal of weight in fifteen years.

'Then awake,' he commanded. 'For be sure that I have need of you, Kit.'

'And be sure, Dan, that you will have but to look in my direction, starting from now, and my body, my sword, my pistols and my brains will be at your service. What, raise a man from the dungheap once in a life time? There was a reason for undying gratitude, to be sure. But raise him twice . . . why, that puts you beyond the attainment of any service I might perform.'

Parke frowned at him for several seconds. And then smiled. And there, at the least, nothing had changed. The flash of white teeth was as winning as ever in the past. 'Now take care what you promise, Kit. For be sure I shall call upon you. There is much we must do.'

'Indeed there is,' Kit said. 'If I could but understand how you come to be here, and in such splendour, and blessed with such power . . . I tell you, it must be a dream.'

'Dreams are not very different to nightmares.' Parke got up, paced the room, arming himself with his cane and flashing at imaginary foes as he talked. 'I doubt my life has been less chequered than yours, Kit, since last we met. And believe me, I am fully aware of the ups and downs of your own career. So you married the fabulous Mistress Templeton. My congratulations, sir. Although had you asked my opinion I should have advised against it, even so long ago. And would I not have been right?'

Kit sighed. 'She is perhaps, too much for any one man. Yet is she the mother of my children.'

'Ah. I too have a wife, and children. At least, a daughter. The most beautiful creature you could ever see, Kit. But *I* have not seen her in five years.'

'There is some tragedy here,' Kit said.

'In a manner of speaking, only. You know my pleasure in cards and dice. Believe me when I say, Kit, I understand that to be a curse. Look at me, and see a man who had all Virginia at his feet. When my father died, and I inherited his plantations, there was no buck to stand beside me. And so, like you, dear friend, I married the best woman going. And I fathered her daughter, and I lived, and loved, out as well as in, for what gentleman will not, and I played, as my fancy took me. And you know full well, friend, that I cared not whether I won or lost, for the stake. I would as soon take my winnings and throw them to the poor. But the winning of it. The triumph. The looks of dismay on the losers' faces.'

He paused in his perambulation, and his fingers curled into a fist, held in front of his face, as if he was crushing the very air. 'There was my pleasure, Kit. There was my joy.'

'And so you cheated,' Kit said.

Parke glanced at him, and the fingers slowly relaxed. 'I do not enjoy losing. I have never enjoyed losing. I have no intention of ever losing. What, are my opponents not equally capable of cheating? A man must be prepared for all things. I am ready to back my fancies with my sword or my pistols. But the devil was highly placed, a friend of my wife's family, and influential.'

'You killed a man over cards?'

'And have you never killed a man in anger? They wished to bring me to trial. And who knows what would have happened, Kit. I might have been hanged, for it turned out that the fool, as he challenged me, and made some sort of movement for his pockets, carried no weapon. Yet he was drunk, as indeed was I, and how could I wait to be murdered myself? He might have had a knife, a pistol, anything.'

'Good God,' Kit said. 'And you stand before me, Governor of the Leewards?'

'I am not so easily brought low. When I learned what they

were about, as if every gentleman who picks up a pack of cards does not equally pick up his life at the same time ... 'tis understood by all. 'Tis only the priesthood and the little men who seek to snipe at us. Well, I'd not risk myself in their power, as you did and to your cost. There was a ship in the harbour, bound that night for England. I boarded her.'

'You fled Virginia?'

'At the time it was best. I have not finished with them yet, by God. They have not seen the last of Daniel Parke.'

'But how did you make your way in England?' Kit wondered. 'Had you friends there? Influence?'

'None, sir,' Parke cried triumphantly. 'Not a soul knew of my very existence. Yet am I not a man, sir? With blood in my veins and temper in my steel? I took service with the great Duke.'

'Marlborough?'

'Who else? One should serve only the best. I offered him my sword and my brains, and I am not bereft of military experience. There are savage Indians on the borders of Virginia no less than in Dominica, I'll have you know. I have conducted a campaign against them, and successfully. And with no smell of treachery about it either. Churchill was sufficiently glad to have my prowess at his side. I rode with him on the march down the Rhine. I was at his shoulder at Blenheim. Now there, Kit, did I witness warfare on a scale I had not supposed possible. I forget, you were at Panama. But even Panama can have been nothing, compared with a European battle, especially one as fought by Marlborough. More than a hundred thousand men opposed to each other, red coats and blue, green coats and white, rolling clouds of black smoke from the cannon, the unceasing fusillades, the cries of the victor and the screams of the vanquished. I tell you, that day I felt I stood on Olympus.'

'For you were the victors.' Kit got out of his tub and towelled himself.

'Aye. And more. When my lord of Marlborough surveyed the scene, and knew his triumph, he resolved that the news of it must be got back to London with the earliest possible despatch. And he called me for that deed, as he possessed no better horseman on his staff. I rode like the wind, Kit, bearing two letters, one to the Duchess, and the other to Her Majesty herself. I was admitted to her own privy chamber, Kit. There was the sum of my triumph.'

'By God,' Kit said. 'You have spoken with the Queen?'

'I have kissed her hand, Kit, and been bidden to rise. And do you know what she asked of the Duchess? "Why, madam," she said, "can all your husband's officers be as handsome as this gentleman? Indeed I understand now why no one can stand before him." And then she laughed, and talked with me some more, and told me, as I bore the gladdest tidings ever to enter London since the bells rang upon the defeat of the Spanish Armada, why, I had but to ask of her, and it would be granted to me.'

'And you wished the Governorship of the Leewards?' Kit asked in amazement.

Once again Parke checked his perambulation, and turned to face his friend. And now the humour, the excitement, had gone from his face. 'No,' he said. 'No, I did not wish for the Governorship of the Leewards. These are magnificent islands, Kit. And I would have given much, even then, to see your face again, and enjoy a glass of punch in your company. But they are not yet my home. Nor did I ever suppose they would be. I meant to return to *my* home, in triumph. Then would I have taken those ruffians by the ears. And it was granted to me, Kit. By Her Majesty herself. It was there, and mine.'

'Virginia?'

'Nothing less. But this woman who rules our destinies, she is naught but a cipher. She does what she is told, by her women, by the Duchess most of all, by her ministers. Ask, she had said, and you shall have. I asked, and was given. And yet recalled to her presence before I had properly finished celebrating, to be told the Governorship of Virginia was already in the possession of someone else, and could not presently be removed from his care. Oh, those courtiers, clamouring about her ears, whispering that I was not to be trusted with such a post, with such a past.'

'But ...'

'But they knew my worth, Kit. Her Majesty sought to soften the blow. "Yet," she said, "you shall have your colonial governorship, Colonel Parke, and one where your own special talents can best be put to my service. What of the Leewards?" she asked. "I have been told you know them, and their people. Then you will know," she said, "that they are an independent-minded lot of rascals, who pay small attention to our wishes here in London, and who have recently had the effrontery to choose a Speaker of their Assembly in a man of whom I hear nothing but ill-repute. There is defiance," she said. "And I know more, that they have a long history of smuggling and piracy and downright criminal activities. There is a position more fitted to your temper, Colonel Parke," she said.'

'It could be that she was right, Dan. 'Tis certain these islands need a strong hand. Even Stapleton was perhaps not sufficiently capable of dealing with the plantocracy. They know their wealth, and the power it bestows. They conceive Antigua, at the least, no less a place than England itself, save in size.'

'Oh, she was right,' Parke said. 'There can be no doubt about that. And more, you are now right. Which is why I am here, in St John's, and not setting up my standard in Sandy Point. The centre of the Leewards is in Antigua, and the centre of the intransigent spirits is right here as well. I shall show them the quality of my blood, you may be sure of that. But I shall need men I can trust about me, Kit. Men like you. And you, like me, have a score to settle.'

'Indeed I have,' Kit agreed, frowning. 'Yet I doubt that a spirit of vengeance is the best in which to undertake to rule a people.'

'Ah, you were always nine-tenths of a Quaker, which is why your true interest always lay in the direction of that Danish beauty. She waits to see you now.'

'Lillan? Here?' Kit dragged at his clothes.

'Easy, Kit. Easy.'

'You do not understand. It has been all but a year, and in that time I have not seen her. More, she has not left her father's house, except privily, and at night. I do believe that you are jesting.'

Parke smiled. 'I never jest, about women, Kit. She has obeyed the summons of her Governor, and gladly. But before you go rushing off to her soft arms, we must finish our discussion. I need you, Kit. Will you serve me?'

'I am distressed you find it necessary to ask again, old friend.' Kit buttoned his shirt.

'Then understand what you do. I have commanded a fast revenue cutter to be built, and the work is already in hand. There is an old saw, is there not, set a thief to catch a thief? I remember how well you commanded the *Bonaventure*, and how with your skill and speed and a few sharp teeth you evaded all attempts at capture by that clumsy frigate. I shall put a stop to the smuggling, Kit, by using a similar sort of vessel. All I need is a man who will sail her, and fight her, if need be, as ruthlessly as I would myself. Do I possess such a man?'

A ship, at last. And to be used for striking at Chester. 'Aye, Dan,' Kit said. 'You have such a man.'

'Then am I content. But listen to me carefully, Kit. You and I, we shall bring these proud planters to heel. But it must be done by the strictest adherence to legality and the wishes of the Queen. This point I must make before you offer Lillan any promises you will not be able to honour. You hate these petty upstarts, and perhaps one or two in particular. But you will fight no duels, and you will make no visits to Green Grove, sword in hand.'

'You cannot have heard the full story of that affair.'

'Believe me, Kit. I *have* heard the full story of that affair. Marguerite is your wife, and a wife's jealousy commands respect everywhere. And you did kill a man. Oh, I have no doubt he died with a sword in his hand, yet where Kit Hilton is concerned that is too close to murder. And should we reduce matters to a straight choice, these people may become desperate. No, no. You know, and I know, that these creatures are sufficiently criminal for us to bring them down without resort to personalities. They smuggle, and that is against the law. I put that in your charge. Hale me a planter to court on a proven charge of smuggling, and by God I will fine him all of next year's crop. I know, and you know, that they habitually talk treason. That will be my charge. And the answer there, once proven, is the gallows. Let those be our two objectives, undertaken with the consent, nay, with the blessing—why, what rubbish do I speak—undertaken at the express command of Her Majesty. "Bring them to heel, Mr Parke," she said. And smiled.' Parke smiled.

And Kit stared at him. There could be no doubting his intention. For where Kit's hatred was all anger, to be expiated in a blow, he understood that he was here witnessing a cold and deep-seated venom, not to be alleviated either by success or pleas for mercy, supposing any planter would ever bring himself to that. And inspired entirely because he could not at this moment reach those he really hated. There was a terrifying thought.

'I will let the matter drop, for the time,' he said.

'Spoken like my old friend. Then I have one last charge for you. As I intend to make St John's my headquarters, and I cannot spend the rest of my term of office in these scurvy rented quarters, I mean to build a new residence for the Governor, on that hill outside the town, overlooking it and the harbour and the sea beyond. An eyrie for an eagle, Kit.

That will be your first responsibility, as you know the people here, and your ship is not yet commissioned. Build it high, and build it strong. You know the planters' houses. Eclipse them. Fear not the expense; they will be paying for it in their taxes. And build yourself a wing. Your best protection against careless challenges is the certainty that you and I walk shoulder to shoulder all the while.'

There was a knock on the door. Parke glanced at Kit to make sure he was dressed, and then called, 'Enter.'

The Negro servant bowed. 'Begging your pardon, Your Excellency, but there is a lady to see you.'

'A lady?' Parke frowned.

'Lillan,' Kit said, making for the door.

'Easy, Kit. She has been here this past hour, and patiently awaits your presence. Who is this lady, Jonathan?'

'Mistress Chester, Your Excellency. She is the wife of the Speaker of the House, and calls to bid Your Excellency welcome to Antigua.'

'By God,' Parke said. 'Mary Chester. Why, when last I was here she was just wed, a child of sixteen.'

'She scarcely seems more than that now,' Kit said. 'Despite the high office her husband has attained.'

'Indeed?' Parke demanded. 'Well, well. And she has come to call. As indeed she must, as her husband is Speaker. I must greet the lady, obviously. You'll excuse me, Kit. Jonathan, you will return here immediately, and show Captain Hilton to the chamber where Miss Christianssen waits for him.' He went to the door, looked over his shoulder, and raised his glass. 'To our mutual success, dearest Kit.'

'Tread carefully, I beg of you, sir,' said Wolff the engineer. 'The seed is but freshly laid. But in a month there will be a lawn, stretching from the patio, here, right across to that bluff. Is that not splendid?' He had short legs, and scurried in front of Kit as they crossed the freshly smoothed ground.

Fifty yards from the patio the rocks and earth had been hewn sheer, to make a drop of some twelve feet to the land below, thus creating a glacis on this side. Truly was Daniel building a fortress, Kit thought. The only breach in these defences was the great tree-lined drive running up the side of the hill, and mounting the man-made terrace through a sloped escarpment.

He turned, looked back at the house, already roofed and gleaming with paint. And Lillan, waiting for them in the trap beneath the shade of the great trees which fringed the drive, while the horses plucked foliage from the bushes at the side of the road.

'A splendid sight, is it not?' Wolff was still looking down at the town. 'A commanding eminence, fit for the ruler. Oh, yes, 'twas well chosen.' He discovered Kit already on his way back, panted as he caught up. 'It has been said the verandahs are too deep, Captain. But a house needs deep verandahs, in these climes, to trap the breeze. And what think you of my doors, eh? Three inches thick, Captain. They'll catch a cannonball. You'll see that I have left a good twenty feet between the kitchens and the house itself, although my covered passageway will make sure the Governor's food does not get rained upon. No house of mine will ever be destroyed by fire from within.'

'An admirable concept,' Kit agreed. 'Perhaps you should also build a covered passageway from the barracks, to keep the guard dry into the bargain.'

'Now there is a plan, sir. I will see to it immediately.'

'Then I shall leave you to your duties.' Kit walked beneath the trees, got into the trap. 'What do you think of it, sweetheart?'

'It is a beautiful spot, Kit,' Lillan answered. 'I remember when I was a girl, how I used to walk up this hill, and lie on the grass over there, and look down on the town, and the harbour.'

'And think, about what?'

She glanced at him, and then away again. 'I do not remember thinking at all, Kit. It was just sufficient to lie on the warm grass, and feel at peace.'

And do you think, now, he wanted to ask her? There were so many things he wanted to say, and to do, and ask. Looking at her, seated in the trap, wearing a light muslin gown in pale green, and her favourite broad-brimmed hat, with her fine hair loose and floating in the faint breeze, with every last blemish gone from her complexion, it was impossible to suppose that anything so tragic, so disgusting, as that night had ever happened to her. Yet it lay between them like a brick wall. She was the same woman he had always known, and always loved. With but a solitary difference. For whereas before, when not talking, or smiling, or loving, she had revealed a continual interest in what was going on around her, now, when he left her to herself for but a moment, her gaze and clearly her mind returned into some private sanctuary of its own.

He could gain no inkling of what thoughts she sought in that privacy. Did she give way to hatred of Marguerite, to thinking of the wildest and most hideous ways of revenge? Or did she surrender to a memory of the brutality and obscenity to which she had been subjected? Or did she remember her feelings when she had lain, naked and debased, in the centre of St John's, waiting to be discovered?

These were bad. But there were possibilities which were worse. For did she, in that privacy, blame him for his failure? He had failed so very often, by setting off in anger and haste, bent on doing only what seemed to him to be necessary at the moment. Or then again, did she merely retreat into a world of despair, a world of which she could not help but be continually conscious, for if there was no man dare offer her an insult or even a smile, while she walked by Kit Hilton's side or was so clearly under the Governor's protection, yet was there not a man who did not turn to stare after her, imagining, or worse, remembering. And the women, who feared no physical interference with their pleasures, were more openly interested in her survival, the brazenness, as they regarded it, of her existence, the effrontery of her apparent triumph.

And yet she accepted his embraces, with the same shy reserve which so suddenly blossomed into passion. Whenever he could find an opportunity *to* embrace her. By tacit agreement she had remained these two months in her father's house. But now the Governor's new residence was all but completed . . .

'You have inspected our apartments?' he asked.

'Indeed I have. And I congratulate Mr Wolff.'

'I have already done so. What I meant was, will you be pleased to take your place in them?'

'I will be pleased, Kit, if that is what you wish.'

'Believe me,' he said. 'I wish it could be different.'

She continued to gaze at him.

'But as it cannot,' he went on, 'and as I must leave you from time to time, if I am to give my support to Daniel. I could not contemplate abandoning you anywhere else but under his protection.'

'And I shall be safe, under his protection,' she said, half to herself.

Kit flicked the whip. The horse turned and the trap made its way slowly down the hill. It was the middle of the afternoon, and the heat was intense. 'I suspect that you do not much care for our Governor,' he suggested. To have her speaking, about anything, would be a blessing.

'I am sure my feelings are irrelevant,' she said.

'They are most relevant to me, sweetheart.'

'Well, then, I will say that he is a good friend, Kit. I think he must be about the best friend that a man could have.'

'The best friend that ever this man could have, certainly,' Kit agreed.

'And yet, he is not a good *man*,' she said.

Kit frowned. 'I do not understand you. So he killed a man over a card game. I have killed at least a dozen. Am I then a very bad man?'

'You, I would describe as a good man, Kit,' she said. 'The crime is surely not so relevant as the thought, the emotion, the ambition which inspired it. Mr Parke is a man who seeks to kill, in some form or other, whether it be by sword or by word. He seeks the contest, continually, like some wild bull, galloping round and round his herd, daring another male to look him in the eye, daring any female not to beckon him with hers. Life without contest, without challenge, and without victory, is for him stale and uninteresting.'

'Now that is remarkable,' Kit said. 'Marguerite used similar words of him, oh, a very long time ago.' He bit his lip in anger. How easily words slipped out.

'Like me, I think, your wife is a good judge of character,' Lillan said.

'My wife,' he shouted, dragging on the reins. 'My God, what meaning you put into that. Lillan . . .'

'I would not speak of her, yet, Kit.'

'But it must be done.'

'Please,' she said softly. 'I made a mistake, once. All of my life, I think. I wished only to yield, as a young girl, to a man of whom I dreamed, a formless creature, yet one I never doubted would appear. And then I met you and my dream became reality. Yet still the decision was only to yield. I sought to escape the brunt of life, by belonging. I had not realized that no human being can, or dare, escape the brunt of life. Hear me out, please. In this business you are but the bridge between two spirits, Kit. Even you are no more than that. Yielding, as I thought, I yet put out a mortal challenge to your wife. I thought no more of it, then. I said to myself, it is between Kit and Marguerite, and if he now loves me and not her, then I am content, no matter what sin we commit. Yet how wrong I was. It was never between you and Marguerite, It was ever between Marguerite and me. So she reacted, with the passion and violence which is the part of her character, and, I suspect, first made you fall in love with her. Can I quarrel with her for revealing her true self in such a situation? Would I have acted differently, granted her wealth and position and upbringing? Do you know, I encourage myself with the thought that I would have been more straight with my rival. I would not have had the deed done by stealth, at night, when I was a thousand miles distant. I would have faced her, even had I ordered others to do the deed. But there is flattery, if you like, of myself. I lack her wealth and position, and thus I do not know for sure *how* I would truly have acted.'

She took his hand between hers. 'And then you returned, and rode forth to avenge me, like the man you are. I did not wish to stop you, then. I did not know what I wished, then. I wished only to lie down beneath the weight which oppressed me. Sometimes I wished for death itself. Yet would I not take my own life. Perhaps because of my beliefs. Perhaps because I am a coward. And when I would again flatter myself, I say perhaps because I have more strength than that. But when you failed, and were incarcerated in that dreadful prison, then I perforce has to consider the matter in a more sober light, and I realized that even had you succeeded, had you dragged Marguerite into town and forced her to scream an apology at the top of her lungs, and had you arraigned the murderers of Agrippa and had them hanged, yet would I still be an object of contempt and pity. No one could blame Marguerite for crumbling before the assault of Kit Hilton. But who would ever take the side of a husband-stealer?'

'Then are we doubly damned,' Kit said. 'As I failed in my mission.'

'I doubt that anyone blames you for that, either, for there cannot be a man in Antigua but knows that you acted as he would have done in similar circumstances.'

'Faith, I wish I understood more of human nature.'

'It is not so very difficult to understand,' she said. 'We had best be getting home.'

He flicked the whip, and the trap rolled into town. 'Then where is your solution to our problem, as you have thought so deeply on the matter?'

She sighed. 'I wish I knew. I only know that the solution must be mine, Kit, not yours. So I beg of you, do nothing rash.'

'I have already promised Daniel that, and felt heartily ashamed for it.' He drew rein before the General Store. 'May I come in with you?'

She shook her head. 'It would be better not.'

'Another thing I can hardly understand. Tell me, does your father speak with you in his own home?'

'Seldom. He is as bewildered by events as I.'

'Bewildered. By God, there is an odd emotion.'

'Do you think so? He is a man of great discipline, over himself, and over those who would work with him or live with him. He brought me up in that mould, as he has ever lived with Mama in that mould. Now he no longer recognizes me, and he cannot understand how Mama will care for such an outcast.' She smiled, a sufficiently rare sight nowadays. 'But then, I scarce recognize myself. Can you imagine, Kit, how many pairs of eyes are at this moment watching us, hidden behind their shutters? Antigua has had no such source of scandal since Edward Warner's wife was kidnapped by the Indians, with all that must have entailed, and yet returned here to rule over them. So must I be less of a woman than she?' She leaned forward, kissed him on the lips. 'That will keep their dinner conversation flowing agreeably.' She squeezed his hand as she stepped down.

'Tomorrow at one,' he said.

'Tomorrow at one, Kit.' She went inside.

He flicked the whip and the trap covered the few yards to the Governor's temporary residence. How strange indeed were the patterns life took up. He had wooed her in a fit of drunken passion, and taken her off to be his mistress with heroic violence. And now he was back to courting her like any timid young man, barred from her door by her father's disapproval.

But this time he would do it her way, because he must. And because he wanted to. This time there was no need to fear any sudden cessation in their affairs.

And indeed he had thought of nothing else since his release from prison. Yet so many other things clamoured for his consideration. Marguerite remained an overwhelming factor. Lillan spoke of her own humiliation, and of her inability to deal with it. But he had also been brought low, by the determined animosity of that remarkable woman. And even had he been able to erase her entirely from his mind and his memory, there remained always Tony and Rebecca. He had not seen them for more than a year. What had been told them of their father, he wondered. What did they think of their father? Or did they think of him at all? And did he have any rights, where they were concerned?

And, looking at the larger canvas, there was the certainty of troubled times ahead, which also he was reluctant to consider. For Daniel had wasted no time in letting the planters know where they stood. In his speech to the Assembly, which tradition demanded of a new Governor, he had all but called them rogues and traitors to their faces, had declared his firm intention of governing the colony *as* a colony, had used the phrase, 'I will bring the malcontents to heel,' and had left them gaping in impotent indignation. Edward Chester's face had gone as red as his hair, and he had stared around the room, making sure of his support, and then up at the gallery, identifying his enemies. And flushing to a yet darker hue on discovering Kit. So, what would be the planters' remedy for the predicament in which they now found themselves? Why, a simple one. They had refused to vote any money, not only for the necessary purposes of government, but also for the building of Government House.

Yet was the island governed, and the house all but built. The captains of the ships which brought mahogany from the Mosquito Coast, no less than those which brought fine cloths and fine wines from Europe, no less than Wolff himself, with every slave he possessed working on the site, accepted Daniel Parke's notes without question. They could, in fact, do nothing less, but obviously they also had no doubt that when there eventually was a reckoning, they would have to receive their money; the planters' crops were sold in England, and their London agents handled all deductions, for goods or taxes. No City merchant was going to quarrel with Whitehall on account of a few angry Antiguans. As for the very few civil servants required—amongst whom, Kit realized, he must now number himself—or the soldiers of the garrison, they were well used to their pay being a year and more in arrears.

He trotted the horses beneath the archway, and threw the reins to one of the Negro servants waiting there. He took off his hat and entered by the side door, mounting the inside staircase to the shaded gallery which ran round the seaward side of the house, pausing to marvel at the quiet. St John's in mid-afternoon was like a town of the dead.

He climbed the great staircase to the upper gallery, unbuttoning his coat, and heard a giggle of laughter. He stopped, his heart seeming to climb very slowly into his throat, for he was sure he could recognize the voice. He approached the door, it led to one of the guest bedrooms, and stopped again. Now all was silent once more. Yet had he heard the sound, and he could not believe his ears. He rested his hand on the door knob, hesitated for a moment, and then twisted it and threw the door inwards in the same instant.

Daniel Parke gave a startled exclamation as he sat up, instinctively, reaching for the pistol which waited by his bed. The woman beside him gave a shriek, and reached for the rumpled sheet to cover her nakedness, while Kit stared at her in total horror.

For he had indeed recognized that high-pitched giggle. The woman was Mary Chester.

'By God, Kit, but you are liable to die long before your allotted moment, if you persist in behaviour like that.' Daniel Parke slouched in his chair, his wig askew, his coat and vest unbuttoned. He had drunk better than two bottles of wine with his dinner.

'I doubt I will apologize again,' Kit said. 'For the deed, yes. For the motivation, hardly. The act was downright suicidal.'

'Bah.' Parke snapped his fingers, and the butler hastened forward with another bottle. 'Drink up.' He leaned his elbows on the table. 'I represent the Queen. True or false?'

'Oh, true, but . . .'

'Therefore I am the Crown by proxy. True or false?'

'True, but . . .'

'Therefore it behoves me to act like a king. Name me a king who has lacked a mistress. One? What am I saying. Name me a king who has lacked a harem.'

'Charles I,' Kit said.

'And he got his head chopped off. In any event, as his father's harem consisted of boys, he was doubtless confused. Besides, Mary is what a man like me needs. God, how I need her. Oh, I understand other tastes. I recognize yours, for slender legs and waists which are nothing more than rib covers, and tits which can scarce tickle the palm of your hand. Mary, sweet Mary, is what *I* desire, Kit. There is nothing but flesh. Christ, man, to sink my face in those bubbies is to lose my awareness of the world beyond. To discover my whereabouts below that belly is to travel to unknown planes of delight.'

Kit sighed. 'I have no wish to discuss the lady's charms,

THE DEVIL'S OWN

Dan. Neither hers nor those of any woman. I but wish to remind you that she is Chester's wife.'

'And damned unhappy with her lot. I'll wager you did not know that.'

'Chester and I have not been particularly close these past two years.'

'Aye. Well, you can take it from me that he only seeks her bed to torment her. That often enough he uses his belt on those marvellous hams. By Christ, one day I will take his ugly face and thrust it down his throat.'

'Yet will you be in the wrong, before the law, and I had supposed that was your main concern.'

Parke glanced at him, frowned, and drank some more wine. 'Who's to know, may I ask? Or do you propose to print a broadsheet?'

'Do you suppose for an instant an affair of that nature can be kept privy, in St John's?'

'And why not, sir? We meet three times a week, in the middle of the afternoon. Had you not so unreasonably returned early you would have suspected nothing.'

'And her husband?'

'Like all husbands, suspects least of all. It is his custom to visit the Ice House every day before noon, as you are well aware, his plantation being so close to town, and there to drink himself nearly insensible. Add four glasses of port with his luncheon, and he is retired by one of the clock, in an absolute stupor from which he does not arise before five. Sweet Mary is always back in bed beside him by four, which allows us two hours of delicious tumbling.'

'With the wife of the man who must in any event lead the opposition to your measures. 'Tis utterly indefensible. For find out he will, Dan. I'll wager you that.'

'Then let him step forth as a cuckold. What, Chester challenge me? I'd pin his ears back for him.' Parke set down his glass and struggled to his feet. 'I must be away.'

'What now?' Kit demanded. 'Another lady? It is all but midnight.'

Parke grinned at him. 'Come.' He led the way, a trifle uncertainly, down the corridor to a downstairs sitting-room, and carefully locked the door. From a chest in the corner he pulled out a long black cloak, and a mask, made to look exactly like a human face, with a moustache and somewhat long nose, but not otherwise grotesque. 'I shall go for a walk.'

Kit scratched his head. 'Wearing that clown's garb?'

'This clown's garb is very suitable, Kit.' Parke stood before the mirror to adjust the mask and carry the cords behind his head. 'It needs a roomful of candles, such as we have here, and a close inspection, to tell that it is not flesh, and I will supply those luxuries to no man. But in an hour or so the taverns will vomit forth their custom for the night, and as you will know, these layabouts remain on street corners for some time after they have finished drinking, attempting to regain control of themselves before they seek their horses. There are overseers amongst them, men from Chester's place, aye, and Goodwood and Green Grove as well, who but repeat their masters' conversations. A man who would rule must keep his finger on the national pulse, Kit. 'Tis not a task to be delegated.'

'You go amongst them?'

'I am there. They are drunk, and one man means little to them. Besides, I can provoke comment with quiet asides, which but brings the flow on more. Why, did you know your wife suffers from an affliction of the eyes?'

Kit frowned at him. 'Marguerite? Her eyes were ever clear enough, to my memory.'

'Yet now she complains, 'tis said. Indeed, she never leaves her bedroom without a veil, to shade her complexion from the sun, and the drapes in her chamber are always drawn. Now, Kit, there is news for you. 'Tis said that not even her children have seen her face this last year, so afraid is she of exposing her eyes to the slightest light. As for your plantation, why it goes to rack and ruin, for she will not venture aback, in case a slight breeze disturbs her veil. Thus it is left to her overseers, and as you *are* probably aware, they are a villainous lot, who care less for producing a good crop than for indulging their pleasures at the expense of the blacks.'

'By God,' Kit said. 'You are sure this is not merely gossip?'

'Perhaps it is, in detail. But gossip must always require some foundation in fact.' He turned back from the mirror, only his eyes and mouth visible. 'Does this distress you?'

'I'd have to be half a man not to care about Green Grove and my children,' Kit said. 'But if you do not mind, Dan, I will not believe such tales until I hear them for myself. Meg, neglect Green Grove? If there is a single thing in life that she truly loves it is that plantation. I know. I managed it for her for over ten years.'

Parke nodded, thoughtfully, and pulled on his cloak before adjusting his tricorne low over his eyes. 'If you wish, you could ride out there and see for yourself. What affects Antigua's greatest plantation no doubt affects us all. But Kit, I must repeat, I will have no violence.'

Now, why had his heart commenced to pound at the thought of once more standing on that verandah, breathing that air, listening to those muted sounds? Why, because then too he would once again hold Tony and Rebecca in his arms, and hear their merry voices.

Or was it because, once again, he would hear another voice, beside which all others were as squeaking doors?

'Bring me information of a more substantive nature, and perhaps I shall,' he said.

'Done,' Parke agreed. 'I will do so this night, you may be sure of that. Now come, you see, I let myself out by the side door, and am on the street before anyone can possibly be aware of whence I arose.' He laughed. 'No doubt they think I am a spirit, a messenger from hell. Aye. I will be a messenger from hell for those scurvy rogues, I promise you that, Kit.' He went down the side staircase, and Kit remained, puzzled. He could not make up his mind whether Daniel was indeed changed, or whether this man was but a logical projection of the youth who had set Jamaica and then Antigua, and no doubt Barbados as well, by the ears. Confidence, carried to a logical conclusion, must mean arrogance. And arrogance, carried to a logical conclusion, must mean, what, he wondered? And allied to this, secretiveness, and lechery as well . . . why, such a man would be whipped down the front steps of every plantation in the island.

But then, as Daniel had pointed out, he was not a man, but a Queen's representative. Which was a different matter altogether.

He turned for the great staircase to reach his bedchamber, and checked at the sound of the explosion. For a moment he was uncertain whence the noise had come, although it had certainly been close at hand.

And had alerted the servants. He heard cries from the rooms they occupied at the back of the house, and the sound of feet drumming on the galleries and down the stairs. He turned himself, ran for the inside staircase, and reached the door as it swung open, gazed at Parke. The Governor had lost his hat, and had torn off his mask. Even in the light of the candles his face was seen to be ashen, and he panted.

'Dan?' Kit cried. 'Are you hurt?'

Parke shook his head, still gasping, and pulled himself up

the stairs. 'Blinded, more like. Fetch me a drink.' He blinked at the crowd of servants. 'And get back to bed, God damn you. A drink, Rum.'

He reached the gallery, sat in a chair. Jonathan hurried forward with a glass.

'A shot, was it?' Kit said. 'I'll turn out the guard.'

'They are there already.' Parke drank deeply, and sighed. 'And I have sent them back again. We'll have no publicity.'

'But someone tried to kill you.'

'Aye,' Parke said. 'Someone. Lurking in the street, to aim at me as I emerged.'

'Knowing that you *would* emerge,' Kit said. 'I did not suppose your subterfuge would survive. This island is a quarter of the size of an English county, Dan. Can you suppose English Harbour does not know everything that happens in St John's, within the hour?'

'Aye,' Parke said. 'Maybe you were right. By God, assassinate me, would they?'

'Yet you'd not have the guard chase the fellow?'

'No,' Parke finished his drink and stood up. 'I know now where I stand. Where I had supposed I would always stand, Kit, eventually. Four-square to the devils. You'll be at my shoulder?'

'You have my word. My only concern is that you give them less opportunity, and I do not only now speak of bullets.'

'Words will cause me no harm,' Parke said. 'But by God, I will harm them. May the devil come for my soul, if I do not bring them down. Make no mistake about that.'

'Strange words, for a Governor,' Kit said, and stood, hands on hips, gazing at the house, into which furniture was being carried by gangs of Negro slaves. 'And look, he means what he says.' He pointed to where more Negroes were dragging a cannon into place beneath the flagstaff from which floated the cross of St George. 'He declares war on his own people. I hope he does not set more substance by the Queen's support than really exists.'

Lillan made no reply. This afternoon, even for her, she had been unusually silent.

'But still,' Kit said, 'it is a splendid house. You must admit that, sweetheart.'

'Have I ever denied it?' She mounted the steps to the

THE DEVIL'S OWN

verandah, her hand loose in his. The workmen smiled at them and touched their hats. 'And what of your ship?'

'She will be launched in a week, by all reports. Then . . .'

'Then will you once again be absent from my side, too often.'

'Sweetheart . . .'

'A man must be active. He must *do*. While a woman must wait. Is that not what you were going to say?'

'Well . . . perhaps I would have chosen my words a trifle differently.'

'The substance would have been the same. But tell me this, Kit.' She freed her hand, and turned to gaze at the lawn, already sprouting grass, and the drive, and the labourers, and the engineer, and the red-coated sentry, patrolling the boundaries. 'Did not a great part of your love for Marguerite spring from admiration of her as a woman who stepped beyond the limits placed on our sex by history and convention?'

'Well . . . she is unusual. I will grant you that.'

'She is breathtaking,' Lillan said. 'In the sweep of her personality. Because she refuses merely to confess, I am a woman, and therefore weak, and thereby hindered. She does what a man would do, whenever it becomes necessary or profitable.'

'There is no denying that,' Kit admitted. 'I suppose in many ways she is unique.'

'No human being is unique,' Lillan said quietly. 'They may only think in unique ways. But we all possess the same attributes, and most of us possess very similar feelings. Were you a general, what would you count the stratagem most likely to give you success in battle?'

'Why . . . surprise, I would suppose.'

'And what has Marguerite done all her life, but surprise her friends and her enemies, her creditors and her debtors, by the force and unexpectedness of her action, of her decisions. And thereby she has achieved all her position and her power, and the admiration with which both men and women regard her.'

'I had not really expected to discover you in the role of Marguerite's defender,' Kit remarked.

'I but seek to point out the strengths on which she trades. Because you see, Kit, if I am ever to hold my head up high again, as Lillan Christianssen, and not merely as Christopher Hilton's mistress, then I must match her on her own ground.'

'But that is . . .'

'Impossible? You think too little of me, Kit. Not that you can be blamed for that. I have ever thought far too little of myself. But this last year I have thought a great deal, as I have had little else to do but think. I have tried to understand the point of view of my enemy, for she is my enemy and there is no point in arguing against that. She has reduced me to a contemptible nothing, a fool of a woman. I must either die, for I cannot live in that guise, or I must force her to admit that I am as good a woman as herself. It so happens that I have at last hit upon a way which provides me very simply with one or other of those alternatives.'

'Sweetheart . . .' Kit began uneasily.

'Hear me out, please,' Lillan said, continuing to speak in the same quiet and composed tone. 'I yesterday wrote her a letter, reminding her of my grievance against her, and challenging her to meet me, at a place of her choosing, and with weapons of her choosing, and at a time of her choosing, that we might settle our quarrel once and for all.'

Kit gaped at her. 'You challenged her to a duel? But that is preposterous.'

'On the contrary,' Lillan unfolded a slip of paper she had hitherto kept in her hand. 'Here is her reply. "Mrs Christopher Hilton will be happy to meet Miss Lillan Christianssen, on the beach outside St John's, at dawn tomorrow morning, for the mutual settlement of their quarrel. The weapons she has chosen are pistols.'

13

The Revolution

'You cannot mean to go through with this madness?' Kit protested.

Lillan's frown had an almost Marguerite-like quality of imperiousness. 'Why should you call it madness?'

'Why, because . . . because . . . women do not fight with weapons.'

'It is not customary for them to do so, certainly,' she agreed. 'But I fail to see why they *should* not. In all the essentials required for the usage of arms we are not different to men.'

'Except in the mind,' he said. 'There you have it. Women have not the cast of mind to wish to harm or kill.'

'Then will we do each other no harm,' she pointed out, with maddening logic. 'But I am sure your remark can hardly apply to your wife. I would have said, there is a woman with sufficient presence of mind to harm, and to kill, if she chooses.'

'By God,' he said. 'You are right.' He seized her hands. 'Not only will Marguerite have the mind to maim you, at the very least, but she has the skill. She has challenged you to fight with pistols. Have you ever fired a pistol in your life?'

Lillan flushed. 'It is not my father's custom to have weapons in the house. But it is a simple matter, is it not?'

'God give me patience,' Kit cried. 'Oh, indeed, it is a simple matter. All things in life are simple enough, to those who understand them. Did you know that Marguerite practises with a pistol at least once a week, and has done so since childhood? She has always conceived it possible that the slaves might rise against their tormentors. She shoots with a deadly and heartless accuracy. Why, this will be no duel, Lillan. It will be, it must be, nothing less than murder.'

'Have you no faith in justice?'

'Ah,' he said. 'Trial by battle. Does the God of the Quakers admit to that?'

She glanced at him; her cheeks continued to glow, but she was no longer embarrassed. 'Is it not time we should be returning?'

He flicked the whip and the trap moved down the hill. 'The house is finished. I have no doubt that Dan will wish to move in as soon as possible.'

'My plans will scarcely interfere with his, Kit.'

'But you will move in with me, will you not?'

She gazed ahead of them at the road. 'Oh, indeed I shall, Kit. I am Kit Hilton's woman. Come next week, I shall be Kit Hilton's only woman, or I shall be dead. It seems to me to be a simple solution to everyone's problem. For be sure that with me gone, Marguerite would welcome you back. And I imagine that even you would welcome that situation. But I will at least have died with the knowledge that I am as good a woman as she.' Once again the quick glance. 'Or should I not even consider the possibility of death, before the duel? You could at least give me that much benefit of your experience.'

'My experience?' he cried. 'For God's sake, Lillan, what

experience do I have? Would you believe that I have never fought a duel in my life?'

'You?' Her surprise was genuine.

'You have been listening to too many of your father's strictures. I have come to the point, often enough, but never have I actually had a challenge accepted.'

'Because of your known prowess. That must be a most comforting feeling. Yet you have killed often enough. So what do you feel immediately before battle? Do you doubt your own survival?'

'No,' he said. 'I have never doubted my own survival.' They entered the sleeping town, clattered gently down the street. Curtains moved at the windows, as usual. Captain Hilton and his woman. How they would stir when they heard of this.

'Well, then,' Lillan said. 'I must not consider my own death, either.' She rested her hand on his as the trap came to a halt. 'I am looking forward to moving in with you, Kit. But I could not do so under the present circumstances. When I bring my clothes up that hill I must be able to look any man, and more important, any woman, straight in the eye. I would hope that you could understand that.'

'I understand the sentiment,' Kit said.

'But you still feel it is unnatural. Well, it *is* unnatural, of course. But, then, is not my entire position unnatural?' She smiled at him. 'I have not yet asked you to second me. Is that not the proper thing to do?'

'Lillan . . .'

'Will you second me, Kit? Or must I go elsewhere?'

How steady her gaze. How little he knew, of what he had commenced when he had offered this girl his love. For how selfish is the human mind, how one-sided the human gaze. What *had* he seen, when first he had looked on Lillan Christianssen? A certain beauty, a certain charm, a certain quiet contentment with life? Or merely a woman eager to respond? He had seen no character, no depths of determination, no deep-seated knowledge of herself. Because had he seen those qualities, admirable in a man with whom one will fight a war, but daunting in a woman with whom one would share a bed, he would doubtless have turned and run.

And proved himself a fool. For is not all life a war? Against age, and poverty, and disease . . . and other people who are also seeking their share? And would a woman, lacking those qualities, be worth having?

'I will second you, Lillan,' he said.

THE DEVIL'S OWN

'Thank you. Presumably Marguerite will supply the pistols. Do you think I should practise?'

She smiled at his bewilderment.

'I think not,' she said. 'An unsuccessful rehearsal might dispel what confidence I possess. I will please Papa by spending the evening in prayer.'

'Your father knows of this madness?'

She shook her head. 'No doubt he will learn of it, in due course. But he at the least will not try to stop me. He considers me nothing more than a daughter of the devil in any event, and searches his own past for the unthinking sin which could have produced me from his loins. But I would prefer not to distress him more than necessary. Do you remain at Mr Parke's house, and I will come to you at dawn.'

Kit hesitated. It cannot be, he thought. I cannot let this happen. But I cannot stop *her*. Even supposing I could, that would be to destroy her all over again. For this truly is the only solution she could ever have come to.

'Aye,' he said. 'I will wait for you, at dawn.'

He flicked the whip and the trap rolled away. He cantered beneath the archway and into the yard of the rented Government House, threw his reins to the waiting slave, and ran up the inner staircase. Colonel Parke was in the downstairs gallery with Mr Wolff.

'Kit,' the Governor cried. 'Great news. Wolff tells me everything is in place.'

'Why, so it is,' Kit agreed. 'I have just come from there.'

'Then we shall move up the hill on Monday. Thank you, Wolff. That is splendid news.'

'I did the best I could, Your Excellency.' The engineer bowed to Kit and hurried for the door.

'And indeed he has done well.' Parke leaned over the plans. 'And then, then we shall see what we shall see, Kit. I have been soft with these rapscallions. I have been too aware that while living here in the centre of their schemes I have been open to ambuscade and annoyance. But when I sit in that citadel, looking down on them, with the fort commanding the harbour at the other extreme, by God, sir, then will I call some of them to account. You'll know they have written letters to London, demanding my recall?'

'I had not heard,' Kit said. 'But how . . . ?'

Parke laid his finger alongside his nose. 'The captain of every ship that trades here is in my pay. Why, should they not humour their governor and principal employer? I took care of that aspect of the situation before I ever left England. So they take care that such of the letters as may be of importance to me are made available.'

'You mean you have confiscated them?'

'I am not that shallow, Kit. I but make myself acquainted with the contents, and then they may go their way. Thus forearmed, I am able to forestall their machinations. So they plead for my recall, and more, for my arrest on grounds of tyranny and misconduct. As long as I may inform the Queen that they will follow these lines, and before *their* letters reach their destinations, they are doomed to failure. As they deserve. Oh, make no mistake about it, soon enough they will have to come out into the open and declare their opposition to me, rather than have their people sneaking about in the dead of night attempting murder, or sending clandestine complaints home to England.'

Kit frowned at him. 'You wish to provoke this?'

'Indeed I do. For when they oppose me, they oppose the Crown, and all the majesty of the Crown. Then may I call upon them to stand up and be counted, and then may I take overt measures against them. And then shall I need your strong right arm, Kit.'

Kit sighed. 'And no doubt you shall have it. Although I must say again I find it a strange way to set about governing a people, first to set them at your throat.'

'I will set them at their own throats,' Parke explained, and smiled. 'Nor is the concept as sinister as you would make it sound. For how may a surgeon set about curing a man shot through with ball? Why, first of all by causing the patient yet more pain while cutting away the diseased flesh and removing the afflicting lead. This is no more than I seek to do with these people.'

'Aye,' Kit said. 'No doubt politics of this nature are a shade too deep for me. I would speak to you on another matter, one which is a great deal closer to my heart. Lillan . . .'

'Is pregnant. Say no more. I have expected the news almost daily. And you are distressed, for mother and child. So he will be a bastard. There can be no criticism of that, Kit. Where or how a man is born is of no account whatsoever. It is what he inherits from his parents that matters, in the way of character and personality, and your son will ever possess the best of both. Why, should you ask me to stand godfather, I would be flattered, and I accept, here and now.'

Kit sometimes felt that talking with Daniel Parke was like

trying to walk a lane with his arms round a wild horse. 'Lillan's not pregnant. At least, not to my knowledge. She has found a way, she supposes, to resolve her difficulties, to expiate her humiliation.'

Parke's turn to frown.

'She has challenged Marguerite to a duel,' Kit said. 'And her challenge has been accepted. They meet with pistols on the beach, at dawn tomorrow.'

Parke's frown slowly cleared; it was replaced with a look of blank amazement. 'Two women, I beg your pardon, two *ladies*, mean to fight a duel? With pistols?'

'Exactly,' Kit said. 'A more preposterous idea has surely never been heard.'

'Preposterous,' Parke said. 'Oh, indeed, it is preposterous. Why, it is . . .' he burst into a peal of laughter. 'By God, Kit, but you will have to excuse me. It is the jolliest piece of news I have received in ten years.'

'I have no doubt,' Kit said, 'that it will similarly amuse everyone who hears of it. I will not quarrel with that. I but require you to forbid it, and I will rest content.'

The frown was back, hovering in the middle of that high forehead. 'Forbid it? I?'

'You are the Governor of these islands.'

'Why, so I am. Yet must I obey the law. Is there a law against duelling?'

'Why, no. But women . . .'

'There is not even a law governing the proper conduct of a duel between women. Why, had they elected to meet while stripped naked and armed only with their teeth, I would have no say in the matter.'

'Except that, no doubt, you would find it even more amusing,' Kit remarked coldly.

'Kit, Kit, must you see all life in such sombre colours? So they will exchange fire. What damage can they possibly do to each other? And it will give the gossips something to occupy their time while I mature my plans.'

'What damage?' Kit shouted. 'At twenty paces? Twenty female paces? At twenty paces, Dan, Marguerite could shoot the cigar from your mouth.'

'Oh, nonsense. Because this wife of yours has managed to obtain the advantage over you time and again, through your own carelessness, I have no doubt, you begin to give her the attributes of a goddess. I will hear no more of it, Kit. I do not believe any harm will come of this affair. Indeed, I suspect a great deal of good may result, for you at least. And I have no legal powers to interfere between two adult white ladies.'

'Oh, do not treat me as a complete fool,' Kit said angrily. 'You put your finger on the nub of the matter, from your point of view, but a moment gone. It will distract the people. By God, sir, that you should use two such women for such a purpose.' He picked up his hat and stormed from the room.

And whipped his horse over the roads to the south. That he should be riding on such a mission after all that had happened. Yet what alternative did he have? But could he honestly suppose there would be any succour to be obtained from a Warner, in this matter?

Yet must he try. The alternative was unthinkable.

It was dusk by the time he flogged his horse down the Goodwood drive. What memories came flooding back, of how many visits in the past, in the carriage, seated beside Marguerite. And of that very first visit, so long ago, now, when he had seemed to rise from disaster to scale the heights of wealth and prosperity.

'Halt, there.'

He reined, faced the blacks, armed with staves, and a white man, carrying a pistol. 'Good evening to you, Haley. I seek Colonel Warner.'

The overseer peered at him. 'Captain Hilton? It cannot be.'

Kit dismounted. 'What, will you set the dogs on me?'

Haley's head shook, slowly, from side to side. 'You'd speak with the Colonel? He is in the withdrawing-room. 'Tis no quarrel you're about, I hope.'

'Far from it.' Kit took off his hat and went up the steps, Haley at his shoulder. 'But it is a matter of importance, none the less. Aunt Celestine.'

She stood in the doorway, a slave behind her with a lantern. She was thinner than he remembered, and thus seemed taller than he remembered. A skeleton of a woman, waiting for death. Her mouth was tight, and this he also remembered. Only the presence of Marguerite and himself had ever made that mouth relax. But they had had to be together.

'You will not have the children,' she said.

'The children?' Kit frowned at her. 'My children are here?'

'Papa.' Tony ran out of the house.

'Papa, Papa.' Rebecca was at his heels. 'Mama said you would not come. But we knew you would.'

Kit knelt between them, hugged them tight, looked over

THE DEVIL'S OWN

their heads at Celestine. 'Perhaps you would explain what has happened?'

'You did not know they were here?'

'I did not.'

She sighed. 'Well, then, why did you come?'

'To speak with your husband. But now I would also like to ask a few questions.'

Again the sigh. 'Tony and Becky are staying a season with us. No more than that. Off you go, now, children. Your father and Grandpapa have business to discuss.'

'But we'll see you again before you go, Papa,' Tony said.

'You will,' Kit promised.

They ran inside. Celestine Warner glanced at the overseer. 'You'd best leave us.'

Haley hesitated, and then touched his hat. 'As you wish, Mrs Warner. I'll not be far.'

'Who is it, Celestine?' came the voice from inside. But this tone was scarce recognizable, so thin had it become.

'A guest, Philip,' she said, and lowered her voice. 'You'll understand that he is far from well, Kit. Indeed, I fear for his life. He had a seizure six months ago, and three since. 'Tis all he can do to speak, and movement is next to impossible without assistance.'

'I understand,' Kit said. 'Believe me, Aunt Celestine, I have come to cause him no hardship. I but wished to beg a favour.'

Again the long stare. 'You, wish to beg a favour of my husband?' Her mouth flattened in disbelief, but she turned and led him into the great withdrawing-room. 'You'll take a glass of punch?'

'That would be very kind of you.'

She rang a little bell which stood on the table by the withdrawing-room door, then led him into the room itself. And here he paused, in surprise and embarrassment.

Philip Warner sat in a large armchair in the far corner, close to the green baize topped table on which, in happier days, they had dealt their cards and rolled their dice. He seemed to have shrivelled, to occupy only half of the chair. Perhaps because he wore no wig, and what hair of his own he still possessed was quite white. But more, Kit thought, because his shoulders were hunched, and seemed to be drawn together.

Yet far more alarming was his face, which was mottled purple and white, with no trace of healthy colour remaining, while one side of it seemed to be contracted; when he spoke it was with great difficulty, and from the corner of his mouth.

But there was nothing the matter with his brain. 'Kit Hilton,' he said. 'By God, sir, you've impudence.'

Kit glanced at Celestine Warner. She would not speak, but she begged, with her eyes.

'Indeed, sir,' Kit said. 'You may believe that I would not have intruded upon you had the matter not been sufficiently grave. And I had no concept of how ill you are.'

'Or you would have come sooner?' Warner asked. 'Drink, man, drink.'

Kit discovered the Negro butler at his elbow, but to his dismay saw that the silver tray carried but a single glass.

'We neither of us find any pleasure in drink, these days,' Celestine said. 'But please take yours. And sit down, Kit. Philip has survived sufficient misfortunes in his life to survive a seizure as well, I have no doubt.' But she was speaking for the benefit of her husband. She understood the outcome of this illness.

Kit sat down, straight, like a schoolboy. But then he would always feel like a schoolboy, where the Warners were concerned. 'Yet am I indeed sorry to see you, or any man, Colonel Warner, brought so low.'

Philip Warner's brows drew together. 'You rode out here, at this hour to sympathize with me? Speak plain, man. Speak plain. You have come about the children.'

'Indeed, sir, I had no idea they were here until a few moments ago. I came out to speak about Marguerite.'

'Ah,' Philip said.

'You still consider her a responsibility of yours?' Celestine demanded.

Kit frowned at her. 'I doubt *she* would allow that, Aunt Celestine. I have not spoken with her this last year.'

'You have not?' Celestine inquired, genuinely surprised. 'Why . . .'

'No more have we,' Philip muttered.

Kit's turn to stare in surprise. 'I do not understand, sir. She is your daughter, and . . .' he hesitated.

'And I am dying. But I have not seen her since the day we placed you in that cell, Kit. Nor has anyone else, save her domestics.'

'But . . . what of Tony and Rebecca?'

'They were brought here, some weeks ago, by one of Marguerite's overseers.'

THE DEVIL'S OWN

Some weeks. Thus her decision could not have been influenced by the challenge. 'You mean they were delivered like two parcels?'

'There was a letter,' Celestine said.

'May I see it?'

'No, you may not.'

'But there was a reason given. Is she ill?'

'It would not appear so,' Celestine said. 'She rides aback. Her crop was shipped with the others. Although it was not so rich a crop as you used to produce.'

'But . . . there was some talk of an ailment of the eyes. Mere gossip, I understood it.'

'It does not seem to hinder her greatly. Although I believe she does go veiled much of the time. Believe us, Kit,' Celestine said. 'We are more concerned than you can possibly imagine. I have ridden over there, on several occasions, and been refused admittance.'

'Could you not speak with Miss Johnson?'

'Miss Johnson showed no desire to speak with me.'

'But surely, on her visits to town . . .'

'Like her mistress, Elizabeth Johnson has not been seen in town this last year.'

'But what is the explanation? Elizabeth is the children's governess. Now you say she remains with Meg?'

Celestine glanced at her husband. 'There are rumours.'

'You listen to rumours? Do the women of this island have nothing else to do, but rumour?'

Celestine sighed. 'There must be a cause, Kit.'

'Then tell me some of these rumours.'

She hesitated, and colour flooded her pale cheeks. 'That Marguerite conducts some vast orgy with her blacks of a night, and is too dishevelled and marked by pleasure to appear in the full light of day.'

'Meg?' Kit cried. 'That is monstrous. Meg? Of all possible women? After what happened to her? She'd as soon hang herself.'

'You asked for the rumours,' Celestine said, coldly. 'I give them to you. And perhaps . . . the human mind on occasion works in a mysterious and unhealthy way. As you say, Kit, she has known a black man's embrace. Who can say what that has done to her mind, in her loneliness? Is she not still a young woman, a beautiful woman, a passionate woman?'

'Madam, that is the most disgusting suggestion I have ever

heard,' Kit declared, getting up. 'And of your own stepchild.'

'My husband's bastard,' Celestine said softly. 'Oh, I grieve for her, Kit. Yet must there be some explanation of her sudden desire for isolation. And there can be no quarrelling with the fact that Green Grove has come to resemble a prison, where Marguerite glories in being the principal inmate.'

'If you knew none of this,' Philip said, slowly, 'you have yet to tell us the reason for your visit.'

The reason. 'By God,' Kit said. 'That I had all but forgotten. Well, you may as well know of it. There is to be a duel.'

'Called out, by God,' Philip said. The tight face almost relaxed into a smile. 'Now, who has found the courage, after all these years?'

'*I* am not going to fight a duel,' Kit said. "None of your friends have discovered that much courage yet, sir. Marguerite proposes to fight one. She has been challenged by Lillan Christianssen. You may believe it was done without my knowledge, but it has been done, and the challenge has been accepted. Which certainly disposes of any suggestion that Meg is ill.'

'A duel, between two women?' Celestine cried. 'Why, that is absurd.'

'My own sentiments exactly,' Kit agreed. 'Unfortunately, it appears that there is no legal impediment.'

'It never occurred to my father to pass a law to prevent women fighting,' Philip said.

'So it seems,' Kit agreed. 'Yet it is impossible, would you not agree?'

'Of course,' Celestine said. 'Why, it is indecent, to say the least. Imagine, there will most certainly be spectators, and one of them could be hit . . . who can say where? Why, my mind positively stumbles. You will have to forbid it, Kit.'

'I? Forbid it? By God, I wish life were that simple. You must understand, Meg acted most cruelly, most unnaturally, towards Lillan, and Lillan conceives herself to be forever humiliated, doomed to be tracked to her grave by mocking laughter, unless she can prove herself as good a woman as Meg. This is her answer. In all conscience, Aunt Celestine, I cannot demand of her that she withdraw. That would doubly damn her as inferior.'

'And you came here, wishing that we would intercede with Marguerite?'

THE DEVIL'S OWN

'She is unlikely to listen to me.'

Celestine sighed. 'I suppose I could ride over there once again. If it is a matter this urgent I could attempt to force an entry. Whether I should be successful, I have no idea. I should imagine that if there is a person in this entire world Marguerite truly hates it would be this Christianssen girl.'

'You'll not interfere,' Philip said. 'By God, there is a spirit. There can be little enough the matter with Meg if she will react so eagerly to a challenge.'

'To an invitation to murder, you mean,' Kit said. 'She knows she has nothing to fear from Lillan. The girl has never handled any weapon in her life.'

'Yet did she challenge,' Philip Warner reminded him. 'And must abide by the consequences. And I will tell you what those consequences will be, Kit. She thought to bring Meg low, no doubt after listening to all these nauseating rumours. She thought Meg would ignore her or decline to fight, and then she could trumpet her vindication abroad. Well, she has failed, by God. I'll wager you a hundred pounds *she* does not appear at the appointed time.'

'By God, sir,' Kit said.

'Kit,' Celestine warned. 'You gave me your word.'

Kit sucked air into his lungs, slowly. 'Aye, so I did, Aunt Celestine.' He finished his drink. 'I had thought we would work together in this event, at the least, as it touches us all so closely. If that is impossible, then I must see what can be done by myself. I will take my leave. It grieves me to see you so low, Philip. I wish you good fortune.'

He picked up his hat and went to the verandah. Celestine Warner followed him. 'He hates you too, Kit; nor can he be blamed for that.'

He hesitated. 'And you?'

She smiled. 'Hatred is for more active minds than mine. I doubt not that both Philip and I shall be in our graves within a twelvemonth. We would be better off remembering our joys than preserving our sorrows. I hope and trust that you can stop this madness, Kit, even if I feel no confidence in your success. And Kit, if you can learn anything about Marguerite, or better yet, if you can bring her out of herself, pray inform me.'

He clasped her hand. 'I shall, Aunt Celestine. Be sure of that.'

She nodded. 'Now come and say farewell to Tony and Becky.'

By now it was late in the evening; the brief Caribbean twilight had long disappeared behind the sun, and the moon had not yet risen. The last time he had taken this road had also been at night. Then there had been murder in his heart, anger in his mind. Now . . . there was more alarm than anything else. Alarm for Lillan, or alarm for Meg? Over this past year he had deliberately shut his mind, to Green Grove, to everything on Green Grove, to his children, to the mistress of Green Grove most of all. He was too conscious of his weakness in that direction, too aware that the thought of Marguerite could bring any man up hard and anxious, while for the man, like himself, who could remember, she was the most exquisite of tortures.

And then, too, the whole memory of Green Grove, of the wealth and power, the immunity from law or criticism that it had given him, of Tony and Rebecca, all of these things were calculated to bring a man down from any position he sought to establish. As Marguerite was herself certainly aware. Thus had she waited, for his surrender, as she had early declared her intention of doing.

But he had not surrendered. He could never surrender, for the sake of Lillan. But this, perhaps, had not entered Marguerite's mind. She counted Lillan of no importance. The quarrel was between man and wife, and the other woman was no more than a symptom, not a cause. When he had not returned to his home, she might well have assumed it was because of the unexpected, the arrival of Daniel Parke. There was the rock upon which her plans had foundered, and there was the event which might well have turned her mind with anger and despair.

Because only a turned mind could possibly justify the suggestion put forward by Aunt Celestine. It was quite incredible. It would be incredible, in any circumstances, about a planter's wife. But about Meg Hilton . . . yet why had she sent away her children? Surely there was the most unnatural act of all.

He reined his horse, looked down the hill, frowned at the sound. It rose from the slave compound, where there was a great bonfire, and where the slaves danced and sang. On Green Grove? Or was this some celebration, some anniversary, of which he knew nothing?

Certainly there did not appear to be any overseers in charge.

He touched his horse with his heels. There were no dogs,

THE DEVIL'S OWN

either. There was a surprise; it was difficult to imagine a sugar estate without dogs. Nor did the dancing Negroes pay any attention to the lone horseman who walked his mount up the drive to the house.

But the house was also filled with light. And with people, he was astonished to discover. Half a dozen overseers, with their wives, lounged on the verandah, drinking sangaree and smoking cigars. They glanced at the intruder, carelessly at first, unable to identify him in the darkness. One of them got up and stood at the top of the steps. 'Who goes there?'

Kit dismounted.

'By God,' the man said. 'Captain Hilton?'

Chairs scraped, and the rest of the party hastily got up. 'No ghost, Hodge, you may be sure of that,' Kit said. 'I seem to have lost track of the date. What are we celebrating?'

'No celebration, Captain.' Hodge licked his lips. 'We are but taking our ease after a long day in the fields.' Kit looked along the verandah, at the suddenly anxious men, at the women clutching their sleeves.

'No doubt the blacks, also, have had a tiring day,' he remarked.

'Ah, it does them no harm to dance and sing a little, Captain,' Hodge said.

'And have you no homes of your own?'

'Why, it is the mistress's own wish that we come up here of an evening,' Hodge explained. 'She likes to hear the sound of pleasure.'

'But she does not sit with you?'

'No, sir, she does not.'

'Then may I ask where she is?'

'Why, sir, she has retired, I would say. She is usually early to bed.'

'Then you'll excuse me. Ladies.' Kit went inside. The men exchanged glances, but no move was made to stop him. Then he stopped himself. The huge withdrawing-room, which he had never seen with other than polished floor and gleaming furniture, was scuffed and shabby, and there was dust everywhere. He took off his hat, and heard a sound. Maurice Peter stood at the foot of the stairs.

Maurice Peter. Marguerite's closest confidant. Should he then be slaughtered on the spot? Yet the old man looked happy enough to see him. Happy? He looked overjoyed.

'Captin, suh,' he cried. 'Oh, God, Captin, but it is good to see you.'

'Indeed?' Kit demanded. 'Would you explain to me what is happening?'

'Happening, Captin?'

'I wish to know why the overseers are making free with my wine and my cigars, and why the slaves are being allowed so much noise.'

'Well, Captin, suh, it is Mr Hodge what says what must be done. And he says . . .'

'Hodge? Where is the mistress?'

'She is upstairs, Captin.'

'And you have just come from here? By God . . .'

'I come from the kitchen, Captin.' Maurice Peter was now looking frightened. Well, that was as it should be.

'Captain Hilton? Oh, thank God you are here.'

Kit raised his head, gazed at the woman who stood at the top of the stairs. Elizabeth Johnson? She wore an undressing-robe over her nightdress, and her hair was loose. It was thin hair, pale brown, and it straggled. Her face was no less thin and pale; the primly tight features had dissolved into a permanent look of misery.

'Elizabeth? Where is my wife?'

Miss Johnson licked her lips.

Kit ran up the stairs. 'You'll explain this mystery, Elizabeth. What is happening here?'

She hesitated, and then glanced at her bedroom. 'If we could speak privily . . .'

'Nothing is happening, Kit,' Marguerite Hilton said, her voice penetratingly quiet, as ever.

As ever. Kit turned, faced the bedroom door, reached for the handle and twisted it, without success.

'I wondered whose strange voice it was,' Marguerite said. 'I could not believe my ears for a moment.'

Kit stared at the door. There was no illness here. Although . . . there was a quality of sadness, perhaps even of despair, that he had not previously heard. 'Why do you keep the door locked?'

'And should I not?' she asked. 'Especially with you in the house, sweetheart? The last time you were here you all but broke my arm.'

'And you would not say I had cause?'

'I would only point out that it is unpleasant to be manhandled. Nor can I believe you would intend less, on this occasion.'

Kit hesitated, glancing at Miss Johnson. 'Leave us alone,

THE DEVIL'S OWN

if you will.' He turned back to the door. 'I'll give you my word, Meg. I only wish to speak with you.'

'In that case,' she said. 'A closed door between us is of no importance whatsoever.'

'Meg . . .'

'I was about to go to sleep, Kit,' she said. 'I would be obliged if you would say what it is you wish.'

'To sleep?' he demanded. 'With that racket downstairs?' Although the noise had largely stopped; no doubt they were listening. 'And your slaves under no discipline?'

'They are happy enough, and docile enough,' she said. 'Do you object to people being happy, Kit?'

His big hands curled into fists. He felt as if he were caught in a bog, or in the forest before Panama, assailed by endless annoyances and uncertainties, dominated by the biggest uncertainty of all, any knowledge of where he was and where he was going and how he was going to get there.

He sighed. 'Very well,' he said. 'There are such rumours about you, perhaps I am reading more into what I see than is really there.'

'Have I not always attracted rumour?' she asked. 'There was a time you were proud of that.'

'There was a time I was proud of a great number of things. But I have a purpose in coming to see you, Marguerite. I would beg a favour of you.'

'Your Danish whore challenged me, Kit,' she said. 'Not I her.'

'Yet surely it can do you no injury to withdraw,' Kit urged. 'No one can doubt the outcome of such an unequal contest.' He knew better than to appeal to *her* sense of propriety.

'Well, then, she is singularly rash,' Marguerite said.

'It would be murder.'

'Perhaps not. Perhaps I shall not kill her, Kit. Perhaps I shall just put a bullet through her body, and leave her scarred.' Still he stared at the closed door. 'But you mean to do that.'

'Oh, indeed. If she wishes blood, she shall have it.'

Kit kept his anger under control with difficulty. 'And suppose things should not go as you intend? What of your eyes?'

'What of my eyes, pray, Kit?'

'Is it not true that the reason you go veiled is because of some affliction which affects your sight? What if you find it difficult, or perhaps impossible, to sight your weapon?'

'Rumours,' she snapped, for the first time sounding angry. 'I care naught for rumours. There is nothing the matter with my eyesight, Kit. I promise you that. There is nothing the matter with me at all. Nothing, do you hear? Nothing. If it is accommodation you wish, let your woman stay away tomorrow. Surely she is sunk so low she can fall no further, in her own esteem or in that of the world. Now begone. Get from my house. You left here of your own accord. Do not seek to come back.'

He hesitated, his shoulders hunched.

And once again, she seemed able to read his mind. 'And should you launch an assault upon my door, be sure I will have my overseers at your throat.'

As if he cared for her overseers. But to start a riot, now, when Daniel was already antagonizing all and sundry . . . would that assist Lillan?

He turned, his hands hanging uselessly at his side, gazed at Miss Johnson.

'Elizabeth.' The word cut across the night. 'You'll speak with him no more, Elizabeth.'

Elizabeth Johnson gazed at Kit for a second, but as he moved towards her, she shut and locked the bedroom door.

'She is a remarkable woman,' Daniel Parke remarked. 'But then, so is Lillan. It seems to be your fortune, Kit, to attract females of character. Me, I prefer my bedwarmers to have no character at all, to have no greater ambitions in life than to feel my hand between their legs.'

Like Mary Chester, Kit thought. But he refrained from saying it. Nothing he could do or say, apparently, would dissuade Daniel from this unseemly path on which he was set, although he of all people must be aware that it was common gossip in St John's, so much so that Edward Chester never even attended the Ice House any more, for shame. What went on in private between the Chesters did not bear consideration.

'You are not attending the duel?' he asked.

Parke drew his brocaded undressing-robe tighter around his shoulders, and sipped coffee. 'It would not be right, I fancy, for the Governor to attend an event of this nature. Besides, I will hear of its outcome soon enough.' He stood up. 'Lillan.'

Despite her request to Kit, she had spent the night at the Government House; the news of the accepted challenge had

THE DEVIL'S OWN

been too much for her father. But she had slept alone, and now she entered the room as quietly and gracefully as ever. And despite Kit's suggestion that she wear black, she had elected to put on a grey gown and her wide hat. Her face was paler than usual, but as composed as ever. 'Good morning, Your Excellency.'

'You'll take a cup of coffee?'

She shook her head. 'I doubt my stomach could retain it. I would like to leave now, Kit.'

Hastily he finished his own coffee, and got up.

'I'll wish you all the fortune in the world, Lillan.' Parke kissed her hands. 'You'll be back within the hour.'

'Of course I shall.' She waited for Kit to arrange her cloak around her shoulders, went to the stairs. Jonathan was below with the trap.

'You keep safe, Miss Lillan,' he said. 'But man, they got people down by the beach.'

'Already?' Kit enquired.

'People? Oh . . .' Lillan squared her shoulders. 'But I expected that.'

She sat beside him and the trap rolled out of the archway and on to the street. It was just dawn, and the first tiny fingers of daylight were starting to throw shadows from the houses. It occurred to Kit that the town must have looked just like this on that terrible morning Lillan had lain on this very street, and waited to be discovered, for the humiliation to begin. Not for the first time he had to wonder if this was a way of committing suicide, if she actually hoped for death, knowing that she could never live down the shame.

And yet, she had already lived down the shame. For as Jonathan had said, there were already people about, moving towards the beach, men and women, and children, hoping for a spectacle none of them had suspected possible. And most of these shouted encouragement at the trap.

'You'll give her best, Miss Lillan.'

'Be sure you aim true, girl.'

'She deserves a bullet through the head, Miss Lillan.'

'You'll puncture her pride, girl.'

Lillan almost smiled. 'What a bloodthirsty lot they are, to be sure.' She glanced to her right as they passed the Christianssen's house. Abigail stood on the doorstep, with little Agrippa in her arms.

'Godspeed, Miss Lillan,' she shouted.

Had she hoped to see her parents there as well, Kit

wondered? Or did she know that by adding this deed of blood to the other deed of shame she had finally ended all hope of a reconciliation between herself and her father? And yet, there was a movement at the curtains shrouding the upper window, and there was no breeze.

'Their thoughts go with you, have no doubt of that,' he said.

'I'm sure they do.' She would not meet his eyes. Because he was the only possible weakening of her resolution. She rode like a woman going to her execution. Well, was she not? And why did he not assert himself, whip the trap into a gallop, forbid this hideous masquerade? Because to do that would be to lose her just as much as if she was killed? He kept coming back to that inescapable fact.

Well, then, why had he not broken down Marguerite's door and fought his way through her overseers, if necessary, to force her to withdraw? Because that would not alter the situation either? Because this was something, not beyond his understanding—he understood their rival feelings only too well—but beyond his power to control.

But then, had he not too often found all life beyond his control? As if any man, or any woman, for that matter, could control life. Life was a sea, often turbulent, whipped by winds of tremendous force and capricious direction, and one kept afloat as best one could, or one sank without trace.

He wondered if Marguerite would subscribe to that point of view. She at the least had never had any doubt about her ability to control such aspects of life as surrounded her. So no doubt she would control this morning's event as well.

And Lillan was hoping for mercy.

The beach was crowded, the people massed against the seagrape bushes which lined the sand. And here waited Dr Haines and several other gentlemen, amongst them John Harding.

He nodded stiffly to Kit as he helped Lillan down. 'I am to marshal this event Captain Hilton,' he said. 'At the request of the challenged party.'

'Who I observe is not present,' Kit said, his heart commencing to pound with hope.

'It is not yet time,' Harding pointed out. 'I assume you are acting for Miss Christianssen?'

'I am.'

'And is your client content with the arrangements?'

Kit shrugged. What was there to criticize? The beach

sloped gently down to the even more gentle sea. The sand was even, and the backgrounds at either end were trees. And Harding he knew for an honest man, even if often enough a misguided one. 'She is content.'

'Then here are the weapons.' He opened the case. The four pistols lay on the velvet. 'They are loaded and primed. I did so myself.'

Kit frowned. 'Four?'

'Your client used the words a "final settlement between us" in her challenge, Captain Hilton. By the code I understand, this means the exchange continues until one party cries, "Enough." '

'By God,' Kit said. 'You will have blood, then.'

'It would seem to be what the ladies wish, Captain.'

Kit walked across the sand to where Lillan waited. 'Did you know that Marguerite wishes to exchange shots until one party is hit or withdraws?'

'It is her prerogative.'

'Oh, indeed. But it is madness. Lillan . . .'

'Please, Kit. I will have no more of it. Besides, it is too late.' She pointed, at the carriage which came rumbling up the road, displacing a cloud of dust.

It halted on the edge of the sand, and the Negro driver jumped down to open the door. A man got out first, and waited to assist Marguerite down, but she waved him away. She had indeed prepared herself well, and was all in black, black gown beneath black cloak, black boots, black kid gloves, wide-brimmed black hat, and a black veil over her face, so that she was, in fact, totally invisible. At the sight of her the crowd started to boo, and her head half turned in that unforgettable gesture, before she came down the sand.

'Show your face,' they yelled. 'Show your face.'

' 'Tis a substitution,' they bawled. 'Have her unveil.'

Marguerite came up to Kit and Lillan. 'Good morning to you,' she said.

'It is customary to show your face, Mrs Hilton,' Dr Haines suggested with some caution.

'Do you doubt it is I, Kit?'

'No,' he said. 'No, I do not doubt that, Meg.'

'Well, then. Good morning to you, Mr Harding. Hodge here will act as my second.'

The overseer nodded to the gentlemen.

'Very well, ladies,' Harding said. 'We had best be about

this business. I must first of all appeal to you to cease this grim intent, and embrace each other as friends.'

'If Mrs Hilton wishes,' Lillan said in a low voice.

Marguerite stared at her. Almost they could see the glint of her eyes through the veil. 'I do not wish,' she said. 'This woman has seen fit to start this business. Let us carry it to a proper conclusion.'

Kit opened his mouth and then closed it again. Nothing he could say could do other than make matters worse.

Harding held out his box. 'Will you select your weapons?'

Marguerite took one of the pistols, and Lillan, after a moment's hesitation, did likewise.

'Now, will you stand back to back, please,' Harding said. 'And when I give the signal, will you walk away from each other for ten paces, and then turn, and fire at will. I will count the paces, ladies, and I must impress upon you that should either of you turn and fire before the count of ten, then she will be guilty of a felony, which shall be murder should her ball strike home, and will be treated accordingly. Do you understand me?'

Marguerite continued to stare at Lillan, whose face had suddenly flushed, red spots clinging to her cheeks, while her mouth settled into an even firmer line. She was summoning all her courage.

'Remember, I beg of you,' Kit said. 'Do not be hurried.'

'It matters naught.'

He bit his lip, let his hands fall to his sides, watched her walk away from him to where Harding waited. She was very nearly a head taller than Marguerite. And now even the rustle of the crowd fell silent, and the only sound was the faint murmur of the surf, as the sun broke out of the Atlantic behind them to bathe an orange light across the scene.

'Now,' Harding said. 'One . . . two . . . three . . . four . . . five . . . six . . . seven . . . eight . . . nine . . . ten.'

Lillan stopped and turned, the pistol hanging by her side. Marguerite had also turned, and once again stared at her enemy. Then slowly, her right hand came up. How slowly it rose. Kit wanted to cry out in sheer anguish. But Lillan never moved, and her face never changed expression. Up and up came the pistol, extended at the end of that black-sleeved, black-gloved hand like an extra finger, absolutely straight. No other part of Marguerite's body moved.

The morning seemed to stop, even the sun seemed no longer to edge its way into the sky. The sound of the explosion, when it came, was a surprise. Black smoke eddied into the air, and Kit realized that he had shut his eyes. He opened them again, and looked at Lillan. She stood absolutely straight, and unharmed. He wanted to shout for joy, and then he looked at Marguerite, who still extended her arm and gazed along the pistol as if in utter disbelief. The second explosion sounded almost before he had realized what was happening. But Lillan had merely pointed her pistol at the sky and fired. And now the crowd relaxed, and a babble of chatter rose into the air.

Neither woman had moved, and Harding was walking forward with the open box. The noise dwindled; the onlookers had not realized there was to be more than one exchange.

Harding went to Marguerite first, the box extended. She gazed at him for some seconds, looked into the box, and then suddenly, in a gesture of remarkable frustration, struck it with the empty pistol she still held in her hand. Taken by surprise Harding dropped it, and the pistols fell to the sand. Marguerite threw her own weapon on top of the others, turned, and walked towards the beach. No one spoke; they merely watched in amazement. The door of the carriage still stood open, and the coachman waited beside it.

'Take me home,' she said, her voice clear and distinct.

The door closed, the coachman climbed on to his box. The crowd woke up to what was happening and started whistling and booing. Hodge scratched his chin.

'Your client has defaulted, sir,' Kit said. 'Mine is vindicated.'

'By God,' Hodge said. He hurried towards the town to find a horse.

'The most remarkable thing I ever did see,' Harding commented. 'And from Marguerite? It is unbelievable.'

Yet had it happened. Kit was already running across the sand to reach Lillan and catch her as her knees gave way and she fell in a dead faint.

So then, even buccaneers and planters can be happy, from time to time. Jean DuCasse had found happiness, like Kit once, in planting. He had retired from the sea he had dominated so splendidly, and grew sugar-cane in the new French colony of Santo Domingo, which had grown out of that same Hispaniola they had haunted as *matelots* so long ago. He wrote letters begging Kit to visit him, whenever this tiresome war would end. But for Kit Hilton happiness was to stand on the poop deck of a stout little ship, and feel the wind rippling his hair while he listened to the creaking of the sheets and the swish of water away from the hull. Her name was *Calliope,* and she was everything he could have wanted: fast, seaworthy, trim, stiff enough to make life aboard comfortable, and armed with four cannon in each broadside and a saker forward. She was a pursuer; a ferret, not a hare.

But there was nothing for her to pursue. The sea was empty of ships save for the three-master bearing down on St John's. But *she* proudly flew the mingled cross of the new union, and was from England. He had already fired a blank charge in salute, and dipped his ensign. Kit Hilton, exciseman. But the planters would take no risks at this juncture. They had no wish to invite reprisals from Mr Parke, and they well knew he only waited the excuse. Even the House had not met in a month. Daniel must be left to fume and fuss, and wait, as they.

So for the coastguard cutter it was just a matter of sailing, and returning home. Why, he might be a gentleman of leisure, with naught to do but amuse himself. For the harbour was opening ahead of him, and Myers the mate was giving the order to shorten sail preparatory to anchoring. And when he was rowed ashore in his jolly boat there would be no frowns to greet him and no boos, at least from the common folk, while the planters seldom came into town nowadays. Although today he saw Harding, and two others, gathered at the far end of the dock, pinching their lips and glancing at him, but offering no greeting. They hoped for mail.

Something to tell the Governor. A horse waited for him, and he nodded and smiled as he rode up the street, exchanging a greeting with Barnee, looking out for Abigail and her baby as he passed the warehouse. Sometimes even Astrid Christianssen was there to greet him. But never Dag. Rumour had it *he* scarcely left his books and his work. An unhappy man. Because his daughter had failed him.

But she had not failed herself. Once through the town Kit could whip his horse into a gallop, and storm up the hill, under the shady trees, to rein before the gleaming white balconies and verandahs of Government House, against which the brilliant red and green of the hibiscus hedge stood out in sharp contrast.

She walked on the lawn, towards him, put up her cheek to be kissed. No, indeed, she had not failed herself. The slight air of defensiveness which had used to accompany her like a cloak had gone, and forever, he hoped. Now she was proud to be seen by his side, proud to live with him as his mistress.

'It is good to have you home, dearest,' she said. 'And did the ship behave as you wished?'

'She is a treasure.' Kit walked towards the house, holding her hand. 'Daniel has done me proud. And how is the great man?'

'He broods, and writes letters. I think he has missed you, Kit. Certain it is he has asked for you to go up to him the moment you returned.'

'Then I suppose I had better do so. But he has no other solace?'

She climbed the wide, shallow steps in front of him. 'Oh, indeed. Mrs Chester comes here quite blatantly now, at least twice a week. I think this island must be so inured to scandal that there is no longer even comment. Not that I should pass judgement. Why, often enough she sits on this verandah with me and enjoys a cup of tea. For we are not two of a kind?'

'Sweetheart.' He caught her hand again. 'You know I would set that right, if I could. I do not suppose . . .'

For they had heard nothing of Marguerite since her tumultuous exit from the scene of the duel.

'Rumour, as usual,' she said. 'How now no one is allowed on to Green Grove at all. I believe even a messenger from Goodwood, informing her of her father's death, was turned away.'

'Philip is dead?'

She nodded. 'A week ago. I think this is what is upsetting Mr Parke. The funeral was used as an expression of solidarity by the planters. 'Tis said there was not a man of them absent. Which makes the non-appearance of Mrs Hilton the more surprising.'

'By God,' Kit said. 'He was clearly dying when last we met. But what of Celestine? And my children?'

'I understand Mrs Warner will sell Goodwood and return to England.'

'With Tony and Rebecca? By God, they'll not be whisked across the ocean. I shall have to pay her a visit. But it is, as you say, inconceivable that Marguerite did not attend her father's funeral. But then, is anything about Marguerite as it seems? I still cannot understand her behaviour that day on the beach. Had her voice not been so clear and sane I would once again have supposed her to be demented.'

'Or sorrowful,' Lillan said. 'Believe me, Kit, I often lie awake at night and wonder at the wrong I have done her.'

'Yet our love had come to an end before I came to you, Lillan,' Kit insisted. 'The affair is now closed. She sought her revenge, most cruelly, and you stood up to her and forced her to admit defeat. And you were right, in everything about her. She admitted how much *she* had wronged you by her action on the day. Can you not forget that?'

'No,' Lillan said. 'I cannot forget her so long as she looms so large in your mind.'

'*My* mind? Why . . .'

'You should not try to dissemble, Kit,' Lillan said severely. 'It is not in your nature. Green Grove, with its mistress, is too deeply embedded in your heart for either of us ever to overlook it.' She freed her hand as they reached the upper floor. 'You had best go to the Governor.'

Kit hesitated. But she would do better when she had been given more time. Even now, happiness was something at which she would have to work. And he could do no more than help her, when she wished help. He knocked.

'Kit? Come in, man. Come in.'

He opened the door. For his office, Parke had appropriated the best room in the house, intended as an upstairs withdrawing room, wide and high-ceilinged, with glass doors opening on to the upper verandah, and standing wide to allow the breeze to enter. A huge mahogany desk faced the doors, and from his chair the Governor could look out across his lawn at the sea and the harbour. Yet he did not appear contented. A sheet of paper and a quill lay on the desk in front of him, and he played with the silver inkstand.

'Kit,' he cried. 'Thank God you are back. You've made an arrest?'

'I have seen but a single ship, and she was out of Bristol. And I even sailed into St Eustatius itself.'

'Aye.' Parke scowled. 'They know you too well, as they know me.' He got up, paced the room. 'They will make no move. They wait . . . do you know, I had supposed it was Warner himself restraining them? God knows I have pushed and prodded and provoked long enough. I had supposed, when their acknowledged leader died, that they would react, and strongly. But by God, they do nothing. Save refuse to grant the necessary supplies. Every day I am assailed with more bills, and every day I possess less funds. By God, this matter must be settled soon or government will become impossible.'

THE DEVIL'S OWN

'I will tell you why they do nothing,' Kit said. 'They are waiting.'

Parke frowned at him. 'Waiting? For what?'

'A letter from England.'

'A letter?' Parke glanced at him, and the frown deepened, and then he turned at the knock. 'Come.'

Jonathan stood there. 'The mail, Your Excellency, begging pardon.'

Parke seized the leather satchel, glanced at Kit again; his face had paled, very slightly.

'And begging your pardon again, Your Excellency,' Jonathan said. 'There are some gentlemen waiting to see you.'

'Gentlemen? What mean you, gentlemen?'

'Mr Chester, suh. And Mr Harding.'

'By God,' Parke said. 'He has come to challenge me. After all this while, by God.'

'I am not sure . . .' Kit began, but Parke was already making for the door.

'You'll second me, Kit,' he threw over his shoulder.

'Oh, I will second you, Dan.' Kit followed him down the stairs. Chester and Harding waited in the front hall, their hats in their hands. And they also had a leather satchel. 'But do you not think it might be a good idea to read your correspondence first?'

'Bah. It can wait,' Parke said. 'I have been looking forward to this day, Kit. Oh indeed. I knew it had to come. Well, gentlemen? Well? You wish to speak with me?'

The planters looked at Kit. 'Perhaps it would be best were we to conduct our conversation in private, Your Excellency,' Harding suggested.

'What? Nonsense. Captain Hilton is my right hand. You'll speak before him, by God, or not at all.'

The planters exchanged glances.

'Very well, Mr Parke,' Chester said. 'If you will have it so. No doubt you are aware, as you seem to be aware of everything else that takes place on this island, that some months ago the planters wrote as a body, over my signature as Speaker of the House, addressing themselves to Her Majesty, and begging her to grant us some respite from the terrible ills that your term of office here has caused us.'

'What?' Parke shouted. 'Why, by God . . .'

'You'll allow us to finish, sir. We complained not only of your manners, but of your morals, and of your obvious desire to ruin the prosperity of this island and the value of its trade with England. Well, sir, Her Majesty is not the lady to turn a deaf ear to the just grievances of her subjects. We have this day received a letter from Whitehall, informing us that you are to be recalled to answer our charge of maladministration, and therefore we wish to inform you, sir, that we no longer consider you as our Governor, and would ask you to hand over the great seal of the colony, together with your appurtenances of power, and to take yourself back to England by the earliest possible means. There is a ship in the harbour now.' His gaze flickered to Kit once again. 'And remove your servants with you.'

'By God,' Parke said, but this time he spoke quietly. 'By God, that any governor should stand in his own house and listen to such unmitigated treason. Kit, you'll turn out the guard, if you please, and have these gentlemen arrested.'

Kit hesitated. 'Dan . . .'

'What? Would you go against me too?'

'No, Dan. You should know me better than that. I would but ask that you ascertain your exact position first. Surely, if there were letters for these gentlemen, there will be letters of similar importance for you.'

Parke looked from his friend to the planters; his face was purple. 'Your correspondence is from the Queen herself?' he demanded.

'From one of her ministers,' Chester said. 'Which amounts to the same thing.'

'You think so, by God?' The Governor went to a marble-topped table and emptied the contents of the satchel. There were several letters and packages, but he sifted through them rapidly, scrutinizing the seals, and at last found what he wanted. 'The Royal Seal.' He brandished it. 'Your answer, gentlemen.'

'Then I suggest you open it, sir,' Chester said.

Parke gazed at the letter for some moments, then slit the envelope and took out the contents, a carefully penned parchment. 'Ha,' he said. 'I fancy, gentlemen, that you have overstepped the mark.'

'May we read that letter, sir?' Harding inquired.

Parke's hand came up. 'No, sir, you may not. It is a personal communication from Her Majesty's privy secretary to me.'

'Then perhaps you will be good enough to tell us its substance,' Chester said.

'I see no reason why I should do so, sir,' Parke declared.

'Suffice it that I see my way clear. But I am a magnanimous man. You gentlemen have been misled, I fear, by some overzealous councillor, not truly privy to Her Majesty's wishes. You may withdraw, and we shall discuss the matter further when next I come down to the House.'

'Withdraw, sir?' Chester cried.

'When next you come down to the House?' Harding shouted. 'Why, sir, we'll have none of it. We are here to demand and obtain your resignation. We'll not leave until that document is in our hands.'

'By God,' Parke said. 'Threats? Call the guard, Kit. Call the guard. Oh, fear not. I shall not waste my time arresting these dogs. I will merely have them thrown from my property.'

'Your property?' Chester shouted. 'Why, sir, this house and this land is the property of the people of Antigua, and leased by them to the Queen's representative.'

'Who stands before you. The guard, Kit.'

Kit moved to the door, but hesitantly. There could be no doubt that each party considered itself to be in the right, and how much more explosive a situation could be reached he did not see.

'Sir,' Harding said, gaining some control over his anger. 'You refuse to obey the dictates of the English government?'

'I obey the dictates of the Queen, God bless her, and no other.'

Kit paused in the doorway. Perhaps the crisis would pass.

'Then, sir, we shall take our leave,' Chester said. 'We did not come here to brawl with you.'

'Then begone,' Parke said. 'But be sure you will hear more of this matter.'

'Indeed, sir, you may count on it,' Harding said. 'As of this moment, Colonel Parke, you have no authority to act as anything but a private person, and we demand that you leave this house and yield up the seals. Think well on this, sir. We shall return tomorrow morning for our answer, and be sure that we shall not come alone.'

'What?' Parke roared. 'You'll have some more snivelling dogs at your heels, will you?'

'Upon receipt of this letter,' Chester said, 'and suspecting your intransigent nature, we despatched messengers to every plantation calling for support. You will see who shall be at our backs, sir.'

'By God,' Parke said. 'You go too far, sir. You preach revolt.'

'On the contrary, sir,' Harding insisted. ' 'Tis you who are planning to revolt. Against the known wishes of the government of England. We shall of course make the facts known to the soldiers of the garrison.'

'By God,' Parke said. 'Never in my life have I heard such treason openly spoken. Well, gentlemen, I give you fair warning. I am a patient man, and as I said, I desire to be generous. You gentlemen hold responsible positions in the community. I leave it to you to return the forces you claim to have raised to their proper stations. For mark my words well, gentlemen, I'll brook no revolution. Should a single armed man attempt to climb that hill out there, be sure I will cut him down.'

'Sir,' Chester said. 'You mistake the situation. It is *we* who are magnanimous, and desirous of avoiding bloodshed. I have here a letter dismissing you from your position. For the good of the people of Antigua, I must insist you respond to those instructions. We shall withdraw. But only to grant you sufficient time to make your arrangements. We shall return tomorrow morning, to escort you to the ship which waits in the harbour. Good day to you, sir.' He turned to face Kit. 'It would be safer for you, and yours, Captain Hilton, to accompany the retiring Governor.'

'By God,' Parke said, half to himself. 'They have played into my hands.'

Kit returned from the verandah, where he had watched the planters out of sight.

'Into your hands? I wish I could understand what is going on. What is contained in your letter from the Queen?'

'From her privy secretary, to be sure,' Parke said. 'Oh, their evil tongues have played their part. There is concern at Whitehall, and I am summoned back to answer certain questions.'

'But then . . .'

'But your friends still mistake the matter, Kit. I have *not* been relieved of my position as Governor of the Leewards. There is my strength. I should return, the letter says, with all haste, leaving a deputy to act in my absence. And should I satisfy Her Majesty, well, then, be sure that I shall be returned here in more power than I now possess.'

'Faith,' Kit said. 'Your waywardness is a mystery to me, Dan. Why did you not let Chester see that letter, and have

THE DEVIL'S OWN

an end to quarrelling? Why, if they do anything rash, this could well come to bloodshed.'

'And what else do you think I desire?'

'You wish them to march on you?'

'Can you name me an easier way to settle this business? Fate has played us well, as she invariably will do, should one but trust her. I see it all. They have their friends in the Privy Council, and the discussion was undoubtedly hot. Thus the planters' friends left the meeting in no doubt that I was about to be dismissed, and sent off their letter to Chester containing that information. But the official letter, written no doubt after due reflection, contains no suggestion of dismissal, at least unless I am convicted of misdemeanours, after my return to Great Britain. So it is that should that rabble down there decide to attempt to remove me by force, they will be guilty of mutiny. Not only will I be obliged to deal with them as I have always wished, but they will have justified my every action since coming here.'

'By God,' Kit said. 'As I may have said before, Dan, you go about governing people in a strange way.'

'And as I have told you, often enough, that is the only way they will understand. You'll not desert me?'

Kit sighed. 'It seems to be the misfortune of my life to stand before lost causes, sword in hand. I'll not desert you, Dan. I think you are wrong. I think you are criminally wrong. But I'll not desert a man who has twice proved the best friend I possess.'

'I expected nothing less. Well, let us prepare ourselves. Turn out the guard, and make sure every man is provided with sufficient powder and shot. Hunt around the servants and select such of them as can be trusted. Impress upon them that our fate is theirs. And send a horseman down to the garrison to inform Captain Smith of the situation, and tell him I expect him to bring his men to Government House at dawn tomorrow.'

'Did not Chester say that they had already been informed?'

'Aye,' Parke said. 'There was a threat of incitement to mutiny if you like. But it matters very little. This house will withstand an assault even from regulars, resolutely defended. We built it for that purpose, Kit. Do you remember? You built it for that purpose.'

'Aye,' Kit said. 'Resolutely defended.' He went towards the front door, met Lillan coming down the stairs.

'Kit? What is happening? There was so much shouting, so many angry words...'

'And now we are past the stage of words,' he said bitterly. 'Once again it seems that we are to be exposed to the caprice of fate. The Governor has provoked a revolution.'

14

The Master of Green Grove

A sound brought Kit awake. And instantly the full possession of his faculties. No doubt he had slept with half of his mind alert.

It was close to dawn; the darkness was already lifting, and the sea breeze was chill. His brain went back all those years, to another dawn, at Panama, when Bart Le Grand had shaken him by the shoulder, and led him to where Harry Morgan had stood. He had been afraid on that dawn, too, and once again without cause. It had only been necessary to do, against tremendous odds, to win.

And certainly Daniel Parke was no more of a rogue than Morgan. But then, was he as much of a man?

The Governor stood in the doorway. 'Awake?' he asked. 'I hear hooves.'

Sure enough there was a faint drumming in the distance. And now Lillan also awoke, and lifted her head from Kit's shoulder. 'Kit? What will happen?'

'I'd give a fortune to know that.' He got out of bed, reached for his clothes, followed the Governor. Parke was already on the verandah, where the sentry waited, and at which Jonathan was dismounting. The Negro panted, and his eyes were bloodshot.

'They's coming, Your Excellency. They's coming.'

'Who?' Parke demanded. 'The garrison?'

'Well, suh, not this minute. The captain down there does be marshalling the men, for sure, but they moving slow.'

'Yet are they moving. I doubt Chester will oppose such a show of force.'

THE DEVIL'S OWN

'But they coming now,' Jonathan wailed. 'Them planters, suh, and a whole lot of others. Man, they got thousands.'

'Speak the truth, man,' Kit said. 'It is important.'

'Well, suh,' Jonathan said, wiping sweat from his forehead with his sleeve. 'They got two, three hundred. I am sure of that.'

'Armed?'

'Oh, yes, suh. They got sword and musket, and pike, and thing like that.'

'By God,' Parke said. 'So it has come to blows after all.' He turned, to find the sergeant of the guard immediately behind him. 'Assemble your men, armed, and with powder and ball, and also load the cannon.'

The sergeant hesitated. 'With grape, Your Excellency?'

'Aye,' Parke said. 'That were the way to dissuade that scum.'

'You cannot be serious,' Kit said. 'Surely ball were the answer, to discourage them without committing more murder than is necessary. We need only hold them pending the arrival of the garrison.'

'By God, Kit,' Parke said. 'I wish I could roll back the years and have a buccaneer beside me instead of a besotted Quaker. Oh, very well. Load with ball, sergeant, but be sure you have a canister standing by for the second charge. And form your men on the lawn there. Kit, you'll marshal the servants. Arm them and place them upstairs as a second line of defence.' He seized his friend by the shoulder. 'You'll obey my orders, Kit. No backsliding. I'll need your best support.'

Kit sighed. 'And you shall have it, Dan. Only, I beg of you, let the first move come from them.'

'You'd not suppose they have made it, by marching on my house?'

'I'd still counsel forbearance, for as long as possible.'

'Aye,' Parke said. 'Perhaps I'll forbear from hanging them all. Now make haste, I beg of you. They cannot be far away.'

And indeed it was possible to hear, swelling up the hill, a confused noise. Kit ran back into the bedroom for his weapons, found Lillan dressed.

'Kit . . .' her voice trembled.

'What we have always feared has come to pass. Those people feel they have right on their side, and Daniel knows he has the law on his. Lock the door and sit tight. Do not move unless I come for you.'

'Can I not stand at your side?' she asked.

'No,' he said. 'And if you force me to it I shall bind you hand and foot to prevent it.'

She hesitated, and then sighed. 'So be it. I should not be of much assistance, that is certain. I can only say Godspeed.'

He kissed her on the forehead. 'Perhaps He may be able to prevent a catastrophe. Certain it is I can think of no other possibility.'

He buckled on his sword belt, checked the priming on his pistols, returned to the great hallway, where a dozen Negroes were gathered, fingering unfamiliar muskets and chattering amongst themselves.

He clapped his hands, and they fell silent. 'Now listen to me,' he said. 'There is a mob coming here, who mean to do your master harm. We must prevent them, which means we must stop them entering this house. We may leave the ground floor to the soldiers. You will come upstairs with me.'

'We going do that, Captin,' Jonathan said. 'We going fight for the Governor.'

He led them up the stairs, arranged them on the verandah, evenly spaced, each man with a musket and a supply of powder and ball, and a pike for close work. 'You'll lie down,' he told them. 'So as not to present a target, and you'll fire through the banisters. Thus there is naught to be afraid of. Remember that those people down there are in the wrong, and you have the law on your side. But wait for the command.'

'You going be here with us, Captin? someone asked.

'You may count on that.' Kit stood on the verandah and looked down, at Parke and the sergeant, marshalling the guard on the lawn. There were a score of redcoats, armed with muskets and sword bayonets, and in front of them stood the cannon, which had been loaded and dragged round to face the top of the drive. Because now the noise was close, and from his vantage point he could see a mass of men starting to climb the hill, and punctuating the dark of the people was the gleam of metal; the sun was just climbing above the horizon and sending darts of brilliant light over the island.

Parke looked up. 'Are you ready, Kit?'

'We are ready,' Kit said.

'Very good.' He drew his sword, and walked in front of the soldiers. Slowly the noise swelled, and a few moments later the crowd appeared at the head of the drive. There were a

THE DEVIL'S OWN

considerable number of them; Kit realized with a pounding heart that perhaps Jonathan had not after all been exaggerating; he would have said there were at least two hundred. They carried an odd assortment of weapons, in the main pikes and muskets, but there were several drawn swords to be seen, and these belonged to the planters. He recognized both Chester and Harding, and frowned as he began to pick out the overseers. Haley of Goodwood was there. And so was Hodge of Green Grove.

Hodge? Then the plantation was not as cut off from events as he had supposed. Because there were other Green Grove men present as well.

But there were also others he recognized. The sweepings of St John's, and already flushed with drink, early as it was. Or perhaps they had spent the night building up their courage.

But whatever force was driving them on, he suddenly realized this affair was not a foregone conclusion. He went into the study, found the Queen's letter lying on the desk, folded it and stowed it in his pocket. Then he returned on to the verandah.

Daniel Parke had not moved. He remained in front of his small army. And now the mob itself checked, to stare at him, at the redcoats and the house, still shouting and laughing amongst themselves. If only the men of the garrison would come, Kit thought, then there would be no risk of bloodshed.

'This is revolution, Mr Chester,' Parke called out, his voice very loud and clear.

'We are a citizens' committee, Mr Parke,' Chester replied. 'We have come to demand your resignation, and your departure from Antigua.'

'And I, sir, demand your dispersal on the instant,' Parke said. 'Or I shall fire into you.'

The planters hesitated, glancing at each other, reluctant to carry events further even now.

'Ten seconds, Mr Chester,' Parke called. 'That is all I will allow you.'

'Sir, you exceed your prerogative,' Chester called, and stepped forward.

'Give fire,' Parke shouted, and the match was applied to the touch-hole. The cannon roared and a cloud of black smoke billowed up to shroud the verandah. There were screams and howls from the mob, and as the smoke began to clear Kit saw that the ball had hurtled through the very centre, decapitating two men and leaving a swathe of scattered arms and legs.

'Oh, Christ,' he muttered. There could be no more talk now.

'Charge them,' Chester bellowed, waving his sword.

'Fire your pieces,' Parke yelled, returning to the line of redcoats.

The muskets rippled, and the mob, emerging on to the lawn, paused; several men fell.

'Retire,' Parke bawled. 'Retire to the house, and there reload. You'll give fire, Captain Hilton.'

'Take aim,' Kit said. 'Do not waste your shot. Fire as you will. Steady, now, lads, steady.'

The Negroes fired, and raised their heads to see what damage they had done, and chattered excitedly amongst themselves as they reloaded. Certainly they had shed their fear, and it occurred to Kit that well led they might make a formidable force. Supposing there were a few dozen of them.

The mob was now advancing at a run, churning up the fresh green of the new-laid lawn. Beneath him the soldiers clattered on to the downstairs verandah, and there turned to face the onslaught, but already he could hear cries of alarm; these people were their friends in more sober moments.

'Stand to,' Parke shouted. 'Stand to.'

'Seize him,' Chester yelled, running at the steps.

'By God, sir, I'll have you at the least,' Parke said, and stepped forward, his pistol levelled.

But someone else fired first; Kit would never be sure who it was. The Governor gave a gasp and fell to his knees, and with a scream of terror the soldiers threw away their muskets and fled through the house, their boots clattering on the polished floors.

Kit stood up in his horror. It was Green Grove all over again. He watched the mob surge up to Parke, who was still kneeling, his left hand pressed to the wound in his body, his right still trying to level his pistol, and seized him as a pack of dogs might seize a bone. And at last Kit came to life.

'Follow me,' he yelled, and ran for the stairs, drawing his sword as he did so. He reached the foot in three bounds and checked to regain his balance, then discovered he was alone. Yet it did not occur to him to hesitate. The mob was baying like wolves now, most howling anger and derision, only one or two voices, amongst them John Harding's, calling for order. Kit burst upon them like another cannonball, swinging

THE DEVIL'S OWN

his sword from left to right. A cutlass came up to meet him, and was swept aside, its owner tumbling down the steps. For a moment Harding himself faced him, and then sprang to one side, while another man fell with a thrust through the chest. Then they fell back and he stood astride his friend.

They panted. 'Shoot him down,' Chester called. 'Hang him high. He is no less our enemy.'

But Kit was looking at Parke. The Governor's clothes were torn and slashed, and to the bullet wound in his ribs there had been added a dozen knife cuts. Even hands had done their worst; there were scratches on his face and one of his eyes appeared to be gouged.

Slowly Kit straightened. 'You are a fool, Edward Chester,' he said. 'Better to have called him out, man to man.'

'He fired into us.' Chester's voice was hoarse.

'He was entitled to do so.' Kit took the letter from his pocket. 'He is Governor of this land, and will remain so until dismissed by Her Majesty.'

'But . . . he was recalled . . .'

'To answer your charges,' Kit said. 'Not to be dismissed, unless he failed to satisfy his peers. You had best read it.'

The shouts had already died, and feet were shuffling. Kit stepped away from the dead Governor, held out the letter. Chester took it; his hand trembled. Hastily he perused the words, then handed it to Harding.

His action accomplished more than a regiment of cavalry would have done. Already men from the back of the mob were drifting down the hill. Now even those from the front shrank back, and the men who a moment before had been shouting for Kit's blood now would not meet his eyes as they slunk across the trampled lawn.

'By God,' Harding said. 'We have committed treason.'

'It was your idea as much as mine,' Chester said.

Harding glanced at him, and then at Kit. 'What do you propose?'

'That you disband that rabble and return them to their proper occupation.'

'And then?'

Kit sheathed his sword. 'The Governor is dead. There is no man of your force can escape the guilt of it, but I doubt there is a man will identify himself as the one who struck the fatal blow. It will lie with the Queen.'

'We are the ringleaders,' Chester muttered. 'And he deserved to die. By God he did. Mary is pregnant. Did you know that, Kit? She carries his bastard in her belly.'

'And for that you should have called him out. This is murder.'

Harding looked past him, at the Negroes gathered on the verandah, at the soldiers slowly returning now the sound of battle had died. 'And you will have us hanged?'

Kit sighed. For all their enmity, he realized, the three of them, standing here on a bloodstained lawn, were all the hope of survival Antigua possessed. 'There was provocation.'

'What?' Chester's head came up. 'You will testify to that?'

'Aye,' Kit said. 'For an end to strife, for an understanding of where your, our duty lies, to the Queen and to our country, I will testify to that.'

'By God, sir,' Harding said. 'There is nothing small in your nature. I'll say that to God Himself.'

Chester squared his shoulders. His right hand started to move, then he checked it. 'You'll have my support, Kit, in whatever you elect to do.' He turned away, and stopped, and looked down at the Governor for the last time. 'But he deserved to die.'

They buried Daniel Parke, together with his victims, that same morning, in the cemetery outside St John's. Six soldiers from the garrison carried the coffin, and a firing squad of their comrades delivered a volley over the grave. Captain Smith stood behind the remainder, armed and looking very stern. He was anxious to quash any suggestion that he had deliberately delayed turning out his men to avoid taking sides. The planters stood in a group, with their wives, and the townspeople gathered in a huge mass beyond. None of them bore arms this day.

Kit Hilton stood by the graveside, next to the Reverend Spalding. Lillan, with Jonathan the butler, and Abigail, were a little distance away. Dag and Astrid Christianssen were also by themselves.

There was no oration by the priest, and Kit did not feel that he could utter one. The first clods of earth fell upon the wood and he turned away, to meet Lillan's gaze. For the moment the island was his. In a most remarkable fashion, he realized, Parke's death was his triumph. He had stood always for moderation and good sense, and for that had been rejected and pilloried. But now at last had the plantocracy gone too far. But only for the moment. Daniel Parke had been his

THE DEVIL'S OWN

support, and now all opposition was crushed by the enormity of his death. But they would recover soon enough.

He walked round the grave, approached the planters. 'I am in possession of Mr Parke's will,' he said. 'Which you may copy, if you wish, Edward.'

'I?' Chester demanded. 'What have I to do with Mr Parke's will?'

'It is simply that he leaves all his possessions to the child of your wife, Mary, whenever it is born.'

'By God,' Chester said.

'Aye. It will be of some service to you, I have no doubt, in proving their liaison. To my mind, it will also serve to prove that his was no mere lust, but a genuine affection. I hope you will do him, and Mary, the honour to believe that.'

'By God,' Chester said again. 'What a remarkable fellow he was, to be sure.'

Kit rejoined Lillan, and escorted her through the crowd, which parted before them.

'Kit.'

He stopped, and turned, and felt Lillan's fingers bite into his arm.

Dag Christianssen's cheeks were red. 'I'd have you know that I honour your defence of the Governor, both for the way you stood by a friend, and for the way you protected a principle.'

'I thank you, Dag.' Kit thrust out his hand. 'It would be my great happiness could we be friends, once more.'

Dag hesitated, then took the proffered fingers. 'Perhaps, after all, there was some sense in what you claimed, and what you did. Perhaps indeed a wrong such as you did Lillan could only be set right by a public flaunting. I wish things could have been different. But I'll bear a grudge no longer.'

'Kit.' Astrid kissed him on the cheek. 'You'll come to our house for luncheon.'

'Indeed, I doubt that we properly belong at Government House in the absence of a governor, Astrid.'

'Well, then,' she smiled. 'You must move back in with us. Oh, we will make room for you, be sure of that.'

'Then we shall be happy to accept,' Kit said. 'And perhaps Dag will help me with my deposition, for I must set down everything that has happened here for the perusal of Her Majesty, and I think the sooner it is done the better.'

'And will that not bring even worse misfortunes upon this unhappy island?' Dag asked.

'I hope not,' Kit said. 'I have promised Chester to be fair to him as well as to Daniel. There was provocation, and misunderstanding, and misfortune. And in any event, it is to Her Majesty's advantage that sugar is grown here, and successfully, and that the planters have some say in the management of their own affairs. I imagine her best course would be to regard the appointment of Daniel to this governorship, however much of a blessing it proved to me, to have been a mistake.'

'If you can even attempt to persuade her of that, Kit, then shall I be your scribe with pleasure. I will prepare my pens.'

He hurried ahead of them down the street, his wife at his elbow. Kit and Lillan followed more slowly. She had said nothing all day, that he remembered.

'Can you not find it in your heart to be happy, at least about the reconciliation with your family?' he asked. 'One would suppose that in Daniel Parke you had lost *your* closest friend. But as I remember you thought little of him.'

'I feared him,' she said. 'If that is what you mean. Perhaps I even foresaw that he must come to a violent end, and feared that he would involve you in his own catastrophe. As he did.'

'Yet do I stand here at your side, now, unharmed.'

'And for that I am eternally grateful. Yet it is also but what I expected, Kit. You are too straight a man to be brought down by rogues, except through an unhappy chance.'

'Well, then . . .'

'I fear you are also too straight a man to live a lie, for all of your life.'

He frowned at her. 'Could you but forget the fact that I am married, I have no doubt at all that I also could manage it.'

'I doubt that, Kit. I doubt that very much. No doubt, knowing that this day of disaster was overhanging us, you slept restlessly, last night. And cried out in your sleep.'

He stopped, and turned to face her. 'Her name?'

'Meg. Time and again. Meg. But you have done this before.'

'By God,' he said. 'That I should have inflicted such a misfortune upon you. It shall not happen again, Lillan.'

'What will you do?' she asked. 'Spend the rest of your life in wakefulness?'

'If I could make you understand. She *is* a part of my life.

THE DEVIL'S OWN

A great part. Like Daniel, she helped to make me what I am.'

'And you love her still,' Lillan said quietly. 'So after all, she is the victor between us, and I must remain a trespasser.'

He stared at her, his mind desperately searching for the words which would have set her mind at rest, and finding none.

'Kit,' Astrid came running out of her front doorway.

'What is it, Astrid? Some more catastrophe?'

'Miss Johnson, Kit. She is here to see you. But Kit . . .'

Kit went inside, to pause in amazement. Could this be the prim middle-aged lady he had known for so long? Elizabeth Johnson was hatless; her hair was loosed and tumbled. Her gown was torn and mud-stained, and there were shadows beneath her eyes. She looked as if she had not eaten in days.

Dag held a glass of water to her lips, and she sipped, and panted. 'He'll not find me here, Mr Christianssen. Say he'll not find me here.'

Dag raised his head, to look at Kit.

'Who'll not find you here, Elizabeth?'

'Captain Hilton.' Elizabeth Johnson half fell out of the chair to seize his hands. 'Oh, thank God. He came into town, you see, to join with Mr Chester and Mr Harding, and most of the overseers came with him. So I managed to escape. I walked all night, Captain, crawled through the canefields to get here.'

He held her shoulders and raised her up. Certainly there was no doubting the evidence of her journey.

'You had to *escape* from Green Grove?'

'I have been locked in my room these last three weeks, fed when they wished. When he wished. I thought he would murder me, but . . .'

'He? Who is this he?'

'Hodge. He manages the place now, Captain. He has since . . . since the day of the duel. Since he . . .' she burst into tears.

Gently Kit forced her into the chair and knelt beside her. 'He has imprisoned Marguerite as well? Is she also locked in a room at Green Grove?'

She shook her head. Her hair scattered to and fro. 'Oh, no, Captain. He would not risk that. He feared her, as we all feared her, until that day.'

Kit frowned at her. 'You mean they rebelled against her because she had not killed Lillan?'

Again the violent shake of her head. 'No one knew,' she said. 'No one, save I, and I was sworn to secrecy. And she was careful, always careful, Captain. She would not go abroad unless veiled, and only I was ever allowed into her bed-chamber.'

Kit stared at her, a terrible lump seeming to swell in his belly. He glanced at Dag; the Quaker's face was rigid.

'But that morning,' Elizabeth said, 'she was in despair. She had gone to die. She thought Lillan would kill her. She expected to die, Captain. And then, when Lillan fired into the air, she knew that she could not. She was in such despair, Captain, she took off her hat and veil in the carriage. And Hodge caught up with her before she regained the house. He saw her, Captain.'

'Oh, Christ,' Kit muttered. 'What did he see, Elizabeth?'

But he did not have to ask, because suddenly he *knew*.

'Oh, God, Captain,' she moaned. 'He saw.'

Kit felt Dag's hand on his shoulder.

'How long had she been ill?' the Quaker asked.

'More than a year,' Elizabeth said. 'It began with a cold which would not dry.'

'My God,' Kit muttered. He remembered Marguerite on board the *Euryalus*, and in the courtroom in Bridgetown, dabbing at her mouth with the scented handkerchief. And he remembered too Martha Louise, and others, whose ailment had begun with a dribbling nose. But neither of them had thought for a moment such a fate could be Meg's. 'You knew of this?'

Elizabeth's head bobbed up and down. 'Soon after she returned from the trial. After that night, when you came out to Green Grove, and were arrested. She fled upstairs when you were gone, and I went in to her, and saw her lying on the bed, in tears. I asked if I could help, and she raised her head, and looked at me . . . oh, God, Captain Hilton, that look I will carry to my grave.'

'There were marks on her face?'

'Not then. On her body.'

'She showed you?' Astrid whispered.

'Aye. She was so alone, in her misery. She knew not what to do. It was I begged her to do nothing. Perhaps it was just a skin disease, I said. Perhaps the yaws.'

'But they spread,' Kit said.

'Yes,' Elizabeth said. 'They spread. And became worse.'

'And would you not send for the surgeon?'

THE DEVIL'S OWN

'She would not, Captain. And she swore me to secrecy. Oh, God have mercy on me, Captain. What could I *do*? What can anyone do, with a woman like Mrs Hilton?'

'But . . . the children?'

'Were not exposed, Captain. I swear it. From that moment she never touched them. She kept herself isolated. No one was allowed near her, except me, and I was to wear gloves whenever I assisted her, and then to burn the gloves.'

'You stayed with her for a year, knowing she was a leper?' Lillan asked. 'Miss Johnson, you put us all to shame.'

'But the children,' Kit said again, his brain a whirl of despair.

'Are safe, Captain. I swear it. I tried to persuade her to send them away, immediately. But she would not. She loved them too dearly, Captain. But when she realized there was no hope for her, then she sent them to her stepmother.'

'Safe?' Kit cried. 'And their mother a leper?'

Dag's fingers still rested on his shoulder. Now they tightened. 'The disease is not hereditary, Kit. All authorities are agreed on that. If they were not exposed, then they are, truly, safe.'

'Oh, God,' Kit muttered. Marguerite, all that beauty, all that strength . . . 'Is that what you would have told me the night I went out there?' he asked. 'But once again you obeyed her.'

'What could I do, Captain?' she asked again. 'By then I loved her as if she were my own sister. God knows, I feared and hated her when first she summoned me to Green Grove. But such courage cannot help but be loved.'

'And she would have had me kill her,' Lillan said half to herself. 'I failed her, in that. But I will put flowers on her grave. Now and always.'

'She is not yet dead,' Elizabeth muttered.

Kit's head jerked. 'Not dead? But . . .'

'Hodge discovered her secret, yes. He was terrified. He summoned two other of the overseers, Lowan and Marks, and they took her to her room. They knew not what to do. With either of us. They wanted to kill her, but they feared her, even then. But then they realized the power that could be theirs, that was already theirs, if no one discovered the truth. Yet they still feared to murder her, to murder a planter, to murder a Warner, to murder Kit Hilton's wife. So at dead of that night they ferried her to the island.'

Kit stared at her, his jaw slowly dropping. 'They took Marguerite to the island?'

'She fought them,' Elizabeth said. 'She fought them and would have screamed for help, but they bound her and gagged her and threw her into the boat, and took her across, and left her on the beach.'

'And you?'

'They threatened to take me with her, Captain.' Tears welled into her eyes. 'I could not. I wept and begged.' She glanced at Lillan. 'You think I am brave, and strong, as she? I stayed because I feared to leave. But when they would have taken us both, I lay on the floor and kissed their boots and begged them. And so they locked me up, at last. I think even then they were afraid of what might happen. They were waiting to hear about the Governor, because everyone knew that Mr Chester had written to England asking for Colonel Parke's recall, and it was felt that if the Governor went you would have to go too, Captain Hilton.'

'Hodge, by God,' Kit said.

'So last night they rode into town to take part in the fight, and I escaped.' She flushed. 'I climbed down the drain pipe.'

'And walked to St John's from Green Grove?' Astrid cried.

Kit stood up. 'You'll get me a horse, Dag. I'll take the trap up to Government House for my weapons.'

'You'll go after Hodge? Can there not be an end to hatred and bloodshed, Kit?'

'Hodge? By God, I'll settle with Hodge, Dag, when the time comes. But I must go for Meg.'

'But . . .'

'She is a leper? Would you have me stay away for that? Yet is that not the true horror of it. Hodge set her ashore on the island where every inhabitant is a victim of her own peculiar method of dealing with the disease. Can you imagine how they must hate her? And now . . . for three weeks, by God, she has been in their power.'

'Oh, God,' Lillan muttered. 'Oh, God.'

'Aye,' Dag said. 'He does pose us some problems, to be sure. You fetch your weapons, Kit. I'll procure two horses.'

'Two?' Kit demanded.

'This day I'll ride by your side. And be happy to do so.'

The sun was still high in the sky when they topped the hill above the plantation. From here all looked as peacefully prosperous as ever in the past. Except that the fields were empty.

THE DEVIL'S OWN

Kit, dragging on his rein to give his mount a respite, and drawing his sleeve across his face to dry the sweat, stared at the empty acres of waving green in amazement.

'The overseers must all have marched with Chester,' Dag said.

'Then may we well discover a massacre.' Kit kicked his horse and cantered down the slope. He had not seen Hodge since immediately before the Governor's death. But then, Hodge would hardly have dared show his face.

The house stood empty, the front door open. But now he could see the activity at the overseers' village. There were wagons waiting, and women standing around giving their menfolk instructions, while the children shouted and played hide-and-seek around their mothers' skirts.

He turned his horse and rode for them, and at the sound of his hooves men, women and children insensibly moved into a huddle. He reined at the gateway, scanned the terrified faces. 'Where is Hodge?'

They glanced at each other, and shook their heads.

'You.' Kit pointed at one of the men. 'Tell me where he is.'

'In town, Captain Hilton.'

'There are two others. Lowan and Marks.'

'In town, Captain. They have not returned.'

'But you were there too,' Kit said. 'Or how do you know to flee?'

The man licked his lips, looked from side to side. 'They sent me, Captain. These people, they are innocent of any harm.'

'Innocent,' Kit spat at them.

Dag touched him on the arm. 'Some of them, at the least, Kit.'

'Did you come here to restrain me, or to aid me, Dag?'

'I'd do both, Kit.'

Kit heard the breath whistling through his own nostrils. 'Then begone,' he told them. 'Let me see your faces again, and by God I'll have his blood.' His gaze scorched at them. 'Or hers.'

He pulled his horse round, cantered down to the slave compound. The blacks were also gathered before their houses, watching. Just watching. What strange people they were, to be sure. How patient, how resigned to their fate. He recalled Tom Warner's words as they had walked through the forests of Dominica, and wondered if the cacique had been right, after all, and there were no more warlike people than the white man.

Someone shouted, 'Is the Captin.'

The cry was taken up, and now at last they moved, surging to the gate of the compound, but not venturing beyond. 'The Captin,' they shouted.

Maurice Peter came through the gateway as Kit and Dag reined their horses. 'Captin, suh,' he said. 'But we is glad to see you.'

'Why is there no one at work?' Kit demanded.

'Well, Captin, Mr Hodge he say to stay in the compound until he come for we. He say so two days now, Captin. And he ain't come.'

'And you have remained here?' Kit asked.

'They are good people,' Dag said. 'They would be better, had they but the opportunity.'

'And where is the mistress?' Kit asked.

'Why, Captin, she must be in the house. Is a fact we ain't see she too much. We ain't see she, why, it must be one month. Is Mr Hodge does manage the estate.'

'Aye,' Kit said. 'Fetch four men, Maurice Peter, and launch the boat. Make haste now.'

Maurice Peter stared at him. 'The boat? But there ain't nobody sick, Captin.'

'Just do as I say.' Kit dismounted, led Dag down the twisting path beyond the slave compound to the beach. After a moment's argument amongst themselves, Maurice Peter followed with four men. Below them the water sparkled blue in the midday sun, and moved with a slow swell between the island and the shore. And on the island itself the green trees, densely packed and hugged yet closer by the snarled undergrowth, looked empty of life, save for the always tell-tale wisp of smoke arising from the seaward side.

The pirogue rested on the sand; the paddles lay in the bottom. Maurice Peter waited at the water's edge. 'But who we carrying across, Captin?'

'Launch the boat.' Kit helped them push the heavy bark down the beach and into the gentle waves, led them over the stern, Dag behind him, Maurice Peter took the steering oar, and the other Negroes handled the paddles. Kit waited in the bow.

Of what did he think, as the island loomed larger? He could not think at all. He dared not think at all. There were too many emotions screaming at his consciousness, demand-

THE DEVIL'S OWN

ing to be loosed, demanding to be expiated in a long burst of fury.

The water turned green, and they could see the white sand only a few feet beneath them. The slaves stopped paddling, and the boat slid to a stop.

'Give way,' Kit said. 'We will have to land.'

'Land there, Captin?' Maurice Peter's voice was high with fear.

'Land me, at least, old man,' Kit said.

'But Captin . . .'

'Wait,' Dag said. 'There are people.'

They waited amidst the trees, watching the boat. Kit's hands were so wet with sweat that they slipped on the gunwale as he stood up.

'Speak with them, Kit,' Dag begged. 'Speak, before doing anything rash.'

But there was more activity on the shore. He had not realized before how many people lived here, waiting to die. On his previous visits no more than half a dozen had ever appeared to greet the new arrival. But now he saw a good score coming down the sand to his right, carrying something between them. They moved slowly and awkwardly, many lacking toes to maintain their balances. They kept their heads bowed, but even at this distance he could make out some of the ghastly mutilations which the disease had inflicted on their faces.

'Land me,' he commanded in a low voice. 'Land me, by God.'

'Stop there, Kit.'

His head jerked at the command, and so did the slaves, rising from their seats to stare at the beach in terror. Maurice Peter reversed the process, and dropped to his knees.

The lepers were opposite the boat, and now they set their burden on the sand. It was a litter on which lay a shrouded figure.

'By God,' Kit said, and thrust one leg over the side.

'Stop, Kit.' The voice was lacking in strength, but in none of the quality he had loved and respected, and perhaps feared, for so long. He rested on the gunwale, staring at the shore, trying to tear aside the shroud with his eyes.

'Have they not harmed you, then?' His voice was hoarse.

'Why should they do that, Kit?' Marguerite asked. 'They are good people. Like me, they wait only to die.'

'But . . .' Good people. Whom she had condemned. 'How are you cared for?'

'By them all, Kit. Here is Henry John. You remember Henry John?'

He remembered Henry John, hanging between the uprights, his back a scarred mass of blood.

'And Martha Louise? Martha Louise cares for me, Kit.'

Martha Louise, whose screams as she had been thrust over the side had been heard even on the mainland.

'*They,* have cared for *you?*'

'Should they not, Kit? As I have cared for them, while I could walk. As I have cared for them, indeed, since fate first conspired to make me their mistress.'

'But...'

'Here I am no longer their mistress,' she said. 'Here there *is* no mistress and no slave, Kit. Here there is no hate and no fear. Here there are only men and women waiting to die. So here there are only friends.'

'You will not die, Meg,' he shouted. 'We will take you home, and fetch Haines, and...'

'Do not be a fool, Kit. I am dying. Faster than any of them here. I have not their strength. There is no cure. I know that better than anyone.'

Tears welled into his eyes. 'But... how?'

The veiled figure moved. No doubt she had shrugged those magnificent shoulders. 'I do not know, Kit. I must have contracted the disease from one of the blacks, or perhaps it sprouted forth from the sheer energy which has always seemed to consume me. I do not know. But I thank God you left me in time.'

'Left you? Meg...' Christ, to find something to say.

'And now you must leave me again,' she said. 'Listen to me, Kit. I long ago lodged the necessary papers with Walker. Green Grove is yours. You were ever more talented at growing sugar, at managing people, than I. It is yours, and the children are yours, and you must bring them to success. But mark this well, Kit. Burn the Great House, and build afresh. It will be contaminated, Kit. Make no mistake about that. Burn it to the very ground, and gut the cellars. Else will you curse yourself forever.'

'Meg,' he cried. 'At least...'

'Let you look at me, Kit? Why do you wish to do that? Am I not the most beautiful woman you have ever seen? Can you not let me go to my grave, as a memory? What would you see, Kit? My teeth are loose, and falling out daily. My hair is white, and all but wasted. My nose is a running sore. I have lost the use of my legs and of my left hand. And I feel the rot eating at my belly. Would you *see* all of that, Kit, to haunt you for the rest of your life?'

'Oh, Christ,' he begged. 'To know, what to *do*.'

'To do, Kit? Why, your duty is to be the master of Green Grove, to be a father to your children, to be a husband to your Lillan. And to be happy, Kit. I charge you with that.'

'And to avenge, by God,' he said. 'I will have Hodge on this beach, on his knees, begging your forgiveness.'

'Hodge did not contaminate me, Kit. God did that, in His wisdom. Hodge did no more to me than I have done to so many others. And Hodge did not even kill your friend Agrippa, or abuse Lillan. I did all of those things, Kit; others but carried out my commands. I would beg *your* forgiveness, Kit.'

'You have it, Meg. God knows . . . but you have it.'

'Then let Hodge go, Kit. Let him go. And know this. I die happier here, with your forgiveness, than I could in my own bed, with your hate. Remember that, Kit. Remember.'

She said something in a low voice to the men around her, and they raised the litter and carried her back along the beach.

* * *

She did not speak again.

Night succeeded dawn, and dawn succeeded night, and the boat rocked gently in the swell, drifting up the passage between the island and the mainland, and being brought back to position by the slaves. At dawn they pulled to the beach where the rest of the slaves had gathered, a vast dark concourse, watching and waiting. Here they were given food, and water, and here Dag left them. He went without a word. There was nothing to say.

Kit remained in the bow. Maurice Peter made him eat, and drink, but for the rest he crouched in the bow, and gazed at the island. On the third day it rained, but the watchers never moved. And now there were others, on the cliffs above. But Kit neither knew nor cared who they were. He had no certainty of time, was aware only that sometimes it was light and at other times dark. He was not even aware that the crew of the pirogue had been changed, although Maurice Peter did not go ashore. The slaves did not trouble him with this matter. They arranged it amongst themselves.

On the sixth day the figures reappeared on the beach of the island.

'Where is her body?' Kit asked.

'It is buried, Captin,' one of the men said.

'Buried? By God, but she must be buried on Green Grove.'

'This island is a part of Green Grove, Captin,' the man said. 'And it was the mistress's wish that she be buried here, and that we do it. She said no white person was to look on her face, Captin.'

'We can go home now, Captin,' Maurice Peter said. He was not asking a question.

Kit sat down, and the boat was turned, and pulled for the shore. The slaves waited there, and some of them were weeping. He climbed the path, and found Dag, and Astrid, and Abigail, and Agrippa, and Barnee, waiting for him. And a little way away, Celestine Warner and Tony and Rebecca. And then Lillan, by herself.

'The overseers have left, Captain Hilton,' Barnee said. 'With their people. They have even left Antigua. They fear your vengeance.'

'But you will let them go, Kit,' Dag said. 'It was Marguerite's wish.'

'Aye. I will let them go.' And Marguerite had had other instructions for him. 'You'll work with me, Barnee?'

'It would be a pleasure, Captin.'

'Then burn the house. Burn it to the ground, and gut the cellars. Then summon Mr Wolff and have him design a new one.'

He went to Celestine, knelt, put his arms round the children. 'Is Mama dead, Papa?' Tony asked.

He raised his head to look at the woman.

'It was Marguerite's instructions, in her letter to me, Kit, that the children were to be brought to you, wherever you were, when she began to die. If only I had understood then what she meant.'

'Aye,' Kit said. 'She is dead, Tony.'

'And will Miss Christianssen be our new Mama, Papa?' Rebecca asked.

Lillan's head jerked.

'That is what Mama said, before we left her, Papa,' Tony said. 'She came out to see us go, wearing her veil, and she said, you are going to have a new mother, children. Miss Christianssen.'

Kit released them, and stood up. Lillan waited, her skirt

fluttering in the breeze. 'I loved her,' he said. 'I could not stop loving her, even when I fell in love with you. Can you understand that, Lillan? I cannot. But there is so little I can understand. Yet it is true.'

'I understand that, Kit,' she said. 'I always did.'

He sighed, and took her hands. 'But she'll not stand between us in the future. You'll be my wife. Although I could not blame you for refusing even that, after so much.'

'Is it not what I have always dreamed, Kit? To act out of pride or pique, now, would be childish. And I hope Marguerite will ever stand *beside* me, Kit. To be the wife of Kit Hilton, with so much to do, can be no simple task.'

Kit turned, to watch the slaves filing up the hill, and into the compound. 'I would say, looking at their grief, that they loved her too. And that also I cannot understand.'

'Perhaps it is because they have known no better life,' Dag said. 'From what Agrippa told me, I doubt their existence in Africa was any less brutal, any less cruel. There they belonged to their kings, here they belonged to Marguerite. But Kit, do they not *deserve* something better?'

Kit hesitated; Lillan's fingers were tight on his own. 'Aye,' he said. 'You'll build a chapel, Dag. In the slave compound itself.'

'I cannot teach them Christianity, with all it implies, unless I also teach them to read and write, and think,' Dag said.

'That has never been permitted,' Astrid said. 'The planters will hate you for it, Kit.'

'They have ever hated me, for something, Astrid. They hated me for being a buccaneer, as they hated me for being Meg Warner's husband, as they hated me for revealing them as they really are, an oligarchy of treacherous scoundrels. But now they will have to love me. Now, now I am master of Green Grove.'

About the Author

Christopher Nicole, who currently lives in the Channel Islands, has traveled widely in Europe, the Orient, and the Americas. The latest of his many novels is the Signet best-seller, CARIBEE, set in the West Indies.